For Sonia, Helen and Margaret.
You know what you did.

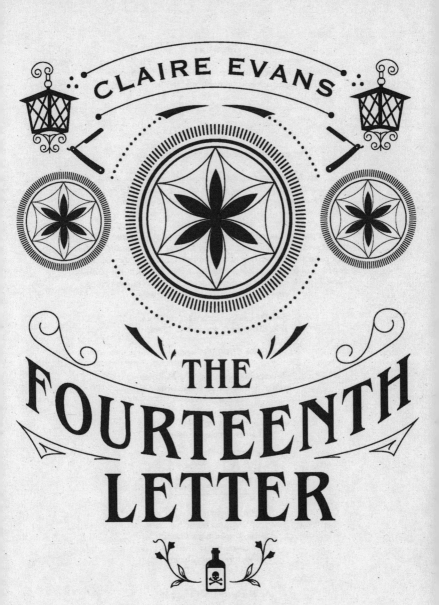

CLAIRE EVANS

# THE FOURTEENTH LETTER

sphere

SPHERE

First published in Great Britain in 2017 by Sphere
This paperback edition published in 2017 by Sphere

1 3 5 7 9 10 8 6 4 2

A CIP catalogue record for this book
is available from the British Library.

ISBN 978-0-7515-6640-6

Typeset in Garamond 3 by M Rules
Printed and bound in Great Britain by
Clays Ltd, St Ives plc

Papers used by Sphere are from well-managed forests
and other responsible sources.

Sphere
An imprint of
Little, Brown Book Group
Carmelite House
50 Victoria Embankment
London EC4Y 0DZ

An Hachette UK Company
www.hachette.co.uk

www.littlebrown.co.uk

Claire Evans is an established business specialist in the UK television industry. After finishing her law degree, she qualified as an accountant, but realising her mistake quickly ran away to work at the National Theatre before finally landing a job at the BBC. Once there, she rose through the ranks to head up operations and business affairs across the TV commissioning teams. In drama, she led the BBC's commercial relationships with the independent production sector and a wide range of international co-producers and distributors.

She left the BBC in 2013 to pursue her writing career. Since then she has advised a number of drama and film production companies, most recently working on *The Honourable Woman* and *Doctor Foster*. She is also now the Chief Operating Officer at Two Brothers Pictures Ltd.

We must, however, acknowledge, as it seems to me, that man with all his noble qualities, with sympathy which feels for the most debased, with benevolence which extends not only to other men but to the humblest living creature, with his god-like intellect which has penetrated into the movements and constitution of the solar system – with all these exalted powers – Man still bears in his bodily frame the indelible stamp of his lowly origin.

CHARLES DARWIN, 1871

CHAPTER ONE

*June 1881*

*P*hoebe Stanbury, blushing, beautiful, and almost in love, greeted the last of her unfamiliar guests and took her seat. As the quartet began to play, she could feel her cheeks paling as her heart retreated to its rightful place; the heart that would, in less than nine and one quarter minutes, pump every ounce of her innocent blood into the flagstones beneath her feet.

The doors to the orangery stood open and a slight chill whispered across her skin. She had asked her mother not to close them yet. The garden's last scent was strong, and she wanted today to be perfect. It *was* perfect. Benjamin held her hand in his limp grasp. This was their engagement party – something she could still not quite believe, nor, she suspected, could their guests. She saw the question in their eyes: why was Benjamin Raycraft, son of Sir Jasper, marrying such a nobody? He was surely one of the most eligible bachelors in London, not for his form or ability maybe, poor Benjamin, but blood is blood after all. She and her mother had endured their interrogations: *are you perhaps related to the Chichester Stanburys?* And even, *wasn't it a Phoebe Stanbury who accidentally hit Prince Alfred with an oar at Henley last year?* No, then smile, then no again. Phoebe wondered what hushed conversations had brought them all to her mother's house on the wrong side of the river. Sir Jasper's pedigree? Or prurient interest in the unknown bride? *No matter*, her mother had said, *they are here*.

As the music danced, Phoebe snatched a glance at their guests. Even the Society Editor of *The Times*, who sat primly towards the back of the room, had smiled in her direction. Now his mouth moved slightly, as if composing the words that would sketch this enchanting evening for his readers. She did not know it then, but Phoebe would never read those words, and he would not write them.

Beyond the open doors, past the cherub fountain that tinkled in the evening sun and down the slope to the river, the curtain of willow trees hid a naked man.

He shivered, his sopping clothes dripping from the branches of the nearest willow. Flat out on the riverbank, he hoped the weakening sun might warm him. He could feel his wet back begin to liquefy the hard surface of the mud beneath him, releasing the earthy smell of decay that the early summer heat had yet to eliminate. It felt appropriate that he should smell like this, of nature, of life and death. Today, he would give the gift of one by bestowing the horror of the other. Today he would right the wrong, the terrible aberration taking place in the house of swirling music and perfume. He would bring the stink of corrosion and finally they would know what had been under their noses: a secret, rotting slowly in the ground for so long.

He rolled on to his front and covered his body with the resurrected muck of the riverbank, pulling it through his pale hair and smearing his face and neck with the rich juice of the earth. He dipped his hand into the chill of the river and wiped some of the mud away, revealing the tattoos that marked his arms and chest. It was important that everyone should see them, particularly the girl. He reached for the leather satchel that hung from the willow bough and removed a bundle swathed in newspaper, sodden and turned to sticky clods of wet ash. Once unwrapped, the hunting knife refused to glint in the evening light as if it knew there was grave business ahead.

It was time. The innocent would die to punish the guilty.

In the orangery, the quartet was reaching the climax of the final movement of Mr Borodin's new arrangement for strings. As cello and viola strode hand in hand through the major scale, Phoebe felt a new gravity enter the room. The betrothal had been celebrated lightly and joyfully, with white roses and white china, and just the merest hint of pink in the tablecloths and in her own simple gown. But no one should undertake of marriage lightly, the music seemed to suggest. Afternoon tea on a late June afternoon is all very well, but a moment of weightiness should be accommodated. The music began to gather pace, and the sombre mood dissipated, brief but acknowledged, exquisitely done. She could almost hear her guests thinking, *these Stanburys do seem to have a certain deftness after all*.

The company rose to their feet and clapped as the quartet took a bow. Phoebe and Benjamin broke their hold of each other and moved among the well-wishers. Joining her mother, Phoebe thanked everyone for their attendance, their beautiful gifts, and their approval, although she tried hard to leave this last part unsaid.

A dozen exchanges broke out across the room but, one by one, the conversations closed down, frozen in time, open-mouthed. Phoebe was the last to stop talking, the last to turn towards the open doors where the figure of a man threw a long shadow that ended at the tips of her pretty pink slippers.

The naked mud man entered, his eyes on Phoebe as he walked towards her. Shock plummeted to her ankles like lead petticoats, rooting her to the floor. Everyone fell still as the man strode forward, the trail of muddy footprints and the stench of the river turning them all into an audience once more.

The intruder stood before Phoebe in all his glory: a sturdy physique, taller by a head than any other man there. Muddy slime dripped from the ends of his long hair and ran down his chest, slicing through the matrix of inked circles that covered his body. Phoebe thought she could hear his heart, thumping fast as he approached her. Or was it hers? She held her breath. Nothing on this earth had ever prepared her for this. She stared at the tattoo that circled his heart like a giant flower. It was all she could see, filling her vision.

The man raised his arm, pointing his hand and the object it carried towards Benjamin. The crowd gasped, the knife a conductor's baton delivering their cue.

The man's gaze followed the line of his outstretched arm as he spoke to Benjamin. 'I promised I would save you.'

Then everything happened at once. Benjamin and two others leapt forward but the dash came too late as the mud man grasped Phoebe by the hair and hauled her to her knees. She was almost grateful to meet the floor, before he slashed the knife through her defenceless neck. She could hear her mother's eternal scream of horror, drowning out the gentle gurgling of her own throat. From somewhere high above, Phoebe watched herself crumble, saw her lost-for-ever life flow red across her dress and into the stone floor. Such a mess. Such a waste . . . Her last thought had nothing to do with pain. She felt nothing. Rather, she realised that she had never seen a naked man before. So that is what it looks like. Ah, well.

And now death. Ah well to that too . . .

The assassin whirled around, responding to the charge at his back. The men, in black tie and dress shoes, stopped before him. As he moved towards the open doors and the river, the knife pointing the way, the men stood to one side, defeat bowing their heads to the floor.

He turned to Benjamin once more. 'Remember, I did this for you.'

But the young man seemed not to hear, his gaze fixed on a trail of the girl's blood that had snaked towards him, vulgar in that pinky-white room of dreams and music. As the naked man reached the doors, he glanced back just once. An older woman was on her knees beside the dead girl, her arms held aloft as if she could draw down heaven itself. The girl's eyes were open, and the bloody gash across her neck smiled up towards the glass dome and the sky beyond, as if awaiting an explanation.

It was sad to see them looking in the wrong direction, for only the devil himself could have told them why.

## CHAPTER TWO

The following morning, just a few miles away, a new day had begun like any other, which was just how William Lamb liked it.

Sarah had opened the bottom sash in the morning room, the clock on the mantel chiming seven thirty as he entered. It really was delightful here, with the lawn perfectly framed by the symmetry of the windowpanes. William and his aunt had planted the garden last spring, and it was responding splendidly to its second summer. It wasn't the biggest of gardens, it wasn't the biggest of houses, but when William's maturity had delivered them enough capital to purchase a home of their own, he had been adamant that buying a small piece of this beautiful country was the sensible thing to do with his inheritance. It was the first time that he and Aunt Esther had owned a patch of land of any size or description, marked out by a high, stone wall from a slab of Hammersmith bog only two years ago. After twenty-one years in an apartment on the Bayswater road, he still felt a thrill to know, whenever the lilac sprouted another branch, that he owned a tree and the earth in which it grew.

A smash from the basement brought William back from his reverie. Sarah was new, and seemed set on a path of destruction. Aunt Esther would be heartbroken if it was yet another of her Wedgwood collection.

'Sarah?'

'Yes, Mr Lamb?' A small, disembodied voice rose up from below.

'Was that a Wedgwood?'

'Um ... I don't think so, Mr Lamb.'

'What colour was it?'

'White, with blue flowers.'

'Oh.'

'Sorry, Mr Lamb.'

They would have to let her go. William could feel the familiar tightening in his chest at the thought. Maybe Aunt Esther could deal with it? But no, he was a man now, twenty-three in a matter of weeks, less than a year away from completing his articles and entering a proper partnership with Mr Bridge. He must handle this alone. A sobbing maid was nothing to be frightened of and, after all, if he were to marry one day, which he so dearly hoped, then he would have to get used to tears and other embarrassments. He could do this ...

'Good gracious, William, whatever is the matter?'

He had not seen his aunt enter the room. As she swept towards him, he let go of the tablecloth, aware that he had bunched the material in both hands in an effort to calm himself.

He cleared his throat. 'Nothing, Aunt, I was just caught up in my thoughts.'

'Well, don't worry yourself so. Your asthma has been much improved since we moved to the country.'

She kissed William affectionately on the cheek and, as always, the papery softness of her skin against his and the warm scent of lavender calmed him once more.

He laughed. 'We are not in the country, Aunt. This is Hammersmith.'

'We own a tree, William. We're in the country.'

She sat down as Sarah arrived, a tray of fresh supplies wobbling in her hands. Her impossibly thin wrists seemed woefully unsuited to the task. He gazed across at his aunt as she poured her tea, reassured as always by the pleasure she took in this morning ritual. I will marry a woman just like her, he thought, but where does one look?

'Will you read to me from the paper, William?'

William picked up that morning's copy of *The Times*. Without a full complement of thumbs, it was still the hardest part of daily life to navigate, no matter how much practice he had. Where his left thumb should have been, he was born with nothing but smooth skin – no indication of trauma, or of something that had started and then, for some reason, stopped. When he was younger, he had asked Aunt Esther whether his father, her brother, or his mother had suffered the same *absence*, as it were. She frowned at the time, as if trying to remember, although obviously it was not something you were likely to forget about a person. They both had all their thumbs, she said.

William moved his breakfast things and laid the paper flat on the tablecloth. He began with the lead article of the day. 'The nation prepares for Cornelius Tinbergen. Sunday will see the arrival on British shores of the Vice President of the United States. Tinbergen will sail the Thames on his new steam yacht *The Seed of Life*, totem of the vast shipping and railroad fortune that the Tinbergens have amassed in recent years. Vice President Tinbergen, the richest man in the world, will be greeted at the Tower of London by Prime Minister Gladstone. The Foreign Office has confirmed that the German Chancellor, Otto Von Rabenmarck, will also be present; a surprising addition to the welcome party considering his frequently voiced animosity towards all things English ... '

William broke off to voice his own thoughts. 'Why does *The Times* insist on deepening tensions? These days, they barely stop short of suggesting a German invasion is imminent!'

He squinted at the paper, finding his place once more. 'Von Rabenmarck has been busy of late rebuilding the League of the Three Emperors, the historical pact between Germany, Russia and the Austro-Hungarian Empire. Brought together by Rabenmarck, the emperors met for the first time last month. The newly crowned Tsar of Russia, Alexander III, appears far more willing to concentrate on international matters than his father, assassinated by his own people in March. The convergence of these three nations on colonialism and the scramble for Africa has alarmed the less acquisitive Gladstone.'

William sighed and stopped reading. He had never met a journalist and didn't care to. Even if the subtext of the article was correct, and the Germans came calling, the men of England would see them off. It was a ridiculous notion.

Aunt Esther bit into her toast. 'Another article, perhaps?'

William flicked his eyes down the page. 'Death of Society Bride. The betrothal of Sir Jasper Raycraft's son, Benjamin, last night ended in tragedy following the unexpected demise of his betrothed. Miss Phoebe Stanbury, of Barnes, London, was pronounced dead at her home yesterday evening by the Hammersmith coroner, following a party given in honour of the newly engaged couple. The cause of death has not yet been made known.'

'How terrible! That poor young girl!'

'Indeed.' William felt something other than just sympathy – at least she had loved. He felt the familiar surge of impatience; a growing and at times overwhelming desire to advance forward in his life. Why must he wait a year to become partner in the firm? And just how long would it be until he was married when he didn't even know any girls, let alone the right one? Neither Aunt Esther nor Mr Bridge, the two most important people in his life, appeared to be in any rush to see him settled.

A familiar rat-tat-tat at the front door caused William to fold the paper as neatly as he could and rise from the table. He took out his watch, feeling the weight of its excellence in his hand, and flipped open the case. It might be old, but the watch kept good time, one of the few possessions salvaged from his parents' house after the fire that took them both when he was yet a babe in arms. He had accepted years ago that this watch, along with a faded daguerreotype of his mother in a scratched wooden frame, was all that was left to him of Mr and Mrs Lamb, the couple with four thumbs that he never really knew.

He pulled on his black frock coat and turned so that his aunt could smooth the material over his shoulders. He tugged at his cuffs and checked all was even before planting a kiss on her cheek. In the hallway he paused by the mirror. The early morning sun beamed through the red skylight above the door, highlighting the auburn tint that came and went of its own accord from his wavy brown hair. He was not a tall man, slight of build maybe, but his face was decent enough, he thought, open and symmetrical like his mother's. Did women care about such things?

A second jaunty knock had him heading for the door. At the last minute, he turned and plucked his furled umbrella from the hat stand, for one never knew when a beautiful day might turn for the worse.

'Morning, young William, what a glorious day!'

William returned Mr Bridge's benevolent smile and joined him on the pavement for their customary stroll to the train. His employer lived nearby, in a large dingy house that William had seldom visited. Since he could remember, it was Mr Bridge who had visited him, three times a year at first, to make sure all was well. Sunday school reports were inspected, health was enquired after, and financial matters were discussed in hushed tones. A friend of William's deceased parents, Mr Bridge had administered his trust, releasing the funds when he reached his majority. William could not remember when the assumption was first made, or by whom, that he would follow Mr Bridge's childless footsteps into the legal profession.

'Have you read *The Times* this morning, sir?'

Mr Bridge didn't respond at first and William had to crick his neck to look at him, for almost all of Mr Bridge's excess weight accumulated on his stomach, giving him a tendency to lean backwards for the purpose of balance.

'Not yet. Another late night at the office caused me to oversleep again.'

William could see the strain about his eyes. 'You must allow me to help more, sir. I am capable, I know it.'

'All in due course, young man. Do not be impatient, William. The big wide world will trouble you soon enough.' Mr Bridge grasped him on the shoulder, as much, William sensed, to propel himself forward as to deliver encouragement.

The eight eleven to Farringdon was its customary three minutes late. William shook his head. 'I don't know why the authorities don't just update the timetable!'

Mr Bridge smiled. 'I suspect that timetables are written for people of the opposing disposition to your good self, those who live their lives in a perpetual rush. Obviously they need a two-minute grace period to manage themselves on to a train. We all have our flaws, William.'

Mr Bridge loved to argue a good defence, but William was unsympathetic. 'The latest I've ever managed to be was on time.'

For some reason Mr Bridge found that highly amusing and he was still chuckling as they took their seats. Once they were settled, William's employer opened his briefcase and began to pore over a file in preparation for his meeting at Lincoln's Inn that morning. The Shropshire Affair, as they grandly called the case, had been going on for months, a complex and dull negotiation regarding land rights.

Knowing he needed to let Mr Bridge concentrate without

interruption, William allowed his own mind to wander. He thought of the society bride-to-be who had died at her own engagement party. A fiancée, an intended, a betrothed – such power those words held, of ownership and belonging all at once. Would that be him one day?

His attention was caught by a lovely young woman with pale gold hair who had just entered the carriage and taken the last remaining seat. Her blue tartan dress looked stiff and new and she tugged at the collar as if it itched. She sat upright and her mouth moved silently in her pretty face, as if she were rehearsing something. She looked up, caught his eye, and frowned.

William looked away, his cheeks burning. He found himself looking at girls constantly, but they so rarely even smiled in his direction. Without thinking, he covered his left hand with his right. Could they sense it, he wondered, even before they saw? *Something damaged about that one, something irreparable.*

The train pulled into Baker Street and half the carriage emptied, replaced immediately by double their number. The woman in the tartan dress cried out and stumbled to her feet, obviously at risk of missing her stop. She pushed her way through the crowd and just escaped through the closing doors, tripping on to the platform as she did so. William rose instinctively, although he could do nothing to help her as the train was already moving. He watched her as they pulled away: she held a shoe in her hand, and glowered at it as if she had just caught the ringleader of some dastardly conspiracy.

When he turned back to his seat, it had already been taken by an opportunist, who refused to meet his eye. Mr Bridge put his papers away and rose to stand by him in solidarity.

'There is no need, Mr Bridge. I am fine as I am.'

'Of course you are.'

Mr Bridge's indulgent smile annoyed William. Was he simply a joke to everyone? He pushed the thought aside; it was unwelcome and uncharitable.

At Farringdon, they said their goodbyes. As Mr Bridge ambled towards Lincoln's Inn, William strode towards their chambers on Kirby Street. The two rooms occupied the top floor of the building, with large sash windows overlooking a small garden. He paced himself as he climbed the five floors.

'Morning, Mr Lamb.'

'Morning, Sedgwick. Mr Bridge has gone directly to Lincoln's Inn.'

'Ah, the Shropshire affair ...' Sedgwick nodded his head gravely.

William shared the outer office with their elderly clerk Sedgwick while Mr Bridge took the inner office for himself. William settled at his desk, surveying the neat stack of papers in front of him. He opened the topmost file from the first stack, yet another redraft of a will for a wealthy widow who was for ever falling out with her relatives. It was the sort of task that made up the bulk of his workload: wills, trusts, deeds and assignments, domestic in nature. The fees were barely enough to sustain his own salary, let alone that of Sedgwick or Mr Bridge. Although he didn't like to enquire, William suspected that the vast majority of their revenues came from just one client.

Ambrose Habborlain.

Mr Bridge attended to the account personally, visiting the man several times a week and never once asking William to perform even the most menial of tasks in support. William knew that Mr Bridge had inherited both the account and the practice from his father. William had worked for Mr Bridge for three years and never in that time had Ambrose Habborlain visited the office. William wasn't even acquainted with the nature of the work, knowing only that it was terribly time-consuming for poor Mr Bridge.

It really was time that his employer shared the workload. William was a man now, and perfectly capable of shouldering more of the burden within the practice. Mr Bridge was not getting any younger and William was determined to prove himself a worthy partner. He set about drafting the new will with vigour and had it completed within the half-hour, just as a messenger boy entered the office.

'One should knock, you know.' Sedgwick barely looked up as the boy approached.

'Sorry, sir, but I was told the message was urgent.'

Sedgwick held out a hand, his eyes never straying from his work.

'It's not a "message" message. I mean . . .'

'Yes?' Sedgwick finally locked eyes with the boy.

'I was told to ask for Mr Bridge and to tell him that Mr Habborlain would like to see him. *Now*, sir. That was it, sir.'

'You will need to take a message back, I'm afraid. Mr Bridge has been held up on an urgent matter. He will return before luncheon, whereupon, I'm sure, he will make arrangements to visit Mr Habborlain later today.'

William leapt to his feet. 'No, it's all right, Sedgwick. I shall attend to Mr Habborlain myself!'

'Are you quite sure, Mr Lamb?'

William wasn't at all sure, but he needed to make the most of this opportunity to help. Habborlain had obviously become stuck in his ways, only wishing to deal with Mr Bridge himself, and it was time to show them both that the burden could be shared.

'Yes, I'll go immediately. Do you have the address, Sedgwick?'

'No, sir, Mr Bridge keeps all the Habborlain files in his office.'

Mr Bridge kept his office locked at all times if he wasn't there.

'Surely we have a note of the address in the general records?'

'Strangely not, sir.'

'Sixteen, Red Lion Square, sir,' the boy threw over his shoulder as he ran out of the office door.

William put on his coat and looked back at his desk, feeling the need to take something with him. He really should purchase a briefcase; not that he had needed one so far. He never took his work home, nor had he attended a client meeting without Mr Bridge. Well, that was about to change. Still feeling the urge not to turn up empty-handed, William pointlessly picked up his umbrella instead.

'Right, Sedgwick, let Mr Bridge know my whereabouts. I shall return presently.'

William hesitated at the doorway. Was this really a good idea?

'Goodbye, Sedgwick.' And with that, William Lamb said goodbye to many things.

# CHAPTER THREE

*S*avannah Shelton tramped down the street towards Red Lion Square, looking everyone she passed straight in the eye. Most of them immediately looked down, or found their attention caught by something rather interesting *over there*. Some managed to hold her gaze for a fraction, long enough to see the olive skin, the jet black hair scraped into a ponytail, the fierce almond eyes, and a thin red scar that meandered from her temple to beneath her left cheekbone.

A small minority looked a little longer and saw other things, none of which she suspected would improve upon their basic perception: a leather coat that swamped her small frame and grazed the top of her sturdy boots, a tweed skirt and petticoats that barely skimmed her ankles; a waistcoat trimmed in grubby gold and a red neckerchief completed the ensemble. The only people who truly met her gaze were kids and mad folks. Or should she say, *other* mad folks? Because that is what they clearly thought of her here, in this cold, cruel, class-crippled hellhole of a city.

A few more weeks on the payroll, though, a month at the outside, and she could be on her way south again. Just follow the sun, Shelton.

She approached the garden in the middle of the square, took a key from her pocket, and opened the wrought-iron gate. Peculiar, she thought, rich folks who couldn't afford a garden of their own.

Back in Arizona, land was cheaper than liquor. All it took to own acres of the stuff was a gun and the stomach to use it. Although she had been visiting the garden every day for weeks, the current inhabitants still watched her suspiciously – mostly weary women in uniform, endlessly walking perambulators about the circular path that wove between the shrubs and trees. Fortunately, most of the nannies didn't seem to know each other well, exchanges between them limited to a few curt nods and the odd 'lovely weather we're having'. If they had felt more inclined to chat, they might have thought to debate why a reprehensibly dressed young woman of a brown persuasion had a key to one of the most exclusive gardens in London.

At the far end of the park she could see an older boy, sitting alone on a bench, facing the houses on the south side of the square. She wove towards him through the shrubbery, but as she cornered a particularly large ceanothus, a wooden hoop clattered into her.

'Goddamn it!'

'I am sorry, miss!'

The boy was dressed in a sailor's outfit; or rather, what these idiot people thought a sailor's outfit might look like, complete with a jaunty cap, blue pom-pom dangling stupidly off to one side. He certainly didn't look like any sailor she had met on her long trip to this godforsaken island.

A matron marched towards them, panting in her stiff grey uniform. 'Thomas, come away now, we should be getting home.' The woman held her hand out towards the boy as she approached, keeping half an eye on the leather-clad stranger.

'May I have my hoop back please, miss?'

Savannah was holding the offending object in her hand, swinging it up in the air and catching it as it fell. She was weighing up whether to throw it at him, lasso style, and knock the silly cap of his silly head. Clearly sensing the threat, the woman grabbed hold of the boy's arm and spun him round.

'Never mind, we'll get you another one, dear.'

The boy started to cry as the nanny dragged him back towards the path. Maybe it wasn't his fault, being one of the rich folks. He probably hadn't chosen that ridiculous hat, more likely his mother picked it out on one of the few afternoons she could be bothered to pay attention to her kid. Maybe she should follow the boy home and throw the damn hoop at his mother instead. She ditched the idea as soon as it formed. She was under strict instructions not to draw attention to herself. She had promised Obediah Pincott that she would blend in as best she could. She had even pinned her hair up in the current style and worn a dress of the correct length for a few days – an unsettling experience, as it meant she couldn't run, and you never knew when running like hell was going to be a key requirement of your day. But what was the point of trying to conform? People stared anyway, and she would rather look as if she didn't care.

With casual stealth, she approached the boy on the bench from behind. JJ was good, but even he could do with a test now and then. The dewy grass and the constant chirrup of birds hushed her footsteps, or so she thought.

'You're late.' JJ spoke without turning around.

'Damn it.'

Grabbing the back of the bench with one hand, Savannah lifted her petticoats in an unladylike way and swung herself over in one lithe movement, landing next to JJ, her boots thudding softly on the turf.

'What's that?'

She was still holding the hoop. 'A present for you. I was going to get you a cute little sailor boy hat too but the moment sort of passed.'

JJ took the hoop. 'It'll make good kindling, dry and that.'

'Good boy.'

Savannah took a tin from her pocket, placed a pre-rolled

cigarette between her lips and struck a match. She blew the plume of smoke directly outwards towards 16 Red Lion Square, a salute of sorts. Surely the old man had noticed her out here by now? Day after day, watching and waiting, staring until her head burned with the boredom of it all.

'Anything to report?' she asked.

'Message boy came and went, and a new bloke pitched up with a delivery, got me all excited. Olly followed him, turned out to be just the usual drop from the grocer on Harpur Street. Seems they fired the last bloke cos the customers didn't like having a nigger around – no offence, Shelton.'

'None taken.' Not entirely true, but what the hell. Her mother had belonged to the Navajo tribe, her father as white as snow, although not so pure. Her mother's people saw only her paleness, whereas white folks saw only her colour. She had hardened herself to it years ago, hadn't she?

'Where's Olly now?'

He pointed to another boy huddled by the basement steps of a nearby house, waiting for a signal to move off and follow someone if the need arose. JJ seemed to have an endless supply of boys even smaller than himself, urchins that could blend into the background as they followed any and all visitors to number sixteen. Habborlain entertained only rarely – impoverished artists, musicians, that kind of thing. The old man obviously fancied himself as a bit of a patron. There was no family, no friends really, unless you counted the fat lawyer that bumbled through Habborlain's door several times a week. Habborlain himself only occasionally ventured out and the comings and goings of various servants was pedestrian. There was nothing going on here that she could see and she couldn't for the life of her understand why a man like Pincott had her conducting such a meticulous investigation of such a mundane life.

The man who had overseen the operation before her had been

doing the job for years apparently. He had found JJ and put together the group of boys that shared shifts and did the grunt work. She had inherited an efficient machine, but to what purpose?

She turned to JJ. 'Come back at four and bring one of those patsy things.'

'You mean a *pasty*.'

'Whatever.'

'I can stay a bit longer if you want.'

She looked down at him. The boy was skinny as a winter calf, with pale skin but hair almost as black as hers. Irish, probably, somewhere way back, but now a son of the city. With his big blue eyes he could easily make a better living begging on the street.

'You got folks, JJ?'

'Nah, must've done I suppose, don't remember.'

'How old are you?'

'Dunno.'

There were other questions too. But what was the point when she would be gone soon? Don't give a damn, Shelton. Giving a damn is what got you here.

'Scram.'

JJ slipped off the bench, and turned back across the park, rolling the hoop playfully alongside him. In that moment he could have passed for a normal boy. The lottery of birth, she thought – someone rolled the dice for you and you ended up where you ended up. Savannah ground her cigarette stub into the grass and sank back in her seat, another day of watching yawning in front of her.

She closed her eyes and tipped her head to the sun. Her thoughts shifted around, landing in difficult destinations, places she didn't want to be. She pushed the past away and turned her attention to the present. What was Pincott after? If this scrutiny were a precursor to a robbery, she would understand. After all, there must be some valuable pickings to be had. But if that was the plan, her boss would have been in and gone by now. No, they were waiting for something to happen, but she didn't have a clue what that might be. Pincott, or whatever his name really was, had refused to tell her what she was looking for. Just look, follow, and then look some more. The money wasn't bad, although she was owed two weeks' wages. She calculated that in another fortnight or so she would definitely have enough to head to the port and take the first boat south.

'Beautiful morning, wouldn't you say?'

Savannah looked up from the bench and her heart tipped into her stomach. Damn it, she should have been paying attention. An English bobby stood before her. Normally she was alert enough to spot them coming and temporarily disappear from sight, for they advertised themselves clearly enough in their blue uniforms and custodian helmets.

'Surely is,' she replied, tight-lipped.

'An American! You must be here on account of Mr Tinbergen?'

Savannah suppressed a you-must-be-kidding snort. The world of Tinbergen and the politicians of Washington was even further from her own than this sad patch of grass on the other side of the world. The fact that they would both soon be breathing the same air in the same city was astonishing enough.

Nevertheless, she put on her best Wild West drawl. 'That sure is correct, officer. We're doing a show for your Mr Gladstone, 'The Wonders of the Wild West', in honour of Mr T's visit to this fair country. Our patron lives over there at number sixteen. He suggested I come sit out here and partake of your fine English summer.'

'Excellent! Excellent! You must be one of them sharpshooters. I heard you can shoot the apple off the head of a man from a hundred yards away!'

Savannah could feel the cold weight of her Colt Peacemaker jammed down the back of her skirt, pushing against the small of her back. She forced a grimace and hoped it could pass for a smile.

'Very well, madam. Maybe I shall see you again before you leave? It's my first day on a new beat. I'll be strolling through regularly. Enjoy our beautiful country and good luck with your show.'

'Thanks. You take care now.'

Savannah sat as still as she could until the policeman reached the corner of the garden where he turned back, made his hands into two pretend guns, and shot her with a one-two. She returned the gesture: *Pow! Pow!* With a big grin on his face he saluted and then was gone. The moment he was out of sight she sprang from her seat and exhaled. That was absolutely the last thing she had needed to happen. She told herself that he had bought her story, of course he had. If he had known who she was, then he would have to be a pretty cool customer to play out that little pantomime right there. She wasn't sure whether they were even looking for her in London.

Her new friend would be back – day after day. And what then? One thing was for sure; she had to ditch the job. It was too exposed. London was only ever meant to be a stopping-off point, a brief respite on the journey to nowhere, but she had stayed too long. Pincott's money was all right but she needed to be doing something more covert, something that used her skills better, paid better. Surely he could find a worthier use for her talents? She would talk to him today, she couldn't just sit here any longer, out in the open. As much as she loved the sun, she needed the shadows to survive.

She strode towards the nearest exit, the one that faced directly on to the house, the one they never used. The young boy, Olly, still hiding on the cellar steps a few doors down, spoke to her with big round eyes: *this is not how the game works, where are you going?*

Savannah marched brazenly past the front door of number sixteen, and for the first time since her arrival in the city, failed to catch the eye of the single passer-by – a young man, carrying a useless umbrella in his thumbless left hand.

## CHAPTER FOUR

Number sixteen Red Lion Square belonged to a terrace of townhouses built in the classical style to which William's own, much smaller abode was intended to pay homage. The only difference he could see between the Habborlain residence and its neighbours was a simple matter of maintenance: a smattering of rust on the cast-iron railings and a certain grubbiness compared to the freshly painted sills of the other houses. William was startled when a young woman hurried past him, a long leather coat wrapped tightly about her. Her head was cast down but he could still see the livid scar that disfigured her striking olive-skinned face. She seemed rather out of place in this affluent part of the city.

His pace slowed as he approached the entrance to the house, his earlier misgivings returning once more. Mr Bridge would not be happy that William had taken it upon himself to visit old Habborlain. However he tried to rationalise his decision, this was really a small act of rebellion, dressed up by his conscience as a charitable deed intended to alleviate the heavy workload that bore down on his employer. He paused at the door. Coming here had been a rash decision, born of the frustration he felt at his own isolation. Patience was a virtue and William was cross with himself for giving in to its errant opposite. The sensible thing to do was to return to the office and resolve to have a proper dialogue with Mr Bridge about his advancement.

He turned to go, just as the door in front of him yawned open.

'May I help you, sir?'

Oh dear. The butler must have seen him hovering and wondered why he had yet to knock. How on earth would he explain himself?

'Good morning to you, sir. I do apologise for loitering but I was admiring the brassware on your door. I have just myself purchased a house of similar design. In the country. We have yet to decide on the exact nature of the door knocker that would most complement the appearance of our home, but I think this might be just the ticket! I shall order one just like it today! It is ridiculous, I know, that we have lived there for so long without a knocker. We do, however, have a bell . . . ' William's speech drifted to a sad end and he coughed to fill the silence.

'May I help you, sir?'

William felt the flush of hot humiliation as the butler repeated his question, the trace of a German accent in his disdainful drawl. William had never met a butler before but the man's appearance conformed exactly to expectations: arms poker-straight at his sides and mousy hair slicked back revealing stripes of pale scalp beneath. As much as William wanted to run away, he could see no path but onwards.

'I'm here to see Mr Habborlain. I am Mr Bridge's soon-to-be partner. He has been held up on urgent business and asked me to attend Mr Habborlain in his place.'

The butler eyed him with outright suspicion. 'Do you have a card?'

'I most certainly do!' William dug into his breast pocket and presented the butler with a rather dog-eared card: the first time he had ever had cause to use one. Months earlier Mr Bridge had indulgently given in to William's request to have the cards printed, just in case an opportunity presented itself. He had kept a few in his coat pocket ever since.

The butler examined the card thoroughly, turning it over although there was nothing on the back, making quite an unnecessary show, William thought.

'William Lamb, Esquire. Articled Clerk. Bridge and Sons.' His voice dripped with incredulity, as if the card had announced William to be an elephant catcher stopping by on the off-chance one was lurking in the hallway.

William was fairly sure that butlers were not supposed to be this impertinent. He puffed himself up. 'I am in rather a rush. If I could see him now, please?'

The butler met his eyes once again before making his decision. Then he opened the door wider and bade William to enter.

William felt the change in temperature as soon as he entered the hallway, leaving the June sun outside as the front door closed behind him. The hallway was shabbier even than the exterior of the house. A grandfather clock took centre stage against the back wall of dark flock wallpaper, the grand staircase curling up and around it. The clock seemed overloud in that echoing space, the pendulum clunking back and forth as it proclaimed the passage of time. William resisted his usual habit of checking his own timepiece against any clock that he came across. Something told him that his watch was likely to be more accurate. This seemed to be a household where it wasn't particularly necessary to have an up-to-the-minute knowledge of the exact time of day.

The butler placed William's card on the hall table. 'My name is Fischer, sir. May I take your hat and umbrella?'

'Very well, Fischer.'

William handed both items over. As the butler grasped them, William turned to examine the hallway in more detail. An empty hatstand and a large mahogany table with a tired-looking arrangement of dried flowers completed the look of faded grandeur. Habborlain obviously lived alone; there was no woman's touch at work in this withered place. The thought made William even more despondent that he had come, but what to do? If he left now, he would still have to explain himself to Mr Bridge. The damage could not be undone.

Turning back towards Fischer, William was surprised to see that the man had not moved. He still held the hat in one hand and the umbrella in the other as he stared down at William's thumbless left hand. William was used to the odd look, the sly double take and the occasional raised eyebrow, but this outright gaping in astonishment was something new and absolutely not something one expected from a servant. How dare the man gawp like this!

William found his voice. 'It's really nothing, just a slight deformity from birth. I have to say that your reaction, Fischer, is a little upsetting.'

The butler looked into William's eyes, still mute, his gaze roaming across William's features. With a cough, he pulled himself together, stored William's umbrella and hat and gave a sharp bow. 'Apologies, sir. I should not have been so startled. You are a fine-looking young man and it is but a small imperfection. Unexpected, that is all. Shall we proceed, sir?' With a new-found briskness the butler waved William towards the doorway on his right.

The heavy oak door opened with a whine, the brass hinges unable to disguise their age. William's eyes struggled to adjust to the gloom as he followed the butler into the room. There were only two sources of light: an oil lamp turned low on a large desk to his left, and the glowing embers of a fire at the far end of the room. Even in the darkness, William could tell the room was generous in size, the tall windows smothered by thick brocade drapes that puddled on the floor. He felt a strong urge to open them and let the daylight slice through the warm, soupy atmosphere. The contrast to the heady freshness of summer he had left on the street only moments ago could not have been more marked.

He could make out two wing chairs silhouetted against the enormous fireplace, above which hung a great painting, partly hidden in the shadows. As the butler's stately pace brought them nearer, a plume of smoke floated across the fire – tobacco, but also a smell that William did not recognise, sweet and exotic.

A voice broke through the dust-logged air. 'Sit down, Bridge. We have much to discuss. Did you read about the girl?'

The voice was thin, yet curiously resonant, almost as if in straining to hear it, it was all that one *could* hear. Before William could correct the misapprehension of his identity, the butler cleared his throat and, belatedly in William's view, announced that he was not, in fact, Mr Bridge.

'Sir, I'm afraid that Mr Bridge was not available. His assistant, a . . . a Mr William Lamb, has come in his place.'

Again, William found the butler's tone inappropriate. The pause he gave before William's name had made him feel like an imposter. With a flourish of his right hand, Fischer indicated that William should take his seat by the fire. William did so, but not before he caught the butler's obsequious smile.

As William sank into his chair he sensed the butler back away through the gloom. He turned towards his companion by the fire and struggled to focus through the smoky haze that swirled between them.

'Good morning, sir. I'm afraid that Mr Bridge has been held up at Lincoln's Inn. I thought I would assist him by attending you, sir. Your message suggested that the matter was urgent. It is a pleasure to meet you at last, I have to say.'

It wasn't a pleasure at all, being here in this strange dark place. He could just make out the long white hair and beard that adorned the gaunt face, the aquiline nose and the large, walnut-lidded eyes turned down at the edges. It was an old face, not just advanced in years, at least eighty he suspected, but old in a classical sense. For the first time that morning, William found himself pondering the origins of the Habborlain name – an ancient name to match that ancient face. He felt horribly out of his depth in this faded, dank atmosphere. William couldn't believe that Mr Bridge, with his jolly outlook and bustling temperament, was any more at home here than he was.

'William Lamb, did you say? Bridge has not mentioned you.'

William had to lean forward and strain to hear the old man's words. It was hard not to feel affronted by Mr Bridge's omission. Was he really so insignificant to the practice?

'Nonetheless, sir, may I be of service in some way?'

They both heard the gentle thud of the front door closing and the old man frowned before tipping his head back and closing his eyes for what seemed a long time. William was on the point of repeating his question, assuming that the old man had temporarily drifted off.

'They watch me, William. Every hour. Every day.'

'Your servants?'

'Servants, yes. Mine? No.'

William really wasn't sure this conversation was worth pursuing but felt at a loss to do anything else. 'Then whose servants are they, sir?'

'They belong to the devil, William.'

Unexpectedly, Habborlain began to chuckle. It started deep in his chest then rose an octave, ending in a long sigh.

'I don't understand, sir.'

'Ah, I have no explanation, not any more. I used to have all the explanations in the world, but they died on me, William, they died on me.'

William wondered whether Habborlain didn't entirely have

his wits about him. Maybe that was why Mr Bridge had kept William away? It was clear that he was to learn nothing of the nature of the work Bridge did for Habborlain, not even a hint to be gleaned from this vaguest of messages. No mention of wills, deeds, assignments, trusts. No information at all.

This was hopeless. He stood up. 'Well, sir, I should take my leave of you. I apologise if I have wasted your time.' William tried and failed to keep a wounded tone from his voice.

'Stop with me a while, William Lamb. I have few visitors these days. Let us pass a few minutes together.' Habborlain rose slowly from his chair, his great height unfurling before William's astonished gaze. The man was well over six foot, despite the stoop in his back. He placed a bony hand on William's shoulder to steady himself. 'Let me show you a few of my things, knick-knacks, I suppose, a random collection from the glorious history of mankind.'

Habborlain chuckled once more as he disappeared in the gloom. Was the man intoxicated? William could smell no alcohol on his breath. The oil lamp on the desk started to move, casting a ghostly glow as Habborlain shuffled back to the fireplace, his long red robe swishing across the floor. The old man turned the flame to its maximum and William was dazzled by the sudden burst of light, revealing Habborlain's attire in full. A noose of chains hung around his neck; under his robe, he wore a bright silk tunic that hung to his ankles, and delicate slippers encased his feet. Habborlain swung the lamp up high, revealing the great painting above the fireplace. A seated youth, wearing a crown of leaves, gazed up at a red-headed woman, her eyes downcast in a look of subjugation and rapture.

'Alexander the Great and Roxanne, the woman he married for love,' Habborlain grandly exclaimed.

William felt compelled to comment, although his knowledge of art was somewhat limited, another symptom of his sheltered existence. 'It is very beautiful' was his lame contribution.

'What is beautiful, William? The painting? Or love?'

'Both,' was William's instinctive response.

'Faith, hope and love, and the greatest of these is love. Remember that always, William. The painting is by Pietro Rotari. Have you heard of him?'

Oh dear. William decided on honesty. 'No sir, I'm afraid I have not.'

'Pity. Not many have these days.' William stifled a sigh of relief that he was not alone in his ignorance as Habborlain continued, 'He was well known in his day, of course. He was, in fact, my great-great uncle on my mother's side.'

William realised how unused he was to making conversation with strangers. Small talk. He rattled his brain for something to say. What would Aunt Esther do? 'He was obviously a very talented chap. Do you paint, sir?' William was pleased with himself for thinking of an intelligent question to ask, a normal question in this strangest of dialogues.

Habborlain's gaze shifted to the distance. 'No, William, I do not. Nor do I write music, or poetry. I have made nothing of beauty in my life, at least not anything that lasted. Instead I collect, I curate. I *preserve*. I have a talent for that, at least.'

Before William could think of something suitable to say, Habborlain moved towards the window near the fire. The lamp illuminated a statue of a man's head that William hadn't spotted in the all-prevailing dusk of the room.

'Come, William, come and see.'

Habborlain's tone was hypnotic and William did as he was bid.

'Do you know who this is?' Habborlain stroked his hand gently down the cheek of the bust before them, as if it might feel his touch.

William's knowledge of history and art was being severely tested. He interrogated the face carved in marble, a noble face, yet unassuming. Before he was forced to admit ignorance, Habborlain answered for him.

'This is Plato, the father of all of us.'

'Ah!' William exclaimed. 'I have heard of him!'

Habborlain chuckled again, a throaty, warm sound this time, his moods as changeable as the wind. 'Indeed, William. You must have read his work?'

'Of course.' The lie came out as a squeak.

Habborlain leant forward. 'In the original Greek, I hope?'

William smiled and nodded, not trusting his voice.

'And do you favour him, or Aristotle?'

On the precipice of another deceit, William pulled himself back. 'I have yet to read Aristotle, sir. I was tutored at home by my aunt. I suspect it was an unconventional education. I have only a rudimentary grasp of the classics.' Well, none at all if he was being entirely honest. It was clear to him now that this might be a setback in his pursuit of a wife, for that would involve, he suspected, quite a bit of small talk. He resolved to visit the booksellers in Farringdon today and broaden his knowledge of such things.

Habborlain had already moved to the far wall, holding up the lamp once more to reveal a cluster of smaller portraits. At least a dozen paintings hung in two concentric circles. Fortunately for William, the paintings were identified by small brass plaques attached to the ornate frames. At the centre was a portrait of the poet Lord Byron, his plaque revealing that he died over fifty years ago. The other portraits were of much younger men and women and bore only first names. William spotted an Erasmus, an Alexander, a Christina and other less common names. One more exchange, he thought, and then I can go.

'I recognise Lord Byron, of course.'

Habborlain smiled to himself. 'A man out of his time. To

this day, they refuse to commemorate him at the abbey.'

'Ah! Poet's Corner at Westminster Abbey! I have been there many times, sir!' Countless Sunday-school trips had at last furnished him with a truthful contribution. Emboldened, he asked, 'And these others?'

'My family. My children.' Habborlain leant his head in close beside William as he examined the portraits, the pungent hum of sweet smoke still clinging to him.

'My word! How many children do you have, sir?'

'None.'

'But—'

'Dead, William. All dead. As dead as all the ideas I ever had and as dead as all the things I ever believed in.'

William opened his mouth and closed it again. He felt quite sure that this statement would be a stretch for even the most skilled at small talk. They stood in silence, gazing at the faces of Habborlain's lifeless children. So many. How unlucky to have lost such a number, how terribly sad.

Habborlain's voice dropped to a whisper, as if not to disturb the dead. 'It is all connected, don't you see?'

'What is connected, sir?'

The old man waved his free arm about the room. 'All this. All of it! Me!'

Habborlain's eyes urged him to grasp something, but William remained lost. The old man sagged, his eyes closing as he spoke once more. 'I have kept you too long, young William. Perhaps you would ask Mr Bridge to call on me as soon as he is able.'

William held out his hand. 'Then I shall say goodbye.'

Aware of a stray thread dangling from his cuff, he automatically reached out with his left hand and pulled the sleeve of his jacket down. Habborlain's eyes snatched towards William's missing thumb.

Would the humiliation of this meeting never end?

William waited for the usual barrage of questions: How did you lose it? Do you sometimes misremember and feel it still to be there? But instead Habborlain's arm shot out and grabbed William's left hand, pulling it up to the light.

'Good God!'

William wrenched his hand away, shocked once more by the excessive reaction.

Habborlain stared at him hard, eyes wide, his voice a mere whisper. 'The fool! The absolute fool!'

'Who, sir? I have to say this is a lot of fuss over something quite insignificant!'

The front door slammed once more and Habborlain's trance was broken. He withdrew the light and cast the lamp back down on the desk. 'I should have known when Fischer left. Stupid, so stupid! Come, William, we don't have much time. We have tarried too long.' He heaved open the door to the hallway. 'Come!'

More bewildered than ever, William allowed Habborlain to usher him through. Fischer was already in the hallway, hands on his hips as he fought for breath. He addressed William, 'Leaving so soon, sir?'

Habborlain replied before William could. 'That's right, Fischer. In fact, I thought I might join William for a stroll. It is a beautiful day, after all.'

Fischer looked quite flustered at this turn of events. 'Are you quite sure, sir? Maybe after luncheon, after you have rested?'

Habborlain was all energy, reaching for William's coat and umbrella and thrusting them into his confused hands. He opened the front door and bundled William through, as the butler looked from one to the other, clearly not quite sure how to influence the situation.

'But your coat, sir! Your hat!'

William couldn't help but agree with Fischer. Surely

Habborlain was not intending to leave the house in his robe and slippers?

'I came into this world without them, Fischer, I shall leave it without them, no doubt. But not just yet, I think. Good day!' Habborlain slammed the door behind them and marched them away from the house.

'Where are we going exactly, sir?'

Habborlain swung round to look at William and grasped his arms forcibly with both hands. 'There is no more time. We must part here.'

In daylight, he was an even odder sight. The rope of gold around Habborlain's neck glimmered, but failed to enliven the grey pallor of his face. It was as if the fresh air could dissolve him to dust in an instant, although his grip was strong. William had no idea what had animated him so suddenly. Surely the man was truly mad?

'Tell Bridge that *the Finder knows*.'

'Pardon, sir?'

'You heard me. Tell him that the Finder knows everything. Or will do very soon.'

'What does that mean, sir? Just so I'm clear?'

'Forgive him, William, he did not think. The lamb who went to the slaughter willingly, who would have conceived of it? We are old fools. We always were.' Habborlain grasped William's bewildered face between cold fingers. 'You should not have come here, William Lamb.'

'I don't understand.'

'Go, tell Bridge everything. He will help you. Go quickly!'

William wrenched his eyes away and turned back the way he had come. There was clearly no point in convincing the man to return inside. Was it really only half an hour ago that he had first passed this way? He could make no sense of this strangest of encounters with the strangest of men.

He looked back over his shoulder, but Habborlain had already turned in the opposite direction.

'Where are you going?' William shouted after him.

Habborlain's robe flapped in the June breeze as he strode on.

'To hell, William, where I belong.'

*D*etective Inspector Harry Treadway held up his magnifying glass and tilted the fossil towards the window, turning it in his hand to catch the best light.

'So what horror of history have you discovered now, Harry?'

Harry shuffled everything back into the top drawer of his desk as Colonel Silas Matlock approached, smiling broadly.

'Just something I found a few months ago but have yet to categorise, sir. It nags at me occasionally and I can't resist a peek.'

'Jolly good. Well, Harry, I have a case for you, a special case.'

'Oh?' This was most unusual.

A few others had also looked up from their work to follow the conversation. Why would Harry *Traitor* Treadway be given a special case?

Matlock unfolded the sordid details of Phoebe Stanbury's demise the previous evening. 'When the locals sent the summons, I attended the scene briefly myself. The culprit seemed to have melted into thin air so I called it a night. My hands are full with the Tinbergen arrival, so I need you to take over, Harry. My notes are all here.'

Harry found himself losing track of the conversation. 'Why me, sir? Why not Dolly?'

Harry could see Detective Dolly Cunningham, their star man, loitering near the filing cabinets at the far side of the room. He was attempting to feign disinterest, but he was clearly as taken aback at this turn of events as the rest of them.

Colonel Matlock smiled at Harry. His rosy cheeks always glittered with bonhomie, even when discussing the most distressing of cases. 'A case such as this needs your forensic attention to detail, Harry, your dog-with-a-bone attitude. I want no stone left unturned, and no one else here, including Dolly Cunningham, has your tenacity and thoroughness.'

Harry was unused to praise of this sort. It was a long time since he had been given a murder case, let alone one as high profile as this. His attention to detail, as Matlock had called it, was usually vilified as an inability to see the bigger picture, or to move his investigations forward to any sort of conclusion. The last time he had been in Matlock's office, it was to be half-heartedly berated for the volume of his unsolved caseload. He hadn't made an arrest for almost a year. Mostly, he was left alone with his stack of files, all marked open, poring over the details again and again, searching for what he may have missed.

'Thank you, sir, I'm flattered.'

Matlock placed a slim folder on his desk. 'Take all the time you need, Harry. If you need any support, just let me know.'

Stranger and stranger. The unwritten rule of the detective division was that Harry Treadway worked alone. Not from choice, but rather that no other member of the force was willing to work with him any more. Three years earlier it had been Harry who had inadvertently uncovered the corruption within the division while checking timesheets. In many ways, it was his finest moment. Until then Harry had been seen as a plodder, the bespectacled, elderly man in a tweed suit and a polka dot bow tie who seemed more interested in his fossils and biding time until retirement than in sacrificing everything to the cause of justice. Nine detectives had lost their badges and four of them had gone to prison, but it was Harry who had lost everything, his friends on the force and, eventually, his family.

Matlock strode back to his office, and Harry's fellow detectives turned to their work once more. The show was over.

Harry inspected the file he had been given. Matlock's notes were random and his handwriting took some deciphering. Harry's attention kept returning to the portrait of Phoebe torn from the *Illustrated London News*, published at the time of her engagement to Benjamin Raycraft. The girl's smile was engagingly lopsided, turning one corner of her mouth higher than the other and revealing a single dimple on her right cheek. Yet the image yielded no clue as to why she had been murdered the night before in cold blood by a naked stranger at her own engagement party.

'Think you can solve this one, eh?'

Dolly Cunningham's red face leered down at him.

His words stung but Harry simply smiled. 'I shall do my best to find the truth.'

Cunningham guffawed. 'The truth, Treadway? It's felons we're after, not the bleeding truth.'

## CHAPTER SIX

ildred Whitfield hobbled up the grand steps of the Langham Hotel. She paused at the top and fanned herself with her hand. The new dress had been a mistake, made from a thick blue tartan that was more suited to a brisk autumn morning in the Highlands than a summer's day in London.

She looked down. She should have spent her money on new footwear, not the dress. The sole of her right shoe had chosen that morning to partly detach itself as she stumbled from the train at Baker Street. She had been so caught up in her preparations for the coming interview she had almost missed her stop.

*Adversity is opportunity*, her father was fond of saying, and this really was the opportunity of a lifetime. Shoulders back, head up and march on. It's what the Whitfields always did.

Mildred pushed through the revolving door and into the busy reception, ignoring her flapping shoe. 'I'm here to see the Vicomtesse de Bayeau. She is expecting me.'

'Of course, miss.' The receptionist bowed low, as if Mildred were the vicomtesse herself. 'Please take a seat.'

The Vicomtesse Adeline de Bayeau, such a grand name. Mildred had been thrilled to receive the vicomtesse's letter in response to her own advertisement in *The Times* seeking employment. Much secrecy was involved in the arrangements for the interview, which was hardly surprising considering the vicomtesse was half-sister to Otto Von Rabenmarck. Mildred had been instructed not to tell a soul who she was meeting with, or where or when. If successful, she couldn't wait to tell her father she had landed a role as governess to an aristocratic family. He might not be too happy about the German connection, but he was bound to be pleased with her advancement.

It had all happened so quickly, there had been no time to conduct much research beyond discovering that the vicomtesse had been her half-brother's escort ever since the eighty-two-year-old Vicomte de Bayeau had died, leaving her a rich, titled widow before she was even twenty-one. Her brother, the German Chancellor, was almost twenty years her senior. They shared a German father who had died when the vicomtesse was little, her mother having perished in childbirth. There had been no mention of children in the papers, but there must be some, otherwise why would the vicomtesse be hiring a governess?

A maid collected her from reception and she was led up to the fourth floor. As they approached the door to the corner suite, Mildred was grateful for the lush carpet that dulled the impact of her broken shoe.

The maid entered first. 'Miss Whitfield is here, madame.' She moved aside and waved Mildred in.

The vicomtesse stood by a table where the remains of a half-eaten breakfast curled in the morning sun. She was reading a neatly ironed copy of *The Times*, frowning as she did so. Dressed only in a loose silk robe, her appearance took Mildred's breath away. A cascade of red, glossy curls fell across her porcelain skin, and her willowy frame was fashionably thin.

'Guten Morgen, Madame Vicomt—'

'Oh please! Only English or French. Anything but German. Such a ghastly language!'

The vicomtesse swept across the room and retrieved Mildred from her curtsy. 'Come. Sit on the sofa with me.'

Mildred allowed herself to be led to the leather chesterfield in front of the window, caught in a waft of jasmine perfume. As she settled across from the vicomtesse, she could just see through the half-open doors to the bedroom. Two matching calfskin trunks spilled their contents across a Persian rug, and a chaise longue was almost invisible beneath a pile of discarded clothes.

Following Mildred's eyes, the vicomtesse gestured vaguely at the carnage of her boudoir. 'Shut the doors, Isabel, and leave us alone.'

Once the maid had departed, the woman flashed a dazzling smile at Mildred, her beautiful green eyes appraising her beneath finely arched brows. Mildred smiled back, waiting for the vicomtesse to begin the conversation, although she appeared in no hurry to do so. The woman's gaze raked over her unblinkingly, surveying Mildred's form.

Mildred grasped her leather bag on her lap and fixed her eyes on the gold silk drapes behind the vicomtesse, a flush creeping up her neck as she avoided the woman's scrutiny. Was this usual, she wondered, to be inspected in this way? She had only had the one previous employment and she didn't remember Mr and Mrs Unsworth examining her in such a manner. Mildred reminded herself that the vicomtesse was an aristocrat, and foreign to boot. Maybe they did things differently.

'So, Miss Whitfield, your father is a soldier, I believe?'

'Yes, madame. He is a sergeant major in the Fifth Regiment Northumberland Fusiliers.'

'I understand he is a brave man, highly decorated?'

How did the vicomtesse know so much about her father? Mildred had made scant reference to him in their correspondence. 'Indeed, he recently received the Distinguished Conduct Medal for his services in Afghanistan. We are all most proud of him.'

'And your brothers are soldiers too, is that so?'

'Yes, madame. You have obviously researched me well.'

'Well, family background is so fundamental. Where you come from almost always determines where you will end up, don't you think?'

Mildred didn't think so at all but kept the thought to herself, feigning agreement with a smile.

'And are you intact?'

'I beg your pardon?'

'Are you a virgin, Miss Whitfield? Unsullied?'

Mildred swallowed. 'Of course, madame.'

'There's no of course about it, not these days. But I believe from the ridiculous colour of your face that you are probably telling the truth. So, there we are!'

The vicomtesse continued to beam her beautiful smile, forcing Mildred to wonder if she wasn't a little touched. Maybe she should introduce a new subject, move the interview in a more conventional direction?

'Perhaps I should talk a little of my experience to date, madame? I have a broad range of expertise, I believe: geometry, algebra, Latin and Greek, French, some Italian. Drawing is my particular passion—'

The vicomtesse rolled her eyes and jumped to her feet. 'Yes, yes, that all sounds marvellous! You're hired. Someone will come to fetch you and your things later this afternoon.'

Mildred stood up, eyebrows raised. 'But there is so much to discuss! Your children, how old are they? Where am I to live? And terms, we should discuss—'

'Money. Yes of course. Shall we say two guineas a week? Plus room and board and so on.'

'Two guineas a week!'

'Five if you'd prefer? Sundays off. Oh, and Christmas! Young Wolfgang is eleven, and adorable, he really is. He is away with his grandfather right now but I shall rent a house when he returns and we shall all live very happily together. Shall I send someone to collect you at three?' The woman grasped Mildred by the elbow and began walking her towards the door.

Mildred hung back. 'Shouldn't we wait for him to arrive in London?'

'Who?'

'Wolfgang.' The vicomtesse furrowed her brow so Mildred continued, 'Your son?'

'Ah yes!' The woman smiled wistfully, as if attempting to convey an unerring impression of motherly love. 'My sweet darling boy. Let's not wait for him, though. Join me today and we can start house hunting together! Oh it will be such fun!' She kissed Mildred on the cheek.

Before Mildred could be ushered out, there came a sharp military rap on the door. The maid bustled through from the bedroom and opened the door to the suite.

A soldier swept into the room and bowed deeply in front of the vicomtesse, gallantly removing his bronze helmet in one smooth movement. 'Captain Karl Ziegler, at your service!'

Mildred knew her uniforms, and this man wore the distinctive red uniform of the German chancellor's elite personal guard. His blond hair, parted on top, was shorn close around the back and sides above the high collar of his tunic.

'You're new,' said the vicomtesse, her eyes appraising him in the same fashion they had earlier scrutinised Mildred.

'It is a pleasure to make your acquaintance, madame. I must inspect your chambers before the chancellor arrives.' He spoke impeccable English but in a thick German accent, the voice deep and confident.

'What exactly are you looking for? A Turkish assassin beneath my bed? Now wouldn't that be exciting!' The vicomtesse giggled.

The captain didn't respond, and Mildred watched the smile slide from the woman's face as she gave a curt nod towards her bedroom. The soldier returned her gesture and strode towards the doors.

'I really should be going . . .'

The vicomtesse turned towards her as if she had forgotten Mildred was still there. 'Why not wait a while and meet my brother before you leave?' Mildred opened her mouth to protest but the vicomtesse grasped her arm. 'He'll be delighted to know that I've found such a capable young lady to look after his nephew.'

Captain Ziegler returned from the bedroom and swept past them without another glance. The captain marched back down the hotel corridor, yelling, '*Frei*!'

The vicomtesse watched him leave, then leant down to whisper in Mildred's ear. 'What did you think of our Captain Ziegler? *Très magnifique*, wouldn't you say? I'm sure my brother thinks so too.'

'He seemed a fine soldier, madame.'

'And so he is.'

They turned to see Otto Von Rabenmarck standing in the doorway. Dressed in grey flannel, a white rose in his buttonhole, his thick hair was iron grey and immaculately coiffed. A slow smile crinkled around his eyes as he held his arms out wide. 'Adeline, my darling, you look exquisite.'

The vicomtesse entered his embrace and hugged her brother. They were almost the same height, Mildred noticed.

'And who might this be?' he asked, his smiling eyes never leaving his sister's.

Mildred clasped her hands together and cast her eyes downwards. Her father had once called the German chancellor the most powerful man in the world. He'd called him other things too.

The vicomtesse skipped towards her, seizing both of Mildred's hands in hers. 'Otto, my dear, this is Mildred Whitfield, the new governess! I just hired her this morning. Isn't she marvellous? I think we will like her very much!' She pulled Mildred towards her brother.

Mildred was uncertain whether she should curtsy or not, compromising with a dip of her head to her chest in acknowledgement.

He looked at her with amusement – presumably she had mis-judged the protocol. Abruptly, Von Rabenmarck reached out and cupped her chin firmly in his hand. Shocked, Mildred's eyes grew wide but the man seemed oblivious to her discomfort. He tilted her head from side to side, his cool fingers digging in to her cheeks, his examination as intense as his sister's.

The vicomtesse placed a hand on her brother's shoulder. 'Her father is a soldier, highly decorated, her brothers too.'

The chancellor nodded, and dropped his hand to his side. 'It was a pleasure to meet you, Miss Whitfield. I look forward to seeing you again.'

As Mildred shuffled backwards towards the door, the vicomtesse piped up, 'Don't forget, Miss Whitfield, three o'clock this afternoon!'

Mildred managed another stiff nod before closing the door behind her. She bumped straight into the maid, who grasped an envelope in her hand.

'Oh heavens!' Mildred realised she had left her bag behind. She had no desire to re-enter the room she had just left. 'It's Isabel, isn't it? I've left my bag. On the sofa, I think. I really don't wish to interrupt them again.'

Isabel looked her up and down. 'Wait here.'

The maid knocked and entered as Mildred withdrew from sight.

'The young lady left her bag behind. And there's a note for you, madame, marked urgent.'

Mildred could hear the envelope being torn open.

'What is it, my dear?' The chancellor's voice was greeted with silence. 'Adeline? Tell me, is something wrong?'

A guttural cry and something smashed against a wall. Mildred shrank back further as the vicomtesse ranted, 'I knew they were not to be trusted! Didn't I say? All these years, I knew they were hiding something. Losing faith, I could tell. I was right to be watching them, but this? I never expected this! They weren't with us, Otto, they were *never* with us!'

'Give me that!' Von Rabenmarck again. Seconds later he spat a single word, 'Betrayal!'

Mildred heard the maid's voice. 'Can I get you something, madame?'

'Get out!' The vicomtesse's voice choked on the words.

'Pardon, madame?'

'Get out!'

The maid yelped and ran back into the corridor, slamming the door and thrusting Mildred's bag into her hands.

'Are you all right?'

The maid nodded, her face reddening as she breathed away her tears.

Mildred turned and marched down the corridor. What a display! Of course she had no intention of ever seeing them again, not after the way that man had looked at her, as if she were an insect beneath a microscope at the Royal Society. She would tell whoever they sent to collect her that she had changed her mind. The Lord only knew what further transgressions she might have to tolerate for her ludicrous five guineas a week. It really didn't bear thinking about.

## CHAPTER SEVEN

William was in no hurry to return to the office and face Mr Bridge, so he took a diversion via Gray's Inn Gardens and found a secluded bench, watching as the shadow of sycamore leaves ebbed and flowed across the lawn. He replayed the meeting with Habborlain in his mind. He could make no sense of it, and yet he had a feeling that it had made sense in some way, if only he could grasp the thread.

Habborlain's physical presence remained with him: the haggard face, the bizarre costume, his surprisingly lofty stature and the sudden burst of physical energy as they made their hurried exit. William could still smell the exotic, smoky scent that had filled the space, more a mausoleum than a drawing room. He leant down and sniffed at his lapel, suspecting he would need to air his coat outside overnight. He was saddened once more to think of all the children Habborlain had lost – the poor man, living alone with his art and his grief. The butler had not been respectful to either of them; his tone when Habborlain left the house was that of a parent addressing a child he felt little affection for. He must ask Mr Bridge about Fischer. Surely Habborlain, at his time of life, deserved a little warmth and care about him?

There was no point sitting here, ruminating alone. Quite possibly Mr Bridge would give one of his hearty laughs and dismiss the whole thing as the ramblings of an eccentric old man. It was worth facing his displeasure in exchange for a rational interpret-ation of events. He stood up, straightened his coat and walked smartly the rest of the way to Kirby Street.

When he arrived, he took the stairs two at a time such was his keenness to share that morning's proceedings with his only friend in the world. He had to slow down on the second landing as he felt the familiar constriction in his lungs at the slightest physical exertion. He held on to the banister until the tightness passed, nodding and smiling close-lipped as two rowdy clerks from another chambers swung around him and bounced down the stairs.

He arrived to find Sedgwick still hard at work, as if he had not moved since William's departure. William was disappointed to learn that Mr Bridge had yet to return from Lincoln's Inn. He glanced at his watch: only a quarter past eleven. There was noth-ing for it but attempt to act normally until Mr Bridge returned. Fortunately, Sedgwick was as taciturn as ever, asking no ques-tions. With some effort, William managed to concentrate on the drafting of a new trust. He found himself slipping back into the papers he had been so eager to leave behind, pushing thoughts of Habborlain to one side. He found comfort in the routine, the logic and plain sense of it all. This was the world he knew, the world he liked.

Eventually he heard the familiar sound of Mr Bridge clam-bering up the final flight of stairs outside their chambers and his nervousness returned. His employer was a kind and patient man, not easy to anger, but William knew in his heart that Mr Bridge would be displeased with William's actions that day.

Nathaniel Bridge puffed his way into the office, his round face glowing with effort. Removing his hat, he rubbed at the small of his back. 'Remind me never again to take on a client from Shropshire. One would think that all that country air would breed calm temperaments and a willingness to compromise. I thought it was we city folk that failed to realise that life is most definitely too short to spend three hours and a small fortune in lawyers' fees arguing over a ditch. I mean really, a ditch!' Bridge fumbled his key into the lock of his office door.

'Perhaps it is a particularly eye-catching ditch, sir? A ditch of merit?' Sedgwick could be really very dry at times.

William stood up. 'Could I have a word please, Mr Bridge? In private?'

'Of course, William, of course. Come inside.'

William trailed Mr Bridge into his office, closing the door softly, but not before he caught Sedgwick's sympathetically raised eyebrow.

Bridge sighed as he sat down at his desk; clearly it was a pleasure to take the weight off his feet at last. 'So, dear boy, I hope your morning has been more interesting than mine?'

It was an opening of sorts, yet William couldn't quite bring himself to dive straight in. Context was required if he was to explain himself fully. 'I found myself thinking this morning ... about, well, about the future. My future, that is. I am very happy to have taken up the law as a profession. It suits me well, I think, and I suit it, as it were. And I'm ready to take on more work, sir, to prepare myself for partnership maybe one day in the not too distant future? I see you working so hard and thought I really should be helping out more, shouldering more of the burden.'

Nathaniel Bridge let William talk, a fond smile lighting his rosy face. 'Dear boy, of course you must progress! You are doing fine work here, and I am glad that the legal profession agrees with you. Let us dine together one night next week and discuss your advancement. Tell me, have you spent all these hours stewing on this topic whilst I discussed ditches? In that case, I'm not sure which one of us had the most fruitful morning.' Bridge leaned back in his chair, threw his head back and feigned deep exhaustion.

Another time, it would have brought a laugh to William's lips but all he could manage was a listless smile. He had to press on. 'That's not all I did this morning, sir. I went to see a client.'

'Hmm?'

'You see, there was a message and – and you weren't here.'

Bridge was quiet for so long, looking up at the ceiling, that William thought he might actually have fallen asleep. Without moving his head, his employer slowly rolled his eyes down, finally locking hard on to William's. 'Who?'

William could tell there was only one answer that Mr Bridge did not want to hear, and that was the only answer he could give. This was worse than he had thought: the look on his employer's face was crushing.

'Mr Habborlain, sir.'

Bridge didn't move, and his gaze did not waver, boring holes into William's brain. William had expected exasperation, a flash of anger even, but not this cold dread that filled Mr Bridge's eyes. He ploughed on. 'I thought it might help matters. It was, however, as I'm sure you would have warned me had you known of my plan, not the most productive of encounters. He clearly would far rather have seen you than me, although I think he had some affection for me by the time we parted on the street. He showed me his collection, paintings and such, and told me of his family, which of course is very sad. He didn't want to talk about legal matters, at least not with me. I realised very quickly that I should not have gone. He told me in no uncertain terms that he thought so himself. He said to tell you everything and that you would help me.'

Bridge rose from his chair and came around the desk to stand in front of William. 'What other things did he say, William?'

'It didn't make much sense, sir.'

'Try! We don't have much time.'

*We don't have much time?* What on earth did that mean? William did his best to recall the conversation. 'There were so many strange things. He said you were a fool. He said the lamb went to the slaughter willingly. He told me to tell you all of this, and that he had no beliefs of any kind left in him any more because they died with his children. It is even more bizarre in the retelling, sir.'

Bridge grabbed William's lapels. 'A message, William, *he must have given you a message for me.*'

This was fast becoming a stranger encounter than the meeting with Habborlain a few hours earlier, but it was a good prompt, otherwise William might have forgotten. 'Oh yes, he said to tell you that the Finder knows.'

Bridge let go of William and stepped backwards, nodding to himself. He moved over to the window and looked down into the enclosed garden, scanning from side to side. Then he ran to the door and locked it.

'Please, Mr Bridge, tell me what is going on, I don't understand.'

'You said you parted in the street?'

'Yes, he decided to go for a walk, in his slippers, against his butler's wishes, I might add.'

'Fischer. Yes, of course, that would make sense. What time was it, William? When did Habborlain leave?'

William fumbled for his watch. 'About two hours ago. Please tell me, Mr Bridge, what don't I—'

'Two hours ago? Two whole hours?' Bridge had collapsed once more into his chair. 'Oh goodness, William, I am undone. We all are. How foolish!'

'I'm sorry, Mr Bridge. I should not have gone, but I did. Please explain what is going on? Why do you look so frightened? If you're worried about losing Mr Habborlain as a client, I'm sure we can—'

William's employer cut him off with a soft, end-of-the-world kind of laugh that made William feel quite alone.

'Please, Mr Bridge!' William was surprised to see that

Nathaniel Bridge, benefactor and guardian, was crying. He felt his own chest constrict in response. What had he done?

'Ambrose should not have burdened me with this! He is so much stronger than I. You caught him unawares. He had to escape. And so do I, William. I have no time for explanations. They will come for me before I am done. Take this.' Bridge bent down, opened the deep bottom drawer of his desk and removed a small wooden casket. He pushed it across the desk towards William.

William looked at the casket. 'What is it?' he wheezed, the asthma beginning to drag at his chest.

'It will explain everything. See it as your inheritance, William. And the list, it is there too. Keep it safe, it might protect you in the end.' Mr Bridge pushed the casket across the desk. 'Tell no one you have it. Not even the police.'

'The police? But I don't understand!' Frustration was boiling over, and something else – the tang of fear. 'What are you afraid of? Please tell me, sir, I beg of you!'

Bridge's eyes bulged wide as he replied, 'History! The weight of it bearing down, heavier with every generation!' He opened the top drawer of his desk, then wiped the tears from his face. 'Forgive me, William, it has to be like this. I am a coward, you see, and what I fear is the price of betrayal. Ambrose was right: we were such fools. Now take the box. And run, William. Run for your life!'

Somehow, a gun had appeared in Bridge's hand. William stepped forward, arms outstretched. Something precious was slipping away. A visceral howl sucked the air from William's lungs as Nathaniel Bridge held the weapon to his own temple and, without hesitation, shot himself in the head.

## CHAPTER EIGHT

*S*avannah walked to Chancery Lane before picking up the
omnibus to Whitechapel and Pincott's compound. She
hated the omnibus. Back home, you never had to get real close to
other folk, not ones you didn't know, not unless you chose to. She
sat upstairs, her head turned up to the sky and her eyes closed,
that way she could avoid the fetid stink of the streets and the
fetid curiosity of their residents. She heard, rather than saw, their
arrival in Whitechapel. The summer chatter of birds gradually
faded, replaced by the hum of industry and the shouts of hawkers
and brawlers. As they rounded a corner, she caught the strident
bark of a street preacher, telling whoever listened that they were
damned to eternal hell for their sins. Savannah figured the petty
criminals and streetwalkers of Whitechapel knew that already.
He was wasting his time.

She walked the last few hundred yards to the Pestle and Mortar
on Dodd's Lane, buying and eating a pie from a street seller on
the way. The meat was noticeable by its absence but the gravy was
first rate. Not for the first time she marvelled at how a city this
size kept itself fed. She hadn't seen a single cow since she got here.

The tiny street of Dodd's Lane was hemmed in on all sides by
ramshackle buildings that leaned inward. The narrow strip of
sky above looked to be pushing with both elbows to prevent the
street from closing in altogether. As she entered the pharmacy,

grateful to escape the squeeze of people and carts that bumped along the narrow lane, the familiar sound of the shop bell rang out above her head. It was cool in here, quiet too. On the dark walls either side of her, shelves rose from floor to ceiling, crammed with jars of all shapes and sizes gathering dust, the labels long since faded. Many of them, she suspected, contained only ash or dirt or nothing at all. She moved to the counter and pressed the bell, her eyes focused on the grimy curtain that hung over the door to the back room, but no one appeared. She rang again, keeping her finger pressed down.

'All right! All right! Give it a rest, will you!' The pharmacist yanked the curtain to one side and shuffled forward, his head barely reaching the level of the counter. She had met the dwarf before, many times, but he always insisted on the pretence that he had no idea who she was.

'Can I help you, madam?'

She wasn't in the mood for this today. The tension had been building inside since her encounter with the policeman and she was impatient to get to Pincott and say her piece. She searched her mind for the right words.

'Tincture of Theobroma oil.'

'Is it for you, madam, or for someone to whom you are tending?'

'Pardon?'

The pharmacist clearly wasn't happy. He preferred it when a little realism was added to the situation, a little dramatic embellishment. Savannah's bald use of the Friday password evidently felt disrespectful. Nonetheless, he moved the curtain back and nodded to her to come through. Beyond was a storeroom, poorly lit, but Savannah knew her way by now. On the far wall, her fingers felt for the edge of the concealed door. She released the catch and shoved hard. The door flung backwards and the shock of daylight blazed in her eyes.

Before her lay Pincott's compound, a huge yard of maybe a

quarter acre surrounded by rickety buildings of different heights, some newly erected, the planks pale in the sunlight. Others were older and black with soot, inclining this way and that. A confusion of walkways and rope bridges linked them all together.

The yard was all bustle, with the main event a dogfight taking place in the far corner. Savannah could hear the snarling and yelping, although the crowd of men and women who circled the action obscured her view. In another corner, a ruddy-faced youth cracked his whip enthusiastically at a sweating dray horse which jolted forward, dragging a cart packed with crates to toppling point through the archway that led out into another Whitechapel lane. The cluttered, twisting streets of the borough bordered the compound on all sides. Only the birds, and the angels that could bear to look, would know it was even there.

On the other side of the yard stood the main building; at least, it was the place where most business seemed to be conducted. She had no idea what lay behind the other doors. In places, the compound rose three storeys high, but she had never been invited to look around. She imagined airless storerooms, full of stolen goods, or whores.

As Savannah crossed the yard, a familiar figure emerged from the door opposite. 'What are you doing here?' She narrowed her eyes at JJ as he sauntered in her direction.

'What are *you* doing here? Thought you were on shift?'

'Something came up.'

'He won't like it.'

'He can go fuck himself.'

'Language, Shelton. I'm a minor.'

They stopped in front of each other.

'Seriously, JJ, are you doing other work for Mr P?'

'Nah, could do with it, though, was just pleading my case. You know how it is.'

'I know how it is.'

'That why you're here?'

'Maybe.'

They looked at each other, faces full of mistrust, eyes as old as the hills.

'Where's your hoop?'

'Got a penny for it.'

'See you, JJ.' Savannah slapped him on the shoulder and wearily launched herself in the direction of Pincott's lair. She paused at the threshold, pulling in air. She felt an overwhelming desire to sleep for ever. Instead, she pushed open the door.

The twin skulls of Obediah Pincott swivelled in her direction as she entered the room. The waxy shine of his shaved head and Slavic cheekbones caught the light from the single dusty window, casting the rest of his face into stark shadow; the whites of his deep-sunken eyes glimmered only vaguely. The better likeness was revealed by the tattoo on his bare white chest, a life-sized portrait of the face above, but easier to see and far easier to read. His long limbs spilled over the sides of the simple wooden chair, one arm grabbing a nearby beam, another leg slung over the counting table that faced the door, the sole of his boot looming large in Savannah's face.

'So you is here, and the boy is here. I must ask, who is *there*?'

She had to hand it to him, the man got to the point quickly enough. His stubborn refusal to acquire more than the rudiments of the English language, despite having arrived here from the Ukraine as a boy, gave Obediah Pincott a straight-to-the-heart-of-it eloquence.

'No one is there. I'm resigning my post.' Savannah slumped into the only free chair, the others being occupied by clerks hunched over the piles of money that littered the table. They continued counting, only quietly now, placing each coin delicately on top of the other.

'You resign? You work in bank?'

'No.'

'Factory?'

'I told you I wouldn't do this for ever. I said six months.'

'Two months, Miss Shelton. You give me two months. No deal.'

'I'm better than this and you know it.'

Pincott's laugh hit a single note, like a groan, not a laugh at all. 'I know nothing. You come to me off boat. Someone tell you to find me. You say lots of things. *I do this. I do that.* I don't know what is true and what is not. I make you watch. Now you give up. You can't watch, you can't do anything.'

Savannah found herself adopting the same simplicity of language: there was no point in subtlety; Obediah Pincott heard only words. In some ways it was a relief to find her voice again.

'I need more money. And I can't be out in the open like this. You pay me to watch an old man do nothing, but it's not enough to meet my needs. I'm willing to take risks, but not this one, being exposed day after day. I don't fit in. I know you pay more for other work, out of sight, when the lights are out. I have the stomach for it. I need the money. I need to get out of here. Soon. Or they *will* find me.'

'Who will find you? The men who cut your pretty face?'

She said nothing and he didn't push her. He seemed to be pondering her request and her hopes rose as he opened his mouth to speak.

'No.'

'Why?'

'Why is stupid question. You're a woman. I have men to do things in the dark. A clever puppy is still a puppy.'

'Let me prove it to you. Give me something else to do, something you'll pay good money for. I'll show you what I can do.' Savannah didn't care about the desperation in her voice. She sensed Pincott would have minded more if she had tried to hide it.

'Show me now.' The clerks jumped up in unison as Pincott

slammed his leg to the floor and reached towards her with an outstretched arm, coins jumping to the floor.

Her heart sank. It wouldn't be the first time she had arm-wrestled a man, but she knew she could not win against the strength that lay in those arms, naked beneath the Russian great-coat he wore. His eyes had emerged in sharp focus as he leaned forward, red-rimmed, full of challenge. Weariness took hold of her again. He would know this was no contest, but maybe if she showed the bottomless pit of fight within her, he might see something he would pay for? Money, Shelton, money is what you need. Money is freedom.

She removed her leather coat, revealing her own thin arms. She wanted him to see how hard her muscles strained before he slammed her fist into the splintered wood. The clerks stood to one side, but one of Pincott's hard-faced goons with dirty red hair had now entered the room and stood over them, hands on hips, presumably summoned by the excitement of spilled coin.

The Ukrainian grabbed her hand in a solid lock. 'Dub will make the count.'

The goon called Dub sniggered, but her eyes were locked on Pincott's, nothing behind them but the years he had lived.

'Three. Two.' Dub counted down in his dense Scottish brogue. 'One!'

Savannah pushed first and almost took Pincott by surprise before he steadied himself. Once their clenched fists were upright again, she knew it would soon be over. She could feel her elbow jamming into a groove in the wood, beginning to bleed, her face contorting, but she would not look away, not ever. At least when you take me down, you cannot say I gave up. Surely that must count for something.

'Let me know when you have had enough.'

Savannah resisted the temptation to speak, focusing every mote of energy into locking her muscles, joints and sinews into Pincott's hand. She could feel the blood squeezing up into her face, filling out the scar tissue in her cheek until she felt she might burst. She knew that the slightest exertion from Pincott, the merest increase in pressure, would have her down in a second.

'You think you are strong. Not in your arms, but in your heart. You are right, Miss Shelton. You have strong heart. You say *I am survivor*. I do not admire survival. Is just a name you give your story until death calls you on.' Then he slammed the back of her hand into a pile of shillings, sending them tumbling to the floor.

Dub started clapping as Savannah rubbed her hand, seeing no reason to hide the pain.

'You return to your job. Watch Habborlain, but, I double your wages. Hide if you need to. Find a bush, use the boy more, something.'

It was a victory of sorts, she supposed. Double wages meant halving the amount of time she had left before she could leave. It's not what she'd come for, but it would do.

'You owe me two weeks already.'

'Come back tomorrow. I have cash-flow problem.'

The clerks were already down on their knees, carefully picking coins from the sawdust. Savannah refused to look at them, refused to acknowledge the lie in his words. Very well, she would return to Red Lion Square. She would do the job. Let Pincott have his small victories, she could wait for payday. She looked once more at his inscrutable face and something made her ask, 'What's your real name?'

He leant forward once more, his eyes unblinking. 'Obediah Pincott. Two t. Now get out.'

She pulled on her coat and moved to slide past Dub, but he grabbed her ponytail and spun her round to face him. His breath reeked of garlic and she could see the broken red veins that clustered over his pudgy nose as he leered down. 'There's other ways of making money, darling, if you're that hard up.'

Savannah slammed her knee hard into the man's crotch and he fell to the floor, howling in pain. She turned back to Pincott with a triumphant smile.

'Do your job, Shelton.'

Savannah rubbed her arm as she walked back across the courtyard. Pushing through the door to the pharmacy, there was a yelp from beyond.

'Damn it!'

On the other side she found the dwarf scrabbling around in the sawdust. The light from the courtyard illuminated a cream envelope, now partly wedged under her foot. Savannah bent down to retrieve it, dusting her muddy footprint from the fancy gold insignia of the Langham Hotel and the single name *Obediah* written in an extravagant script.

'Give it back!'

'Why? I'm sure you've read it already. Now it's my turn.'

The pharmacist paled and his mouth hung open.

Savannah laughed. 'So, I'm right! You sneaky devil. What would Mr P say?'

'Please. Don't.' The little man looked genuinely afraid.

She handed the envelope over with a smile and moved into the shop. 'So who's it from? Fancy letter like that.'

'I shouldn't have opened it.'

'Why?' she called over her shoulder. 'Is it a love letter?'

His reply was almost lost as she opened the door to the sounds of Dodd's Lane.

'A death sentence.'

*I*t was late morning by the time Detective Harry Treadway reached the Stanbury house. The villa was built in the grand style, with two stone lions sitting high on posts either side of the wrought-iron gate – well, they had clearly failed in their guardianship the previous night. It seemed a peaceful neighbourhood, making it hard to believe what had happened here. Nor were there any gawpers standing about; that would come later when the cause of death became known. It was surprising that the papers hadn't yet been alerted, despite the number of witnesses who could have relayed the sordid story, not least the Society Editor of *The Times* himself. The Stanburys could not have exerted the influence necessary to keep this quiet: that had to be the work of Sir Jasper, future father-in-law to poor Phoebe.

Harry crunched across the gravelled sweep of the driveway and approached the front door where a uniformed constable greeted him warily. As Harry introduced himself he could see that the young man looked rather disappointed. Harry was used to it. The relatively new Criminal Investigation Department of Scotland Yard was famed throughout the Metropolitan police. Their reputation as brave investigators who valiantly fought the toughest of villains and kept the streets safe was undimmed by the scandal of a few years ago. Most bobbies therefore had certain expectations of what a CID detective might look like: Harry wasn't quite the ticket.

'This way, sir. She died in the conservatory, out the back.'

The constable led the way through the house. The hallway was surprisingly bare; a grand staircase such as this one was normally adorned with a myriad of family heirlooms and portraits, accumulated through the generations. He rather liked this uncluttered look, and it wasn't as if the place was unhomely. A large vase of white roses stood inappropriately resplendent on the hall table, and a cushion lay on the single chair that sat to one side. Harry picked it up and admired the careful embroidering of the two entwined letters, picked out in pink thread: B and P. He knew, from all of those years watching his wife contentedly sewing by the fire, how many hours must have gone into making this pillow. He wondered who had worked it: Phoebe, or perhaps her mother? There was no sign of Lydia Stanbury yet. He would leave that encounter until he understood more of what had happened here.

They entered the conservatory. He glanced around the impressive room, noting the overturned chairs and the abandoned china. The scent of roses filled the room still, sickly now as it mingled with the sweet odour of half-eaten fruit cake and the faint tang of congealed blood.

A large area of the stone floor was virtually black. The poor girl must have lost most of the blood in her veins before her heart had stopped. Her body was now in the Hammersmith morgue, although there was no real doubt about the cause of her death.

'Tell me what we know.'

The constable talked Harry through the witness reports. 'Everyone was too scared to follow the man and see where he went. The trail went cold, sir.'

Harry picked his way around the blackened stone tiles towards the doors. 'May I have the key, please?'

'Um, I don't know where it is, sir. Perhaps the doors are still open?'

Harry twisted the handle down and, to his surprise, the door opened. He turned back to the constable, who looked appropriately shamefaced. 'Sorry, sir, we should have locked it. Suppose we didn't think the murdering so-and-so would have the gall to come back again.'

Harry thought that this particular murdering so-and-so, who had killed a defenceless girl in front of so many, had clearly had enough *gall* to do just about anything. He said nothing and walked out into the garden.

The air felt fresh as Harry followed the gentle slope of the garden towards the river. As he came closer, he could make out the muddy footprints of the last man to walk this way, faint at first but growing more distinct as he approached the bank of willow trees. Harry placed his foot alongside one of the prints: the killer had indeed been a large man.

He pushed through the canopy of trees until he reached the riverbank. The mud at the water's edge was packed down, except for a patch close by which had recently been disturbed but was now beginning to harden in the morning sun. Standing as close to the edge as he dared, Harry strained to look as far as he could in both directions. He could see no evidence of a boat having recently come aground along this particular stretch of the river. Upstream, the river disappeared into a large bend towards Richmond. Downstream, however, less than half a mile away, he could see the towers and suspension wires of Hammersmith Bridge. It would have been a difficult swim, fighting the tide all the way.

Harry returned to the house and found the constable loitering in the hallway.

'I'd like to see Mrs Stanbury now. Is she awake?'

'Hasn't been to sleep as far as I know, sir. She's in the upstairs drawing room.'

'Is she alone?'

'Yes, sir. A cousin is arriving this afternoon on the Oxford train to be with her, I believe.'

'Has anyone been with her since this happened?'

'Only the maid and us locals, sir. I came on shift at six this morning.'

'And where is this maid now?'

'Sleeping, I believe, sir. She was up with Mrs Stanbury all night.'

Harry gave the man instructions to conduct interviews with all local residents who had a view of Hammersmith Bridge yesterday evening, and anyone who might cross the bridge at the same time this coming night.

'Of course, sir. What would we be asking them, sir?'

'Whether they saw anything unusual.'

'Such as, sir?'

Harry removed his spectacles and cleaned them with a hand-kerchief taken from his pocket. 'I suggest you start by asking whether any of them saw a tall man jump off the bridge and swim upstream, possibly naked, and then see where the conversation goes from there.'

'Of course, sir. Right away.'

Harry climbed the stairs with sombre footsteps. It was surprising that after such a trauma, Lydia Stanbury had been left alone with her bereavement. Surely, if she had no relatives nearby, the Raycrafts themselves would have seen fit to attend to her in some way. After all, she was almost part of their family. Harry braced himself for the avalanche of grief that he knew must wait for him on the other side of the door.

He knocked lightly. 'Mrs Stanbury? I am Detective Harry Treadway. May I come in?'

He waited a decent interval, but hearing nothing, knocked again. 'Mrs Stanbury?'

'It's open.' The sadness of the world weighed heavy in her voice.

Harry stepped into the room. He was taken unawares by the bright sunlight that poured through the windows, expecting instead to be greeted by drawn curtains and gloom. The walls were painted a pale grey and the two light blue sofas and the white flowers on the table in the bay window stood in stark contrast to the dark-haired woman, clad head-to-toe in black, who sat ramrod straight on the sofa that faced the door.

'Please take a seat.'

Harry did so, making himself comfortable before he spoke. 'Mrs Stanbury . . . Firstly, I would like to offer to you my heartfelt condolences on your loss. This must be a terrible time for you. I understand you have family arriving later today?'

Lydia Stanbury closed her eyes. 'My family is dead.'

Harry nodded. He knew what she was trying to do – to stare into the bottomless pit of sorrow and face the truth. Harry had done the same himself. He knew that it wasn't bravery that had made him do it, but rather cowardice – the mistaken belief that if you looked grief in the eye it would reward your nerve and shrink away. It didn't work, of course, grief remained for as long as it wished to stay, whether you looked on it or not.

'When did you lose your husband, Mrs Stanbury?'

'A year ago today.' She looked at him defiantly, as if daring the world to send her some fresh awfulness, just to see how much she could stand.

Harry nodded again. To the point then. 'I need to ask you some questions about the events of last night. I know you have already given a statement, but it helps enormously if I hear the details first hand.'

'Of course.' She took a deep, slow breath and sat up even straighter.

Taking a small notebook and pencil from his pocket, Harry patiently asked his questions, starting with who had been there, and establishing the timings of all the comings and goings.

'So, Sir Jasper himself was not present?'

'Apparently Lady Raycraft was taken ill.'

The questions and answers continued. Her recall was impressive, but it didn't surprise him. Rather than shrink from the details, Lydia Stanbury was the kind of woman who would play the scene over and over in her head until everything was sharp and blinding.

'Tell me more about the tattoos.'

'It was the same image repeated. A large one I could see on his chest, smaller ones elsewhere – his legs, his lower arms.' She paused, as if pulling the image of her daughter's murderer back to her. 'I think he must have made them himself. They were only in the places he might reach. I know very little about tattoos but they looked uneven, amateur.'

'Might you be able to draw the shape for me?'

'I can try.' She took the pencil and notebook from his out-stretched hand. She drew a shape but scratched it through angrily and started again. Moments later, she handed the notebook back to him.

'It was quite intricate. I'm not sure I have all the details. It was like a flower within a circle. Something like that.'

Harry looked at the geometric shape she had drawn: circles layered upon each other, seeming to form petals. Harry tucked the notebook and pencil neatly away in his breast pocket.

'Is there anything else you recall, Mrs Stanbury? Anything that you think may help?'

Lydia Stanbury nodded, uncertain. 'I'm not sure if I have this right. I meant to ask Benjamin, but there wasn't time and it didn't seem important. Sir Jasper arrived here so quickly once we sent the alert . . . ' She paused again, wading through the last moments of her only daughter's life.

'Go on.'

'I really don't know if this is correct. My mind has played so many tricks on me in the hours since . . . ' Momentarily, her backbone sagged and her hands fluttered before she once more regained her iron control. 'He knew him.'

'I'm not sure I follow.'

'The man who killed Phoebe. He knew Benjamin. He spoke to him – and the look in his eyes … he *knew* him.'

'What did he say?'

Her eyelids closed once more, and again he admired her bravery as she tried to bring a piece of something back.

'He said, "I did this for you … I promised I would save you."'

'Are you sure?'

'Yes.' Her voice was clear and confident once again.

Harry tapped his fingers lightly against his mouth as he pondered the woman's words, a gesture his wife had always claimed to find annoying but which he also knew she thought endearing in equal measure. He put the memory back in its place and turned the key.

So the murderer knew Benjamin Raycraft, or at least had claimed to.

'Thank you, Mrs Stanbury, you have been very frank and most helpful.' He rose to his feet and bent to shake her hand lightly. It was dry and cold. 'I will keep you informed of the progress of our inquiry.' He knew better than to try to offer further words of comfort.

As he opened the door, her voice called him back. 'You lost them too, didn't you? Your family.'

Harry turned around to face her once again. He said nothing.

'Yet you go on.'

He nodded briefly before turning away.

*Yes, I do.*

## CHAPTER TEN

William sat on the stairs outside the office, huddled against the banister, his arms wrapped around his knees to calm the worst of the trembling. The policemen had asked him to leave the room while they interviewed Sedgwick. Mr Bridge's body lay slumped over the desk in his office while a man from the coroner's office examined the scene and took notes.

William's ears still rang from the gunshot, and every few minutes or so he saw and heard it all again, his own hands rising too late. *Run for your life, William.* It had been less than an hour since Mr Bridge had shot himself, and in that time William had done no more than watch as Sedgwick stumbled through, first summoning the police and then coaxing William to relate the bare facts, his voice a monotone. When had it happened? William wondered. At what precise moment had the real world slid away to be replaced by this imposter? Had this new world been there when he awoke that morning, masquerading as the life he knew, lying in wait to shout *Surprise!* the moment he knocked on Habborlain's door?

Sitting on the stairs, he tried to muster his rational lawyer's mind so he could begin to explain the inexplicable, but that part of him stubbornly refused to come out of its hiding place. Numb and cold, he strained to focus on the conversation taking place on the other side of the door.

'And how would you describe Mr Bridge's behaviour when he returned to the office?'

'Normal, sir.'

'And what was normal for this particular gentleman?'

Sedgwick paused before answering. 'Happy. Looking forward to luncheon, no doubt. Normal.'

'So what did you hear after Mr Lamb followed Mr Bridge into his office and closed the door?'

'Nothing. Not for a few minutes. Then the gunshot.'

'I see. No raised voices? No indications of disturbance?'

'Disturbance, sir?'

'A fight, Sedgwick.' There was a pause before the inspector spoke again, an angry note in his pompous voice. 'This is no laughing matter, Sedgwick. May I remind you that your employer is dead!'

'Of course, sir. I didn't mean to smile, sir. It is just the thought of young William and Mr Bridge *brawling*, sir. Well, it is amusing, and highly unlikely in my opinion, sir.'

'Then how do you explain a man who is perfectly happy in one moment, and then suicidal the next?'

'I cannot, sir. That would be your job, I believe.'

Another pause. 'Very well, Sedgwick. You may go.'

'Go where, sir?'

The office door was flung back, and the inspector strode out into the hallway. He was a portly man, with short black hair slicked with oil and a sharp widow's peak. His pallid face was now marked with two red spots of colour high on his cheeks. The inspector sniffed as Sedgwick shuffled past him into the hallway.

'Come with me please, Mr Lamb.'

William and Sedgwick traded places without looking at each other as William followed the policeman back into the office.

'Sit down.'

Sedgwick's chair had been placed in the middle of the room. It seemed an inappropriately intimidating approach to interviewing the witnesses, but William did as he was told. The two policemen stood over him. Inspector and Sergeant something-or-other, William couldn't recall their names.

'Tell me again exactly what happened when you followed Mr Bridge into the office.'

This time, William concentrated harder on the details, trying to find his own explanation for the madness of Mr Bridge's behaviour. 'I told Mr Bridge that, in his absence, I had been to see one of his clients, Ambrose Habborlain. He was very unhappy with me. I don't know why. I gave him a message from Mr Habborlain, *the Finder knows*. I didn't understand what it meant but that is when Mr Bridge started to act very strangely. He rushed to the window and looked out. Then he came back to his desk, and—' William glanced at the casket on his chair, Mr Bridge's warning in his head: *tell no one you have it*. 'Then he took out the gun and . . .' William swallowed the words down, his hands twisting in his lap.

'Smiley, go and see if the coroner has finished.'

That was it, *Sergeant Smiley*. As Smiley opened the door to the inner office, William caught sight of the picture on the back wall, an ordinary landscape. He had seen it every day for the last five years but had never thought to ask Mr Bridge why he had chosen it or what it had meant to him. For the first time, William felt a tremendous sorrow roll against the wall of shock that had risen about him the moment he had seen the gun in Bridge's hand.

Smiley called the inspector into Bridge's office. 'Dolly, coroner wants a word.'

*Dolly?* William remained seated while the three men conversed in the other room. He thought of Sedgwick waiting outside and fervently hoped that the clerk would know what to do next. A funeral would need to be organised. They would have to find the will, contact the clients and make arrangements. He would have to tell Aunt Esther. How on earth would he do that? William could feel his breathing grow shallow as the enormity of the situation began to break through.

The inspector returned to the room. 'So, Mr Lamb, the coroner's initial view is that this was quite possibly a suicide.'

Quite possibly? With a jolt, William realised the police had to consider all options. Even he, who had seen the act with his own eyes, could understand how hard it was to believe that the avuncular Mr Bridge would do such a thing.

'Arrangements will be made to move the body. For now, I suggest both you and Mr Sedgwick go home for the day. You will be able to clean up and get back to normal from tomorrow, I would say.'

Get back to normal? The man clearly didn't understand anything. The inspector thrust a card in William's face. 'We will be in touch in the next few days to confirm the formalities. There will need to be an inquest, of course. In the meantime, you can contact me if you should feel the need.' The tone in his voice implied the opposite. The man clearly didn't care what might have caused such agony for Mr Bridge that suicide had seemed his only option.

As the inspector let Sedgwick back into the room, William studied his card: Detective Inspector Adolphus Cunningham, Criminal Investigation Department, Scotland Yard.

William rose from his chair and took his coat from its hook. He reached for his umbrella. Every action seemed profound and pointless all at the same time.

'One more thing, are you both sure that there is no family?'

'Quite sure, sir,' Sedgwick replied.

Only me, thought William. As he waited for Sedgwick to prepare to leave, he glanced back at the casket on his chair. Maybe the answers would be contained within. The box was plain walnut, clearly old. The only decoration was a symbol carved into the lid: a series of overlapping circles, like a flower.

With his back turned to the detective, he picked it up and folded his coat over his arm to keep it hidden.

'He was so terribly scared.' William's voice caught.

Inspector Cunningham sighed. 'Of what?'

Bridge's words returned, the snap of gunshot, the smell of burning. 'He didn't want to die. I know it!' William pleaded, close to tears.

The inspector patted William's shoulder with an outstretched hand, as if William's tears might be catching. 'In my experience, son, if something looks like a spade, behaves as if it were a spade, then in all likelihood it is a spade. And if by any chance it isn't, then it only has itself to blame if it is branded as such.'

Sedgwick looked as bewildered as William felt. The final pat on William's shoulder seemed more like a slap as the inspector continued, 'Most men are afraid of something. Go home, son.'

The two clerks walked together in silence down the stairs and out into the street. William was surprised to see people dashing on with their lives as if nothing had occurred: a woman scolding a red-faced child, the tailor next door shouting at the men unloading a cart in front of his shop. William felt a heavy cloud of sorrow scud across the hot afternoon sun.

'What happens now, Sedgwick?' William could barely hear himself.

'Let us leave those questions for tomorrow, sir.'

William nodded, not trusting himself to speak.

'Go home to your aunt, William.' It was the first time the clerk had used William's first name. 'Tomorrow, we shall engage with what is to be done. There are always solutions, you will see.'

'Why did he do it, Sedgwick?'

The clerk shrugged. 'I don't know. But you mustn't blame yourself. The seeds of such a deed ... well, they must take time to grow so deep within a man.'

'But the inspector was right, Sedgwick! Nobody is happy one moment and without hope the next!'

Sedgwick smiled ruefully. 'No, indeed they are not. Tell me, William, if Mr Bridge was so content, why did he keep a loaded gun in his desk?'

The thought slapped William hard in the face. The gun had been placed there deliberately, the need anticipated.

'Go home, William. We will talk tomorrow.' The clerk patted William on his arm as he took his leave.

William, weighed down with his umbrella and the mysterious casket, hailed a cab to take him home and to the conversation he was dreading.

Normally, William felt joyful when he saw his own front door, the newness of it all welcoming him home, but his heart was in his boots as he climbed the steps. Mr Bridge had been like a father to him, but had also been the closest thing to a friend his Aunt Esther had. He couldn't think how to break the news to her. Hopefully, she would just look at his face and know something terrible had happened, the words redundant as they embraced each other.

He entered the cool, familiar hallway and slammed the door behind him, bringing Sarah running up the stairs from the basement.

'Mr Lamb! Whatever are you doing here at this time?'

'I have a headache, Sarah. Where is my aunt?'

'She went out after lunch, Mr Lamb, for a stroll along the river, it being such a lovely day.'

William was strangely disappointed. He had built himself up to this moment of revelation and had almost been looking forward to sharing the burden he carried. He realised how selfish that was, that he shouldn't begrudge his aunt another few hours of innocent happiness.

He refused the offer of tea and trudged upstairs to his room, taking the box with him. Lying down on the bed, he stared up at the ceiling and willed his mind to look back objectively on the day's events. Mr Bridge had killed himself. Was it William's visit to Habborlain that had triggered it, or the message he had brought back, *the Finder knows*, or something else entirely? Was William somehow responsible for Mr Bridge's death? The thought tore through him and he covered his eyes with his hand as he felt the tears begin to flow. Shock and grief swelled within him and demanded release, so he allowed the sobs to come, hoping Sarah wouldn't hear.

After several minutes he lay still, listening to the gentle wheezing in his chest. Vaguely, he sensed how hungry he was and how tired. As he began to nod off, his mind floated back to the last words of that doomed conversation in Mr Bridge's office. *It will explain everything. Keep it safe.*

William's eyes snapped open. He jumped to his feet and picked up the box from his dressing table. Taking a deep breath first, he opened the hinged lid.

He unfolded the first sheet of paper: a list of a hundred or so names in three columns. The name Ambrose Habborlain jumped out, a few well-known names too, but a cursory glance indicated there were no other clients on the list. He laid it to one side to examine later and withdrew the next sheaf of papers from the box. They were yellowed with age and, as he unfolded them, they almost fell apart along the lines of the deeply scored creases. He concentrated on the top page, but couldn't decipher a single word. He scanned through the other pages with increasing frustration – they were all written in another language, one that used an entirely unrecognisable alphabet.

William looked in the casket again. At the bottom lay a very thin layer of paper, parts of it crackled away into smaller bits or crumbled to dust completely. Carefully, he lifted out what he could: it felt like skin, old and dying. Any words it still held on its surface had faded to wisps of grey, and he replaced it before the paper could turn to powder in his hand.

He was about to return to the list of names when Sarah knocked at the door. 'I found a letter on the doormat, sir.'

William took the envelope. His name was written on the front but there was no address, no postage. Someone must have delivered it by hand. A client, perhaps, who had already heard of Mr Bridge's death?

He withdrew the single sheet of paper.

*Leave. Do not return. Meet me.*
*Cosmati*
*Hena Kai Nea*
*Hespera*
*A.H.*

William ran to the window, pushed open the bottom sash and looked up and down the street. No one was there.

*Run for your life*, Mr Bridge had said before turning the gun on himself, and now Habborlain too had delivered the same instruction, for surely the note came from him. William felt a hot flash of anger towards them both, with their cryptic messages and explanations written in a language he couldn't understand.

He crumpled the note in his pocket and replaced the other papers in the casket, slamming the lid shut. He had had enough of mysteries for one day. He had not been thinking clearly – he should have gone straight back to Red Lion Square. With new purpose, William left his room. Breaking the news to Aunt Esther could wait, for only one man had answers for him now.

## CHAPTER ELEVEN

Harry wondered what to expect as the hansom carriage rumbled through the wealthy streets of Hampstead towards Ridgeside, the famous residence of Sir Jasper Raycraft. The general population viewed Sir Jasper Raycraft as a modern magician, encouraged by constant newspaper stories of his most recent inventions, and his home was rumoured to utilise the very latest in scientific developments.

As the carriage twisted up the hill beyond the heath, the traffic thinned and Harry caught only the occasional glimpse of the vast estates behind the thick canopy of trees that shielded the rich from prying eyes. The air here was fresh despite the mid-afternoon heat. The carriage rounded a corner and turned left into a plain driveway, the horse's hooves crunching loudly through the gravel.

Harry leaned out of the open window and called up to the driver, 'Are you sure this is it?'

'Certainly, sir. Every cabbie in London knows Ridgeside. The tourists like to come here. If you stay on the road you get a really good look from the next bend. Mind you, first time I've ever been this close. Quite excited, sir.'

The driveway cut narrowly through a dense thicket of fir trees as it meandered along, and Harry found himself growing impatient to finally set eyes on this palace of modernity. Having telegraphed ahead earlier, he hoped he would find both Benjamin and Sir Jasper himself in residence.

The house came into view, catching Harry by surprise. It resembled a medieval castle, the massive central structure towering several storeys high. The house sprawled in all directions, a rebellious gesture towards the symmetry and order of Georgian London. The building jutted and receded randomly, the Gothic gables and mullioned windows all at different heights. Harry could only marvel at the complexity of the red-tiled roof that had to shield such an arbitrary range of architecture. In front of the house, the land sloped downwards. Behind, a tree-covered hill rose sharply, the crags forming the backdrop to the assorted red brick chimneys that drove up to the sky. It was difficult to believe the house was only a few decades old.

The horse snorted through the exertion of the last steep climb towards the tall wooden gates of the central tower. As they pulled to a stop, a servant came out to greet them and spoke to the driver. 'You may take your carriage around to the stables. Your horse can rest and eat there.'

The driver thanked him and, leading his horse, trudged slowly towards the stables, gawping at the house as he went.

The servant spoke to Harry. 'You must be Detective Treadway. Master Benjamin is expecting you. Follow me, please, sir.'

In the hallway, a chaos of ornately carved staircases led in different directions, confirming his earlier perception that nothing was on a level in this house. The servant took him to the left, climbing five steps up to the room next door, a cosy morning room with a large inglenook fireplace of brick and a low, beamed ceiling. As they passed through another door, Harry noticed that, up close, the wood was not as old as it appeared, rather it had been charred evenly and varnished to give the impression of great age.

Beyond the door, a staircase led steeply downwards, turning at right angles back on itself. The stairwell was lit by a large globe that hung from the ceiling and Harry paused, allowing himself to be impressed at his first glimpse of electric light. The servant followed his gaze and smiled. 'Fascinating, isn't it, sir?'

With as much pride as if he had invented it himself, the servant flicked a brass switch on the wall and allowed the globe to fade to darkness before turning it back on. In a matter of seconds, the globe was as bright as it had been before.

'Most extraordinary!' Harry offered.

The servant flicked the switch once more and darkness descended. Harry heard the switch click again, but this time no light followed. After a few more clicks, the servant cleared his throat.

'Oh dear, it appears to be broken.'

Harry could hear the anxiety in the man's voice. 'Do not worry, I shall not tell.'

Muttering his gratitude, the servant led on through the gloom toward another antiqued door and they stepped into daylight once more. Harry found himself in an enormous library, twenty feet high at least. To his left, a massive window rose up to the ceiling, the stone casing several feet deep as if built to withstand a war. The other three walls were lined with books, broken by narrow ledges from which hung a complex matrix of wooden ladders. In the centre of the room, dwarfed into insignificance, sat two armchairs and a low table that perched on a faded rug, a life raft in a sea of polished wood.

Harry circled the room as the servant left to fetch Benjamin Raycraft, gathering his thoughts for the coming interview. His eye was immediately drawn to the back of the room, where a large shape glittered in the shadows. As he approached, the object revealed itself to be a magnificently carved silver swan, several feet high, each feather separately detailed. The amazing sculpture sat on a bed of thin glass rods surrounded by delicately made leaves of silver. Harry leaned closer, and saw tiny silver fish beneath the rods, the whole structure effectively mimicking a stream. It was truly beautiful, he thought. Behind the swan was a silver casket. Finding it hard to resist, Harry touched his fingers to the box. Caught up in his own fascination, he lifted the lid.

Out of nowhere, a tinkling melody filled the room. Harry nearly jumped out of his skin when the head of the swan turned towards him. The glass rods had also started to move back and forth and the fish beneath twisted and turned, creating the illusion of running water. The graceful neck moved fluidly as the swan dipped its head toward the water. How was this possible? How could something made of solid metal move in this way?

'I was terrified too when I f-f-first saw it.'

Harry whirled around to find Benjamin Raycraft standing behind him.

'My apologies. I have a well-developed sense of curiosity, as you can see, but it can be a dubious quality.'

'A rather good one in a police officer, I w-w-would have thought.'

'Indeed.'

The music stopped and the swan returned to its original position, static once more.

'It's called an Automaton. My great-grandfather had it made in S-S-Switzerland. The mechanism is c-c-clockwork. It's over a hundred years old.'

'No electricity? That is what I assumed, of course, once I got over my fright!' Harry smiled, hoping to relax the stuttering young man before him.

'Father says that one day everything w-w-will run on electricity. Carriages, houses – even servants – will be replaced by m-m-machines.'

Harry thought that unlikely, but if it were the case, then he was glad that he would likely not be alive to see it happen.

Benjamin turned towards the chairs in the centre of the room. 'Shall we sit?'

'I think that would be a good idea.'

A look of resignation crossed Benjamin's face as he eased his thin frame into one of the chairs. His fine blond hair was beginning to recede and Harry felt a stirring of pity for him.

'I would like to offer my condolences for your loss, Master Benjamin. This must be very hard for you.'

The young man shrugged, conveying a clear message: many things in life were hard for Benjamin Raycraft.

'Perhaps you could take me through, in your own words, the events of last night.'

Benjamin Raycraft nodded but took his time before speaking again. Gazing into the distance, he recalled the bare facts of the night before: a short speech, the words clearly carefully chosen. Only towards the end did his composure seem to fracture a little. 'I didn't r-react as soon as I sh-should have done. By the time I reached him, he had d-d-done the deed. He turned on us then, w-waved the knife so we backed away. Then he was g-gone.'

For the first time it occurred to Harry just how brave Benjamin had been. When he had first heard of Benjamin's rush to intervene, his actions had conformed to what one might expect of a young, vigorous man compelled to save his fiancée, but that was before he had met this stumbling youth whose suit drooped from his shoulders as if it would slide off him at any moment. Benjamin was no man of stature. To confront the mystery assassin would have required an extraordinary nerve.

The headlines of Benjamin's story confirmed what countless witness statements had already set down, but he had made no mention of the words that Lydia Stanbury claimed the murderer had spoken to him.

'Did he say anything to you?'

Benjamin looked down at his hands. 'I don't think so.'

'Are you sure?'

'I don't know.'

'Had you seen the man before, Benjamin?'

Benjamin's eyes flicked up to meet Harry's and his voice was stronger this time. 'No. I do not think so.'

Harry tapped his fingers to his lips. 'How did you meet Phoebe?'

'My f-f-father introduced us. Mr Stanbury used to w-w-work for him. He ran the export side of the b-business.'

'I see.' Harry smiled to cover his thoughts. Although Benjamin was clearly not the son that a man such as Jasper Raycraft would have wanted, he would nevertheless have expected him to make a more socially ambitious marriage for Benjamin than the daughter of one of his managers.

Harry pulled his notebook from his pocket and passed Lydia Stanbury's drawing to Benjamin.

'Do you recognise this?'

Benjamin glanced fleetingly at the page and then handed the notebook back to Harry. 'No.'

'No? I'm surprised. Most of the other witnesses saw the man's tattoos clearly. This was Mrs Stanbury's attempt to draw the likeness.'

Benjamin sat upright in his chair. 'Oh, the t-tattoos? Yes, they looked something like that. I didn't see them c-closely.'

Harry dropped his voice. 'Where else have you seen this image, Benjamin?'

Benjamin sagged again. 'Nowhere. I've n-never seen it before.'

That there were lies in Benjamin's answers was abundantly clear, but why? Benjamin visibly squirmed in his seat under Harry's benign gaze. Again, Harry felt a jolt of sympathy for this boy who couldn't even dissemble with any competence.

Harry rose from his chair. 'Very well, Benjamin, that will be all for today. May I speak with your father please?'

'He isn't here. He's at the f-f-factory.'

'Then I shall call for him there.'

'I'll let them know you are c-coming.'

Presumably, Ridgeside was also equipped with a telephone. Colonel Matlock had just had one installed although Harry had yet to see it used.

'I'll ask someone to sh-show you out.'

Benjamin wiped his palm quickly on his trousers and rose to offer Harry a limp handshake. He reached down to the coffee table and pressed a large brass button atop a wooden box. When nothing happened, he pressed it again.

'Oh dear, the c-circuits must have failed.'

'Don't worry, I shall find my own way out.'

As Harry reached the door, he turned back to smile at Benjamin, who stood stiffly with one hand on the back of his chair, insignificant in the cavernous space of the library.

Harry watched his steps as he climbed the unlit stairs, retracing the way he came. As he approached the morning room, he heard a woman's voice singing softly within, a performance that was clearly not intended for any audience. He stood on the landing, in two minds as to whether to enter. He cleared his throat loudly and knocked on the door. The singing stopped abruptly, but no one responded. He waited a few moments before opening the door and jumped in surprise at the sight of a woman standing immediately in front of him, eyes staring.

Harry quickly arranged his face into a smile but feared that his initial reaction to her had been all too visible. Her head was mostly bald, with a few stray wisps here and there. There was a particularly livid sore just above her right ear, and another on her cheek. The brutal shadows under her eyes added to her macabre appearance.

'I'm sorry to have interrupted you, madam, but this is the only route I know back to the hallway. I am Detective Treadway and I have just been visiting Master Benjamin.'

The woman continued to stare and showed no sign of moving out of his way. He was about to retreat to the library and find another exit when she spoke.

'My son. Benjamin is my son.' Her cultured voice contrasted with her monstrous visage.

So, this was Lady Raycraft.

'May I pass through, madam? I wouldn't wish to detain you any longer.'

She stepped to one side, never taking her eyes from his. The effect was unsettling.

'Thank you, Lady Raycraft.'

'Why are you here?'

She clearly had not been told of Phoebe's murder, and Harry felt no desire to update her on events. 'Just a routine query, nothing to worry about. Good day, madam.'

Harry moved gingerly across the room and started down the steps to the hallway, just as a nurse breathlessly clattered into the room from the other direction.

'There you are! I wish you wouldn't wander off so!' The nurse clucked her tongue and steered Lady Raycraft back towards the door. 'Who were you talking to?'

Harry had by now reached the hallway but could still hear the conversation.

'They've come for him at last!'

'Who are you talking about?'

'The police. They are going to punish him for what he has done to us.'

'Shh, now, no one has done anything.'

'He is damned – and now the world will know!'

'Calm yourself!'

Harry heard the door to the library slam shut behind them,

leaving him alone in the hallway. Lady Raycraft clearly did not have all her wits about her, but her words cast a chill nonetheless. It was often the case, of course, when investigating a crime, that one became intimate with the family affairs of witnesses and suspects. Most family dramas that unfolded in this way were mundane: a touch of cruelty maybe, or a secret from long ago grown stale in the darkness. The Raycrafts were no different, the only surprise being the illustriousness of the household in which the story unfolded. That Lady Raycraft hated her husband was not in itself surprising, but the reason certainly was.

She was dying of syphilis.

The Raycraft Armaments factory sprawled over several acres of prime waterside beside the Regent's Canal. As the cab approached the main gates, a small group of men and women, wearing the drab, grey Raycraft uniform, raised their banners while a single policeman stood idly to one side. Harry caught the eye of one of the strikers, one half of his face distorted with blisters. Harry looked away, but not before observing in the man's gaze both challenge and resignation in equal measure. The strike had clearly been continuing for a while and had now sunk into stubborn defiance, but he could see the defeat in their faces.

Intrigued, Harry asked the driver to drop him outside the gates. The strikers looked at him with suspicion as he approached, more so when he showed them his badge.

'We've told your lot before, we ain't moving—'

'I just wish to speak with you, that is all. Why are you here?'

The group needed little prompting to discuss their experiences of working in the huge brick building behind them, as its three towering chimneys belched clouds of toxic smoke into the sky. The ringleader, a scrawny individual named Tom, listed their grievances, which included a startling number of accidents that had befallen workers in the last few years. 'I make it seven deaths in two years and over twenty serious accidents. No compensation was offered. Most of the injuries were caused by machinery, but a few of them came from the weapons' testing itself. Stray bullets and fires and the like.'

The man with the blistered face interjected, 'And them is only the ones we know about. You need special clearance to work in the basement – they pay more down there, but only a few get asked. They say some have gone in there and never come out again.'

'What happens in the basement?' asked Harry.

Tom dropped his voice. 'More weapons development, from what we know, but the secretive kind. Last year there was a leak and a gas of some sort escaped into the main building, near the women's facilities. Three of our number were taken to hospital, their skin covered in yellow pustules, screaming in pain they was. Two of them never came back to work here again. Daisy, show the man your arm.'

A big woman rolled up the sleeve of her smock. The skin from wrist to shoulder was puckered and leathery, like a burn that had never healed.

'You poor woman.'

'Yeah, well, I had no choice but to come back. Got four kids at home and no husband alive to feed 'em. Then I got fired for makin' a fuss. So I live on handouts and wave a banner every day. Won't be long till we're all on the workhouse steps.'

'Murderers . . .' muttered Tom, his gaunt face full of conviction.

With a promise to talk again, Harry left them behind. He entered the complex and picked his way through the activity of the central courtyard to the management offices located nearby. The crisp air of the Hampstead hills felt like another country.

The office building was the tallest, rising over the compound like a lookout tower. Harry was greeted on the ground floor by a suspicious guard, whose manner didn't soften when Harry introduced himself as a CID officer here on urgent business. He was kept waiting for twenty minutes, jammed into the corner of a crowded bench with nervous salesmen and impatient proprietors waiting for their appointments to materialise.

Harry had spent most of the journey pondering his encounter with Benjamin Raycraft and his mother. Between them and the strikers he had conjured a portrait of Sir Jasper Raycraft that was less than flattering. Benjamin's stutter and apologetic demeanour was surely testament to an overbearing paternal influence, and the less he thought about Lady Raycraft's unspeakable predicament the better.

It was important that he meet Sir Jasper without preconceptions obscuring his view, though it was proving difficult to put them aside. He thought of how he had cherished his own precious wife, dead for three years now, and of how he had nurtured and supported his only son, bolstering his strengths and helping him overcome his weaknesses, so different, he suspected, from Sir Jasper's approach to parenthood. Thinking of his son immediately summoned the sweet faces of his two grandchildren and he fingered his bow tie, a gift from both of them three Christmases ago. It had been the last time he had been allowed to see them.

Harry swept the pain aside and focused on the task ahead, for he suspected that Sir Jasper would be a less straightforward interviewee than young Benjamin.

Eventually a debonair young man in a pinstripe suit arrived to rescue him from the holding area. 'Good afternoon, Detective Treadway, I am Sir Jasper's private secretary. Please follow me.'

Harry followed him through a door into a small but grandly decorated lobby. The thick carpet hushed the sound of their footsteps as they approached a pair of recessed doors.

The secretary inserted a key into the wall and Harry's eyebrows rose as the doors automatically slid back, revealing what looked to be a small closet.

'After you, sir.'

Harry looked at Raycraft's secretary, unsure how to frame his response politely.

The man smiled. 'It's a *lift*, sir, powered by hydraulic electricity. It goes up and down to each floor, sir. It's really very safe, I assure you.'

'Of course.'

Harry stepped into the closet, feeling foolish. He had always been more interested in the past and paid scant attention to the newspapers' fevered reaction to the latest scientific novelties. Maybe he should turn his magnifying glass on himself – a fossil in the making.

Once they had stepped in to the tiny room, the secretary pressed a button and the doors closed seamlessly, sealing them in. He grasped a large brass lever to the side and with both hands pulled it dramatically through a half turn. Immediately, the closet began to rise. Harry stared forward as the doors slowly disappeared beneath them leaving only the brick walls of the shaft as they travelled upwards at a stately pace. The journey took only half a minute and they rode in silence. The experience was curiously intimate, Harry thought, and consequently he was unable to think of anything to say as both men stared fixedly at the brick wall passing in front of their eyes. The physical exertion of climbing stairs had been replaced by the embarrassment of being trapped in a small space with a stranger. He really wasn't at all sure whether he would call this progress.

They arrived at a set of identical doors. The lift stopped and the doors stuttered open. Relieved, Harry stepped out into another reception area flooded with light. Floor-to-ceiling windows on either side were filled with massive single panes of glass, as if there were no glass at all. Uncomfortable with heights, he felt slightly giddy and was glad to be offered a seat.

Raycraft's secretary knocked discreetly on the door to the inner office before opening it and poking his head around the corner.

'Sorry to interrupt but Detective Treadway is here to see you, sir.'

'A moment, please.' Raycraft's voice carried clearly to the next room. It had a low, breathy quality, rather like an actor's, Harry thought.

The secretary gave Harry a tight smile before sitting at his desk and officiously shuffling some papers. Harry leant forward, daring to peer out of the nearest window, judging himself to be at least five flights up. The group of strikers looked tiny and insignificant from these lofty heights, easy for Sir Jasper to ignore. Tom's words whispered through Harry's mind. *Murderers . . .*

Harry turned back as Sir Jasper emerged from his office.

He was an impressive man to behold: tall and slim, his suit exquisitely cut and fitting his frame perfectly. As he greeted Harry, he ran his hand through his thick blond hair. 'You must be Detective Treadway. I can hardly believe what has happened, such an awful business. Murder . . . ' He closed his eyes and shook his head. 'Just saying the word makes one shudder.'

## CHAPTER TWELVE

William stumbled on to the train at Hammersmith and took a seat, uncertain which stop would take him to Red Lion Square. He didn't even know if the train was early or late – in fact he had no idea what time it was. He removed his pocket watch – half past four. Was that right? He hadn't checked the time since before Mr Bridge returned to the office, the routine act of another lifetime.

He glanced around the carriage, seeing only two other passengers, so unlike his normal rush-hour commute. William suddenly felt very alone, and the emotions that he thought he had purged earlier in his room threatened to overwhelm him once more. He took the crumpled note from his pocket. *Cosmati. Hena Kai Nea. Hespera.* The first word rang a bell of sorts, although he could not place it. The rest was incomprehensible. Greek, maybe? It was his own fault, he supposed, claiming that morning to be something he wasn't: an educated man of the world.

He alighted at Euston but stopped at the foot of the stairs. Maybe he should return home and wait for Aunt Esther to make sense of it all? He thought of the speech he had rehearsed that morning before any of this had happened, *I'm a man now, Mr Bridge.* Had he been a fool to think so?

A porter clattered into him from behind. 'Watch where you're going, lad!'

William took a deep breath and walked up the stairs towards the daylight and the answers he hoped to find. He walked with purpose, framing the questions he would put to Habborlain, for he would accept no obfuscation or riddles this time. He wished he had thought to bring the casket with him. Maybe Habborlain could make sense of its contents?

William stopped as he realised he was in front of Habborlain's house already. He looked around the square. The garden was almost empty now, save for an urchin boy perched on a bench facing the house. The afternoon heat had most likely chased everyone back to the cool of their homes. He raised his hand to knock on the door, girding himself for the confrontation ahead.

Surprised, he dropped his hand to his side. The door was ajar. He pushed it open and took several steps into the hallway.

'Hello?'

There was something in the silence that made the hairs on the back of his neck stand up. He stepped further into the hallway and glanced quickly around. He realised that the grandfather clock, which on his previous visit had filled the room with a rhythmic thud, was the source of the silence. The clock face was smashed, the hands registering the time as twenty minutes past three. Uncertainly, he approached the drawing room and knocked gently. 'Mr Habborlain?' But there was no reply.

William opened the door. The room was almost in darkness. Only a few dusty beams of sunlight shed any light through the gaps in the heavy drapes. William waited until his eyes adjusted to the shadows. Where was everybody? Maybe he should find the kitchen or the servants' quarters. As he began to turn, his heart froze: a movement, in one of the chairs before the fireplace.

Someone was sitting there.

'Mr Habborlain?'

No answer came. William could hear the sound of his own breathing, wheezing up through his chest. For the second time that day, he could feel the beginnings of an asthma attack. Just then, he saw a plume of smoke drift up from the chair. Habborlain, it must be, playing more games no doubt. Well enough was enough. He marched forward, impatience making him brave.

'Now you listen to me, Mr Habborlain! I have had enough of your—'

William sprawled to the floor as he tripped over a heavy object in his path. Landing flat on his chest, he struggled once more for breath as he tried to pull himself up in the darkness. He leant on the object that had caused his fall – and felt its softness.

The figure in the chair had shot up when William tripped and had now moved to the window.

'Mr Habborlain?' The words barely made it out of William's mouth before the figure ripped back one of the curtains, flooding the room with daylight. William shielded his eyes and looked down at the floor, before reeling back in horror as he saw where his hand rested. Fischer, the butler, lay dead before him.

William shuffled backwards, slamming hard into the desk. Bile burned his throat but he couldn't tear his eyes away from Fischer's dead stare and the soft pinkness of the man's own genitalia protruding from his mouth. The image blistered William's mind, holding him in its grasp.

He was dimly aware that the figure was moving towards him now, blocking the sunlight, its shadow flitting across the floor. He tried to find his voice but his lungs were locked tight. He dared to look up as the figure advanced steadily, arms forward, holding something.

A gun. It was another gun.

'So, why don't you tell me who you are?'

A woman's voice, foreign. Fischer's eyes pulled at him once more. No air, anywhere. Just Fischer's gaze, gripping him like a fist. His chest a lifeless vacuum, William stared back, slowly suffocating, unable to look away until he heard the distant ratchet of the trigger.

'Who do you work for?'

The gun, unwavering, was all he could see now, his airways glued together in the face of it. The fear of death in one direction, the horror of it in another. A scraping rattle escaped his throat. A single thought, *I am dying*.

The woman sighed, dropped the gun to her side and came towards him. His legs jerked forward in defence, helpless without oxygen.

The woman knelt down and pushed him on to all fours as his chest froze and his mouth hung open for the air that wouldn't come. She circled her arms around his stomach and squeezed tightly, forcing his diaphragm upwards. The pressure in his chest increased tenfold. She repeated her action, squeezing harder this time. The world was bleaching to white, a thrumming in his head, the last beats of his failing heart. The pressure was unbearable. This is it. Goodbye to Aunt Esther, to this day, to everything that made absolutely no sense at all ... She squeezed again, and suddenly he let out a great sigh. The woman let go and his body instinctively gulped in a lungful of sweet, sweet air.

'Slowly does it. Breathe out. Breathe in. Breathe out. Breathe in. There you go.'

The woman slapped him lightly on the back and stood up. William took several more breaths before pushing back on his haunches, the danger still present. The panic threatened to return as he caught sight of Fischer's body on the floor nearby, the mutilation compelling him once more. Dragging his attention away, he focused instead on the woman who was now pacing the room, this woman who had pointed a gun at him before saving his life. Who was she?

His voice rattled when he spoke. 'Thank you.'

'You're welcome.'

She looked down at him suspiciously, arms wrapping her leather coat tightly around her. A curious creature, with dark olive skin and large almond eyes. A long scar stretched down one side of her face and her dress was rather short. A remote part of his fractured brain noted that this day had brought many firsts: guns, dead men and now a woman's ankles.

'Are you going to kill me?' Exhaustion made him blunt.

The woman snorted. 'Depends if you annoy me.'

'Who are you?'

'I asked first.'

William couldn't resist glancing back at Fischer. He whispered, 'Did you kill him?'

'Nope,' she said, clearly not caring if he believed her or not.

William finally felt able to stand. He grasped the desk and pulled himself up. 'My name is William Lamb. I'm looking for Ambrose Habborlain.'

'You're not the only one, by the looks of things.'

'Why are *you* here?'

'A question I have been asking myself for the last two months.'

William slumped into the chair behind the desk. The desire for answers that had propelled him here was reasserting itself, a primal need that would not be denied, whatever it meant for his own safety.

'Why did you point a gun at me?'

'When in doubt, it's what I do.'

'Well, that's just marvellous, isn't it? Jolly good for you.' Despite his shaky breathing, William's anger broke the surface. 'Maybe I too should stride about waving a gun at people. Then maybe, just maybe, somebody would answer a straightforward question with a straightforward bloody answer!' He thumped the desk, not caring if his heatedness angered her or brought on a relapse.

The woman stared back at him. 'I think I preferred you when you couldn't speak.'

William sighed. 'I apologise. My language was inappropriate. It's been a rather trying day, I'm afraid.' He almost laughed. A trying day?

The woman shook her head and looked back towards the window, biting her lower lip. 'All right, this is what I know. I'm here because I am paid to watch the house. When the door was left open, I got curious. Fell over the same thing you did, looked around, found nobody and nothing. So I sat down to think. Then you arrived.'

'Who is paying you?'

The woman leant across the table. William caught a glimpse of the swell of her breasts, and quickly looked away as she said, 'If I told you that, then I really would have to kill you.'

She pulled back but continued to stare at him. 'Why were you looking for Habborlain?'

'I needed answers.'

'What were the questions?'

What was the point in trying to explain? He couldn't even explain it to himself. Wearily, he summarised his predicament. 'I visited Mr Habborlain this morning for the first time. He is a client of my employer—'

'Bridge?'

'You know . . . *knew* Mr Bridge?'

'Not exactly. Go on.'

'It was a strange meeting. I thought he was simply a trifle eccentric. When I returned to the office and told Mr Bridge, he was scared of something. The weight of history, whatever that means. He shot himself.'

The woman raised her eyebrows. She almost looked impressed.

'I don't understand any of it.' William rubbed his eyes.

'No, neither do I. But I think you should go.'

William cleared his throat and stood up. 'We should alert the police first.'

'Of course.'

'Very well, I shall go immediately. We are bound to find an officer somewhere nearby.'

'Tell you what, why don't I do that? You've had a trying day. You said so yourself. Best get on home, pour some brandy into that chest of yours.'

William normally didn't like the taste of alcohol. In fact, he hadn't tried it since Mr Bridge had bought champagne for his twenty-first birthday luncheon and William had spent most of the afternoon in his room with a terrible headache. Right now, however, the thought of a brandy almost appealed. It was certainly tempting to leave this woman to notify the police. After all, she seemed a lot more comfortable than he was standing only yards from the mutilated body. He could see Fischer's feet from where he stood, had to stop himself from looking further.

'Wouldn't that be fleeing the scene of a crime?'

The woman seemed to ponder the question. 'Well now, maybe it would. But I was here first, it's my responsibility to report it.'

'Who would have done this? Why would anybody do this?'

The woman shrugged once more and looked over to where Fischer lay. 'A jilted lover, perhaps?'

'This isn't funny.'

'I wasn't laughing.'

His faculties were beginning to return, and William realised he had seen her before: outside Habborlain's house when he had first visited that morning, which lent credence to her story that she was watching the house for someone, but he really wasn't sure if he could trust her or not. The urge to leave the room was, however, overwhelming.

'Very well, I shall leave you, if you don't mind, to deal with the police.'

William fished out a card from his breast pocket. 'If they

wish to contact me, this is my office address. And if Mr Habborlain should return, perhaps you would be so kind as to let me know.'

The woman didn't even look at the card before thrusting it into her own pocket. She looked him straight in the eyes. 'What happened to your thumb, by the way?'

William looked down at his hand, adding up the number of times today he had been asked that question one way or another. It was yet another reminder of how many people he had met today, compared to his usual narrow existence. To think he had bemoaned that fact over breakfast that morning. Now he wished he hadn't met anybody new at all.

'Nothing happened to my thumb. It never existed.'

The woman nodded, obviously not caring either way.

William felt emboldened. 'How did you come by your scar?'

'In a fight.'

'How dreadful. I am sorry.'

'You should've seen see the other guy.'

Reminded of the woman's propensity for violence, William made his excuses. 'I had better leave. If you're sure.'

'You can rely on me.'

William was grateful to leave the room behind him as he entered the hallway, his legs still trembling and strange. Was he right to leave a female here alone? William sensed that the normal rules of courtesy did not apply to a woman who wielded a gun and held her own modesty in such low regard.

At the threshold he turned around. 'Thank you for what you did. Not for pointing a gun in my face, obviously. I mean the . . . squeezing . . . '

'Anytime.'

William blushed despite himself. 'Good day to you, madam.'

The woman grinned at him and dropped into an elaborate curtsy. 'You are very welcome, kind sir.'

William straightened at her sarcasm. 'You didn't tell me your name.'

'I guess I didn't.'

Her face was impassive and William felt it was pointless to push her on this. After all, she might change her mind about killing him. With the stiffest of nods, he walked away.

## CHAPTER THIRTEEN

*S*avannah took one last look at the butler's dead body.

Despite the brutal mutilation, the killing had been quick and efficient. A single knife wound under the ribs, angled upwards towards the heart. Death would have been instantaneous. The dismemberment, thankfully, looked to have taken place after the man died. Why did they bother with that bit of decoration, she wondered? Maybe it was a message, but for who? Habborlain?

She had seen Dub and another of Pincott's men enter the house not long after she had returned to her post. They had stayed barely five minutes before leaving again. Dub had looked over to the bench where she sat, dutifully watching the house. Their eyes met, and Dub left the door ajar with a tantalising smile. *Take a look, why don't you?* She had resisted the temptation to explore until JJ returned at the appointed time for his shift. It was clear that something was very wrong, but what she found when she entered the house was still a shock. There had been little time to assess the situation before the young lawyer had stumbled in, but clearly she had missed something of significance here during her unhappy encounter with Pincott that morning.

She slammed the door of number sixteen behind her and strolled across the square to where she had left JJ ensconced on the bench. He was eating the pasty that she had turned down in favour of indulging her curiosity.

'So?' JJ managed to get the word out despite having his mouth full.

'Not much to tell.'

'No one there, then?'

'No one alive.'

'Ah. The old man's snuffed it?'

'Nope. The butler. Knife through the ribs and his cock in his mouth.'

JJ's eyes grew wide. Still, he tore off another large mouthful of pasty before he spoke again. 'Shouldn't we tell Pincott?'

'I think he already knows.'

JJ had arrived after she had seen Pincott's men enter and leave the house and she didn't feel inclined to share the information.

'What did you see, Shelton?'

'Just some men.'

'Did Olly follow them?'

Savannah had forgotten all about the bemused young boy she had left behind that morning. He hadn't been here when she finally returned. Presumably, in the absence of JJ and herself, he had scampered off in search of other employment.

JJ's questions continued. 'Why did you leave earlier? It's not allowed.'

'Got ants in my pants.'

'I'm surprised Mr P didn't kill you for it.'

'Yeah, well, the day is yet young.'

'Who was the bloke who went in after you? Was gonna warn you but he seemed harmless enough.'

'A nobody.'

Harmless was as good a word as any to describe William Lamb, lawyer of this parish. Most Englishmen seemed tethered to an invisible post, domesticated. She wondered how people like him actually survived in this world, before she remembered that there were two worlds: the world of William

Lamb and her own world of shadows. She wasn't sure what had shocked him more, falling over the butler's body or her choice of attire. Surely he must struggle to last a day in this city without something or other bringing on the ludicrous hysteria she had witnessed. She'd struggled hard not to laugh in his face when he suggested that they inform the police. Maybe people like that believed so wholeheartedly in their own innocence that it never occurred to them that others might not take the same view. *I just happened upon a dead butler, Mr Policeman. Nothing to do with me, of course.* William Lamb was clearly incapable of committing such an act, and that would be a last line of defence against a lawman's probing questions. Savannah, on the other hand, lacked the same quality. Any policeman worth his salt would see it in her eyes.

That said, this William Lamb might not be as innocent as he claimed to be. He had obviously visited the house while she was absent. Maybe it was one big coincidence but three things had happened since: Habborlain's lawyer had ended his days with a bullet, his butler had been murdered, and Habborlain himself was obviously missing. The stakes had been raised in a way that made life more interesting and a lot more dangerous. Maybe Pincott would need her other services after all?

JJ licked his fingers and brushed some crumbs from his jacket. 'What do we do now? Better not hang around here with a dead butler and all that.'

'Good question. How about I go back to see Pincott and you do what the hell you like?'

JJ nodded, staring ahead at nothing in particular. 'We missed something, didn't we?'

Savannah laughed. 'Sure did, JJ, sure did.'

She pushed herself off the bench and turned to say goodbye. She probably wouldn't be seeing him again. 'Take care of yourself, kid.'

'Maybe I could look you up later?'

Once again, Savannah saw the boy behind the delinquent, but she had no room for passengers. So once again she turned away.

## CHAPTER FOURTEEN

*S*ir Jasper chose to sit behind his desk for the interview, rather than the comfortable arrangement of sofas and chairs near the fireplace.

'I'm not sure how much I will be able to help you, Detective Treadway. Obviously, I wasn't *there* and I didn't *see* what occurred.' His voice was pure theatre, emphasising words with a dramatic flourish.

Harry nodded. Sir Jasper's statement, like his choice of seating arrangements, conveyed a clear, defensive message.

'Perhaps you could relate your experience of last night, Sir Jasper?'

'Very well. I was at home yesterday evening when a police officer arrived and broke the news to me. It must have been about eight o'clock. I left immediately and arrived at the Stanbury house about an hour later, I suppose. The girl's body—'

Harry interrupted. 'You mean Phoebe?'

Harry detected a twitch in Raycraft's cheek as he continued. '*Phoebe's* body had been removed already to the morgue. I stayed until the police had finished their preliminary investigation and then brought my son home. He was most distressed, obviously.'

'Obviously.' Harry paused to consider his next question but Sir Jasper was keen to proceed.

'Terrible business as I said, quite *horrid*. Will that be all? I'm a *very* busy man.'

'Why were you not present, Sir Jasper?'

'I beg your pardon?'

'Your son's engagement party, why were you unable to attend?'

Sir Jasper pursed his lips and ran his hand through his thick mop of hair. 'My wife was unwell and I thought it best not to leave her. Benjamin was in agreement. I missed the engagement party, detective, not the wedding.'

'I met your wife this morning. How long has she been ill?'

Sir Jasper's eyebrows flew up and his face began to redden. 'I hope you did not question her, Detective Treadway. I won't have her upset by any of this. Anna suffers from a rare condition.'

'I simply ran into her as I left the house. It was a very brief encounter.'

Sir Jasper sat back in his chair and eyed his opponent. 'Will that be all?'

Harry ignored his question. 'I understand Phoebe was the daughter of one of your managers?'

'Yes. John Stanbury had been an excellent employee for many years.'

'How did he die?'

'I really can't see how that might be relevant.'

'Two deaths in one family within a year *is* unusual, unless natural causes are responsible, of course. Did he die of natural causes?'

The silence hung in the air as Sir Jasper openly appraised Harry. He laced his hands and placed his index fingers to his lips, almost mirroring Harry's own telltale gesture. 'No, he did not. He died in a coaching accident near his home last year. It was a sad loss for all of us.'

'Back to happier times, then. How did Phoebe and Benjamin meet?'

'Phoebe came with her parents to our spring party at the

house last April. We hold one every year for senior employees and their families. She and Benjamin liked each other immediately. They were engaged shortly afterwards. Obviously, when her father died a few weeks later, the celebrations were postponed.'

'So you approved of the match, Sir Jasper?'

'I don't see how that is any of your business.'

Harry held his hands up. 'I am sorry, sir. I had no intention to offend. I am simply trying to understand as much as possible about the situation.'

'Surely it's very simple? A madman broke into the Stanburys' house and murdered a poor young girl. I don't suppose you have apprehended him yet?'

The challenge in his voice was unmistakable and it was Harry's turn to feel defensive. 'No, we have not. We shall be questioning other residents and passers-by this evening. For now, we have no idea where the man went. One final question, Sir Jasper, do you recognise this symbol?'

Harry handed over his notebook where Lydia Stanbury had drawn her recollection of the tattoo that covered the murderer's body. Sir Jasper looked more prepared than his son had been for this particular question, making a big show of placing his large black-rimmed glasses on his nose and holding the book at exactly the right distance to demonstrate maximum scrutiny. You would have thought he was studying a particularly complicated recipe. 'I'm afraid I do not. Sorry.'

Sir Jasper removed his glasses, handed the notebook back to Harry, and stood up, buttoning his jacket. With a close-lipped smile, he gestured Harry towards the door.

Harry rose from his seat, taking his time to put the notebook back in his pocket. In truth, he wasn't quite ready to leave yet, but Sir Jasper was making it very difficult for Harry to probe much further. Looking around the room, his eyes immediately alighted on the display case that dominated one wall: on the central shelf sat a row of human skulls.

Approaching the macabre exhibit, Harry smiled at Raycraft. 'I hope these aren't former employees, sir?'

'Unfortunately not, detective. Some of them are thousands of years old.'

Harry noticed that all of the skulls were identified by small brass labels tacked to the case: *New Guinea, 16.9 centimetres. Black Forest, 17.6 centimetres.* 'The dimensions of the human skull are of interest to you, Sir Jasper?'

'They were. A little project of mine that came to naught, but I thought they made a fetching display.'

A large metal contraption with adjustable spokes occupied the end of the shelf, no doubt the tool used to measure the skulls accurately. Harry hoped the previous owners of the skulls had not been alive when it was used.

'I myself have long been fascinated with the writings of Mr Darwin. Do you follow his work, sir?'

'I follow my own work, Detective Treadway, not anyone else's. I don't mean to hurry you but I'm afraid I have other matters to attend to.' Raycraft opened the door to the outer office.

Rather than following the direction of Sir Jasper's gesture, Harry walked over to the far window, another single large pane. Swallowing his queasiness, he looked below into the busy yard and again saw the group huddled despondently by the gates.

'How long have these workers been on strike, sir?'

Sir Jasper was still waiting impatiently for Harry, his hand on the doorknob. 'Almost six months.' He shook his head. 'The fools.'

'They must care passionately for their cause, sir.'

Sir Jasper laughed. 'Never make the mistake, detective, of confusing passion with rightness. The passion with which one believes something does not, thank the lord, make that thing true. There are men all over this land who desperately want more:

the vote, higher wages – or whatever else their little hearts and half-baked chartist, pulpit education demands. But wanting it, and being entitled to it, remain two very different—'

A loud crash from the outer room interrupted his speech. Sir Jasper screamed and slammed the door, almost falling over a chair as he backed away. Seconds later, the door flew open once more and the secretary looked at his employer in surprise. 'I apologise for alarming you, sir, I simply dropped a vase. I shall clean up immediately.'

Sir Jasper nodded dumbly and straightened his waistcoat, his cheeks blushing violently. 'Very well.' He cleared his throat. 'Perhaps you can show Detective Treadway out. He was just leaving.'

Harry bade farewell as he shuffled past. Sir Jasper nodded in reply but avoided his gaze. No matter; Harry didn't need to look him in the eye to know that Sir Jasper Raycraft was terrified of something.

Or someone.

It was almost six according to the overly large clock that dominated one wall of the CID office of Scotland Yard. Harry sometimes thought that it was meant for him: a constant guilty reminder of the seconds and hours that ticked by as he perused his caseload for clues and solutions. Often he thought he could hear it, tick-tock, but in truth it made no sound.

The late June sun slanted across the office floor. Harry watched the dust motes dance in mid-air as he waited to update Colonel Matlock on progress so far. He had arranged to meet an old friend who worked at *The Times*, Finian Worthing, at half past six, but suspected he would be late.

He glanced down at the notes on his desk, written in his small neat script. There would be a lot to cover. Unfortunately, he wasn't the only one waiting to see Matlock. Dolly Cunningham was loitering near the colonel's office, recently returned from an apparently brutal murder scene in Red Lion Square. Two men from the Lord Mayor's office were also waiting impatiently for an audience: the preparations for Vice President Tinbergen's visit on Sunday were occupying most of Matlock's time and energy. Harry was tempted to leave his update until the morning but knew that he would be unlikely to sleep unless he was able to chew over the day's investigation with another enquiring mind. He had always found Matlock's insight extremely helpful – there had been many a case where he had helped Harry see the wood for the trees. Lord knows, he needed help now.

Harry picked up his notes and wandered over towards Matlock's office, hoping to catch his attention first when he finally emerged from his previous meeting. Dolly Cunningham frowned at him, but then Dolly Cunningham always did.

'Productive day I hope, Harry? I presume the murderer is already clamped in irons?'

Cunningham laughed and Harry smiled back good-naturedly. He was used to this sort of ribbing from his colleagues. 'So tell me, Dolly, how many villains have you put behind bars today?'

It was a genuine question but Cunningham took it as a slight, turning his back on Harry. Obviously the answer was none, unusual for the handcuff-happy detective.

The door to Matlock's office flew back and the colonel stepped out, still smiling affably despite his long day of meetings. He said goodbye to various soberly dressed men that Harry didn't recognise, probably civil servants from the Foreign and Home offices.

Matlock looked at the assembled crowd waiting to see him, rubbed his hands, and with an apology to everyone else, called Harry in first.

'Let's talk police work, Harry – it would be a welcome distraction from security towers and manpower deployment. These Americans are a nervous bunch, I have to say. The assassination in Russia has them flapping. Glad they don't come here too often or even I might stop smiling.'

Matlock flopped into his chair and leant forward across the desk in expectation. The smile was still there, but Harry could see shadows under his eyes. Strictly speaking, as head of the CID, the colonel would not have been involved in such matters, but Silas Matlock was widely tipped to be the new commissioner of the Metropolitan Police when the current incumbent stepped down in the New Year. As one of the few senior army officers who built rather than destroyed their reputation in the Crimean war, he was an obvious candidate to oversee the logistics of managing large crowds and orchestrating unprecedented numbers of security personnel.

'It must be quite a challenge, sir,' Harry sympathised.

'That it is, Harry. These days, our standing army is dispersed across the globe. The might of this country actually consists of small huddles of men dotted here and there, keeping the imperial show on the road, an illusion, if you will. We don't have the manpower for this sort of thing, at least not here, not any more.' Matlock shook his head. 'Take my mind off it, Harry, have we found the brute who killed poor Phoebe Stanbury?'

Harry placed his notes carefully on the desk in front of him. 'It's been an interesting day, sir, but I'm not sure what it all amounts to.'

'Go ahead, Harry, I'm all ears.'

Harry laid out the bare facts of the case and the version of events that most of the witnesses seemed to agree on. He showed Matlock the drawing Lydia Stanbury had made of the naked man's tattoos and outlined the instructions he had given to the local police to question anyone that passed over Hammersmith Bridge at the same time that evening in the hope that they might pick up the trail of the naked murderer.

Matlock seemed happy with Harry's progress. 'Jolly good,

Harry. Let's hope your approach gives us more to go on in the morning. Let us speak again tomorrow.'

Harry paused. 'There are a number of complications, however . . .'

Matlock's smile broadened. 'There always are, aren't there, Harry? Come on then, out with them!'

'Four things concerned me, sir. Firstly, Lydia Stanbury heard the murderer speak to Benjamin Raycraft, suggesting that he killed Phoebe in order to protect him. She got the strong impression that he knew Benjamin, or at least thought he did. Benjamin denied the man had spoken to him, but I didn't believe him. Secondly, Benjamin and his father both denied that they recognised the tattoo symbol, although it seemed to me that they clearly did. Thirdly, Phoebe Stanbury's father, who worked for Raycraft, died in an accident a year ago. I've had the Hammersmith coroner check the records, sir. An open verdict was recorded. Not everyone was convinced it was an accident although nothing could be proved at the time.'

Harry paused to allow Matlock to take all this in.

Matlock leant back in his chair and stretched his hands behind his head. Harry could almost see the cogs of his brain whirring. 'So you think the Stanbury family may have been deliberately targeted, and that the Raycrafts know more than they are letting on?'

As ever, Matlock had summarised Harry's suspicions perfectly. 'It is one interpretation, sir.'

'You need to tread carefully, Harry, and you will need to dig up more evidence. Focus on finding our murderer. If there is a conspiracy here, he will be the key. I doubt much will come from pushing the Raycrafts until you have more to go on. Sir Jasper will make life difficult for us if we don't play this right.'

Harry nodded; it was good advice. There was no point reinterviewing the Raycrafts until he had more justification for his suspicions. Finding the naked man was still the priority.

He rose to leave, unsure how to approach his final concern, but Matlock made it easy for him.

'You said there were four things that worried you, Harry. I can count, you know, and you have only given me three.' Matlock's eyes glittered with sharp humour.

'Outside the factory I met a small group of striking workers. Their story made my hair stand on end, quite frankly, sir. Injuries, deaths even. The work is clearly dangerous and the accidents are being covered up. I thought I might investigate, sir, when this matter is concluded.'

The habitual smile on Matlock's face had, during Harry's speech, worn thin. 'Very well, Harry. Can you make some detailed notes of exactly what they claimed? I would have to justify the allocation of resources.'

Harry plucked a sheet of paper from the pile in his hand. 'It's all there, sir.'

Matlock took it from him, the smile returning to his face. 'Good old Harry. What would we do without you?'

Harry turned to go and Matlock rose, following him to the door. He slapped his hand on to Harry's shoulder and squeezed.

'Good work, Harry. Although it seems we have ended the day with more problems than solutions.' His smiling eyes grew more serious. 'Be careful, Harry. We do not have the resources to open another Pandora's Box.'

As she rode the omnibus to Whitechapel, Savannah tried to piece together the order of events, based on her own observations and those of the young lawyer, revealed between gasps of air. None of it made sense and her decision to leave her post for the second time that day made her nervous. Maybe she was supposed to have stayed at the house, watching for Habborlain's return? But there had been something in Dub's smug smile that implied the game was up and she had no intention of hanging around the square waiting for someone to discover the body.

Maybe it was a mistake to return to Pincott's at all, but without knowing more, she couldn't judge whether now was the time to run. At the very least, she needed to get paid and, ideally, Pincott might have some interesting work for her now that the situation had escalated in some way.

Her ruminations occupied her all the way to the door of the Pestle and Mortar. As the bell above the door sounded, it pulled her back to the moment and the conversation ahead. She felt under-rehearsed, anxious as ever before an encounter with the man with two skulls. The pharmacist was already behind the counter, cleaning his fingernails delicately with a rusty scalpel. He pretended not to notice her approaching the counter.

Savannah leant down so her face was close to his and spoke softly in his ear. 'Boo.'

The dwarf didn't look up. 'May I help you, madam?'

'Don't worry, I can help myself.' She placed both hands on the counter and swung herself over to the other side, nudging the pharmacist as she did so.

'Ow!' The little man sucked the blood from his finger.

Savannah bent down and kissed him on the top of his head. 'Just checking you bleed like the rest of us.'

Despite his protestations, Savannah marched through the back room and out into the hidden compound. The sun was still bright although low in the sky, cutting the yard sharply in half. Savannah walked into the shadows and towards her second meeting of the day with Obediah Pincott.

Before she could reach the door on the other side of the compound, Pincott strode out to meet her, his face screwed up against the sunlight in his eyes. Savannah stopped in her tracks as he approached, pondering what her opening line should be, but Pincott maintained his stride. She realised what he was about to do a fraction of a second before he swiped her hard with the back of his hand and sent her sprawling to the floor.

She landed brutally in the sawdust, her shoulder crunching in to the solid earth beneath. The smell of dung filled her nostrils as she gently levered herself to a sitting position. She remained on the ground, rubbing her shoulder. Let him see that he hurt you then he might not hurt you again; a lesson learned young and never forgotten.

Pincott stood over her. '*Seven years* we wait for something. Seven years I take money from client. Then something finally happen and I know nothing! *Nothing!* Stay in the dirt, Shelton.' His boot connected with her bruised shoulder and she bit down the pain, but the touch was lighter than it could have been.

'I'm sorry.' The simple statement was directed at Pincott's boot.

'The world is full of sorry. Sorry mean nothing.'

'Let me make it up to you.'

Pincott laughed, a hollow sound. 'How you do that? Turn back clock? See what you should have seen? A lawyer with no thumb?'

'Is that what I missed? I saw Dub go in and come out, I know what he did in there. Why?'

He knelt down beside her, his large face close to hers. 'Too late, Shelton, you are leaving the jamboree as they say.'

'Let me help. Let me put it right.'

Pincott's eyes remained flat. 'You really believe in second chance, don't you, Shelton?'

He leant towards her, and Savannah had to use all her will-power not to shrink away. 'I should kill you. I won't. Consider that your second chance.' Pincott rose and turned back across the yard, his greatcoat swinging out behind him.

Savannah scrabbled to her feet and ran after him. 'No wait, please. I know where he is! The lawyer! I can take you to him!' Guilt crushed in but she pushed it aside. 'Or I'll leave if you want, just pay me for the work I did. The last two weeks. You owe me that at least!'

Pincott swung round and grabbed her by the throat with both hands, pulling her down to her knees. Savannah felt the blood rush to her head and the air squeeze out of her lungs. 'You wanted to know my name? Maybe I tell you just before you die. The last word you hear. My name.'

'The girl is here!' A voice interrupted and Pincott let go.

Savannah fell back on her haunches and gasped for air. Pincott's head was silhouetted against the sun, only the skull on his chest returned her gaze.

'Go away, Shelton.' The words were spoken softly, the best she could hope for.

Pincott turned his back and strode towards the large doors at the other side of the yard where earlier she had seen the fading dray horse whipped within an inch of its life. She got to her feet and rubbed her neck, her skin chafing where Pincott had almost crushed her windpipe. The doors opened and two men entered, carrying a trussed-up bundle between them. They dropped it heavily to the ground and began to unravel the ropes. The bundle started to move and moan, kicking hard at every target. Finally, the rough sacking was removed, revealing a dishevelled blonde woman in a tartan dress, her hands and feet bound tightly, her mouth gagged beneath wide, staring eyes. Savannah began to back away towards the pharmacy, in two minds as to whether she should run or stay and try to help this woman, but what could she do?

Pincott bent down and pulled the gag from the woman's mouth and immediately she started shouting. 'Help! Please help!'

Pincott and the other men laughed loudly. Even if the woman's voice carried outside the compound, this was Whitechapel, not Kensington. Everybody was looking for help but very few were willing or able to offer it.

'God can't hear you,' said Pincott, and the woman's shouts became weaker. Then her eyes lighted on the retreating Savannah and she raised her voice once more.

'Please, please help me! My name is Mildred Whitfield. I have been brought here against my will. These men work for the Vicomtesse de—' Her speech was cut short as one of the men stuffed the gag back into her mouth, but her eyes continued to plead with Savannah until Pincott threw the woman over his shoulder and strode towards a nearby stairway.

Savannah looked around the yard as Pincott retreated with the woman into a doorway high above. She counted at least six other men watching the scene unfold. She was powerless to intervene. After all, only seconds earlier, it had been her writhing in the dirt silently calling for help that would never come. It was no shock to her that women were mistreated here, but this Mildred Whitfield seemed to be in a different class to those who usually suffered such abuse in this miserable part of the city. She knew that

Pincott would be involved in all sorts of skulduggery, and hadn't Savannah herself offered to help him out in his darker activities, whatever they might be? But she would have drawn a line at this.

'I'm sure I heard the boss asking you to leave.'

Savannah turned around and found the dwarf standing behind her, arms folded and a smile on his face. He had probably witnessed her earlier humiliation and enjoyed every minute. She would have to leave, abandoning her wages for the last two weeks, her dignity, and a woman in trouble. She wasn't sure which of these most fuelled the fire of bright anger that burned within her. She pushed aside the pharmacist and marched across the yard towards the hidden door. As she reached it, she turned once more to survey the yard, taking it in with new eyes: the layout, the passageways and the entrances. Maybe she would return and bring down a hell's worth of trouble on the head of Obediah Pincott.

Savannah looked up at the doorway through which Pincott had taken the woman, Mildred Whitfield. Surprised, she saw a different young woman gazing down at her through an open window. The afternoon sunlight lit up her red hair like flames that licked around a strikingly pale face. Savannah couldn't help but stare back. The woman's ruby red mouth smiled down at her and Savannah shivered despite the heat of the day.

She tore her eyes away and walked through the pharmacy and out into the squalid streets of Whitechapel. Only when she had gone some distance did she pull William Lamb's crumpled card from her pocket. Pincott was not the only one who might pay for her services. Something her father had once said came unbidden to mind.

*The enemy of my enemy is my friend.*

## CHAPTER SIXTEEN

Despite the smoky, crowded atmosphere, Harry spotted Finian Worthing immediately. The Old Bell tavern was a long panelled room, the wood blackened over the years by the oil lamps that glowed permanently along the walls, whatever the time of day. The tavern backed on to St Bride's church and both buildings shared the task of tending the weary souls of Fleet Street.

Finian was sitting at his usual table at the back, nursing a glass that contained two fingers of single malt whisky. Harry jostled his way to the bar and ordered two more from the flustered barman before weaving his way through the raucous banter towards his friend.

'Apologies, Finian, I thought I would be here earlier.'

'Not at all, dear chap, not at all. I was a little late myself.'

As Harry sat down he doubted this last statement was entirely true. Judging by his rosy sheen, Finian had likely been here for at least an hour. Harry had known Finian Worthing for years, since his days as an assistant crime reporter for *The Times*. Most crime reporters cultivated relationships with detectives, lubricating mutually beneficial exchanges of information with their company expenses. Harry didn't know precisely at what point his relations with Finian had turned to genuine friendship.

When Harry had first faced the barrage of press attention as

the whistle-blower who brought down the previous CID administration, Finian had guided and protected him. When Harry's
wife had passed away, worn down by the stress of Harry's isolation
and rejection, it was Finian who had laid a firm hand on Harry's
shoulder at the funeral; the only gesture he had received that day
that wasn't laden with recrimination.

'How goes it at the paper? That editor of yours seems excited
by the Tinbergen visit – all those editorials on the state of play,
he must be quite exhausted already.'

The joke was lost on Finian, and his eyes gleamed. 'Just think
about it, Harry, revolution is everywhere in old Europe. The fight
is on. A united, autocratic Germany, a new tsar in the Winter
Palace, the League of the Three Emperors – but how long can all
that last? The world is changing, Harry. Power grows, spills, and
consolidates at a pace we are not used to. The state of play, as you
call it, changes tenfold from one edition to the next!'

'I forget what a radical you are.'

Finian laughed. 'Oh, I am far worse. I am a journalist. We are
united in curiosity, you and I. To our respective professions!'

Finian clinked his glass clumsily against Harry's, almost spilling the fine liquid. Despite the bonhomie, Harry had to stifle a
yawn.

'Working late, eh? Does that mean old Matlock has finally
passed something interesting your way?'

Harry couldn't help a wry smile. 'I suppose he has.' He would
need to navigate this conversation carefully. As much as he trusted
Finian as a friend, he knew that this case would be catnip for any
journalist. He needed information though. Not the information
of hard facts, but rather the kind of information that journalists
traded in daily: opinion and rumour.

'What do you know about the Raycraft family?'

Finian let out a long whistle. 'You're sniffing around the
Raycrafts? Blimey, Harry, I'm impressed. Does this have anything

to do with the unexpected demise of young Benjamin's fiancée? Our chap was there, apparently, but no one has seen hide nor hair of him today.'

There was little point in denying it, but Harry stopped short of confirming that he was investigating Phoebe's death. Instead he pushed Finian for as much background as he could and his friend duly obliged.

'Our very own chief of industry and endeavour is a bit of a cad, of course. The ladies like him, all that blond hair, and he keeps himself trim. Committed to his work, though, almost evangelical some would say. Electricity is his latest thing – supposedly has electric lights up in that creepy house of his in Hampstead. Even heard he's invented a machine for washing dishes! My char shall be wanting one of those!'

'What else do you know?' Harry pulled Finian back to the point.

'Well, that factory of his does a lot more than manufacture guns and cannon, but they are highly secretive. I've heard some bizarre stories over the years: machines that fire a jet of flame, poison gases that could take out an entire army, that kind of thing. They produce medicines too, to be fair. Sir Jasper supposedly cured himself of syphilis fifteen years ago, but if he did, he's never made the remedy available to other afflicted souls.'

Harry thought of Lady Raycraft's sunken cheeks and diseased mind. 'What of Sir Jasper's wife and son?'

'Very little is seen of them. Sir Jasper is often out and about, very much part of it all. But his wife hasn't been at his side for a number of years. And by all accounts young Benjamin is a bit of a disappointment, can't even string a sentence together, they say, so not exactly a chip off the old block. He is an only child, stands to inherit everything, I believe. So what's the story with the fiancée? Have second thoughts, did she?'

Harry smiled enigmatically. 'We're not sure at this stage. Just investigating every avenue, that's all.'

Finian grinned. 'I'll buy it for now, Harry. Don't keep me waiting too long though.'

'So tell me, when he is seen out and about, who is he out and about with?'

'Just about everyone, I'd say. Good pals with the great and the good. Did you know he's related to Cornelius Tinbergen? The Raycrafts will be stabling the horse that Tinbergen is transporting to race at Newmarket and I'm sure Sir J will be milling around at the welcome bash. And of course, he's been seen with the vicomtesse, lucky fellow.'

'Who?'

'Where have you been, Harry? The Vicomtesse Adeline de Bayeau. Stunning redhead, the widow of an old French aristocrat, though still a young woman. She's been flirting her way around London since the autumn; no one's quite sure why she's here and no one seems to care so long as she attends their soirées. Only thing going against her as far as British society is concerned is that she also happens to be Otto Von Rabenmarck's half-sister.'

'He's a well-connected man, I see.' No wonder Matlock had warned him about antagonising the Raycraft family.

'What are you up to, Harry?'

Harry held his hands up in surrender. 'You know me, I like to explore every avenue of conversation.'

'Don't play the innocent with me, Harry. Your boss might fall for that, but I don't.' Finian smiled at his friend, but receiving no smile in return, he relented. 'Look, Harry, ask what you want to ask outright. I won't pose any questions of my own or expect any explanations, at least not tonight. I'd like to help if I can.'

Harry gave up the pretence of idle chatter. 'Do you think Sir Jasper Raycraft is capable of murder?'

'I think men such as Sir Jasper are capable of anything.'

## CHAPTER SEVENTEEN

O nce he had left the horrors in Habborlain's house behind him, William picked up his pace, going nowhere in particular. Walking the crowded streets soothed him, a reminder that the world still turned. Before he knew it, he had arrived once more in Gray's Inn Garden. He sat on the same bench as he had that morning and watched the early evening hubbub unfold; clerks his own age filed out of the red-brick buildings, some talking excitedly in groups, punching each other's arms playfully as they ribbed their colleagues over minor infractions and faults. He envied the easy geniality that some young men seemed to be born with. Even at Sunday school, he had been an outsider, unsure how to be anything else. Insignificant William Lamb.

His thoughts skittered randomly, keen to avoid the image of Fischer that emerged from nowhere and flashed across his brain like lightning, intense but fleeting. He found himself thinking about his parents, something that rarely occupied him. Would he have grown up very differently if they hadn't perished in that fire? He had no memories of his own and had rarely asked Aunt Esther for anecdotes and reminiscences. He had always supposed that, much like his thumb, one didn't miss what one had never known.

The shadows lengthened, their fingers reaching out to him across the green lawn. The thought of returning home to Aunt Esther and relating the madness of the day had become increasingly unappealing. Fischer's barbaric murder had heaped questions upon questions. He was glad to have left the woman behind to deal with the police. Presumably they would contact him at the office in the morning and take a statement. Maybe Fischer's case would rekindle their interest in what might have caused Mr Bridge to take his own life? William had no idea what the connection might be between the two terrible events, but surely it had to be more than coincidence?

William knew he should go home and face his aunt. Instead, he took Habborlain's note from his pocket once more. Where had the old man gone? Maybe he had another address in London, somewhere other than the gloomy residence of Red Lion Square. William thought of all the files in Mr Bridge's office. Maybe he could yet track Habborlain down, take him the casket of papers and demand explanations. The thought of finding at least a few answers before the sun set on the day put a spring in his step as he hurried towards their chambers in Farringdon.

As he climbed the stairs, William wished he had accepted the offer of a lamp from the porter before the old man left for the evening. The narrow windows of the staircase faced east and what little light they let in was quickly absorbed by the dark mahogany that encased the stairwell. Approaching the door to their office, he noticed afresh the brass plaque that announced *Bridge and Co, Solicitors*. William paused with his hand on the door, swamped by a fresh wave of sentiment. Taking a handkerchief from his pocket, he wiped the plaque, removing some of the smears and spots that he hadn't noticed before.

Once inside, he reached for the lamp on Sedgwick's desk and lit the taper, turning the light up high. Giving himself no time to consider, he entered the inner office.

It was the first time he had been there since Mr Bridge's body had been removed. He held the lamp out before him, throwing light on to the small, neat bloodstain that covered most of the rectangular blotter in the centre of the desk. It was not the scene of devastation that William had expected. Mr Bridge's pen and inkwell, his leather address book, the grand brass lamp that had once been his father's and an ebony tray of well-sharpened pencils all occupied their usual place. If it weren't for the stained blotter, one would have thought Nathaniel Bridge had simply left for the day.

William covered his mouth with a shaking hand as tears rolled down his face. He put the lamp down and tore the top sheets of blotting paper away. The blood had dried and he scrunched the sheets in a ball and threw them into the wastepaper basket. The stain might have been small but it had gone deep and William had to tear off many more sheets before it was completely gone.

Deciding to explore the desk first, he lifted the lamp but almost dropped it again immediately. An enormous spatter of blood and gore had been revealed on the wall behind the chair. The memory returned sharply: the effusive gush of red, Mr Bridge's head snapping to one side before falling forward. Cleaning up the mess would not be a simple matter of throwing away some blotting paper.

William swallowed back the tears and yanked open the drawers that had previously contained both the gun and the box of incomprehensible old papers, but he found nothing more than paperclips and a bag of mint creams. He flipped open the address book, but found no entry for Ambrose Habborlain.

William picked up the lamp once more and looked around the office, feeling overwhelmed at the thought of his next task. Against the opposite wall sat a whole row of oak filing cabinets, each drawer marked with the label 'Habborlain'.

Maybe all this was best left until the morning? With Sedgwick's help, the task of finding anything useful would take half the time, and he could already feel the tiredness pulling at the back of his eyes. His stomach had also begun to rumble, but he couldn't think about food, not now. William set the lamp down on top of the first cabinet.

He was surprised at how easily the top drawer slid open on its rails.

It was empty.

Well, at least that made the task less daunting. The next drawer down was as bare as the first. In fact, the whole filing cabinet contained no files whatsoever, nor did the next. William wrenched open all of the drawers in all of the cabinets with increasing frustration.

They were all empty.

He slammed the last drawer shut with such vehemence that he had to catch the lamp as it toppled over. Had someone else been here, the police maybe, or Sedgwick, and removed the files? Or maybe there had never been any files in the first place. Maybe this was all some kind of charade. Yet again he could feel his chest tightening with claustrophobia as he struggled to make sense of why Mr Bridge would have six filing cabinets marked Habborlain with nothing in them at all.

The door to the main room banged open so hard, it crashed against the wall. William barely had a chance to stand before three broad-shouldered men strode towards him. He backed away, trying to keep a confidence in his voice that he didn't feel. 'What on earth . . . ?'

The tallest of the three men advanced, his thin red hair sticking to his forehead. He showed William a mouthful of cracked, stained teeth as he smiled down at him and spoke in a thick Scottish brogue. 'William Lamb, I presume?'

William could feel the blood draining from his face as his brain tried to decide what to say. All he could manage was the truth. 'Yes.'

'You're coming with me.'

William froze. He could smell the threat that exuded from the Scot. The man seemed to be waiting for him to say something, and again William resorted rather pointlessly to the truth, stammering, 'But I don't want to come with you. I need to go home.'

The man turned towards his accomplices and gave a hearty laugh. 'Well, isn't that lovely,' he said, before shaking his head. 'What the hell does Pincott want with a boy like you?'

Who was Pincott? Before William could respond, the man took a knife from his waistband and pulled William towards him by his throat. 'All we need now is the bookkeeper's box, so tell me, laddie, where do I find it? And don't tell me you don't know, or I'll gut you like a pig.'

William tried to swallow, his Adam's apple compressed by the man's clammy grip. Fear and incomprehension entwined around his lungs once more.

'The bookkeeper's box, lad, tell me where it is.'

The bookkeeper? William could feel the point of the blade pressing in to his side, every muscle tensing in terror. Bridge had told him to keep the box safe. He had to fight for time. His voice was a whisper as he spluttered for air. 'It's not here, it's at home. You may . . . may have it tomorrow.' As he forced the words out he realised the danger of what he was saying. These men would not want to wait until tomorrow.

'Where do you live?'

He couldn't let these men go to the house – the thought of exposing Aunt Esther and Sarah to these vagabonds brought fresh horror.

'I said where do you live?'

The blade dug further into his side, at any moment it would penetrate his clothing and cut him. His chest was restricting and he struggled for air. 'I can't breathe!'

The red-headed man pulled the knife back, but the relief was temporary as he raised the blade and placed it flat against

William's cheek, the tip pressing against the delicate skin beneath his left eye. William screwed his eye shut, aware he was whimpering, unable to stop.

'Got it!'

The Scot let him go and William slumped forward, his breathing ragged as the room spun around him. He saw that one of the men had torn a sheet of paper from Mr Bridge's address book.

William's address!

The Scot grabbed the paper from the other man's hand. 'Bloody Hammersmith! I'll see to it myself, you get Mr Bumble here back to Pincott's.' He started for the door before remembering something. He grabbed William once more and began to search his pockets.

William tried to push him away and received a slap across the face as a reward. The man quickly found what he wanted: William's keys. Still reeling from the slap, William lunged to retrieve them but it was too late, the Scot was already striding towards the door, followed by one of his thugs.

'No, wait! Please! Leave them alone!' William's thin voice made no impression. The men were gone, leaving him alone with their accomplice, who was busy eyeing up Mr Bridge's other possessions.

William had to get home. The thought of these men accosting his aunt was unbearable. If he ran to the station, then ran home, then maybe he could get there first. He knew the way, they didn't. *Run?* said a voice in his head. *You won't be running anywhere.* But he at least had to try.

His captor was examining Mr Bridge's pen and inkwell. Then he opened the drawer and withdrew the bag of peppermint creams. 'Nice, very nice indeed,' he muttered, his mouth full.

The man was too close to the door for William to get past him and the precious minutes slipped by slowly as the villain munched his way through the whole bag of peppermints.

When he was finished, the man tipped Mr Bridge's pencils out of their ebony tray and moved towards the window to examine it more closely in the fading light.

William, seeing his opportunity, bolted for the door and dashed through the outer office towards the landing. He practically fell down the first flight of stairs, swinging round the newel post to the next level. He could hear the thundering footsteps behind him, spurring him on despite the fire in his lungs. He could barely see where he was going, his head felt as if it might float away in search of air, but instinct drove him forward as he let gravity pull him downwards towards the street. He had no hope of success, his lungs would give out before he could outrun his pursuer, but he would rather die trying to protect his aunt than think about what might happen when that rogue opened the door to his home.

Finally William could see the door to the street; he had made it to the first floor. As he prepared to jump the last few steps, William felt a crushing weight land on his back, propelling him forward. He landed with a sickening crunch in the hallway and felt the last of the air in his lungs forced out of him by the weight of the other man's body.

The man sat up and turned William's pliant body over, a grin plastered across his sweating face. 'Didn't think you had it in you.'

William lay prone beneath him. The fight was gone and he felt oddly calm. It was over and he was drowning slowly inside himself.

The man slapped him lightly, first on one cheek and then on the other. William had no strength left and his head lolled from side to side.

'You're lucky that Pincott wants you alive.' The man was clearly enjoying his capture, toying with his prey.

William opened his eyes as he heard the front door push open and felt a rush of cool air ruffle his hair. The man looked up and frowned briefly before the sharp retort of a firing gun snapped through the air. William looked into the surprised eyes of his captive, at the blood that dripped down his face from the small hole in the centre of his forehead. The man fell backwards, his head coming to rest on William's feet – his third encounter with death, knowing that without air in his lungs, his own could soon follow.

A shape emerged from the gloom, someone standing over him. He saw her ankles first, then the swinging leather coat. A hand extended towards him.

'Get up, William. We need to talk.'

## CHAPTER EIGHTEEN

*A*deline glanced around the room, trying to see it through Otto's eyes, hoping it would do. They had needed a safe place, far from prying eyes. These rooms in Pincott's labyrinthine warren were perfect: large and sufficiently high up so that the noises and smells of the yard outside could not penetrate. And yet, as today proved when Mildred Whitfield had decided to yell the place down, they were in a part of the city where no one cared how they occupied themselves as long as the rent was paid on time. She had done an excellent job, she thought, in turning the rather basic accommodation into something far more *charmant*. Thick purple velvet swathed the rough-hewn windows, an elaborate chandelier hung overhead and the large pewter bed frame that governed the room next door, with its rich brocade comforter, could have graced any palace.

She skipped over to the window at the sound of shouting outside and pulled the drapes apart. A grand carriage had entered and the graceful horses arched their necks downwards as they puffed to a halt. Otto was here at last! Pincott pulled open the carriage door and Captain Karl Ziegler bounded to the ground. Otto followed and two more guards brought up the rear. Pincott ushered them forward to the staircase that would bring them to her, talking quietly to Otto as he did so. She felt a lurch in her stomach as both Captain Ziegler and Otto examined the compound. Although the light was fading, she knew her brother's eyes would be glassy with distaste.

She checked that all was in order one last time. The candlelight in the bedroom was magical, almost romantic, and the glass phial had been placed on the nightstand. She sincerely hoped the girl would not make this too difficult. It should be beautiful, in its own way.

She returned to the other room as Pincott led in the new arrivals. She felt a stab of annoyance that Pincott had not changed his clothes in honour of the distinguished guest that now graced his iniquitous den. His sheen of sweat glinted in the candlelight and the skull tattoo on his chest seemed to grin in her direction.

Adeline raised her arms outwards in a hospitable gesture. 'Otto, Captain Ziegler, welcome to our very own secret boudoir!'

Otto said nothing, merely glancing around as if he didn't yet trust himself to speak. Ziegler glared at the back of Pincott's head, clearly sensing a threat. Pincott himself made no attempt to fill the silence, instead he observed everyone with his usual laconic smirk.

'So,' Adeline spoke to Pincott, 'perhaps you could leave us for a quarter hour or so and then bring the girl?'

'Of course, madam. You need anything else, yell out of window. I may or may not hear.'

Ziegler's frown deepened as Pincott rolled past him and out of the door.

Adeline clapped her hands together. 'Some wine, maybe?'

She began to pour from the decanter of claret that had been left to breathe on the bureau. 'Will Captain Ziegler be staying?'

Otto turned towards his companion. 'Leave us, Karl. Wait outside. I may have need of you yet.'

Otto placed his hand on Ziegler's arm and Adeline quickly looked away. Once he was gone, she held out a glass towards her brother.

'I hope you're excited!'

'Adeline, we need to talk.'

She turned away and walked briskly towards the bedchamber, throwing open the doors. 'At least come and admire, Otto. I've worked so hard to compose *un arrangement séduisant*.'

Otto sat down on the chaise. 'Adeline, my love, we will come to all that soon enough. We need to talk of other events, however briefly. Pincott has informed me—'

'Yes, I *know*! Habborlain is missing and Bridge has cheated us of his punishment, the coward, may he rot in hell. Today or tomorrow they will recover the damned box, which, by the way, you should never have allowed Bridge to keep in his sole possession, whatever his reasoning. And as for that deformed mutt, once Pincott has him in his fist we can decide what to do with him.' Adeline threw herself down beside her brother, her face bright with determination.

Despite her intensity, Otto pursued the conversation. 'Tell me, why did they kill Fischer? He's been with us for years. Without him we would not have known the truth.'

'You said no loose ends.'

'But—'

'Shhh.' She placed her finger against his lips. 'No more. Not tonight. Tonight is about the future, not the past.'

Adeline twisted away and sprang to her feet. 'So! What of Mildred? You should have seen her today when they brought her here, wrapped up like a Christmas gift. She yelled and yelled.' Adeline laughed as she spun round. 'The gumption! I tell you, Otto, we have chosen well. *I* have chosen well.'

She curtsied before him and she could see the Chancellor of Germany was charmed by his little sister.

'Very well. No more salesman, however. *I am buying*, as they say. I trust you will make it easy for me?'

Adeline saluted her brother, an old joke that brought a sweetness to his smile.

'Very well, I will do this, for you.'

They heard the door between the bedchamber and the hallway bang open and the muffled cries of someone being dragged across the floor. Otto frowned, revulsion flooding his countenance.

Adeline immediately backed away towards the bedroom, blocking his view. 'Do not worry, brother, all will be well, I promise. I will come for you in ten minutes.' Her hands fluttered towards him as she stepped backwards. 'Prepare yourself.'

Still smiling into his eyes, she closed the doors slowly until his face disappeared from view.

Pincott and another man secured Mildred's wrists to the railings above the bed. Despite the cloth binding that gagged her, Mildred's chest heaved with the sounds of protestation as her body writhed and twisted, her every movement as proud as it was pointless.

Adeline waited patiently for Mildred to see her. When their eyes finally locked, the captive woman gave a low growl and the fight in her eyes was a joy to behold. The men were taking no chances as they secured her legs with chains to each bedpost. Dressed only in a white shift that had ridden up during the struggle, Mildred's pale calves and thighs glowed in the soft candlelight.

Like a practised physician, Pincott removed the stopper from the glass phial and nodded at his accomplice. The man removed the gag and grabbed Mildred's nose with one hand and her throat with the other. He tipped her head back as Pincott poured the noxious fluid down her throat. As the other man forced her to swallow in audible gulps, Pincott pulled himself up and addressed his client, his face impassive.

'Enjoy yourself, Vicomtesse.'

Did she detect something in his tone, a flicker of distaste perhaps?

Adeline waited for them to leave before meeting Mildred's

eyes once more. The girl had stopped struggling now, her gag replaced and the chains pulled tight. Adeline sat on the bed next to Mildred's helpless body.

'Hello, Mildred.'

No response.

Adeline considered removing the gag, but had no doubt that Mildred would recommence her shrieking and caterwauling. She would have to content herself with a one-way dialogue. No matter, there were many ways to communicate.

Slowly, Adeline traced the back of her index finger across Mildred's cheekbone, feeling Mildred shrink away as she did so.

'It's all right, you know. He is a good man, my brother, he will not hurt you.'

Adeline laid her head on the pillow next to the frightened governess and placed her hand on Mildred's stomach. 'This is the core of you, Mildred. You think you feel things in your head or in your heart, but you don't. This is where all feeling lives.' Adeline's hand drifted across Mildred's belly.

Gently, Adeline's fingertips grazed upwards over Mildred's breasts and she smiled to herself as she heard the catch in the young woman's breath. Mildred stared up at the ceiling, her eyes wide.

Adeline continued to mutter in her ear. 'There there, my darling. Can you feel it? Can you feel your womb stirring?'

Adeline's fingers moved down the length of Mildred's body. On reaching her goal, she grabbed hard. Mildred's eyes exuded hatred and fire, so unlike the prim young lady she had first met that morning.

'You must have done this before, my dear, or wanted to. It's what we have in common, rich and poor, young and old. It's the secret we dare not share, our own private joy.'

Adeline's fingers moved rhythmically, patiently waiting for the response she knew would eventually come, however hard the young woman fought.

'Oh, Mildred. There is a fire inside you, burning. We can quench the fire. Trust me, my darling, trust me, trust me, trust me.' Hypnotically, Adeline continued her ministrations, waiting for the first sign that Mildred was indeed ready for what would come next. She had to admire once more the girl's stoicism and refusal to surrender.

Finally, Adeline's fingers felt what they had been waiting for and she stopped, pulling her hand away abruptly. She took a linen cloth from the end of the bed and wiped her hand meticulously, deliberately ignoring the fury in Mildred's stare.

'Let's make it as comfortable as possible, shall we?'

Adeline picked up a silk cushion from the bed and pushed it beneath the governess. 'I would loosen the chains so you could raise your knees but I don't think we can trust you yet. My brother is not the strongest man. You might decide to squeeze him to death!'

Adeline's laugh tinkled as she opened the door to the drawing room. Her brother was not alone. Her laugh caught in her throat as Otto hastily dropped his hand to his side, the hand that moments ago had clasped Captain Ziegler's head in affectionate embrace. She closed the door to the bedroom behind her.

Otto was immediately on his feet. 'Is the girl ready?'

'She is.'

He drained his wine glass and deposited it on the bureau with purpose. 'Then I am ready too.'

'So I see.'

'Adeline . . . ' The heat of embarrassment in his eyes had turned ice cold at her last remark. There were some things that had not, and could never be, discussed between them.

'Go to her, Otto. She is as ready as she will ever be. Try not to look her in the eye would be my counsel. There is spirit in her still.'

'Very well.' Otto removed his jacket and looked around for a place to put it. Adeline took it from him, removing the rose first before folding his jacket neatly in her arms. He straightened his cuffs and pulled his waistcoat down.

'You might want to remove more?'

'I am fine as I am.'

'All set?'

'All set.'

Moving closer, Adeline planted a kiss on his lips. 'Thank you, dear brother, you know what this means to me. If I could have children of my own then . . .'

Placing his hands on her arms he closed his eyes and nodded. 'I understand. Perhaps you will pour me another glass of wine for when I am done?'

They smiled at each other, friends again. Briskly, Otto entered the bedchamber and closed the door behind him.

'I should leave, madame.'

Adeline had forgotten Ziegler's presence. 'No, Captain, why don't you stay? A glass of wine perhaps?'

'Thank you, madame, but not while I am on duty.'

'Are you ever off duty, Karl? Is it all right if I call you Karl? My brother does.'

Captain Ziegler looked very uncomfortable indeed, his large form dominating the chaise longue. 'Of course, madame, you may call me what you wish.'

'Really? I can think of many things to call you, Captain Ziegler, but I shall settle for Karl.'

A blush rose up his pale neck and he glanced longingly at the door to the hallway as Adeline hung Otto's jacket on the back of the chair, glided across the floor and squeezed herself on to the sofa beside him. She was still holding the white rose from Otto's buttonhole, twirling it in her hands.

'Isn't this snug?'

They both heard the sound from the room next door,

somewhere between a gasp and a howl. Ziegler stared intently at his boots as Adeline turned towards him and stroked the petals of the flower across his ear.

'You must have heard that sound many times, Karl?'

'No, madame. I . . . we shouldn't talk of such things.'

'I didn't know soldiers were such prudes. Surely a man of your stature and countenance has heard the sound of a young maiden surrendering her virginity on many occasions?'

Ziegler leapt to his feet. 'I think it best if I waited outside, madame.' He swept out of the room without a backward glance.

Adeline watched him leave, such a powerful grace in his limbs, such a waste. She crushed the flower in her hand, ignoring the thorn that pricked her finger, and dropped the petals to the floor. She picked up the decanter of claret and refreshed her brother's glass. Casting around the room, she could not see where she had left her own, so with a quick glance towards the bedroom door, she swung the decanter to her lips and drank deeply. She smiled to herself, imagining the appalled look on her brother's face if she had dared to do something so inelegant in his presence.

She hoped that Otto would soon emerge from the bedroom. Any longer and she would fear he had been unable to complete the act. It would not be the first time.

When Otto returned, he looked as starched and well dressed as he had five minutes earlier. If it hadn't have been for the muffled sound of soft weeping that came from the other room, she would have doubted that the deed had taken place at all.

'It is done?'

Otto put on his jacket. 'It is done. You are right, my dear, she has much fortitude and strength of mind. The results should be interesting, I grant you that.'

'We should try again before the week is out and you have to leave, just to make sure.'

There was a knock at the door, but before she could call out Pincott breezed into the room.

'That is good timing, Obediah, we are done. You can take her away.'

'Is not why I come, Vicomtesse.'

Otto's tone was sharp. 'The bookkeeper's box, the boy, you have them?'

Pincott looked down at him. 'We have one of them, and something else of value, I think.'

~

William grabbed the woman's hand and pulled himself to his feet. The pain in his shoulder was excruciating. 'Savannah Shelton. We met before, at Habborlain's, remember?'

Of course he remembered. Why was she here?

'Why are you here?'

'You gave me your card.'

William looked across at the dead body of the man who had chased him down the stairs and attacked him. His face was thankfully obscured at this angle and William steeled himself not to look. He needed no more images to haunt his memory.

'I have to get home! There were two others, they went there to retrieve the box.'

'The box?'

'My aunt is there! I have to get home.'

William ignored the pain in his shoulder and lunged for the door. The train would still be the quickest way of reaching home. He stumbled on to the pavement and lurched towards the station.

'Hey!'

He turned back towards the woman.

She stood uncertainly on the pavement, hands on hips, as if in two minds what to do next. 'What are you going to do when you get there, William?'

It was an answer into which he had no intention of putting much thought. 'I don't know!'

She met his eyes and, with a shake of her head, trotted down the street to catch up with him. 'I'll come with you; if they're still there you won't stand a chance on your own.'

'Thank you. You've been ... most helpful.' William wasn't sure that was quite the right word for what she had done. She had killed for him.

'But I'll need something.' She looked down at the floor.

'What?'

She cleared her throat. 'Payment.'

'Of course! Yes!' He nodded vigorously, as if hiring a killer was something he did every day.

She met his gaze then. 'So let's go.'


The train journey was agonisingly slow. No one else seemed to be in any hurry, rush hour had ended long ago. They found an empty third-class carriage and sat in silence. William tried to avoid all thoughts of what might now be happening behind the door of his cherished home. All the previous cares and curiosities of the day receded, the only thing that mattered now was Aunt Esther. Please God the brutes leave her alone.

The acrid smell of tobacco reached his nostrils and he coughed.

With a roll of her eyes the woman threw her cigarette on to the floor and ground it with her boot, muttering to herself, 'Well, this is fun.'

He had been glad when she agreed to join him, now he wasn't so sure.

The woman broke the silence. 'So what does this other villain look like?'

'A brute.'

'Aren't they all?'

'Tall, Scottish, red hair.'

'I see.'

'And the smell was hard to describe.'

'Whitechapel.'

'Pardon?'

'Just guessing. The smell of the streets.'

When the train finally reached its destination, William felt recovered enough to partly run the rest of the way to the house. The woman kept up with him easily.

As they turned into his street, the woman stopped abruptly and pulled him back. Silently, she removed the gun from the back of her skirt.

'No!' William hissed loudly. 'No guns. Please. My aunt is of a delicate nature, as am I, for that matter. Please don't wave that thing around!'

'Fine,' she hissed back. 'But if he's still there he ain't gonna leave because you ask him nicely!'

She tucked her gun away and they stared at each other for a few more seconds before she spoke again. 'All right. So, you open the door as quietly as you can, then we creep in. I'll go first.'

'I don't have the keys. He took them. Can't we just knock? We're wasting time.'

'You don't know what you're up against, William. Can we get around the back?'

William thought of the side alley that led to the rear of the gardens, but surely the walls were too high? 'I don't know how we'll get over the walls and the door to the alley is locked. The key is in the other side.'

'Leave it to me. Come on.'

They cut through the alley and arrived at the door that led to William's garden. His house looked ominously dark. The enormity of the situation hit him hard. 'Maybe we should fetch the police? Constable Ennis lives in the next street, he hasn't retired yet.'

'Constable Ennis? And what does he have, William? A

truncheon and a whistle? What's he gonna do if those men are still here? *Deafen* them into surrender? You go for the police and I'm out of here. You decide.'

William swallowed. This strange woman really was his only chance of rescuing his aunt if that villain was indeed still here. 'So, how do we get in?'

The woman stood up on her toes and surveyed the wall.

'Help me up.'

'How?'

'Like this.' The woman cupped her hands in front of her. 'You know, like you did with your friends when you climbed trees as a kid.'

'I've never climbed a tree.' In fact, had never had any friends.

'Just do it.'

William cupped his hands in front of him and winced as her thick-heeled boot landed on his palms. He was further alarmed when she grabbed his shoulders in an embrace and it took all his willpower not to shrink away.

'When I say go, you push me upwards, got it?'

'I think so. But is this decent? I mean . . .'

'Just close your eyes and think of England, William.'

'Very well.'

'Now!'

William heaved with all his might and the woman managed to grab the lip of the wall with both hands. 'Push, William, I need you to push!'

The woman's feet hung four feet off the ground. 'Push what?'

'My ass, William, push my ass!'

It was the single most shocking thing that William had heard all day. Stunned into obedience, he closed his eyes once more and did as he was told, hoisting the woman upwards as she swung a leg over the wall. When he heard a soft thump on the other side, he decided it was safe to look.

'I do hope you're all right,' he whispered hoarsely.

'I'm just dandy. Where's the key?'

'In the door.'

'Great. No one would ever think to look there.'

Seconds later, the door swung open and William was in his garden. They hastened towards the back of the house and the steps that led down to the kitchen door. Once again the woman pulled him back, placing an index finger to her lips. Quietly, he crept down the stairs and placed his ear to the door.

He couldn't hear a sound but his own breathing in and out. Or was there something? Something soft? A woman weeping!

Without further thought he grabbed one of his aunt's seedling pots and hurled it through the glass pane of the back door. There was a scream on the other side. William shoved his left hand through the broken window, ignoring the pain that sliced along the side of his hand where his thumb should have been. Turning the key from the inside, he pushed the door open wide and stepped into the kitchen. He could just make out a shape huddled in the far corner.

'Please, please don't hurt me. I haven't moved, I promise!'

'Sarah? Is that you? It's me, it's Mr Lamb.'

'Oh, thank God! Oh, sir! Thank God you're here!'

Sarah ran towards him, her feet crunching on broken crockery, and threw herself at him, weeping. The woman entered behind him and lit the lamp on the kitchen table, the soft light revealing the devastation around them. The dresser had toppled forward, propped up only by the corner of the table – the dresser that had contained row upon row of Aunt Esther's neatly stacked Wedgwood tableware.

William held the weeping maid in his arms. With a heavy heart he asked, 'Where is she, Sarah?'

'Oh, Mr Lamb!' Through her snuffles, Sarah's sense of decorum was returning. 'They took her! Two men came and took her away!'

William slumped into a nearby chair, sagging with despair. If only they had arrived sooner.

The woman took over the situation for him. 'Sarah, sit down. Where's the whisky?'

'We don't have any whisky, only brandy – it's in the pantry.'

The woman busied herself, returning with the bottle of brandy. She removed the stopper with her teeth and took a large swig before handing the bottle to the startled maid. 'Go ahead. Don't look like there are any glasses left so we'll have to do this the Arizona way.'

Uncertainly, the maid took a large gulp, wrinkling her eyes as the liquid burned her throat. The woman passed the bottle to William, keeping her eyes on the maid. 'Tell us what happened – quickly, we might not have much time.'

Sarah recounted her story. A Scottish fellow and another man had knocked at the door barely ten minutes ago, before letting themselves in with a key just as Sarah reached the door. They pushed her aside and demanded to know where a certain box was. Sarah pointed them towards William's room. By the time the Scottish one came back down the stairs, the casket in his arms, Mrs Lamb had come out of the drawing room to see what the commotion was. She had been very brave and challenged the men, ordering them to leave the house. They laughed at her and then the Scot struck her across the face.

William had already drunk deeply from the bottle of brandy. On hearing that his aunt had been physically assaulted and then taken, he took another long swallow. The loss of the box Mr Bridge had entrusted to him barely registered. The woman took the bottle from his hand. He didn't resist.

'Sarah, did they say why they took her? Or why they wanted the box?'

'The man just said, "You're coming with me, you're my insurance", and then he called her a horrible word, miss. They took her scarf from the hallway and tied it around her mouth and then they took her away. Oh, it was awful! There was nothing I could do! Honestly there wasn't! They told me to stay in the kitchen, that if I moved a muscle they would know!'

'It's OK, Sarah, it's not your fault.'

Sarah's crying had subsided and she was beginning to look at William's companion with open curiosity, brazenly gawping at her scar. 'Who are you, miss?'

The woman ignored the question. 'You need to leave here, Sarah. Is there somewhere you can go?'

'Shouldn't we call the police?'

The woman smiled. 'Constable Ennis is a good friend of mine. Leave it with me.'

William looked around the kitchen, focusing for the first time since he had found Sarah cowering in the corner. 'Why is the dresser pulled over? You didn't mention the men had been in here?'

Sarah blushed, colour replacing the pallor of shock. 'I'm afraid that was me, sir. When the men left, I was so scared, I ran to the basement and I—'

'It doesn't matter, Sarah. None of it matters any more.'

Savannah left William in the company of the brandy bottle and bundled Sarah out of the house – she had a sister she could stay with who worked in one of the grand houses in Holland Park. Savannah promised that the police would probably speak to her in the morning.

She found the housekeeping tin easily and removed its contents. She counted out what was needed for the cab fare before stuffing the remaining notes and coins into William's coat pocket. Payment for services rendered would have to wait.

Although it would be a good while yet before Pincott discovered that William had escaped his clutches, they needed to leave right away. Who knew what the neighbours might have heard? Right now, someone could be rousing the constable to come and investigate.

Judging that William would be next to useless, she went in search of his room so that she could pack some things. The bed was neatly made and a small vase of purple peonies sat on the nightstand. It was a lovely room. A lovely room in a lovely life of tea, and cake, and merry Christmas, one and all.

She found a soft leather bag inside the wardrobe and packed some shirts, underclothes, and William's shaving things. She looked around the room, and saw the daguerreotype propped on the chest of drawers – his mother, she presumed. She shoved the photograph into the bag, closed the clasps, and returned to the kitchen.

'William, we have to go. Once they realise you got away they'll come back.'

William put the brandy bottle down, his eyes glassy as they attempted to focus on Savannah. 'What about the police? I need to find my aunt. The box, too. I was supposed to take care of it.'

'I know, William. We will find her, I promise, but not tonight. Tonight you need to rest.'

'But this is my home. Where will I go?'

The words were out of her mouth before she could stop them. 'You can stay with me.'

'But you're a woman! It wouldn't be right.'

Savannah laughed and sat down opposite him. 'My reputation is no longer an issue of concern to this world, William.'

It was then that she noticed that William's left hand was sticky with blood. She found a first aid box in the pantry and returned to the kitchen. The cut was deep but thankfully the blood had congealed. Once she had rinsed it carefully with water, she tipped some iodine on to a cloth, pressed it on to the cut and wrapped a bandage tightly about his hand. William barely winced. Savannah glanced at the brandy bottle and saw it was half empty.

'Why are you helping me?' he slurred.

*Money, curiosity, revenge, information . . .*

'What do you know about a man called Pincott?' she asked.

'Pincott? That brute mentioned his name. He said it was a Mr Pincott who wanted the box, and who wanted me.'

'What was in the box, William? Why would Pincott want it?'

'Old papers, Greek or Latin maybe, and a list of names.'

'What names?'

William waved his hand. 'Habborlain was on it. I didn't have time to read the rest because this came.' He pulled a piece of paper from his pocket.

Savannah read the note. The instruction to run away was clear enough but the rest meant nothing to her.

'I need to go to the police and find my aunt.'

Savannah sighed. 'There's no point, William. The police can't protect you against Pincott.'

'But my aunt!'

'I know where she is, William.'

'What?'

'I know where she is. I know the man who took her, he's called Dub. He works for Pincott. He killed the butler today. He will have taken your aunt to Whitechapel.'

'How do you know all this? Did the police tell you?'

'The police?'

'When you saw them today? About the butler?'

'Oh, William.' There was no point lying any more and she couldn't keep him away from the police for ever. 'I didn't go to the police today. I knew who killed the butler because I saw him go into the house. And I knew he worked for Pincott because so do I. At least, I used to.'

William stumbled to his feet, uncertain with drink. 'I'm going to wake Constable Ennis!'

'Please, William, don't do that. Talk to them in the morning once we've worked out how to keep me out of the story. You can't tell them about me, William. I'm an illegal immigrant and they may be looking for me. I did something bad once.' The understatement of the year.

'Dear God!'

'I've saved your life twice today! Doesn't that count for something? They are not going to hurt your aunt, William. Can't you see? They have taken her for leverage, to make you cooperate with whatever they want from you. One night won't make a difference! I know where she is. They won't hurt her while they don't have you. And if you talk to the police, you might endanger her further because they might bungle it. But we need to leave now. Trust me when I say the police won't be any use if these men come back. They are killers, William, you know that.'

'The police will understand. I'll *make* them understand. That man was attacking me and you gunned him down to protect me.'

'It won't work, William. I'm not some country squire who shot a poacher on my land. The law ain't on the side of people like me. If you tell them, I'll swing.'

'I won't mention you. But I want their help, I won't not go to them.'

'Whatever. Right now we're leaving.'

William swayed slightly, bleary-eyed.

'I've packed your things.' She held out the bag.

William burped. 'Thank you.'

The driver of the carriage she flagged down looked at them both with suspicion but nonetheless accepted the coins Savannah brandished as she bundled William into the cab.

William had insisted on bringing the brandy with him. Now he sat beside her in silence as they sped towards the attic room she rented on the Cromwell Road. As they alighted, William was sick on the pavement and the smell of stale brandy made her wrinkle her nose as the carriage departed.

Savannah led William up the stairs to the attic. Once inside her garret, all of William's previous misgivings seemed to be forgotten as he flopped on to her narrow cot and curled up, his arms still wrapped around the bottle of brandy as if it was a child's doll.

Savannah took the blanket that was folded beneath William's feet and arranged it over him. Then she removed her coat and threw it over herself as she settled into a battered armchair, the horsehair coming loose and poking through one of the arms. She'd slept in it many times before, after waking from one of her nightmares, feeling too vulnerable to lie down again.

She listened to William's soft snores and watched his face in the moonlight. He must be in his early twenties, she thought, not much younger than her, and yet he had the maturity of a boy half his age. Where she came from, boys grew up fast. By the time they were William's age, most of them were fathers or murderers or both.

What had she done, saddling herself with such a burden? In the morning she would ask William to settle up and then they'd go their separate ways. His housekeeping funds wouldn't get her out of the country, even if she took them all, which she couldn't bring herself to do.

She would need to find a way into Pincott's and take the money she was owed. There were at least two women being held captive there, William's aunt and the girl in the tartan dress, and that stirred her too. Maybe William's desire to involve the police could serve her well. With any luck, if the authorities acted promptly, Pincott's compound would be wide open when she returned the following night. The spoils would then be hers, Pincott would be on his way to the gallows at Newgate and the women would be free.

Of course, she felt a certain curiosity as to why Pincott was after William and what was so valuable about that box and its list of names, but satisfying that curiosity was not a priority. As she drifted off to sleep she hoped everything would turn out well for poor William Lamb, that his silly life of please and thank you might be restored to him once more, but she couldn't afford to care.

She really couldn't.

Somewhere in the distance she heard a clock strike midnight. The day was over and Savannah Shelton fell asleep.

## CHAPTER TWENTY

*T*he man awoke, shivering. Since his mighty swim to the house by the river he had struggled to find warmth even when he looked squarely into the face of the sun. At least he now had dry clothes. It had been surprisingly easy to scrabble unseen through the back alley of a tenement row on the outskirts of Fulham, taking his pick of the garments hung out to dry by the chapped hands of the fat peasant matriarchs who were making the most of the early summer heat. The rags he now wore were hardly what he was used to, but they fitted well enough and, unlike his previous attire, didn't stink of the polluted river. The only possessions he had retained were his boots, his satchel, and his hunting knife.

He had no money and no food but he didn't care, it was enough to be free at last, breathing fresh air for the first time in decades. The other waifs and strays who had been his companions for the last two nights beneath the arches of Waterloo had shown only a mild interest in him – enough to share what little food they had with a fellow wretch but without the need to ask bothersome questions such as what was his name or where was he from.

Where was he from, indeed? The answer disgusted him, his name disgusted him. He came from hell, from sins committed in this world but which had been born of another, long ago. With his finger, he traced the outline of the symbol he had carved into his forearm the previous night. He had no ink, so he had dug deep with the knife and the scar tissue had yet to form. The physical pain barely registered, the real pain flapped within him like a trapped bird. The relief he felt when he carved his flesh was always temporary. When he had slaughtered the girl two nights ago, he had hoped the release would last for ever. As he swam back along the river towards the setting sun, he had felt strong, and free, and right. The only part of the evening that didn't fill him with elation had been the look on Benjamin's face. Had he really cared for the girl? If that were the case, then her death had been even more necessary than he had previously thought.

*I promised I would save you, didn't I?*

This morning, however, the relief was fading, bleaching out to nothing as the sun's rays crept relentlessly towards him across the grimy floor of his hiding place.

It hadn't been enough, it was never going to be.

He knew what he needed to do, before he had even roused to consciousness. There was only one deed that could truly purge him. He had tried before, but now he would try again, in the knowledge that he was capable not only of summoning death, but that death would hear and skip gladly under his command.

He looked at the knife that lay next to him, shining in the brightening dark. It would be his ally once more – and this time the devil himself would perish.

CHAPTER TWENTY-ONE

* co*

William kept his head very still. It had all been a bad dream, of course it had. A terrible nightmare summoned up from who knows where within his fevered brain. He was obviously very ill. His head was gripped in a vice of searing pain and his mouth was feather dry, his tongue swollen and stuck to the roof of his mouth. His eyes refused to open, although he didn't try too hard. However poorly he felt, inside he wallowed in the joy that the terrible visions that had plagued him were now over. The relief was only partly dented by the pain in his head, and by the knowledge that illness had summoned forth a rather dark side to his imagination, hitherto unexpressed. What on earth had inspired his mind to create the madness of Ambrose Habborlain, or the terrible demise of Mr Bridge and the unspeakable mutilation of the butler's corpse? Not to mention the American girl. He knew he was fascinated and fearful of women in equal measure and marvelled at how his mind had created such a dark invention. He would have smiled to himself if it hadn't hurt quite so much.

'Wake up, I brought breakfast.'

The voice sounded startlingly real. Maybe he should try to sleep again, that would be nice, but the pain in his head was showing no sign of lessening. Maybe he was getting worse, not better?

She was there! Staring at him. She looked so real – just how sick was he? And where was Aunt Esther? The apparition had moved to the back of the room, out of view, but soon returned, holding a wooden tankard in her outstretched arm.

'I even found you some clean water, guessed you might be in need.'

'You're not real.' His voice sounded like nails on a blackboard and a cough ripped through his chest.

'Bad luck, sweet pea, I'm as real as it gets.'

Still doubtful, William took the tankard of water from her hand and gulped it down. The water felt real enough, as did the pain in his foot when she roughly sat down on the end of the bed.

William scrabbled to his feet and headed straight into the opposite wall as a swell of dizziness pulled him down. He steadied himself, his head resting back against the peeling paint. The smell of mould swam around him and he thought he was going to be sick.

'I'm going to be sick.'

There was a wooden pail next to the bed and the woman shoved it roughly towards him with her boot.

'Here.'

William retched hard into the bucket. There was very little content, but the sour smell of brandy was overwhelming and he retched again. The pain in his head was excruciating as he bent over the bucket, gripping the sides for support. For the first time, he noticed his damaged left hand, the thickly wrapped bandage obscuring his deformity. The memory of putting his hand through broken glass tugged at the corner of his mind.

'Water, I need more water!'

'Too bad. It was in the bucket.'

William slid down the wall and faced the woman on the bed who was hacking through a large pound cake with a small knife. She placed the resulting lumps on to two pieces of brown paper and passed him one of the bundles.

'Eat. You'll feel better.'

William looked at the stale hunk of cake with distaste, but after a few tentative bites, realised he was ravenous. Once he had finished eating, he didn't feel so thirsty and the throbbing in his brain began to diminish. The realities of the day before were landing with a thud, one by one, ending with Aunt Esther's kidnapping. He remembered nothing after that, beyond his first pull of brandy and the accompanying desire for oblivion.

'Is this your room?'

'Yep.' Savannah answered with her mouth still full of cake.

'I slept in your bed?'

'Yep.'

William pulled himself up, embarrassment taking the place of his earlier disorientation. 'I apologise. That was the most terrible imposition. I shall leave immediately. It is most inappropriate for me to compromise you in this way.'

Savannah laughed, and he wondered at her ability to react with such flippancy to the most extreme of situations. His next words were out of his mouth before he could check himself. 'Have you no standards?'

Her face darkened. 'Maybe you have so many of your own that you left none for the rest of us.'

'I'm sorry. I didn't mean to be rude. I was simply curious.'

She dusted crumbs from her skirt. 'Where will you go, William? Habborlain is right. You can't go back to the house, or to your office.'

'I shall go straight to Scotland Yard. I should have gone last night.' Guilt and shame weighed him down. While he'd slept like the dead in a stranger's bed, would Aunt Esther, in whatever place she now found herself, have slept at all?

'What will you tell them?'

William thought it a stupid question. 'That my aunt has been kidnapped, my property has been stolen and that some man called Pincott is clearly out for me for a reason I cannot fathom.'

'You can't tell them about me, William.'

Her voice was hard. Was she threatening him?

'I don't have to mention you. I can say that I found the butler's body on my own, that I escaped the men on my own, that
I returned home on my own and found Sarah sobbing and my
aunt gone.'

'Your maid *saw* me, William, and who will you say shot the
goon who jumped you on the stairs? You'll need to do better
than that.'

William slumped down in the battered armchair and tried
to think it through. He had to go to the police, his aunt was in
danger, but he didn't want to land this woman in trouble. She had
done so much for him that he had to behave honourably, whatever
her reasons for avoiding the authorities might be.

'I don't know, Savannah.' It was the first time he had used her
name and it felt strange to him. 'But how can I not go to the
police when my aunt is missing?'

Savannah nodded. 'I want you to go. I want the police to take
Pincott. There are other things going on there, William, bad
things. Whatever he is doing, he needs to be stopped.' She smiled
then. 'And who knows, once the police have cleared out the compound maybe I can sneak in tonight and avail myself of the money
he owes me, perhaps with interest.'

So that was it, she was simply a common thief. Part of him
was disappointed. Why, he wasn't sure. Was a thief worse for him
than a murderer? However much she had helped him, he needed
to remember what she was. The thought provided him with a
dose of cold clarity. He stood up, ignoring the wooziness, and did
his best to arrange his clothes and hair into a semblance of order.

'Very well. I shall not mention that Sarah was still there when
I returned. My aunt was alone when she was taken. Sarah can
remain with her sister until this business is over. I did not see
who shot the man who attacked me – and as for the Habborlain

residence,' William tightened his tie against his throat, 'you were never there.'

Cautiously, Savannah nodded. 'That could work.'

She bent down and retrieved something from beneath the bed. William recognised his travel bag, a birthday gift from Mr Bridge that he had never had cause to use.

'I packed you some things.'

William took the bag and inspected the contents: thoughtful, and unexpected. 'Thank you for everything. I mean it. Thank you for all of your help yesterday and for putting a roof over my head.'

'Aren't you forgetting something?'

'And thank you for the cake.'

She rolled her eyes and he realised his mistake. 'Apologies. Of course.' He patted his pockets, searching for money.

'The right one.'

William removed a fistful of notes and coins and rummaged through them. What was the going rate for whatever she was?

She sighed and crossed towards him, picking out a number of the higher value coins from his hand. 'Is this acceptable?' She looked at him as if he were a child.

'Yes. That seems a fair sum.' He stuffed the remaining funds away and smiled at her, uncertain how to take his leave. Eventually he offered his right hand, fully expecting some humorous comment in return, but the woman resisted her usual impulse to mock him, taking his hand in a firm grip and shaking it formally.

'Goodbye, Miss Shelton.'

'Goodbye, William Lamb.'

It took some time to open the door – a fiendish combination of locks and bolts had to be navigated. He looked back into the shabby, neat room where he had spent the night and felt a twinge of pity. There were no pictures, no flowers, no signs of home.

As he turned to go, Savannah spoke again. 'Be careful, William. They might not believe you.'

'Don't worry. I will keep my promise. I will not mention you.'

'That's not what I meant. It's you they might suspect. They'll have only your word.'

William smiled confidently. 'An Englishman's word is always enough.'

## CHAPTER TWENTY-TWO

*I*t was gone eleven in the morning before Harry finished reading all the statements that had been taken in Hammersmith the previous evening. The local police had done a better job than expected. Twenty-nine local residents and passers-by had been interviewed in detail, although only two seemed to recall a man loitering on Hammersmith Bridge in the hour before Phoebe Stanbury's murder. Both witnesses had remembered him for the same reasons: he was tall, dressed like a gentleman, and in the words of the dowager who lived alone in the corner flat overlooking the Thames, the man was also *striking handsome and fair.*

Unfortunately, neither witness had seen the man enter the river, nor were there any sightings at all after the murder had taken place. There were no leads for him to follow.

Harry tapped his fingers against his lips. Colonel Matlock was right, the key to this case lay in finding the murderer. All his suspicions regarding the Raycraft family would go nowhere unless this man could be found and his motives established. Until then, pressurising the Raycrafts would yield nothing but grief for the department.

He decided a cup of tea was in order to clear the fog, so he stood up and slipped on his coat. The tea cart was not due for another half an hour so he would have to track it down on the floor below. The break would do him good.

As he walked through the small CID reception area and approached the top of the stairs, a young man came bounding up the flight below, bashing Harry on the shoulder in his haste.

'I do apologise, sir. I'm afraid I didn't see you there.' The young man's words were accompanied by a vague whiff of brandy.

'No harm done.'

As Harry descended the stairs in search of tea, he overheard the young man asking to see Detective Cunningham on important business. Harry knew his haste would have been in vain. Dolly Cunningham had been called to yet another murder scene early that morning in Farringdon and was unlikely to return until lunchtime. Murder was everywhere these past few days.

It took him a quarter hour to locate the tea cart. Its surly custodian, a young widow named Pamela, was initially reluctant to dispense a cup of tea to an interloper from another floor. After all, if everybody acted as he had done then the smooth workings of the refreshment operation of Scotland Yard would grind to a halt, mired in chaos. The devil in him requested a buttered scone as well.

Harry climbed back up the stairs with his ill-gotten gains. The young man was still sitting in reception and he wondered whether he should offer to speak to him rather than have him wait for Dolly to return, for he seemed decidedly agitated. He was not alone, however. Perched next to him was a dowdy young girl in a grey nurse's uniform, her eyes flitting back and forth nervously.

The constable in charge of reception today, an old-timer whose name Harry could never remember, lifted his head as Harry approached. 'Ah, Detective Treadway! This young lady asked to see the detective investigating the Stanbury murder.'

Harry frowned and turned to look at the girl. *The Stanbury murder?* There had still been no coverage in the papers that morning. The world at large knew only that Phoebe Stanbury had died of unknown causes.

Harry turned back to the constable, his voice matter-of-fact. 'Is there a room available, please?'

'Of course, sir, number three.'

The man handed Harry a key with a wooden tag. Harry put his cup and plate on the desk, no longer in need of the distraction.

Room three was the largest interview room on the CID floor, with opaque windows that overlooked Whitehall, the only furniture a table and four plain chairs. Harry beckoned the girl to sit.

'Why don't you start by telling me your name?'

The girl licked her cracked lips. 'Jenny. Jenny Smith.'

'And you work as a nurse, I take it?'

'No, sir. Not exactly, sir. That is, I'm an orderly. Today is my day off which is why I come 'ere.'

'What did you want to see me about, Jenny?'

'I read about it, sir. Yesterday. About that girl, Phoebe Stanbury, that she'd died.'

'And what made you think that Scotland Yard was involved in an investigation?'

'Well, you would be, wouldn't you, sir? All murders in the city come to you, don't they?'

Harry paused before dropping his voice. 'What makes you think that Phoebe Stanbury was murdered, Jenny?'

The girl licked her lips again. 'Because I think I know who done it. He wanted her dead, I heard him say it. When he escaped that day, I worried he would do something like this. I should have said something earlier, but the warden didn't seem concerned, sir, didn't even report him missing, sir. And then I started to hope that nothing bad would happen. You see, I like Edward, sir. We all do. You should see his paintings, sir, he's left them all behind. They're so beautiful, although they're not everyone's cup of tea. Maisie Pilkington says they're the devil's work—'

'Edward who?'

'He doesn't have another name, not that I know of, just Edward.'

'Where do you work, Jenny?'

'Bedlam.'

William wondered how much longer he would have to wait for Detective Cunningham to return. It was already gone eleven and there had been no sign of him. Maybe he should ask to speak to another detective? The thought of having to start the story all over again was off-putting, but he needed to report Aunt Esther's kidnapping as soon as he could. He had already lost twelve precious hours to a bottle of brandy and, as he began to recover physically, the loss of his aunt and his fears for her safety began to overtake him once more.

He looked up to see Detective Cunningham ascending the stairs, somewhat out of puff from the climb. William got to his feet, uncertain of how to begin. He wondered whether the detective would even still remember him.

He need not have worried. As Dolly Cunningham reached the final step, their eyes met and the detective paused, his foot in mid-air.

'Mr Lamb,' he said wearily. 'We have been looking for you.'

'I need to speak with you urgently.'

'As do I need to speak with you, young man.'

'My aunt is missing. She's been kidnapped!'

'Really? You *are* having an eventful time of it, wouldn't you say?'

William stood to one side as Dolly Cunningham obtained a key to one of the interview rooms and left instructions for someone to track down Sergeant Smiley and inform him that Mr William Lamb had been found and the search could be called off.

*The search?* Why would they be searching for him? Then he realised: the body in the hallway at the chambers would have been discovered hours ago. Sedgwick would have arrived for work although William, of course, had not. He had completely forgotten about Sedgwick. He should have sent a message, a warning not to return to the office while these thugs were still at large. Thankfully, the police would likely have arrived first.

The room they entered was small and stuffy, the window was dirty but the strength of the morning sun had found its way through. Detective Cunningham was now sweating profusely, tiny drops forming across his widow's peak. He pushed open the door, which led to a fire escape, and propped it open with a wastepaper basket.

The moment they were seated, William began his story. He covered it all, from the discovery of Fischer's body (too shocked to go to the police straight away), the three rogues who came to the office, the death of one of them (too dark to see the perpetrator), Aunt Esther's kidnapping and the stolen box. William stopped at that point, proud of the succinctness of his summary of events, and no mention of Savannah's role in any of this.

'And then?'

'And – and then?'

'So, your aunt is taken and your property is broken into. Presumably you didn't think it worth troubling us at such a late hour? So you hopped into bed, maybe with a glass or two of brandy,' Cunningham paused with his eyebrows raised, causing William to blush, 'and waited until the morning before coming to tell us about two dead men and a kidnapped aunt? I trust you slept well?'

'I know it sounds peculiar but as I said, I was in shock yesterday, and I admit, I probably had too much to drink last night. Trust me, sir, I feel very ashamed indeed of my—'

'Do you drink often, Mr Lamb?'

'Of course not! What are you implying?'

'I'm not implying anything. But you have to see things from my position, Mr Lamb. Three suspicious deaths have been reported in the last twenty-four hours. First, Nathaniel Bridge commits suicide with you as the only witness. Then Mr Habborlain's butler is murdered in the most gruesome fashion – yes, I have seen the body, Mr Lamb – in a household visited by your good self only a few hours previously. Then this morning a man is found shot dead in the lobby of the chambers where you are employed. Do you see what all these deaths have in common, Mr Lamb?'

The pause felt worse the longer William left it. 'Me,' he said, just one syllable that drew the madness together. William was conscious that he too was now sweating, the open door providing little relief.

'What happened to your hand?'

'I cut myself when I broke into my house. I had to smash the back window to open the latch.'

'I would have thought a key was a more conventional way of obtaining access to one's own abode.'

'Obviously, detective, but the men I told you about took my key when they went searching for this damned box!'

'The box you failed to mention yesterday.'

William thought of Bridge's warning: *tell no one you have it, not even the police.* But Aunt Esther mattered more. 'I know this all sounds highly unusual, I do not blame you in the slightest for treating my testimony with scepticism, but the fact remains that my aunt is missing! For whatever reason, this man Pincott has taken her. Do you know anyone of that name, detective?'

Cunningham paused, clearly in two minds as to whether to answer William's question. 'He is a notorious operator in the East End of the city. Many people know of him. It is said that the children of Whitechapel grow up believing him to be the bogeyman.'

Cunningham's inference was clear. William could have conveniently chosen an already infamous name as a diversion for the police. Surely they couldn't really suspect him of anything? What on earth would his motive be?

'Please, detective, if I have behaved erratically in the last day, understand that it is simply a function of the misfortunes that have heaped upon me. I have been reeling from the moment I met Ambrose Habborlain yesterday morning. I am a gentleman of honour, sir. I acknowledge that I should have come to you sooner. I cannot explain it.' William silently cursed himself for trusting Savannah to go to the police yesterday afternoon. Keeping her out of his story was making his own actions look at best absurd and, at worst, downright suspicious.

Detective Cunningham shook his head slowly but said nothing. William hoped the gesture reflected that he was appalled only by William's stupidity, nothing more.

'Please. I need you to look for my aunt, sir. It is all I care about. Clearly none of this makes any sense to either of us, but a woman's life is in danger. She is all I have!' His voice choked on these last words.

'Very well. Are there any other witnesses we can call on to these events you describe?'

William thought of Savannah and the maid, Sarah. He had never told a lie of any significance before. He dearly hoped it would not have dire consequences for either himself or Aunt Esther. 'No. There are no witnesses. You have my word alone.'

Dolly Cunningham looked into William's eyes without blinking. William held his gaze, hoping it conveyed the sincerity and desperation of his position.

'I will send some men to your home immediately.'

William sighed and leant back in his chair as the detective left the room in search of something to write down William's address. At last, action would be taken and he felt an urge to cry. Maybe he should find a hotel for the next day or so, somewhere where Aunt Esther could rest once the police released her from her ordeal? She would not want to return to the house, at least not yet. He had enough for a modest set of rooms somewhere nearby. Meanwhile he could arrange for someone to fix the broken window as a matter of urgency, and he should contact Sedgwick. Even someone of Sedgwick's composure would surely be alarmed at the current state of affairs and require some explanation.

It felt comforting to be making plans again. He couldn't bring Mr Bridge back to life, but he could bring order to the chaos that descended after his death. It was still only a day ago that poor Mr Bridge had taken his revolver in hand, and yet so much had happened since, it felt like a lifetime ago.

He felt in his pockets, pulled out Habborlain's crumpled note and flattened it on the table before him. He should show it to the detective.

He read the words again: *Cosmati, Henna Kai, Nea Hespera.*

The word Cosmati definitely rang a bell but the others meant nothing to him. Maybe he could ask at the booksellers in Farringdon? If someone recognised the language, the note could be translated.

Eager for matters to progress, William stood and poked his head around the door, looking for a sign of Detective Cunningham, and saw his round form at the other end of the long corridor. The detective was in the reception area, deep in conversation with an animated colleague, whom William recognised from the previous day as Sergeant Smiley. The men had their backs turned to him as he approached.

William was about to clear his throat to interrupt, when Smiley's words stopped him in his tracks.

'Dolly, just arrest the man! There is almost certainly no aunt, this story is ludicrous. Let him rot in the cells for a few days and maybe he will come to his sense and confess all. We don't have the resources to look for a missing aunt who almost certainly isn't real. In a week's time, he'll be singing a different tune, no doubt.'

A week! William was about to protest and demand they search for Aunt Esther immediately even if they locked him up for the duration. But what could he say? What else did he have to convince them? The note, maybe, or would that just be further evidence of his madness? Sarah's testimony? But that would mean revealing Savannah's role and further damaging his own credibility. There was no guarantee they would search for his aunt.

He turned around and crept back to the interview room and the propped-open door to the outside. He grabbed his bag and strode into the sunlight. Halfway down the steps he paused. Below was a narrow alley that led to the busy streets of Whitehall, only twenty yards away. If he left now, he would be a fugitive, alone in his search for his aunt. If he stayed, what then? It would be Aunt Esther who was all alone, her disappearance ignored by all. It was too much to bear.

He pushed himself on towards the crowds, expecting at any moment to hear Cunningham's voice behind him.

The traffic on Whitehall was moving swiftly and without pausing, William threw himself into a passing hansom carriage and called up to the driver, his voice shaking, 'Don't stop, please, I'm in a desperate hurry!'

As he leant back in his seat, the doubts came quickly. Should he have run?

The driver called down. 'Where to, sir?'

William closed his eyes. Where to indeed? Loneliness wrapped about him as he took the note once more from his pocket.

'Farringdon Road, please.'

Twomey and Field, booksellers. The name came back to him as he stood beneath the awning. He had passed here so often on his daily commute, and only yesterday, at his fateful encounter with Habborlain, he had thought of this place, resolving to visit to improve his conversational ability. How frivolous a desire that seemed to him now. His office was only two streets along, but felt a million miles away, much like everything else. He wondered if Sedgwick was there, clearing up the mess. My mess, he thought.

William pushed open the door and went in. The air was old, dusty and dry. Immediately he coughed and reached for his handkerchief to control the spluttering.

'May I help you, sir?'

The man who stood before him was so uniformly pale in colouring it was hard to see where any one feature ended and another began. His hair was white, and his eyes were rimmed with pink, like a rodent's. He could have been twenty or seventy or anywhere in between.

William cleared his throat and pulled Habborlain's note from his pocket. 'I was hoping you might recognise this language?'

The man moved closer to peer at the note and William fought the desire to take a step back.

'Why, of course, sir. The last two lines are Ancient Greek!' His tone implying that William had failed to recognise something as clearly identifiable as a giraffe.

Normally such scorn would bring a hot flush of shame at his own ignorance but William was too tired and desperate to care. Besides, it was that same sense of shame that had caused him to lie to Habborlain in the first place, and pretend knowledge of a language he did not have.

'Do you have a dictionary I might purchase to aid a translation?'

The man smiled, yellow teeth against white skin. 'That won't be necessary, sir. I know what this means, at least in part.'

'You do?'

'*Hena Kai Nea*. From the Attic calendar, used in ancient Athens. It means the "old and the new", and it refers to the day before the new moon. It's a date.'

'Do you know when that is?'

'It occurs every month, sir. Here, let me look . . . ' The man went to his desk and picked up a large leather diary. He leafed through it until he found what he was looking for. 'Here we are. The next new moon is on the third of July. So Hena Kai Nea is on the second. That is this Monday night. *Hespera,* which of course gives us our word vespers, means dusk.'

'Of course.' William was beginning to enjoy the man's patronising tone, so inured did he feel to it. 'And Cosmati?'

The man frowned. 'It will be the name of something, a place perhaps. It sounds familiar but I can't identify it, I'm afraid. Italian, probably. Maybe an atlas will help us.'

*Cosmati*. Something William had heard at Sunday school perhaps?

As the man searched through his bookshelves, William sank into the all-too-familiar frustration of anything to do with Ambrose Habborlain. The man communicated in nothing but riddles. *The lamb who went to the slaughter willingly.* William should not have gone to the house on Red Lion Square and he should not have been seen there. True, but inexplicable, for he lived such an ordinary life, in plain view, without secrets, or so he thought. But with Mr Bridge dead and Aunt Esther taken from him, he was truly alone in the world. They had been his whole life, the only two people for whom William's existence meant anything more than a *good morning* or a *how do you do*? His frustration of a few days ago that he knew no young women of marriageable status now gave way to a deeper insight. In fact, he knew nobody. Had his aunt and his employer made it so?

The pale man thumped a huge tome on to his desk. William tried not to cough as a dust cloud erupted in his direction. 'That is a sizeable atlas, sir!'

The man looked up. 'This is simply the index.' He pointed at a row of similar books on a high shelf.

'How impressive!' Feeding the man's pride was yielding quite a lot of free information so far.

But the man was frowning again. 'I'm afraid I can find no place called Cosmati.'

So, he had a date and time for a meeting with Habborlain, but no notion of where to go.

'Is there anything else I might help you with, sir?'

William was about to shake his head but felt it might be unfair for him to leave the shop empty-handed. He recalled his original intention when he first met Habborlain to visit this very shop. 'Do you perhaps have a small volume of Plato's works? My classical education is clearly lacking.'

The man smiled and gave a small bow, evidently pleased that his patronage had opened William's eyes to his own failings. 'I have the very thing, I believe. A short summary of the great man's key writings. It skims the surface, of course, and wouldn't satisfy the more trained mind.'

William ignored him as the man searched the lower shelves for this child's guide to philosophy. He recalled the delicately carved bust of Plato he had seen in Habborlain's drawing room – *the father of all of us.* Everything that was wrong in the world led back to that meeting, those lost moments in the shadows with Habborlain's collection. *It is all connected, don't you see?*

He must leave no stone unturned. William called across to the bookseller, 'Tell me, sir, you seem an astonishingly well-educated chap. Are you aware of any connections between Plato, Alexander the Great and Lord Byron?'

The man leapt to his feet with a small volume in hand, his eyes shining. 'Ah, a game sir! Very well, let me try.' He tapped the book against his bloodless lips and closed his eyes, clearly enjoying himself. 'Well, the first part is easy of course. Aristotle was a student of Plato, who in turn became tutor to Alexander the Great. As for Lord Byron . . . Ah, I have it! Lord Byron had an obsession with finding Alexander's grave, which of course was common to many travellers in his day. Nonetheless, the connections are complete, I would say!' He looked expectantly at William, as if he might have a prize to offer.

William could find nothing relevant in what he had just heard. 'Truly astonishing, sir, I am honoured to have met such a scholar.'

The man glowed as he handed William the book. William was glad of the bandage on his left hand, which meant he did not have to endure the customary sharp intake of breath and inevitable questions.

'How much do I owe you, sir?'

The man waved his hand. 'It is a gift, sir. I am always happy to help bring the light of learning to those who live in darkness.'

How on earth did this man make any money in his trade? William felt a tad guilty that he had manipulated the man's vanity in such a way. After sharing a few more superlatives, William thanked him and turned towards the door. At the threshold, he held up the book and couldn't resist asking, 'I don't suppose it has pictures?'

*

Back on the street, William trudged the familiar route towards the station. How tempting it was to take the train home, to see his front door once again. He repaired to the tea shop on the concourse, ordered a pot of tea and some bread and cheese, and tried to concentrate on the book he had been given, but it was no use. His thoughts strayed again and again to his aunt. His sojourn to the bookshop and partial translation of the note had been a small distraction, but now the bald facts of his predicament hit him hard and his food felt laced with the bitter taste of hopelessness.

Sarah had mentioned that the men had taken Aunt Esther as some kind of insurance, but heaven only knew what use either William or his aunt were to this man Pincott. The thought of waiting two days until Monday to obtain information from Habborlain left him feeling utterly powerless. He didn't even know where the meeting would be. And what of poor Aunt Esther in the meantime? Was she, and he hardly dared think it, even still alive?

He took out his watch. It said a quarter past three but it was surely considerably later. He didn't really care what time it was. Knowing the time belonged to another world, a world that William had destroyed, for somehow he himself had brought the walls crashing down.

He got to his feet. He had to do something, however reckless. His aunt was in Whitechapel, the box too most likely, and that is where he would follow, whatever the consequences.

He jingled the coins in his pocket. There was one person left in this world who could help him, and he knew her price.

## CHAPTER TWENTY-FOUR

*H*arry had been eager to leave immediately for Bedlam but had been delayed by a commotion at Scotland Yard. Angus Smiley, the arrogant young sergeant who shadowed Dolly Cunningham, had been apoplectic over the young suspect who had absconded from an interview room and had demanded the assistance of all in searching the surrounding streets. Even Dolly had seemed embarrassed at Smiley's excessive reaction, although his mortification may have had more to do with the fact that it was Dolly himself who had left the door to the fire escape wide open, allowing the criminal to flee easily.

So it was mid-afternoon before Harry found himself standing before the gates of the Bethlem Royal Hospital, to give it its proper name. There had been an institution with that title for over six hundred years and Harry was aware of its fearful reputation as a place where the aristocrats of centuries ago would come to laugh at the antics of the wretched and the insane, a place where once committed, one might be trapped for ever. The very word *Bedlam* seemed synonymous not just with madness of the brain, but with chaos of the worst kind, where the natural order of things might unravel and the world itself might go mad.

Harry could see little relationship between the myth and the reality. The new hospital had been built in an appealing quarter of Southwark. Set back from the main thoroughfare by an expanse of well-tended lawn, the grand building took its place gracefully, like a giant wedding cake, adorned with a pleasing dome and large portico. If there were horrors within, the building hid them well.

As he entered, sunlight poured through the glass dome fifty feet above his head. He wondered whether the inmates were ever allowed into this part of the hospital, or whether it was reserved only for family members visiting the distressed. Maybe the grandness reassured them that the hospital took its mission seriously, that such an inspiring entrance hall would not have been built if inmates were to pass through it only once, never to see the door again.

After a short wait, he was ushered through a brightly lit corridor and into the warden's office. It was a pleasant room, with a large low window overlooking the gardens behind. The bottom sash was raised and the aroma of honeysuckle filled the room.

Captain Barnaby Drummond was a surprisingly young man, no more than forty, Harry guessed. Judging by his title and the firmness of his handshake, Harry suspected the man had spent much of his life in the army and had only recently turned his well-connected hand to the task of caring for the tormented.

'Apologies for keeping you waiting. What can I do for you, detective?'

The warden's tone was all business and Harry responded in kind.

'I believe an inmate of yours is missing, sir, a man who goes by the name Edward.'

'And what makes you believe that?' Captain Drummond shot back.

The warden was clearly not intimidated by the presence of a detective asking questions, but then Harry was not easily intimidated by men like Captain Barnaby Drummond.

'It was brought to our attention in relation to another matter we are investigating.'

The warden left a long pause, clearly hoping Harry might say more. He didn't.

'You are right. We do indeed have an inmate called Edward. He is entitled to come and go as he pleases. His incarceration here is entirely voluntary.'

'When was he last seen?'

The warden gave a good impression of thinking hard. 'I believe it would have been Thursday afternoon.'

'And where would he normally go?'

'I'm sorry?'

'When he comes and goes as he pleases, where would he normally go?'

'Edward does not leave us often, I believe he likes it here. I myself have not been in post for very long.'

'When did you take up the position, sir?'

The warden paused again before speaking although his face still did not betray any discomfort. 'Three years ago.'

'So, you were not concerned when this man left your care for the first time in three years and failed to return that night?'

'No. I was not. Edward is a grown man, and not considered by a court of law to be incapable of making decisions for himself.'

'So why is he here?'

'Edward is a sensitive soul, an artist. He is given to bouts of whim and despondency. I daresay he finds the environment ... nourishing.'

'Indeed. Just how long has he been nourished here, sir?'

The warden stood up and came around the desk. 'I don't wish to be unhelpful, Detective Treadway, but I cannot share confidential patient information with you without a patient's, or their guardian's, consent.'

'Does Edward have such a guardian?'

'No, sir, he does not.'

Harry stood up and held his hand out once more. 'Then I shall trouble you no more, sir. Thank you for your help.'

The man was all smiles then. 'Not at all, detective. I am sorry I couldn't furnish you with all the information you desired. Rules are rules and to bend them, in my experience, often leads to no end of trouble.'

'How true, sir. I will just conduct a brief examination of his quarters before I depart. Perhaps you could arrange for someone to show me the way?'

'I really don't think that would be appropriate.'

'Oh, I assure you, it is *highly* appropriate. You see, a murder has been committed by a man who matches Edward's description. I think you would agree that Edward's appearance is most distinctive.'

The warden opened his mouth to object but Harry continued. 'I have my man, sir, I know it. I could return in a matter of hours with a warrant, of course – after all, rules are rules.' Harry could do no such thing, it would be Monday before the paperwork could be completed and a judge's signature obtained.

Like all good army men, Captain Drummond knew when it was time to beat a retreat. 'Very well, Detective Treadway.'

An orderly with a round bald head took Harry to Edward's room. Harry attempted to engage the man in conversation but, as expected, the warden had selected the most truculent and tight-lipped employee he could find for this particular task. At first they had passed a number of inmates gathered together in groups, either in the corridors themselves or in large day rooms where a variety of activities seemed to be taking place. The only indications that this was a hospital for the mentally ill were the alarm bells that lined the corridors at strategically placed intervals, their thin cords hanging within reach above his head. He caught a glimpse of a sizeable orchestra rehearsing behind one particular open door, and the resulting sound was surprisingly competent and pleasant on the ear. The number of patients he saw outside their rooms lessened as they descended to the basement level and entered a corridor which contained only a series of locked doors. As they walked, the atmosphere shifted: a sudden bark of callous laughter and the desperation of a woman weeping shaped an anthem of human distress.

There were two locks on Edward's door, Harry noticed, one more than he had observed on the others they had passed. The idea that this man could come and go as he pleased was clearly an absurd lie. But if that was the case, just how had Edward been able to leave the building in the first place?

The answer presented itself clearly the moment Harry stepped into the room. Four windows were set high in the opposite wall. The late afternoon sunlight strained through three of them, weakened by the film of dust that covered the windowpanes, but poured through the fourth opening, where the pane had been smashed. A large cupboard had been pushed askew under the window and a chair balanced on top.

It was almost impossible to tell the exact size of the room, crammed as it was with paintings. The walls were covered from top to bottom, and stacks of canvases sat twenty deep on the floor, leaving only narrow paths through which one could pass. Even the small cot in the far corner was littered with sketches and inks. Nearest to him was a large canvas set on an easel. Harry removed his spectacles from their case and placed them on his nose to take a closer look.

The work was incomplete, but of astonishing technical brilliance and detail. Painted in the colours of the earth, it depicted a world of many figures where proportions were skewed out of kilter. Men and goblins appeared to stand on nothing while clouds drifted across the bottom of the canvas, depicting an upside down sky, and oversized acorns and daisies littered the ground randomly. It was a dark vision of chaos painted by a restless, brilliant hand. In the centre of the painting was an unmistakable symbol. Harry withdrew his notebook and found the drawing Lydia Stanbury had made the day before of the murderer's tattoos. The image was the same.

As he looked about the room, he saw the symbol repeated everywhere, incorporated into the paintings in a variety of ingenious ways: a globe here, or a flower there. Harry picked his way through the stacks of canvases and painting equipment towards the bed in the corner. Before he had come close, his eye immediately caught on to something.

Lying on the bed was a copy of the *Illustrated London News*, opened to the page containing the lithograph of Phoebe Stanbury on the day the engagement party had been announced. It was the same page he himself had perused yesterday morning, examining the image of the victim closely to see if it revealed anything of the future tragedy that was to befall her. In the copy of the paper that now lay on the bed, the image was gone, obliterated by a pen that had scratched across it, over and over, until it had scored through to the page beneath. The viciousness of it made him shiver and instinctively he looked over his shoulder to where the orderly stood by the open door.

'How did Edward come by this newspaper?'

The man weighed up whether to answer or not, evidently deciding that no harm could come from it. 'He liked to get the papers – took *The Times* every day and the *Illustrated London News* every week.'

Harry surveyed the room. Selecting the stack of canvases nearest the bed, he began to flip through them. They were large and cumbersome to manipulate. Before he had reached the middle of the stack he was about to give up on the task. He would assess one more painting and then move on. As he manoeuvred it into view, he saw at first that it was a simple portrait, without any of the dense, meticulous anarchy of the man's other work, but when he caught his first full view of the canvas, he was astonished.

Before him was a portrait of Phoebe Stanbury.

The beauty that had been hinted at by the small image printed in the paper was here amplified into a breathtaking likeness: the same wry smile, the same dimple on the right cheek of her heart-shaped face. She wore her hair differently in each image, but Harry was struck by something else. The illustration in the paper had been gouged, yet this portrait had undoubtedly been painted with the utmost tenderness. What had changed, he wondered? The painting had been lost in a stack of others, forgotten maybe. What had turned that vision of love into a nightmare of hatred and murder? He had his man, all right.

Harry asked the orderly to return him to the warden's office.

'Captain Drummond said you would be leaving after you had seen the room, sir.'

'And so I was. I have, however, changed my mind.'

The journey back to the warden's office was conducted at an infuriatingly slow pace. Harry found himself keen to escape from the maze of corridors. The warden was not pleased to see him again, but Harry persisted nonetheless. There was now no time to lose in this investigation. He might have discovered the murderer's identity and seen his lair, but he did not have the man himself, and if Harry hadn't entirely believed it before, now he felt sure that the madman would continue to be a real danger if he remained at large in the city.

'I would like to see Edward's records, please.'

Captain Drummond matched Harry's frankness with his own. 'I'm afraid I cannot do that, Detective Treadway. I am going to have to insist on a warrant before I give you such access.'

The man had changed his tune. Had he spoken to someone in the meantime? There was a telephone on his desk, after all.

'It is hard to believe that Edward is the voluntary inmate you suggest, Captain Drummond. There were two locks on his door and he evidently had to break a window in order to abscond.'

Captain Drummond remained unruffled and instead patronised Harry with a tight-lipped smile. 'You would be surprised what patients ask us to do for them, detective. Edward wanted to be locked up, to be kept safe from the world and for the world to be kept safe from him. It does not change the fact that he was a voluntary patient.'

'I would like to know who is paying Edward's bills here.'

The warden skipped a beat before replying. 'No one. His residency is funded by the Bethlem charity.'

'Really? But you said his incarceration was voluntary?'

Checkmate.

The warden eyed Harry with open hostility. 'Return with your warrant on Monday, detective. You will receive your answers then, sir.'

Harry knew that the last thing he would be given on Monday was an answer to anything. Whatever records existed would surely have been destroyed by then, an accident that would be blamed on some unreliable filing clerk. He had to get his hands on those records tonight.

'Very well, Captain Drummond, until Monday morning.'

Harry turned on his heel and strode into the corridor, where the orderly was waiting for him.

'Don't worry, I shall show myself out.'

Harry walked with conviction back towards the main entrance hall but the moment he heard the door behind him close, he turned around. The orderly had disappeared. Harry seized the moment, turned the handle of the nearest door, and entered the room.

Four empty desks sat in the middle, facing each other; it being a Saturday the occupants had presumably left for the day around lunchtime. The back wall was lined with filing cabinets, but Harry knew better than to become excited at the coincidence of stumbling into the room where the asylum's records were kept. He suspected Edward's files were currently somewhere in the warden's office, if they had not been destroyed or tampered with already.

He moved to the far side of the room and unlocked the bottom sash of a small window and, with some effort, pushed it open a few feet. Beneath the opening was a neatly planted flowerbed; it would be a soft landing.

Back at the doorway, he took a few deep breaths. He was far too old for such antics, and his heart was beating fast. He didn't much care if he was discovered after the fact. He just needed to see the file, however briefly. After all, what could the warden actually do to him? Colonel Matlock might discipline him in some token way for causing a disturbance and not following the letter of the law, but Silas Matlock would also know that needs must in such a situation.

He opened the door and swiftly looked up and down the corridor; it was empty. He tiptoed across to the nearest alarm bell, reached up to grab the cord, and pulled as hard as he could. The noise was deafening and he ran back into the room and closed the door. Already he could hear shouts in the corridor and the thump of running feet. He hurried to the window and pushed himself through. He navigated the flower bed, staying low, until he stood next to the warden's window.

He peered in. The room was empty.

Harry had to nudge the window open further before he could climb into the office. The door to the room was shut and, when he checked the handle, he was pleased to find that the warden had had the perspicacity to lock it behind him before running into the corridor at the sound of the alarm. At least now Harry would have some warning if Captain Drummond returned. He turned his attention to the warden's desk, forcing himself to remain calm. He was a firm believer in the saying, more haste, less speed.

He need not have worried. There was only one pile of folders, positioned at the end of the desk. Harry looked through them methodically until he found the one he wanted. The name on the file and a quick flick through the contents told him all he needed to know.

He replaced the file and checked to make sure that he had left no telltale footprints on the floor. He could hear the warden's voice in the corridor, snarling instructions to check the other rooms. Harry climbed out of the window once more, taking care to lower it back to its original position.

He worked his way around the long building, staying close to the wall, still expecting someone to see him and demand an explanation for his presence in the garden. He suspected that he might encounter a steel gate, heavily bolted, that would require him to surrender himself and admit to his actions like an errant schoolboy.

As he came to the edge of the building he was surprised to be faced by no more than a neatly clipped hedge, through which he could clearly see a gravel trail that would lead him back to civilisation. The sun had begun to dip towards the horizon as he lay on the ground and used his head to push a path through the hedge. It was neither elegant nor comfortable, but it was easily done.

Once on the other side, he brushed himself down and removed the twigs from his thinning grey hair before smoothing it back into place. He kept to the shadows as he walked back towards Southwark's busy main road.

'Hampstead, please, driver,' Harry shouted up as he found an empty cab. 'To Ridgeside, if you will.'

He was south of the river and the journey would take some time. He settled back into the warm shabby leather, and wondered why, twenty years earlier, the most powerful industrialist of the age had imprisoned a boy of eight in the most notorious mental asylum in the world, and had continued to pay the bills ever since? The only clue had been in Edward's surname, printed in block capitals on the front of his file.

Raycraft.

$\mathcal{S}$avannah cut through the streets of Kensington towards Hyde Park Corner. She was in no rush to pick up the omnibus to Whitechapel. The light was fading, but what she had planned needed the cover of darkness. She just hoped that William Lamb had done his bit and persuaded the authorities to raid Pincott's lair. With Pincott removed and his empire weakened, she would have a chance tonight to partake of the spoils and take what was rightfully hers.

As she turned down a familiar alleyway, she tried to focus her thoughts on the task ahead. Get the money and get out, Shelton. But, as ever, the solitude of her walk through these affluent streets brought the past crowding in. She knew better than most to avoid wasting her time with regrets. They lined up before her like rabbit holes and she could easily spend a lifetime climbing out of one and into another. She had to believe that if she kept running, her past would give up and let her go. The visual image of history stalking her made her skin prickle. She ripped the gun from her skirt and spun around.

'What the hell?'

William Lamb dropped his bag to the ground and put his hands in the air, his eyes round with fear.

'Are you following me?'

'Yes,' he stammered. 'I went to your home. I saw you leave, so

I followed you. I was waiting for the right moment to stop you. But then I thought you might lead me there, without my having to ask . . . '

She lowered her gun and narrowed her eyes. 'Lead you where?'

'Whitechapel. Pincott.' He swallowed. 'I need to rescue my aunt, and retrieve the box. It's the key to everything, I think.'

She wanted to laugh. The notion of William Lamb rescuing even a kitten from a tree was dubious. And as for her plans, well, since when did they ever work out? She moved towards him. 'Let me guess. It didn't go so well with the law.'

'I thought at first they believed me, but then, the next moment, they were going to lock me up and not even look for Aunt Esther. So I ran. I didn't know what else to do.'

'And you thought you'd go ask the nice Mr Pincott to give you your aunt back?'

He shrugged, and she saw the tears in his eyes. 'I have no choice.'

Savannah sighed. 'I'm going there tonight. I told you, he owes me money and I mean to get paid. If your aunt is there, I'll see what I can do. No promises though.'

'I have money. I can pay you. And I'm coming with you.'

Savannah laughed and shook her head. 'Don't be a fool, William. You won't help your aunt if they find you. We don't know *why* they want you but we sure as hell know that they do.'

'I can't just do nothing and wait for a meeting with Habborlain on Monday when I don't even know where it is!'

William told her of the partial translation of the note. Mystery was piling on mystery, but why should she care? Savannah paced around him, talking as much to herself as anyone else. 'I don't need passengers. I'm on my own, that's how this works, do you understand?'

'I understand that you care about money and very little else!' He ran his hands through his hair. 'I'm sorry, that is both unfair and untrue.'

Is it? she thought. She didn't know any more. 'Listen, I'll take your money. Money matters when you ain't got none. But I'm not your partner. I'll help you tonight, but your troubles are your own. I don't have a dog in this fight.'

They returned to Cromwell Road to leave William's bag in her room before catching the crowded omnibus. As they rumbled through the streets, the city seemed more claustrophobic than ever, and she felt a stout desire to be alone once more. Why was everyone turning to her to throw them a rope? Couldn't they see that she was drowning too? It was all right for William Lamb — one look at his confused, pleading eyes and the cavalry arrived from nowhere to rescue him, herself included. All people saw when they looked at her was that damned scar and the hard set of her mouth. Now she was forced to enter Pincott's lair with its defences still intact, accompanied by a man who would likely be more hindrance than help. Still, payment was payment, and the irony hit hard; she was risking her life to acquire the funds she needed to find a safer haven.

'Why are you smiling?' William asked.

'Because I'm an ass.'

'Oh.'

'Just feeling sorry for myself. Waste of time.' And so it was, she thought.

'Tell me more of this rogue, Pincott.'

Savannah shifted in her seat. 'He's not a good man, William. He's from the East, and I doubt Obediah Pincott is his real name. He has a life-size tattoo of his own face in the centre of his chest.'

'Really? How astonishing!'

Savannah glared at him. 'He's dangerous, William. That's all you need to know.'

'So how did you make his acquaintance?'

'When I arrived in the city, someone suggested he might have work for me. He sent me to watch the Habborlain house. That's all there is to tell.'

'What work do you usually do? How did you earn a living in America?'

She picked at her nails. 'This and that.'

'Domestic work?'

'Whatever I could get.'

'Does everyone in America carry a gun? Just in case?'

'No, William, they don't.' Savannah sighed and pulled herself up. 'We're here.'

She jumped down into the road and watched as William tentatively reached out a foot, searching for solid ground like an animal about to be released from captivity, although he still managed to land in a grimy puddle.

'Stay close to me – and try to look as if you know your way around. If anyone looks you in the eye, you look back, no casting your eyes down like a submissive maid.' William looked at the ground. 'Exactly like that, William, that's exactly what you do *not* do.'

'But surely, if I look away, a ruffian is more likely to leave me alone?'

'They're more likely to stab you in the guts and take your purse.'

William turned pale and Savannah took advantage. 'You can still back out.'

For a moment, William looked to be in two minds before grimly shaking his head. 'I have to find my aunt and try to recover the box, whatever it involves.'

Savannah had to admire his bleak determination. God help her but she could see something strengthening within him, something small, but growing in the darkness.

As they trudged towards the back streets of Whitechapel, William kept his promise and stayed close to her. She tried to see it all through his eyes: the open sewers that ran in muddied lines through the streets and the many barefoot residents that skipped around them without having to look down. As she passed the garishly painted women who stood in doorways and on street corners, the glacial expressions they flicked in her direction obviously softened when William filed past, judging by the calls of *why don't you buy me a drink* and *c'mon, dearie, only a shilling to you*. She could just imagine the horror those words were inspiring in William. Some of the girls were impossibly young and tugged at her heart when she saw them.

Their pace slowed as the roads narrowed and filled with an ever greater variety of humanity – traders wheeling their barrows home, clusters of children playing in the dirt, and negro sailors, fresh from the ships docked at Limehouse Basin and in search of a good time. The air about them grew thick, exotic and foul all at once. They had to push their way through the last few hundred yards, single file with Savannah in the lead. She lost count of the number of times she heard William say *sorry* or *pardon me, sir*, although eventually he became silent, worn down by the torrent of expletives that each apology seemed to provoke.

As they jammed into another alley, Savannah had to shove hard to make any progress. Something up ahead was blocking their path. They were very close now to Pincott's compound. As they neared the obstacle the alleyway widened into the square just outside the Hog and Spike alehouse, a local landmark that Savannah had passed many times. A large crowd had gathered, and the sound of catcalls, boos and cheering meant only one thing.

A prize fight.

Savannah was immediately apprehensive. Pincott ran all the fights in this part of town: terriers, cocks, men . . . whatever beast he could persuade to bare its claws and teeth for money. If there was a fight taking place here tonight, then Pincott's men were bound to be present and any one of them might recognise her.

The crowd was pressing in from behind as more people arrived in the square. William was thrust close to her and he rasped, 'I can't breathe!'

With her arm around William's shoulder, she drove them forward through the crowd. Keeping William close, she pressed on until they reached the clearing.

Two men squared up to each other, one much fatter than the other. Both were half-naked and sweating profusely. The smaller of the two had blood running down into one eye, but dared not drop his guard to wipe it clear. The large man took a heavy swing at the other, narrowly missing him. The smaller one may have been bleeding but he seemed to Savannah to be younger and more nimble. She cast a glance at William and saw he was making a conscious effort to breathe deeply through his mouth. Obviously the distinctive smells of Whitechapel were assailing his senses as hundreds of unwashed bodies pressed in around him. It was fully dark now, and great torches burned furiously on the walls surrounding them, a smouldering straw occasionally breaking free and dropping down on to the shrieking heads below.

The crowd gasped as the fat man landed a heavy blow on his opponent, who fell instantly to one knee. The fat man grinned and began to gather his strength to land the knockout punch, just as his opponent threw his fist upwards, catching his rival under the jaw with a terrible crunch. The fat man fell instantly on to his behind, the rest of his body crumpling to the floor soon after.

The crowd showed no signs of dispersing: evidently another bout was scheduled. Savannah looked around to get her bearings. The quickest route to Dodd's Lane would be straight on and then right up ahead. They would have to cross the circle before the next fight started.

'Follow me and stay close.' Savannah began to step out into the clearing when her blood froze in her veins.

Dub was standing on the opposite side of the makeshift boxing ring, his red face and hair glistening in the firelight. His arms were folded across his chest as he laughed and jostled with two other men. Judging by the rattling gasp she heard at her side, William had seen him too.

Savannah thought quickly, summoning the images of Pincott's compound that she had tried so hard to imprint on her mind the day before. Dodd's Lane was not the only way they might be able to get in.

Keeping her eyes on Dub and willing him not to look in their direction, she spoke to William. 'To our right is an alehouse. We're going in, right to the top, just keeping going up. I'll follow you.'

William mobilised with more haste than Savannah expected, striding through the door of the alehouse and up the first flight of stairs. She half expected him to collapse and tumble, but he kept up a steady stride as they pounded up the stairs, to the bemusement of the pub's inebriated clientele. Savannah fought the urge to look back over her shoulder. Had Dub spotted them at the last moment? She pulled the gun from the back of her skirt.

On the top floor William came to an abrupt halt, his breathing ragged. They were in a deserted attic room, filled with broken furniture, overturned mattresses and piles of old crockery. At the far end they could see a gabled window, so ensnared with cobwebs that it was impossible to make out what was on the other side. William reached the window first, undid the latch and pushed hard. A waft of night air from the open window blew the cobwebs back into his face. Savannah put her gun away, raced towards the window, and looked out. There was a drop of about seven feet to the roof below and she just hoped it would hold their weight. She turned back to William. 'You first.'

William climbed on to the window sill and dangled his legs over the edge outside.

'Jump!'

'It's so high!'

'Oh, for God's sake.' Savannah shoved William hard in the back and he fell forward out of the window with a yelp. Savannah climbed into the window frame and jumped, feeling the hard crunch of slate beneath her boots.

William was rubbing furiously at his ankle, although Savannah suspected any damage suffered in his fall on to the roof had more to do with pride than broken bones. 'Can you reach the window?'

Injuries forgotten, William rose up on his toes and just managed to push the window closed with his fingertips. Savannah drew her gun again and they hunkered down behind a large chimney stack, out of sight of the window above.

William spoke in an impassioned whisper. 'If they follow us, I won't go down without a fight!'

Savannah shushed him but couldn't resist smiling at his words. Maybe the bare-knuckle punches they had witnessed in the square had almost brought out the fighter in him. She exhaled slowly and closed her eyes, allowing a few more moments to pass before deciding they were safe from pursuit. If they had been seen, Pincott would know they were here in Whitechapel, and that she was helping William Lamb.

'Look, it's so beautiful.' William's tone was flat but his words held conviction.

Savannah opened her eyes and looked at the subject of William's rapt gaze. All around and below them lay the city, its lights spilling out into the distance like a million candles set afloat on a calm night sea. They must have run up four or five flights of stairs and now, out on the rooftops, there was nothing to hinder their view. Savannah stood up and walked to the edge of the roof, careful not to lean too far over and risk being observed from the alleyway beneath. The building across the street was more or less the same height, and close enough almost to touch.

William's enthusiasm was growing. 'Look, I can see St Paul's!

That line of shadow must be the river. And there, over there, the Palace of Westminster!' He came to a stop in one place, and Savannah saw a pitiful longing ripple across his face as he looked towards the west of the city. She followed his eyes along the dark snake of the Thames until it disappeared from view.

'Looking for something?'

'Yes . . . ' William's voice faltered.

'Home,' she said.

'Only I can't see that far.'

'Neither can I.'

William turned towards her. 'Where is home?'

Savannah sniffed against the sudden night chill. 'I'll let you know when I find it. Right now, we have somewhere we need to be.'

She turned towards the attic window and retraced her steps. Finding Pincott's compound was hard enough on the streets in daylight, let alone from the roof of the Hog and Spike. She closed her eyes and summoned up the route she would have taken from the front door of the alehouse, calculating distances as best she could. She opened her eyes again and allowed them to focus in the direction her mind had told her to look.

Of course! In front of her, and across to her right, the rooftops and chimneys jumbled together randomly before stopping abruptly at a big black square of nothing: the yard of Pincott's compound. It couldn't have been more obvious from where she stood, and the path they needed to take could not have been more straightforward. For all the protection he employed, and the lengths he went to in order to stay hidden from view, Pincott was brutally exposed to Savannah from her vantage point above the city, like a turtle on its back. She had joined the birds and the angels.

Savannah led them forward as they picked their way across the rooftops. There was only one jump of any difficulty that had to be addressed and she was relieved when William made it without injury or complaint.

As they drew closer, they began to descend, finally arriving on the roof of the compound itself. The yard, at this time of night, was unusually quiet. A few dogs barked in lacklustre fashion and she could just hear the snores of a man lying prostrate on a pile of straw in one corner.

They were on the same side of the compound where Savannah had earlier witnessed the captive woman in the tartan dress being taken: exploring the rooms below them might be a good place to start. Savannah went first, softly dropping down on to the walkway below. She could see the lights on the other side of the yard burning brightly in the room where she usually met Pincott, but on this side, most of the windows and doorways were dark and she hoped they could move unobserved. She pushed open the first door they came to, grimacing as the hinges groaned.

The corridor they entered was dark, only a dapple of moonlight to show them the way as they crept forward. Savannah inched open the first door on the right with a tentative hand.

The room was empty, save for a child's cradle pushed against the far wall and a bundle of clothing bunched in the centre of the floor. William immediately began to rifle through the pile of fabric, presumably looking for evidence of his aunt's presence. Eventually he stopped and held up a tiny knitted bonnet. 'Baby clothes,' he whispered.

As they turned to go, William stepped on a small box and stumbled forward. He caught himself before he fell but a tinny melody suddenly filled the room, breaking the silence they had worked so hard to maintain. It was a child's musical box, the sweet sound rendered flat by a broken spring.

'Turn it off!' Savannah snarled.

'I'm trying!' William fiddled with the box as the haunting tune echoed through the room. Then he stood up and stamped on it once more. The sound dipped abruptly to nothing.

They froze in their places. Had anyone heard the disturbance? Eventually, Savannah's breathing slowed. They had been lucky that no one else had been in earshot.

She led them back into the corridor and tried another door. This time, they entered a much larger room, the moonlight spilling through a floor-to-ceiling opening that must lead to the loading platform in the yard below them. Wooden crates were piled high on either side. One of the crates lay partly open, revealing row upon row of small glass-stoppered bottles, nestled between pads of compacted straw. Laudanum, she realised, probably defective, but still valuable. She shoved a few into her pockets. With the right buyer ...

'Did you hear that?' William, who had remained near the door, whispered loudly over his shoulder.

Savannah pulled out her gun and strode towards the door. 'What?'

'A moan, a woman I think, across the corridor!'

She grabbed William's arm. 'Stay behind me. If it is your aunt, William, she may not be alone.'

William nodded unconvincingly. She hoped he could keep a grip on himself. With soundless steps Savannah approached the room on the opposite side of the landing. Up close, she could see the tiniest drizzle of light seeping out from beneath the door, probably a single candle flame. She took hold of the handle and paused, ignoring the sensation of William's impatience pushing up behind her. She heard the creak of a chair or a bed from behind the door, followed by a soft grunt. Lifting her gun upwards so that it would be the first part of her to enter the room, Savannah turned the handle and stepped into the chamber beyond.

Immediately she saw two women lying prone on cast-iron beds in each corner of the room. Both of them wore thin shifts and lay on their backs, propped up on pillows with their round bellies starkly contoured in the candlelight. Savannah raised her finger to her lips, although neither woman looked inclined to raise the alarm, their faces displaying no more than mild curiosity towards the intruders. Neither of them was, Savannah suspected, William's aunt, and the groan of disappointment she heard behind her confirmed it. The woman to the right circled her right arm around her swollen belly, her other hand held aloft by metal handcuffs that chained her wrist to the bedpost. Dark shadows sagged beneath her eyes and her thin, mousy hair clung to her head, one tendril following the line of her sharp cheekbone.

Savannah spoke to her. 'Who are you?'

The woman stared back and Savannah shivered to see the emptiness in her unblinking eyes.

'She doesn't speak English,' said a cultured voice.

Savannah turned her attention to the other woman. She too was handcuffed to a bedpost, but her belly was smaller, and her raven black hair spilled out across the pillows. Although she looked healthier than the other, the look in her eyes was somehow even harder to return.

'What's your name?' It was William who spoke to her, his voice gentle.

She laughed as if it was the funniest thing she had heard in a very long time. 'I don't have a name any more.'

The rich voice seemed in stark contrast to their rudimentary surroundings. There was a bucket in a corner of the room and a single candle burned on an upturned crate between the two beds, next to a glass and a jug of water. William stepped forward, filled the glass and handed it to the dark-haired woman. She didn't say thank you but drank nonetheless.

Savannah sat down on the edge of her bed. 'Why are you being held here?'

The woman stroked her belly. 'For this.'

Savannah glanced up at William as he closed the door softly

and leant against it, his eyes averted. The sight of two heavily pregnant women chained up in such squalid surroundings was gruelling for anyone to see. She returned her attention to the woman with no name.

'Pincott?'

'No.' The woman's eyes flicked across to her companion, who stroked her belly and hummed softly to her herself.

'Then who?'

The woman's eyes darkened into pinpricks. Savannah recognised the surge of hatred and instinctively grabbed the woman's hand as she spat out the name. 'Raycraft! The devil's child!'

Savannah heard William's sharp intake of breath but kept hold of the woman's hand. 'We'll get you out of here. We'll find the keys and come back for you.'

The woman withdrew her hand. 'No. There is no point. Where would I go? I am nothing.'

Savannah felt a familiar anger swell within her. 'I don't believe that.'

'Then you're a fool, whoever you are. There is no place in the world for me now.'

For Savannah, the woman's words fell like rocks, and she knew the truth of them. She pulled her eyes away and stood up, swallowing back the bile of her own story. Not trusting herself to speak, she nodded at William, indicating that they should move on, at least for now. William opened the door and tentatively poked his head out into the corridor, signalling that it was clear for them to slip out. At the door, the woman's voice called her back.

'My name is Rebecca. I was a scientist. I worked at the Raycraft factory before they brought me here. There are others – a new girl came yesterday. Save her, it might not be too late.'

Savannah nodded before she stole out once more into the corridor. Once outside the room William's agitation became clear and in an accusatory tone he whispered harshly to Savannah, 'What monstrous outrage is going on here? Those poor women!'

She spat back, 'I didn't know, William! I saw a woman taken here yesterday, but it's the first time I've seen anything of—'

William talked over her. 'We can't leave them here! We must find a local constable!'

Savannah couldn't stop her voice from rising. 'The police don't care what goes on in places like this, William, and they don't care about women once they've been *soiled*, which I think is the charming phrase that—'

William's eyes grew wide. 'Someone's coming!'

They could hear voices and see the faint glimmer of a moving light. Savannah's focus snapped back in to place. She pulled out her gun once more and crept forward until they reached yet another doorway. There was no time for caution and they tumbled through into the darkness.

With the door closed, they struggled to adjust their eyes to the gloom. Unlike the other rooms they had entered so far, heavy drapes hung over the windows, the moonlight only just peeping through. Their footsteps were muffled by a thick carpet and she could no longer smell the stink of the yard outside, masked as it was by a lingering scent of jasmine and musk in the air. There was something incongruous about this space. Savannah could make out a richly upholstered sofa and a polished tray of cut glass that glinted in the dim light. The room connected to another and instinctively she gestured William towards it, pulling him down so that they huddled close to the floor on one side of the doorway. They were in another luxurious space, dominated by a large bed. As they hunkered down, she could just see the first room through a thin crack between the door and the wall.

The voices grew louder: a man and a woman. One of the voices was unmistakable and she felt herself flinch.

'Pincott,' she muttered under her breath.

The door to the main room flew open and the young woman with red hair that Savannah had seen at the window the day before entered with an oil lamp raised high before her, lighting her tresses as if they were the flames of hell itself.

*A*deline had already made up her mind not to offer Pincott any refreshment. It wouldn't be wise to create an overt display of her displeasure, he was still of great importance to her after all, but a snub of some kind was in order to reflect his mishandling of the situation so far.

To her annoyance, as she bustled around the room lighting the lamps, Pincott was already helping himself to a glass of claret, clearly immune to the irritation she hoped she was demonstrating through the sharp rustle of her silk skirts.

'A drink, madame?'

'No . . . Oh, very well, a small one.'

Adeline arranged herself on to the chaise longue, her smile icy as she accepted the glass from Pincott's outstretched hand.

Pincott wrapped his limbs into a delicately carved chair meant for someone half his size. The effect was ridiculous and she tried not to laugh at him. Their relationship was one of opposites. He represented the coarse underbelly of the world they both occupied, with his face untouched by sunlight and his features unsoftened by childhood frivolity. She, on the other hand, sparkled even in the crabby dark of Whitechapel, the best and most beautiful that could be fermented from humanity's organic rawness. Yet she needed him, at least for now.

'I don't believe the new girl has taken. We will need to try again soon.'

Pincott supped deeply from his glass. 'These things take time. Even a man like me knows to wait.'

'And a woman like me knows how to tell if a woman is with child or not. I have an instinct for it.'

'And yet you have no children of your own.'

Adeline hurled her glass into the mahogany panel behind Pincott's head. Pincott was unruffled and continued to sup slowly, his eyes betraying nothing. She shouldn't have done it, riling him would not be to her advantage, but the temptation to stamp on his impudence grew stronger every day. She picked up the conversation as if nothing had happened. 'The others are progressing well, I assume?'

'The dark one, her spirit is broken. She will be no further trouble to you.'

'Good, and the other?'

'Lata.'

Adeline waved her hand. 'Whatever, the dead have no need of names. She must be due very soon.'

Pincott swirled the wine around his glass, staring intently at the rich red liquid, his mouth hanging open slightly like a vampire about to taste blood. He drank it down in one go before raising his eyes to hers once more. 'So I believe.'

'Give the midwife everything she needs. The child must be given every chance to thrive.'

'Indeed it must.'

Not for the first time, Adeline doubted Pincott's commitment to her venture. Maybe he thought her silly? That no matter how much he was being paid, his time was wasted in helping her achieve the perfection to which she aspired. That must be it, she thought, a man such as him would have no truck with dreams. He would have left his own behind long ago.

'Once the child is born, you must dispose of the mother.'

'That was not, how you say?' He paused for a moment. '*Articulated*.'

'I thought it obvious.'

'It is not enough to kill them once, eh?'

'I don't like loose ends. Speaking of which . . .'

Pincott rose up and poured himself another glass of wine before he spoke. 'The boy lawyer was seen here in Whitechapel a few hours ago.'

Adeline was immediately on her feet. 'Tell me you have him!'

Pincott shook his head, seeming to enjoy her exasperation. 'No, the trap we set is here. He will think to find his aunt, so he will come.'

'How would he know of this place?'

'He was not alone. A former employee was seen with him. All entrances are being watched. When they come, we will be ready.'

'You had better make sure of it, Obediah. The mutt has proved more resourceful than we thought. Any news of Habborlain?'

'None. He has left no trace, and yet he was in a hurry. Hurry normally means mistakes, a trail. Not this time. Your Mr Habborlain had a plan.'

Adeline sucked in her cheeks and leant back into the soft padding of the sofa. 'Indeed he did. All this time, he had a plan. Have you ever been betrayed, Obediah?'

'Only by everyone and everything I have ever known.'

'Ah, of course, betrayal is a way of life in the gutter. For us, it feels so new.' For days now, she had contemplated Habborlain's capture. She could not wait to spit in his face, to hear him scream. Adeline looked up to where the lamplight danced tricks across the ceiling. 'Do you know where you come from, Obediah?'

'Yes, though it is not important.'

'And that is the difference between you and me.'

'There are many differences between you and me.'

She shook her head with a graceful sweep of her long neck. 'Only one that matters, I think.'

Pincott clinked his empty glass on to the tray, summoning her back to the room. She was going to be late.

'Have them bring my carriage around, I must go.'

Adeline rolled her evening gloves back on, the tight blue satin reaching above her pale elbows. 'Warn the others that the boy may come looking for his aunt. If he discovers she is not here, he might begin to make connections.'

'Yes, Madame Vicomtesse.' Pincott held the door open as she swept out of the room without a backwards glance, leaving him to dim the lamps and cast the two intruders back into the bewildering shadows.

## CHAPTER TWENTY-SEVEN

𝒮

The sky was dusky pink by the time Harry reached the winding roads of Hampstead and the thicket of trees through which the carriage passed loomed dark and ominous, their earlier lush greenness lost to shadow against the setting sun.

His visit to Bedlam had confirmed his suspicions. Both Benjamin and Jasper Raycraft, and possibly Lydia Stanbury, had lied when they claimed not to know anything of the naked intruder. Harry would be lenient providing they now offered their full cooperation in tracking down the missing Edward.

Not all of Harry's concerns were allayed by the discovery of the murderer's identity. The death of Phoebe Stanbury's father almost exactly a year ago was yet unresolved. Could Edward have been involved somehow? It seemed unlikely. Edward's murderous tendencies had so far leant towards the spectacular, slaughtering a young girl in front of fifty guests while dressed in the altogether. Faking a coaching accident did not seem to fit either his methods or his madness.

Harry straightened his bow tie and smoothed his hair in preparation for another fractious encounter with Sir Jasper Raycraft. He was not looking forward to pitting his wits once more against such a challenging mind, but the facts were on his side and this time he would not be rushed through his questioning by Sir Jasper's imperious haste to be done with it.

As the cab approached the massive doors of the house, they plunged into grim blackness. Even the moonlight was obscured by the cliff that hung over the house like a wave about to break. Despite the great number of mullioned windows that randomly littered the front of the building, only a few revealed the faint glow of occupation and no lamps were lit outside the house. Clearly no visitors were expected, or desired, tonight.

Harry instructed the driver to wait and approached the doors. He fumbled towards the bell pull and tugged hard. The thunderous clang reminded him of the ear-splitting noise he had been responsible for earlier at the asylum and the parallel caused Harry to smile. If one had to choose which of the two buildings would make a more suitable home for the insane, most people would have dismissed the neat white stucco of the Bethlem Royal Hospital and opted for the forbidding chaos of Ridgeside.

The same manservant Harry had met on his previous visit answered the door. Although he had been friendly enough on that occasion, tonight he looked at Harry with some suspicion.

'I apologise for the lateness of the hour, but I have some urgent matters to discuss with Sir Jasper.'

'I'm afraid Sir Jasper is not at home. Perhaps if you were to contact his office on Monday, they could schedule an *appointment*.' Each syllable of this last word was cleanly enunciated, implying that the term might be unfamiliar to Harry.

'In which case, I shall speak to his son, if I may. Alternatively, I am happy to await Sir Jasper's return.' Harry smiled, displaying a confidence he didn't quite feel.

The man stepped back and allowed Harry inside. He was shown to a long wooden bench that lined one wall of the hallway and asked to wait. The bench was as uncomfortable as it looked, blending seamlessly into the panelling that wrapped its way around the room. It was as if the whole house had been carved from one massive tree, its roots still alive and breathing in the ground below. When the man returned, he took Harry along a different route, through the back of the house and up a staircase that turned in on itself several times, forming a perfect square. The now familiar globe lights lit the way down a wide corridor, although the radiance they provided was miserly, Harry thought. If this was the future, it seemed a gloomy place.

The man paused and knocked on a door. Harry heard the occupant clear his throat several times, before calling out for him to enter. Harry walked into a small sitting room, a fire blazing in the grate. The room was cosy, but the heat immediately caught in Harry's lungs and he coughed.

'I am sorry, detective, but I feel the c-cold in the evenings. Let me open a w-w . . . ' Benjamin Raycraft opened one of the stone-set windows and didn't bother fighting himself to finish the word.

The servant retreated and Benjamin called Harry forward towards two chairs arranged by the fire. Harry took the one nearest the window and pulled it back as far from the fire as courtesy would allow.

'Your investigation has p-progressed, I assume?' Benjamin sat upright, his hands folded neatly in his lap. One foot tapped rhythmically up and down on the Persian rug and Harry had to admire the young man's attempt to appear at ease when he so clearly was not.

'Indeed it has. I know who killed Phoebe.'

Benjamin's eyes grew wide and he leant forward as his hands gripped the sides of the chair. 'You do? Why that's marvellous! And have you apprehended the felon? Has he offered any kind of explanation or motive?'

Harry smiled at Benjamin's enthusiastic reaction to his news, noting that he had spoken without a hint of his usual stammer. His eagerness appeared genuine, causing Harry to wonder exactly what Benjamin did and did not know about the existence of

Edward Raycraft. 'I'm afraid we have not yet captured the fellow, but we have discovered his identity. The man escaped from Bethlem Royal Hospital on the day of the attack.'

Again, Benjamin's reaction to the news seemed to hold no guile. 'Goodness! An escaped madman? Well, I suppose that makes sense. Surely one would have to be beyond reason to commit so cruel an act. Poor Phoebe.' The excitement of the news receded and Benjamin slumped back in his chair, his eyes cast towards the fire as if he thought it might shed some light on the secrets of the insane.

'Benjamin,' said Harry, recalling the young Raycraft from his trance. 'He spoke to you, did he not? That night? Others who were there, they remembered.'

Benjamin flushed, as if his pale skin was finally responding to the heat of the room. 'Yes. He did. But it made no sense, I . . . It made no sense.'

'What did he say, Benjamin?'

'That he promised to save me, that he did it f-for me.'

The look on his face was full of pain and incomprehension and Harry's heart went out to the young man. Again, thoughts of his own lost family came unbidden, but he pushed on. 'You had seen him before, hadn't you?'

Benjamin looked down, seemingly more confused than ever, and slowly shook his head. 'I honestly don't know. Maybe, if he had been clothed, or his face less c-covered in mud, maybe there was something. A f-flicker. A memory.'

'A memory?'

'When I was l-little. I remember someone, I think.'

'Go on.'

'Those w-words. I remember the words.' Benjamin looked upwards, as if he might find the past etched on the ceiling. 'There was a boy.'

'A boy?'

'Older than me. He promised to save me. I know not what from.'

'Who was the boy, Benjamin?'

Benjamin looked at Harry, his face an open book. 'I don't know.'

Harry nodded reassuringly but allowed the silence to continue, broken only by the crack of wood as it split apart in the fire.

Benjamin looked down at his hands. 'I am sorry I said n-nothing of this before. I didn't understand it. I still d-do not. Who is this man, detective?'

Harry removed his glasses from his pocket and cleaned the lenses with his handkerchief; there was no point yet in revealing Edward's identity to Benjamin. 'I believe you, Benjamin. If you knew this man once, it was a long time ago, but . . .' At this point, Harry withdrew his notebook and once again showed Benjamin the drawing Lydia Stanbury had made. 'I do believe you recognise this. Whatever it might be, this symbol was very important to the man who killed Phoebe. Tell me what you know of it, it may help us.'

Benjamin looked down at the drawing for some time, the tip of his tongue protruding slightly before he said simply, 'I know it, and so do you.' Harry must have looked stumped so Benjamin continued, his eyes glinting with a previously unseen humour, 'It is all around you.' He waved his arm limply about the room.

Harry stood up. The only thing he could see all around him was the oppressive oak panelling. He moved closer to the walls.

And there it was: the symbol, carved into the dado rail that lined the sitting room, the same symbol that Edward Raycraft had stabbed into canvas after canvas, and into his very own skin. Here, the symbol had become a motif, fading into the background with endless repetition. Circles within circles, everywhere.

'What is it, Benjamin?' asked Harry. 'Does it have a meaning?'

Benjamin shook his head. 'You would have to ask my f-f-father. Although I would be grateful if you didn't mention that it was I who p-pointed it out to you. Your skills of d-detection can take the credit.'

Harry chuckled. 'I will do as you ask, although my skills of detection did indeed fail to spot the obvious on this occasion.'

Benjamin allowed a small grin to escape. It slipped from his face almost as soon as it arrived, but its fleeting appearance was heartbreaking.

'My f-father thought it best not to mention the similarity. He thought it might d-distract from the investigation. It is only d-decoration after all. I am sorry.'

Harry sat back down in his chair. 'I understand. He is a daunting man, your father.'

Benjamin cast his eyes back towards the fire, clearly on less comfortable territory. 'He is the most brilliant man I have ever known.'

The words struck a discordant note, the words of an admirer, not a son. Benjamin Raycraft had probably grown up hearing those words spoken by his father's acquaintances and associates, to the point where they had become his own, an acceptable cover no doubt for his true sentiments: rooted deeper, and harder to voice.

Harry glanced at his watch. It was almost eleven. He believed that Benjamin had been completely open with him and decided to reciprocate. 'We have reason to believe, *good* reason, that Phoebe was known to her killer, that he knew enough of her to have formed a strong attachment at some point in the past. Is there anywhere she spent time, or visited perhaps, where an acquaintance might have inadvertently been made?'

Benjamin shook his head. 'I don't know. Maybe she visited the hospital? She was extraordinarily k-kind. I know she supported a local protection league. Swans, I think. Maybe there were other causes. I suppose we didn't know each other that well, n-not yet at least.' Benjamin's voice drifted off.

'It must have been difficult after her father died to come to know each other away from the constraints of family obligations.'

'Indeed,' said Benjamin gratefully. 'His death was quite a b-blow.'

'Tell me, was Phoebe's father happy about your engagement?'

Benjamin frowned, evidently it was not something to which he had given much consideration before now. 'I am not sure. He was a g-gruff man. My father respected him hugely. I had hoped that Mr Stanbury would view the match more f-favourably than perhaps he did. Maybe he was nervous, m-marrying into such a . . . ' Benjamin's struggle for the right word seemed unconnected to his stammer, 'an *illustrious* household.'

It was as Harry had feared. Phoebe Stanbury's father had probably expressed reservations about his daughter's marriage to Benjamin. Had those reservations seen him take a fatal tumble from his carriage that night?

It was time to go. Harry was glad now not to have encountered Sir Jasper himself this evening. The meeting with Benjamin had given him plenty more to chew on before he challenged the man at the centre of this mystery.

Harry stood up. 'Tell me, Benjamin, I am curious. The strikers at your gates. They talk of vicious things, dangerous activities, in the basement of the factory in particular.'

Benjamin raised his eyebrows. 'They do?'

'You have spoken with them?'

Benjamin shook his head. 'My father requested that I do not.' He looked down, a man who obeyed his father without question.

Harry bade farewell and once again offered to show himself out, wishing to indulge his desire to snoop before he left for the city. Instead of retracing his steps towards the staircase, he continued along the corridor in the opposite direction. As he reached the front of the building, he looked out of the window to see his driver still waiting patiently below.

The corridor forked in either direction and Harry opted to turn right. The motif that Benjamin had earlier pointed out continued along the full length of the dado rail; it was even carved into the wood panels below each window he passed. How had he missed it?

A door opened up ahead and Harry drew as close to the wall as he could, grateful for the obscure softness of the electric light. Someone emerged and turned away from him towards the opposite end of the passage. His heart thumping, Harry stepped forward with caution as he watched the retreating form of the nurse he had seen with Lady Raycraft the day before.

Lady Raycraft: what secrets might that decayed mind yet hold? The temptation to grab a few minutes alone with her was strong, but so was the risk of discovery. Sir Jasper was surely a man to be feared and Harry had told no one he was coming here. Creeping through the shadows of this remote castle, that now seemed a foolish decision.

Heavy footsteps sounded on a nearby staircase and the choice was made for him. He dashed forward to the doorway the nurse had emerged from and turned the handle.

A strong scent of lavender greeted him as he entered. It was a ladies' dressing room, and Lady Raycraft, wearing a nightdress of white lace, was seated at a curved dressing table gazing happily at her own reflection. Whatever she was seeing in her mind, Harry doubted it was the terrible visage that he could see captured in the mirror. Her eyes locked on to his. Harry made to speak, to reassure her that he had once again simply lost his way, but was taken aback by the unexpected smile that had spread across her face.

She turned towards him, her hands flirting with the cotton ties of her gown. 'This is most naughty of you, sir.' She cast her chin downwards, the light catching the red sores on top of her head, her voice a mere whisper. 'This is my chamber!'

'Forgive my intrusion, Lady Raycraft, but I was keen to speak with you again.'

She rose and came towards him, the smile still in place. 'Please, call me Anna.'

Harry fought the urge to retreat at her approach. 'Very well, Anna, it is a pleasure to make your acquaintance again.'

Anna Raycraft held her hand out towards him. Swallowing down the revulsion he felt, Harry raised her hand to his mouth and lightly kissed the grey flesh of her fingertips.

Her laugh was still young and unblemished. 'It is a terrible thing to admit, but I am afraid that I have forgotten your name!'

'My friends call me Harry.'

'Then I shall call you Harry also. We are friends, are we not?'

'I would be flattered to think so, Anna.'

'But you really shouldn't be here, you know.'

'Forgive me, but I wanted to ask you about Edward. Do you know where I might find him?'

Her eyes tried to hold his gaze, but he saw them flicker and dart. 'Edward doesn't live here any more. I think you should leave.' Her body sagged as she turned away from him.

'He used to live here, though?'

She turned back sharply. 'Of course he used to live here! After Sybil died, we were his only family. What do you think I would do, throw my nephew out on the street to starve? I am a better woman than someone has had you believe, Mr . . . ?'

'Treadway, Detective Treadway.'

She softened once more. 'Is Edward in trouble?'

'Yes. I'm afraid that he is.'

Her eyes closed and she shook her head with leaden sorrow.

Harry stirred himself to continue, for the nurse might return at any moment and raise the alarm. 'Forgive me, Lady Raycraft, I am not as familiar as I should be with your family history. Sybil was Edward's mother, I take it?'

'Yes. It was kept very quiet, of course. My husband's sister had the child several years before I married Jasper. He allowed them to

live with us, despite the shame. He was fond of Edward until . . . '
Her voice petered out into memory.

Harry's mind quickly absorbed all she had revealed. Edward
Raycraft was the illegitimate son of Sir Jasper's sister. At last,
Harry had made the connection.

'Lady Raycraft, why did Edward leave this house?'

She slumped down into her seat at the dressing table, her back
to the mirror, and rubbed her hands together. 'Sybil killed herself, God rest her soul. She was always troubled, I think. Edward
would have been maybe five. My own son – at least, the one
who lived – had just been born. I suspect that those two events
coming so close together were very hard on the boy. He became
difficult. Not towards Benjamin – he loved my son – but towards
my husband. One Christmas day, a few years after Sybil died, he
set upon Jasper in a frenzy, calling him the devil. The servants
had to pull him away, he was such a strong boy. It was awful.' A
solitary, fat tear rolled down her pitted cheek and she brushed it
away elegantly. 'I never saw him again.'

Harry recalled that Lady Raycraft had herself referred to her
husband as the devil when she had raged to her nurse the day
before. What would make an eight-year-old child believe the
same of his uncle?

'Would you like to see a picture? Jasper had most of them
removed, but I kept one, a small portrait. I was fond of them
both, you see.'

Harry tried to keep his eagerness contained. 'That would be
most helpful.'

Lady Raycraft shuffled towards the panelled wall at the back
of the room. No pictures hung there, and Harry wondered if the
conversation had been too much and her mind had begun once
more to recede underground, but the wall in fact masked a cupboard, which she opened and began to rummage through.

'Here it is! Let us take it back to the light.'

Lady Raycraft had retrieved a canvas held in a simple silver frame, now tarnished with age. She rubbed the sleeve of her nightdress across the picture, coughing lightly as the dust came away, before propping it up against the dressing table mirror.

She gripped the sides of her gown, and swayed gently from side to side, dancing to the music of another time. 'She was very beautiful then.' She lifted one hand to her grizzled cheek. 'So was I.'

Harry barely heard her words above his own resounding heartbeat. Before him was a study of a little blond boy, half standing and half climbing about his mother's knee. It was his first sight of the murderer he had spent days pursuing, but Harry barely glanced at his likeness.

Sybil Raycraft had indeed been very beautiful.

She was also the exact double of Phoebe Stanbury, the girl her own son had slaughtered in cold blood.

## CHAPTER TWENTY-EIGHT

William rushed to the window to see the vicomtesse being helped inside an opulent carriage as four black thoroughbreds stamped and snorted with impatience.

'We have to follow her!'

Savannah stood up, rubbing the stiffness from her back. 'Maybe.'

He turned back towards her. Her presence at Pincott's had been motivated by money rather than any driving need to help him find his aunt.

'Please, Savannah, this woman, I need to know who she is!'

She closed her eyes for a moment, before nodding in his direction, a curt, reluctant gesture. 'Come with me.'

They retraced their steps out of the compound. Savannah reckoned that there were few streets in Whitechapel wide enough to take such a carriage. If they were quick, they could get back over the rooftops and circle round through the smaller lanes, meeting up with the carriage once more on the main thoroughfare towards Liverpool Street.

They kept to the shadows, knowing now that their presence in Whitechapel had not gone undetected. Their progress was slow and William's anxiety rose. What if he were to lose this mysterious lady, the only connection to his aunt? But as they reached the main road, they saw the black and gold carriage in the distance, travelling west. William stepped into the street and stopped the first hansom that came along, shouting to the driver as Savannah squashed in beside him, 'Follow that carriage but keep your distance!'

Just as Savannah had promised, the road itself was chaos and the cab easily managed to catch up without breaking into more than a trot. The two of them were silent for a while and avoided each other's glances, still reliving that overheard conversation in their heads.

It was Savannah who spoke first, although her voice was soft, as if intended for herself alone. 'We have to help those women.'

William shuddered to recall their pale, haunted faces and once again found it impossible to believe that anyone would conspire so deliberately to cause their ruination. 'I'm sure we can find a way to alert the authorities to their plight.'

Savannah snorted. 'The authorities will not care, William, not for unmarried women in their state!'

William bristled. 'That may be true in your country but I can assure you it is not the case here. There are organisations, charities—'

Savannah cut him off. 'Marvellous! Charities, you say? Well, that's just dandy.'

Not for the first time, William found her hard to fathom. He changed the subject. 'Every time we try to solve one mystery, another emerges. I have never met this vicomtesse in my life and yet . . . ' *She hunts me, she calls me mutt.* The words hung in the air, heard but unsaid.

'I've seen her there before,' said Savannah. 'The very last time I was there. Makes sense, though. Pincott had me watching Habborlain for a client, not his own purpose. I wonder who she is.'

William occasionally bought the *Illustrated London News* to peruse on the train, but the gossip about famous aristocrats and their exploits usually washed over him. The vicomtesse was young and beautiful, but there had been such callousness in her dialogue with Pincott. He found himself repeating out loud, 'The dead have no names.'

The cab began to pick up speed and bumped steadily from side to side. William could see the huge walls of St Paul's Cathedral loom beside them. 'At least we have left Whitechapel behind.'

'Does this name Raycraft mean anything to you? The woman, Rebecca, accused him of rape.'

William blanched at the word. 'He is a well-known scientist and manufacturer, some say he is the richest man in the country, but I absolutely cannot believe that a man of his standing would be a part of such an undertaking. Although . . .'

'Although?'

'The list of names in the box. I only glanced at it quickly, saw Habborlain's name and a few others.'

'And?'

'Sir Jasper Raycraft was on that list.'

'What did Bridge say to you?'

'To keep it safe. That the list could protect me.'

'Whatever it is a list of, maybe some do not want it known they are on it.'

'We have to find the box. Maybe this vicomtesse has it in her possession?'

Savannah shrugged. 'So we have a beautiful young aristocrat running a baby farm in Whitechapel with a famous scientist. On top of all that, she's after you, my friend.'

William flinched at Savannah's summary. 'Must you put it so baldly?'

Savannah sat forward. 'They are going to kill those women once they have given birth. It is only the children they wish to see thrive.'

'To what purpose?'

Savannah had no answer and William closed his eyes. 'She

called me a mutt.' The word tasted foul in his mouth. 'But what can this woman know of me? She knew Habborlain, that much is clear, and he was a client of ours, but what does she want with me?'

'Maybe she thinks that you know something, something valuable? Maybe she thinks you read this list, copied it maybe? Or could it be something Habborlain might have said to you, perhaps?'

William searched his brain and once more felt weighed down by the leaden wish that he had never set eyes on Ambrose Habborlain. If only he could turn the clock back, how different things might have been. The knowledge tormented him.

They had been travelling for at least twenty minutes and now found themselves riding along the grand embankment. Majestic buildings rose up to their right and, to their left, ship lights twinkled upon the river. William shifted in his seat. What exactly were they going to do when they caught up with this woman?

As if reading his mind, Savannah spoke. 'We need to isolate her, see if she has this box and find out what we can about where they are keeping your aunt.'

William looked at her, his eyes round with hope. 'Do you think she will tell us?'

'I can be very persuasive.'

William sighed at the thought of her methods, but he couldn't afford to be coy now. They had a lead at last and they had to follow it to its conclusion, whatever that might entail.

The cab turned suddenly to the right, the noise of the horse's hooves rising considerably as they clip-clopped across cobblestones. They had entered some kind of mews so must be close to the woman's destination. Savannah called up to the driver to stop, lest their target hear their approach. As they slipped out of the hansom, they could see her carriage about a hundred yards ahead, turning awkwardly into a stone archway, lit by two large gas lamps either side. William and Savannah followed, keeping to the shadows of the other buildings in the dimly lit street. As they neared the archway, two huge iron doors slammed shut and they heard the sound of bolts being drawn. The carriage had disappeared inside.

'We are somewhere between the river and Whitehall,' William whispered. 'These are mostly government buildings, I would wager.'

'Not this one.'

'You know it?' William asked.

'Sure do. We followed Habborlain here, many times. This is the rear entrance. The front is, well, it's at the front, on the next street. It's a club of some kind.'

'Do you know its name?'

'Yep, and it's pretty goddamned appropriate after what we've seen tonight. It's called the *Olympian Breeding Association*. We shortened it to the OBA in our reports.'

They had reached the archway and the thick iron gates. The building was low, maybe two storeys high, and on this side at least there were no windows, just an expanse of solid brick that surrounded the only opening. Savannah pushed lightly on the gates. They gave slightly before coming into contact with the bolts behind. The sound brought an onslaught of howling and gnashing on the other side. William pulled back as the dogs threw themselves at the heavy iron, which nonetheless shuddered at the ferocity of the attack. Savannah headed quickly towards the corner of the building and William followed.

As they edged around towards the front, the plain bricks gave way to the terracotta sandstone of the building's façade. There were windows here, elegant and simple, dating the building to the last century. This street was equally deserted, but they were careful to duck as they passed beneath the windows. Strips of light could be seen between the cracks in the shutters, meaning that some of the ground-floor rooms were occupied despite the lateness of the hour. They came to the entrance where worn stone steps rose up to a wide panelled door. Tacked to the pillar on one side of the stairs was a plain brass plate spelling out the building's name, *The Olympian Breeding Association.*

But it was not the name that had captured William's attention, for beneath it was a symbol.

Circles within a circle.

'That symbol! It was carved into the lid of the casket. Maybe Bridge was connected to this place too, not just Habborlain.'

William clapped a hand over his mouth to mask his excitement before continuing in a hoarse whisper, 'And I have the answer!'

'You've lost me.'

'Why didn't I think of it before? Cosmati! The location in Habborlain's note. Westminster Abbey! I told him I had been there many times!' Savannah seemed confused so he continued, 'The Cosmati Pavement is in the abbey. It's a mural that encompasses this image many times over. This symbol is the Seed of Life.'

'The seed of what?'

'*The Seed of Life.* Reverend Harker called it the most ancient of religious symbols, signifying the seven days of creation. Seven circles within an eighth, forming a flower.'

At last he had known something of value to help his cause. Briefly he thought of the bookseller and felt a moment of welcome superiority. Cosmati. The day before the new moon. Vespers. At least one part of the puzzle was coming together.

As his excitement began to abate, his mind returned again to the vast number of things he still didn't understand. What did these people want with him? And how had Mr Bridge – humble, benign Mr Bridge – been linked to it all?

Savannah was looking up and around the building.

'Are you assessing potential entry points? You have a plan?'

'Yep,' she whispered, 'and I'm thinking you might just ring the bell.'

He thought she was pulling his leg but she continued, 'I don't like the idea of strong-arming our way in, not until we know who is on the other side.'

He wanted to laugh, thinking of Habborlain's words. *The lamb who went to the slaughter willingly.* 'But they would know me!'

'Would they?' she said. 'How many people know what you look like? I doubt the vicomtesse does. Dub and his men are in Whitechapel. Bridge is dead – sorry – and Habborlain is missing. Your most obvious characteristic is bandaged up. You could be anyone.'

*I could be anyone.* Her words held a strange delight, but the thought of ringing the bell filled him with fear. 'What would I say?'

'I'll stand to the side, in the dark. If only a servant answers then signal me and I'll take them.'

Her gun appeared once more and he baulked at her matter-of-fact tone. 'And if someone else answers? A soldier, or a villain perhaps?'

'Then you apologise, say you have the wrong house, and we leave.'

It sounded so simple, but his heart was in his mouth.

'You've come this far, William.'

And so I have, he thought. He dug his hand into his pocket and pulled out a banknote, pressing it into her hand. 'In case something happens, this is for you.'

She bit her lip. What did he see in her face? Something like shame.

'You deserve it.'

She nodded briskly, refusing to meet his eyes. 'Do it, then.'

They crept up the steps to the door and Savannah tucked herself into the shadows. Without giving himself time to think, he tugged on the bell cord and heard the faint tinkle from within. William reminded himself to breathe as he waited, his legs wobbling so much he wondered if he might topple to the ground at any moment. He thought he heard something over the thrumming in his ears. Heavy bolts sliding back somewhere nearby. Savannah grabbed his arm and, as he turned, he heard something else: dogs. The slathering beasts had been released!

Savannah's shout was already redundant before it had left her lips.

'Run!'

## CHAPTER TWENTY-NINE

'W as that entirely necessary?'

Adeline heard the admonishing tone in Otto's voice but did her best to hide her resentment behind a gracious smile. 'It is late, brother, I doubt it was a delivery boy who had simply mistaken the front door for the tradesman's entrance.'

'Strangers are not necessarily enemies, my dear.'

'Then more fool them for knocking on the wrong door.'

'You take too many risks. It is cavalier of you.'

Adeline ignored the impulse to roll her eyes to heaven like a child. Her brother had been in a cantankerous mood since the meeting had broken up an hour ago. She called out, 'Lampley! More brandy if you please!'

'I think you've had enough.' Otto leant back in his chair.

Lampley stuttered through the door with another bottle of cognac held aloft on a silver tray. She wished he would use both hands rather than insist on keeping one of them behind his back in the traditional fashion. He picked his way unsteadily towards the side table by the chesterfield. She knew better than to leap to her feet to help him. Although not connected to the families, he was a proud man who had served the association faithfully for many years. In fact, her last conversation with Bridge had been to discuss Lampley's retirement. In this, they had both been as weak and sentimental as each other and had failed to settle on a course of action. Once again she felt the involuntary sting of tears as she experienced afresh Bridge and Habborlain's betrayal.

When Lampley had left the room, Otto spoke. 'This man of yours. Pincott. Do you trust him?'

It was not something she had previously thought consciously about. 'I pay him, and he came highly recommended, you will recall.'

'He is a disagreeable fellow in my opinion and I mistrust a man who is motivated solely by money.'

Adeline smiled. 'Then you must trust very little, brother.'

'Just be careful. The man knows much of our affairs and he has bungled the William Lamb situation.'

Adeline's gut twisted at the sound of that hateful name. How could Otto bear it? Ignoring the sensation, she smiled brightly. 'But at least the casket has been returned to its rightful place. We should never have fallen for Bridge's ruse that he wished to work on his own translation; it was obviously his intention all along to give it to the cripple. And that list he had made! If it had fallen into the wrong hands—'

Her brother interrupted as if she had not spoken. 'At some point, we must set Pincott adrift. He is unlikely to keep our secrets without plenty of coin.'

Adeline fired back, 'Plenty of coin is exactly what we have!'

'I do not like debts, even if I have the means to pay.'

She waved her hand dismissively. 'Pincott is a king among thieves, no more. Your Captain Ziegler can crush him like a sewer rat in his iron fist when the time comes.'

'Ziegler has better things to do than tidy up your mess, Adeline.'

'I'm sure he does.' Adeline drank deeply from her glass, averting her eyes from Otto's reptilian glance.

Lampley returned and began to clear away the glasses. She understood the message, for he was probably weary and wished to retire. Adeline stood up. 'Come, brother, we should return to the hotel.'

There was a knock on the door and Captain Ziegler entered the room without waiting for an answer. Otto rose to greet him, a look upon his face which he tried and failed to conceal, a look that Adeline had never seen before but which she recognised deep in her soul. The thought made the bile rise in her stomach.

The men spoke briefly in German and left the room. As they departed, Adeline paced towards the window, although with the shutters closed there was nothing to see. Pointless as it was, she began to untie the drapes from either side of the frame and draw them across, her hands grappling clumsily with the knots.

She heard Lampley's voice behind her. 'You do not like this new man Ziegler, madame?'

Her hands continued their frenzied work. 'No, Lampley, I do not. The man is a distraction, an abomination. Oh, I know there have been others, I do not consider myself a prude. My brother would not be the first general with this predilection. They say even Alexander suffered with such a sickness. I do not like it, but if it is hidden, and stems only from the desperation of a long cold night in the field without female company, then one can turn a blind eye. Perhaps.'

'Madame . . .' Lampley's tone held a note of caution.

'But this! This *love*!' She spat the word, a drop of saliva landing on her busy hands. 'It prevents him from doing his duty. He promised me a child!'

With a sharp tug she closed the final curtain. She turned on her heel to continue her tirade, but froze as she came face to face with her brother, his eyes dull with cold hatred. She opened her mouth to speak without any idea of what she might say, but it didn't matter. Otto whipped the back of his hand sharply across her face, sending her spinning to the floor.

She lay where she had fallen, her breath pushing out against her corset. Touching her hand to her face, she checked for damage, her fingers quick and gentle. No blood, that was good, not like last time, and any bruising could be camouflaged. She so wanted to look her finest at the ball. Lampley bent over her, his shaking hands encircling her waist. He said nothing as he helped her to the sofa. He never did.

Otto stood facing the fireplace, as if to warm himself despite the mugginess of the evening.

Adeline circled her lower jaw. Nothing clicked or seemed broken which meant she could trust herself to speak once more. 'We should go.'

He nodded, his back still turned. 'I have been thinking. Maybe we should continue with just the five of us, ring the changes, so to speak.'

Adeline was off the sofa immediately, her voice high and loud. 'Otto! Surely not! What are we without our traditions?'

'Our ambition may have changed little but the battleground has shifted. We have no use for art and history any more, they are no longer weapons.'

'But we must respect our heritage, our great purpose! It is surely sacrilege to think otherwise. We have always been seven, we must be so again, whatever we thought of Habborlain and Bridge.'

Otto faced Adeline head on. 'And what is our great purpose, is it one on which we all agree?'

Adeline spoke before she could catch herself. 'Perfection. That has always been our goal, Otto. It is the goal we were given.'

She regretted the remark as soon as she made it. She didn't want to provoke him further, but to her surprise, he simply nodded in her direction.

'And how, my dear, will we recognise this perfection when it arrives? Maybe, just maybe, it is already here.' Otto Von Rabenmarck took a slow sip of cognac, his eyes shining in the flickering gaslight.

## CHAPTER THIRTY

*M*ildred wondered what time it was. If the dawn had come yet. Another voice within her wondered if it mattered, but she willed it silent. She would not give in to despair, no matter how it dragged at her, hounding her to be acknowledged.

It was her second night in this place. An airless room, without a window. Her candle had long since burned out and she was grateful for that at least: then her mind could float free from her chains, from the body she was trying so hard not to despise.

They would come for her again, she knew. Would the second time be easier? What of the third? She so much wanted to think of all the things her father would say, about adversity, about courage, about the long night before the dawn. But when she conjured him, the tears came. Would she ever be able to think of him again without them? His heart would crack in a million pieces if he knew what had been done to her, and the shame of it made her growl through gritted teeth even as she wiped the tears away.

She heard voices outside the room. The panic flapped its wings once more and she swallowed it down. She would endure. She was a Whitfield.

The door slammed open and she screwed her eyes against the light. The dawn was indeed breaking. A man sat down on the bed, one face in shadow as the other glared at her from his waxen chest.

'You know of childbirth?'

What was he asking? Her voice caught in her throat, but she knew she had to talk. Talk about anything. Make herself less of an animal to him.

'I know many things. I was – *am* – a governess. I—'

'There is other woman here. She is ripe. I think is time, but we cannot raise the midwife.'

He needed her help. That was good, although she knew little of what might be required. 'Yes! Of course! I will help if I can.'

As if she'd been asked to organise the raffle at the local fete.

He unchained her and handed over her dress, turning his back. A pointless gesture, for he had seen her naked, howling in her disgrace. Once dressed, he led her into the corridor beyond. They climbed some stairs, went outside briefly on a rope walkway where she could see the yard she had arrived in only days earlier. She tried to remember as much as she could of what she saw, at the same time as talking about anything she could think of. He let her talk but didn't answer, his grip firm but not unnecessarily rough.

They finally arrived in another corridor. He took a set of keys from his coat, opened a door, and pushed her forward.

'Do your best.'

She stumbled in to the room and the door slammed behind her.

An impossibly thin woman with a huge belly lay on a bed, shivering, her legs tangled in sodden bed sheets. A dark-haired woman was stroking her brow, and she looked up at the new arrival with suspicion.

'You are the midwife?'

'No. I am . . .' Mildred looked down at the woman's belly, also heavy with child. 'I think I am one of you.'

What on God's earth was this?

The woman on the bed groaned, her eyes vacant, her skin frighteningly pale. Mildred knew precious little of childbirth, but she knew the look of death when it came to call.

She looked back at the dark-haired woman. 'We have to get her out of here. Let us share what we know, see if there is a way. We are three now.'

The woman laughed. 'There is no hope of that. You are as damned as the rest of us.'

Somehow, in all that had befallen her, this woman's bitterness was the hardest thing to take. The words shot through her like smelling salts and Mildred felt her back straightening, her head held high.

'The only person who has permission to damn me is God.'

## CHAPTER THIRTY-ONE

'So, Harry, what scurrilous gossip can I supply you with today, my friend?'

It was early on Sunday morning as Harry Treadway sipped his tea in Finian Worthing's cottage in Pimlico. 'Sir Jasper Raycraft. He had a sister?'

'Ah, yes. I would have mentioned it the other evening but your interest had moved on to more murderous matters, I seem to recall.'

'Indeed. So what do you know of her?'

'Sybil Raycraft. A great beauty, they said, although I think she only managed a single season before she *fell ill*.' Finian's heavy emphasis was accompanied by a tap of his nose.

'Was there any conjecture as to who the father may have been?'

'Plenty, although none of it was conclusive as I recall.'

'Any interesting names?'

Finian thought for a long moment, then shook his head. 'I don't believe so. The brother covered things up pretty quickly. She died several years later. Rumour had it that she hung herself from the rafters in their house in Berkeley Square. Jasper Raycraft was building Ridgeside at the time and the family moved there almost immediately afterwards. It took an age for the London house to sell, the common belief being that it was haunted.'

'And the child?'

'Went with them, maybe, or was farmed out somewhere. The rich don't like to be reminded that their shit stinks as much as ours. Who knows? Benjamin is the only Raycraft of his generation that we know about.'

So Anna Raycraft had spoken the truth. Harry was not surprised. The wilful telling of lies was a skill that belonged only to the sane.

He took his leave of Finian, thanking him for both the information and the tea. He had been sorely tempted to share all he had discovered so far with his friend, but he resisted the lure of spilling all. He was able to escape with only a promise that he would bring Finian up to date before any other newspaper discovered the truth.

It was another beautiful day, the sky nakedly blue without a cloud in sight, but it was still early, and the temperature pleasantly cool. Harry felt in need of a walk. He had spent the previous night sleepless in his bed, unable to stop his mind from turning over. The priority now was to see Lydia Stanbury once more. It was most definitely too early to visit a grieving mother, not yet nine o'clock, but if he went on foot it would take him at least a few hours. It would be a pleasant walk along the river, and not just that: the journey would take him past St Catherine's in Fulham at just the right time.

It had been a few months since he had last hidden under the huge oak tree on the west side of the graveyard, waiting to catch sight of his grandchildren as they skipped out of church, giddy that the service was over and they were no longer compelled to be silent or still. It would have been March, and the ground was hard with frost. Catherine had been in her mother's arms as they emerged into the weak sunshine, wrapped tightly in her winter garments. She had screamed to be let down and Harry had laughed to himself as she toddled away, listing from side to side like a tiny rowing boat on the waves. David, on the other hand, had his hands in his pockets and was scuffing his shoes along the gravel path, as if there were leaves to be kicked up into the wind. His head had been down – a young boy still smarting from a dressing-down of some kind. His father had been the same, the clouds lingering long after the storm had passed. They lingered still . . .

Harry continued along the river. The sun shivered across the water, the Thames empty of its usual traffic, for non-essential boats had been cleared in advance for the lunchtime arrival of Cornelius Tinbergen. His sumptuous yacht was due to dock at the Tower of London at one o'clock. Harry had been sorely tempted to track down Silas Matlock to update him on the latest developments in his investigation, but the colonel's mind would surely be on more pressing matters of national security now that the big day had finally arrived.

As he strode down the embankment towards Fulham, Harry turned his mind back to the investigation. He could conjure no rational explanation for the similarity between Sybil Raycraft and Phoebe Stanbury, although at least it explained the portrait that he had seen in Edward's basement. The canvas had obviously been painted in loving remembrance of the mother who had died so tragically when he was so young. What must he then have thought when he saw Phoebe Stanbury's image staring out at him from the pages of the *Illustrated London News*, alongside the announcement of her engagement to his cousin, Benjamin? It had sent him into a murderous rage, against Phoebe herself, and he had left that bloodied room with a chilling explanation. *I did this for you*, he had said to his young cousin, a boy he had not seen for over twenty years.

Lady Raycraft had made no reference to the similarity and Harry assumed this was because she had never met Phoebe. It seemed abundantly clear that Anna Raycraft was kept locked away as much as possible and would not have played any role in the formalities of her son's engagement. But Jasper Raycraft *had* met Phoebe Stanbury. He would have seen the stark resemblance to his own dead sister.

There was only one conclusion, of course. Phoebe Stanbury must have been a Raycraft: the similarity was too close to be pure coincidence. What secret was Lydia Stanbury hiding, and why had Sir Jasper been so comfortable to see Benjamin wed a woman who obviously shared a close familial link?

Harry raised his eyes up from the pavement, only to be met by the look of intense surprise on his own son's face. He had been so lost in his own thoughts he had come upon St Catherine's church unaware, and with no time to hide himself away. Now, he stood face to face with the son who had not spoken to him for several years.

'Father, this is a surprise.' An unwelcome one, evidently.

'Hello, Philip, I happened to be in the area. I'm in the middle of an investigation, you see.' The excuse sounded weak even to Harry's ears.

'Well, don't let us keep you.'

The rest of the family emerged from the church.

'Grandfather!' David came running towards him, tripping over his own feet as he threw himself at Harry and wrapped his spindly arms tightly around his grandfather's waist.

Harry bent to kiss his grandson lightly on the head, refusing to meet Philip's discouraging stare. He wanted to close his eyes, to give all of himself into this sweetest of hugs. The lump in his throat was as big as an egg and it refused to be swallowed away.

'Hello, Harry.' His daughter-in-law's voice was as soft and round as she was.

'Hello, Felicity, I am sorry to disturb you so unexpectedly. I had business in the area, you see.'

'It is a pleasure to see you, Harry.'

Philip had now turned his wrathful gaze towards his own wife, but, like Harry, she refused to return it. Instead, she looked down at her daughter who was hiding her face in her mother's skirts. 'Catherine, darling, say hello to your grandfather. You remember him, don't you?'

The little girl looked up at Harry briefly, but her eyes darted away again. Harry didn't mind, she was so young after all. It was enough just to have seen the blue of her eyes, so like his wife's before the light had gone.

David pulled away from him and looked up, the apples of his cheeks flushed. 'Will you come and see us again?'

The words he wanted to say caught in Harry's throat. He turned towards his own son, meeting Philip's implacable stare, his anger towards Harry over his mother's premature death still seeping outwards like a wound that refused to clot. The unfairness of Philip's position struck anew. Harry could not have known how the stress of the corruption scandal would eventually take such a toll on his sensitive, loving wife. How had they managed to breed such a lack of forgiveness, such austerity of sympathy and affection? Philip was doing well: a senior manager in a shipping office, although not yet thirty. Felicity was a perfect wife, and the two children were enough to make any other man's heart sing. Yes, Philip had loved his mother dearly and had keenly felt her loss. *But so did I*, thought Harry, *so did I*.

Philip turned away and clapped his hands together in a call to action. 'Come on. David, hold my hand while we cross the road.'

David did as he was asked, oblivious to the emotional weight of the encounter. He shouted a happy goodbye over his shoulder.

'Goodbye!' Harry shouted back, before looking down at his granddaughter. 'And goodbye to you, Miss Catherine.'

'Come along, Felicity, we mustn't dawdle!'

'Coming!' Felicity bent down and picked up her daughter, her voice dropping to a whisper as she hid her mouth from her husband's view. 'Be at home on Tuesday afternoon, Harry – I shall come by and see you. Alone.'

His heart surged. 'Thank you.'

He watched them stroll into the distance, kept watching long after they had turned the corner into another street, hope of a reconciliation rising up within him, loosening its chains.

At the Stanbury residence, Harry was shown out to the garden and passed through the orangery once more. The space had finally been cleared of the debris left behind by the fateful engagement celebration. Chairs and tables were neatly stacked against the wall, presumably awaiting collection by the caterers. Only the unmistakable darkening of a patch of stone gave any hint of the atrocity that had occurred here three days ago.

In the garden, Lydia Stanbury was pruning a rose bush. Dressed in black, she snipped away with enthusiasm, although to Harry's eyes the bush already looked well manicured.

'I hope you don't mind if I carry on, Detective Treadway, there is much to do in the garden at this time.'

'Not at all, madam, it is good to be active, I believe.'

'You have information for me?'

Harry had spent more time pondering the questions he was planning to ask rather than pre-empting those she might ask of him. He chose his words carefully. 'We believe we know the identity of the man, but we do not have him in custody as yet. I cannot say too much more at this stage, but we have made good progress.'

She nodded kindly at him and pushed no further. She was not the sort to fool herself that the capture of Phoebe's assassin would bring her daughter back or provide any meaningful relief to the pain she felt. Harry's silence prompted her to look up. 'So how can I help you today, detective?'

Looking into her intelligent eyes, Harry realised there was little point in attempting to dress up his questions. She would see through him immediately.

'Phoebe was an only child, was she not?'

She returned her attention to the roses. 'Yes, but you know that already.'

'Indeed. I was wondering who she resembled the most, yourself or your husband?'

Lydia Stanbury dropped her hands to her sides and looked at him once more. 'You will need to explain to me the relevance of that question before I answer it.'

Harry maintained the eye contact as his mind whirred. It could be dangerous to share too much speculation at this stage; he had no idea what this woman did or didn't know. It was time to use the force of his authority, something he only ever did as a last resort. 'I'm afraid I can't tell you, madam, you will have to trust me that it is relevant to our investigation. I can say no more.'

Lydia Stanbury took this in her stride and answered his question. 'Then I will tell you that she took after neither of us. Phoebe was adopted. We . . . I couldn't have children.' The same challenge appeared in her eyes that he had seen on his last visit: *this is the life I have been given and I will stand it.*

Adoption. Of course. He had not thought of it. 'And can you recall where Phoebe came from? Which hospital?'

Lydia Stanbury had given up all pretence of pruning and her face puckered into a frown. 'Why is this relevant? You think Phoebe's background might have something to do with her murder? That there is a connection?'

'I can't tell you why but yes, I do.'

She accepted his answer. 'My husband arranged things. We hadn't intended to adopt, had not even considered it for we were still young enough to hope. One day he returned from work and spoke of it as a possibility. Sir Jasper was involved in some kind of refuge, something like that, and they were looking for good homes for unwanted children. Suddenly it seemed like the right thing for us to do. Sir Jasper was pleased, I think, and within weeks my husband came home with a baby in his arms.' Her voice caught and she looked down, her eyes blinking at the roses. 'I didn't ask too many questions. It was selfish of me, I know, so if you wish to know more, you will need to speak with Sir Jasper.'

Wouldn't he just.

Harry could see that Lydia Stanbury was beginning to make connections. There was no point trying to avert the scent so he continued, 'Tell me more about her engagement to Benjamin. They met at the Raycraft staff party at Ridgeside. You were there, I take it?'

'My husband and I went every year, but it was the first year that Phoebe had been invited. We almost didn't go – my husband had come down with a cold and was unwell – but Sir Jasper made it clear that as a senior manager in the business his absence would be noted, so we went.'

'And Phoebe and Benjamin became very taken with each other?'

Her frown returned. 'Not exactly. Sir Jasper introduced them, then asked Benjamin to accompany him as he showed Phoebe the grounds. So they spent quite a bit of time together that day. A week or so later, Benjamin asked if he could call for tea and so the courtship began.'

Jasper Raycraft's behaviour was sounding more and more inexplicable. Not only had he been tolerant of his son's interest in a girl with hidden Raycraft connections, he had gone out of his way to make the match himself.

'Was Lady Raycraft present that day?'

'No. I'm afraid we have never met her; I understand she is very unwell. My husband said she was away in a sanatorium in Switzerland on the day of the party.'

'And your husband disapproved of the match?'

Lydia Stanbury crossed her arms, her hands rubbing at the fabric of her dress as if she were chilly despite the summer heat and the weight of her mourning clothes. 'He was uncomfortable with Phoebe marrying into aristocracy.' Her sharp eyes sought out Harry's. 'Or so I thought.'

Harry did not dare mention his suspicions about her husband's death, although he supposed she might develop her own once he was gone. Without glancing at his watch, he knew it was time for him to leave if he was to make it to the Tinbergen gala in time. As a distant relation of the Vice President of the United States, Jasper Raycraft was to be a guest of honour at the celebration. Harry felt there was a good chance that Edward may show his face among the crowds and try to finish his murderous campaign. It might be the best opportunity they would have to apprehend Phoebe's assassin. Harry had brought his own revolver with him in case of trouble.

'I must leave now, unfortunately. I shall visit again soon, hopefully with more positive news. Thank you for your help; I know this must be very difficult for you.' Empty words, but he said them anyway. 'Good day, madam.'

Lydia Stanbury nodded vaguely, her mind clearly still lost in their conversation. Harry turned to go but, as in their last meeting, she called him back before he could reach the door to the conservatory.

'My husband . . . one night just before he died we were discussing Phoebe and he said something, something I didn't understand. He said that no child is a blank canvas, that there is a watermark, an inheritance that cannot be painted over.'

The words hung in the air between them, a profound truth, a truth that Phoebe Stanbury had died for.

'Who was she, detective? Who was my daughter?'

Harry nodded, for it was the right question, although he had no answer.

## CHAPTER THIRTY-TWO

William awoke in Savannah's battered armchair. His back hurt dreadfully, although he had fallen asleep easily enough after their escape from the hounds of Whitehall. He had never run like that before, had never needed to, and yet his weak chest had not given out on him. If anything, his lungs had never felt clearer than they did this morning.

There was no sign of Savannah and, despite his discomfort, William tucked the thin blanket about himself and stared up at the large damp patch in the middle of the ceiling. Two days had elapsed since Mr Bridge had raised the gun to his temple and unleashed a dark world on his young apprentice. William could find no connection between the city he had always known and the one that had unpeeled before him over the last few days. Was it possible that while he had perused *Dempster's Illustrated Seed Catalogue* and fretted over the punctuality of trains, the likes of Obediah Pincott and the mysterious vicomtesse had breathed the same air, perpetrating murder and subjugation? It was easier to believe that the old world had simply disappeared as the new one arrived, that he had passed through a door without even knowing it was there.

The sun fell through the small sash window on to the bare floor. There was a smear where the window had been cleaned recently, inside and out. What a strange creature she was, this

Savannah Shelton, a killer who cleaned her windows and swept the floor.

He spotted his travel bag in the corner of the room, packed by Savannah as he sat at his kitchen table that fateful night with his head in one hand and a bottle of brandy in the other. He sat up and pulled it towards him, searching for some clean underthings. It was the bag's first outing and it still emitted the rich smell of new leather. What had Mr Bridge been thinking, buying a travel valise for the boy who went nowhere?

He dug deeper into the bag and pulled out the portrait of his mother that he had kept on his bedside table. He placed the frame on the upturned crate at the side of the chair so that Savannah might see he appreciated the thought.

He had just finished dressing when she returned, carrying a large bucket of steaming water that leaked drips across the floor. 'Our neighbour Gerty charges a penny a bucket. Use it quickly, I've lost half already.'

'Thank you, that was most kind of you.'

She landed the bucket on to a small washstand near the window. 'There's a screen you can use.'

William brought the screen across and set to work on his ablutions. He heard the window open and the telltale clank and swoosh of a chamber pot being emptied. We are born to savagery, he thought, unless we are taught otherwise. It was gratifying to give himself over to the familiar ritual of grooming, although it was a cumbersome operation. The cut to his palm still stung, so he left the bandage on his hand, unwilling yet to explore the damage beneath. After all that had happened he was surprised that his face still looked the same. He had expected some impression to be left, a subtle change in shadows and lines, but the face in the mirror was most definitely the one he had brought with him all those days ago. He felt vaguely disappointed.

Savannah cleared her throat. 'So, what next?'

What next indeed. The meeting with Habborlain was tomorrow, but he could not pin all his hopes of finding his aunt on a meeting with a man who, so far, had served up only questions and no answers. One thing was for sure: he was ravenous, for he had barely eaten a thing the previous day. Strange, he thought, how his body still had such needs when his life lay in ruins. Still, a full belly might help him think.

'I believe I owe you breakfast at least.'

He emerged from behind the screen to find Savannah hunched over, her fingers busy as she counted through the coins and notes within a small leather purse. She hastily retied the string and rammed the purse back into her pocket.

'Your employ with this man Pincott, it paid well?'

'Not well enough.'

He looked around the room. 'Well enough for what?'

Her face hardened. 'I can give you one more day of my time. Tonight I go back to Pincott's. Then I'm gone.'

'Very well.' He had no plan for the day yet, but her company at least offered some solace.

As they left the room, Savannah tumbled the myriad of locks and bolts into place. There was a tea shop nearby in Kensington that he had visited with his aunt on numerous occasions. They walked in silence, purchasing a copy of *The Times* along the way.

The place was as charming as he remembered it, respectable but modest, with clean but worn tablecloths and a homely atmosphere. William instantly realised he should not have come here, the loss of his aunt so palpable he had to fold his arms tight across his chest as if his heart might otherwise splinter.

He was greeted by a short round man in a starched white apron. 'Welcome, sir, we are honoured to see you again.'

'Thank you, Mr Pears, a table for two if you please.'

The man's smile slid away when he saw Savannah. Raising

himself up on his toes, he spoke into William's ear with a loud whisper. 'I'm sorry, sir, but we do not usually serve darkies here.'

Savannah dropped her head and turned back towards the door but William reached out and stopped her as he replied to the man, surprised by his own assertive tone, 'By all means put us at the back of your shop, hide us away if you will, but I *insist* that you serve myself and my friend breakfast. Otherwise ...' William looked about him, his eyes roving across the tables of customers who were beginning to suspect an intrigue of some sort. He inclined his head closer to Mr Pears' ear. 'I might feel compelled to make a scene.'

Savannah pushed William's arm away. 'Let's go.'

Mr Pears straightened his apron and put on his welcoming smile once more. 'Perhaps a quiet booth will suit your company best, sir. Please, madam, follow me.'

William took her arm and nudged her forward.

As soon as they were settled at the back of the shop, William ordered tea and kedgeree for both of them. Savannah shrank into a corner of the booth, her coat wrapped tightly about her, her face stony. William tried to find the right words. 'I apologise for my countryman – the man is ignorant, that is all.'

'Ignorance? Is that its name?'

'And you are not a "darkie", your colour is so very much lighter.'

'Oh, I see! Is there a chart, William? I wasn't aware.'

William held up his hands in appeasement. Savannah's eyes shifted to his bandaged left hand and her posture softened. She rubbed her own palm across her face and shrugged. 'Don't worry, William, I knew this city and its people before today, there is nothing new to learn, not for me. The shock is all yours.'

William didn't think so, but changed the subject anyway. 'So, I have over a day until this meeting with Habborlain. I cannot simply wait. I have to find this vicomtesse. My aunt is somewhere, as is the casket, but we have no inkling of where.' His thoughts tumbled about.

Savannah grabbed the paper and kept her eyes down as Mr Pears returned and silently but efficiently filled the table with pots of tea. She waited for him to leave before speaking. 'I'm returning to Pincott's tonight, alone this time. I cannot leave those women there and I need the money. If I can sniff out any information on your aunt's location, then I shall. No promises, though.'

William thought about the two women they had seen last night, both with child and chained to their beds like animals. 'Those women . . . I cannot comprehend it. You called it a baby farm?'

'They're harvesting infants. Who knows why? And the name of that place, the Olympian Breeding Association? Those women are just a means to an end, expendable. That bitch as much as said so.'

William frowned at her language but Savannah ignored him. 'This vicomtesse, have you ever heard of her before? Maybe Bridge or Habborlain mentioned her? Did you see a vicomtesse on this list?'

William shook his head. 'I did not, although in truth I barely scanned it. As for a connection to Mr Bridge, he didn't exactly move in those circles, I would have remembered if we had a vicomtesse on our books. Maybe if I could sneak back into chambers, have another look at the files—'

Savannah cut him off. 'Don't go back there, William, and don't even think about going home. They'll be waiting for you – the police, Pincott. Whatever you do from now on, it must not be predictable.'

Savannah returned to reading the paper. William thought of Sarah and Sedgwick, both now wondering where on earth he was. The police would surely have contacted them by now and lord knows what would be going through their minds. 'Then what can I do?'

'There are precisely two things you can do.' Savannah looked up from the paper and leant forward. 'This afternoon we go to welcome Cornelius Tinbergen's arrival in this great country of yours. Then we follow *her*.'

Savannah folded the paper and pointed to the lead article, FANFARE FOR TINBERGEN. William's attention was immediately caught by the name of Tinbergen's yacht: *The Seed of Life*. Surely it must be some coincidence? Halfway down the page was a list of those who would officially be present. Prime Minister Gladstone, of course, and a host of other dignitaries, but three names jumped out immediately: Sir Jasper Raycraft; the German Chancellor, Otto Von Rabenmarck, and his gracious sister, the Vicomtesse Adeline de Bayeau. Of course! He had heard Aunt Esther talk about her, for she was a darling of society, a widow despite her youth. William's spirits rose, they would be able to pick up the trail again and follow the vicomtesse just as Savannah had suggested.

Savannah sighed. 'This woman, Sir Fancypants Raycraft *and* the German chancellor? And they are all friends of Tinbergen? I don't like these connections, William. Your enemies are powerful.'

'My enemies,' he repeated. The words felt hollow – they were not his. He owned a house, furniture, *a tree*. When had he acquired *enemies*? Savannah looked at him as he stirred more sugar into his tea. The enemies were his alone and he felt utterly forlorn once more. It was madness to think that even with Savannah's help he could take on such powerful adversaries and win the day. 'Maybe I should talk to Detective Cunningham again. Even if they arrest me, I'm sure they will at least investigate what I have to say.' He sipped his tea, milky and grown cold. 'Besides, in a gaol I would at least be safe.'

Savannah shook her head. 'You need more facts, more evidence.'

It was true. What did he really have? Wild conjecture about a conspiracy whose end goal was still unclear. The police would be more convinced of his madness than ever.

'Then we go to the Tower this morning and pick up the trail once more.'

Their breakfast arrived and they ate in silence. The kedgeree was excellent, although William's appetite had diminished. He took the newspaper and read the rest of the front page. There was reference to the police inquiry into the sudden death of the society bride that he remembered reading aloud on his last day in the old world, perhaps the last breakfast he would ever enjoy with his aunt. Again the name Raycraft seemed to be everywhere, for the dead girl had been betrothed to his son. His eyes darted to the bottom of the page when his peripheral vision caught sight of his own name.

> The Metropolitan Police are searching for a missing man, William Lamb, Esquire, who is wanted to assist with their enquiries into two suspicious deaths that took place in Red Lion Square and Farringdon on Friday evening. He is described as being of average height and build, with brown hair and blue eyes. He is missing the thumb on his left hand.

He knew the police would be searching for him, of course, but to see his name in print, branded a murderer for all the world to see, brought the sting of tears to his eyes at the injustice of it all.

He refolded the paper with difficulty and slid it across the table. Savannah frowned as she read the short paragraph, her eyes turning towards his bandaged left hand.

He followed her gaze. 'I had almost forgot these last few days . . .'

'You're being hunted, William. You have been marked out for a reason.' She nodded at his hand. 'It is the only remarkable thing about you.'

William tried not to take offence at her words. Ordinary, insignificant William Lamb.

'It means something. It has to,' she continued.

'Means what?'

Savannah shrugged. 'That is what you have to find out.'

*B*y the time Harry arrived at London Bridge Station, day trippers filled the concourse, many weighed down with picnic hampers and children. The reception ceremony was to be held on the green outside the Tower and Harry joined in the push towards the bridge. He made sure his revolver was tucked securely in his pocket and allowed the crowd to carry him towards his destination.

A man in front of him, who clung to a walking stick with one hand and his wife's elbow with the other, shouted over his shoulder as Harry tried to make sufficient space to remove his wallet from his breast pocket. 'There is no point in pushing me, sir, we can go no faster!'

'I apologise, but you will need to let me through.' Harry held his badge over the man's shoulder.

In this manner Harry forced his way to the north end of the bridge, stopping only to enjoy the view of Cornelius Tinbergen's impressive yacht, *The Seed of Life*, lashed to a specially constructed jetty with thick new ropes. It was a fine vessel, the stern rising up out of the water was black and sleek, the brass fixings gleaming like gold, and the impossibly white sails billowed like swans puffing their chests, although Harry could detect little breeze in the midday air.

At the steps down to the embankment, the uniformed bobbies

were already hot and fractious. He slipped past them and pushed his way towards the Tower. To his right, the tall-masted ships that docked at the Pool of London bobbed silently in the thick soup of the river: all eyes were focused on the black beast moored further ahead. Middle Tower finally loomed before him. The outer green was already full and he had to show his badge once more to gain entry. An enormous cheer went up as the gangplank of the yacht lowered to meet the red carpet that stretched through the green towards the Byward Tower, where a sturdy platform had been erected. The crowd on the green was bigger than he had hoped for, at least five hundred strong, he guessed. If Edward Raycraft had indeed decided to show his face, it would be difficult to identify him. The crowd was bisected by the carpet and held in check by two lines of constables who held hands as if they were on a school outing. Harry scanned the throng, a sea of hats nodding in the sunlight.

Two flags hung above either end of the platform. The Union Jack and the Stars and Stripes both made a poorer show of the insipid breeze than the sails of Tinbergen's yacht. The dignitaries had yet to assemble, but the platform was abuzz with minions repositioning chairs and other decorations with surgical accuracy. Below the platform, a band was tuning up. There must have been thirty or so crammed into the tiniest of spaces, a battleground of arms, drums, legs and trombones.

Harry caught sight of Colonel Matlock. A short man in a white suit, surely an American, was berating him loudly. Matlock's ritual smile remained plastered to his face as if stuck there with horse glue. However tempting it was to interrupt and share his discoveries and concerns, Harry didn't want to burden his senior with any more stress on this important afternoon.

He addressed a nearby constable, shouting to be heard over the crowd. 'Could you tell me who was in charge of the briefing today? I would like to speak with him.'

The fellow directed Harry towards his sergeant, a surprisingly young man who enthusiastically brushed the sweat from his top lip as Harry explained what he was doing there.

'So, you think this murderer of yours might put in an appearance, then?' the sergeant lilted in a strong Welsh accent.

'I hope not, but it is entirely possible. If he is here, then his target may well be Sir Jasper Raycraft.'

'Blimey. Does Sir Jasper know?'

'I don't believe he is aware of a particular threat, and I think it best if it is kept that way. It is only suspicion on my part. Presumably the security around the platform will be tight?'

'As tight as a virgin's fanny, sir,' the sergeant replied cheerfully.

Harry found himself smiling. 'Jolly good, Sergeant. Jolly good.'

'I will tell the chaps to keep a lookout. Tall, you said, with long fair hair, and plenty of loose screws, like?'

Harry mentioned the tattoos but suspected that if Edward were here, he would be fully clothed. He let the sergeant go and surveyed the crowd once more. Most were turned towards the yacht itself, marvelling at its richness and beauty. The anticipation that flickered in the air was for Tinbergen himself, the richest man in the world, rather than for the office that he represented.

A small boy tugged at Harry's jacket. 'Fancy a souvenir, sir? We got flags, pins and models of the ship, copied with pinpoint acc-acc ...'

'Accuracy, you mean?'

'That's the word, sir.'

Harry glanced down at the wooden tray that was tied around the boy's neck with a thick leather strap. Of course, no one had seen the yacht until it had arrived that morning. The sorry lumps of wood in front of him were obviously someone's best guess at its appearance. The sails were made of paper, attached to a matchstick and the hull of the boat was painted red, not black. Harry looked pointedly towards the ship, and then back to the contents of the boy's tray. The boy hoisted his wares higher, as if closer inspection would tempt rather than disaffect a potential buyer. 'We was told the hull is red, underneath the water, the bit you can't see, sir.'

Harry had to admire the boy's cheek – younger in years than his grandson David, but older in so many ways. He bought one of the models for the extortionate price of sixpence and slid it into his pocket. Maybe if he saw David again soon he could make a funny story of it and they would call it *the not Tinbergen's yacht* and laugh.

As the noise of the crowd grew, William and Savannah turned to see a procession of men and women filing on to the platform. There were a dozen or so, walking in pairs. William didn't recognise the first couple, a very fat man with a handlebar moustache accompanied by a dowager who used a walking stick, her hand shaking as she stabbed the ground. But he did recognise the man who followed, whose portrait he had seen often in the papers.

He nudged Savannah. 'That's Raycraft!'

She barely glanced up at the stage. Since they had arrived at the Tower she had kept her face hidden, her collar turned up and her eyes cast down.

The crowd quieted and turned towards the gangplank, now flanked by two tall handsome sailors in bright white uniforms with shiny brass buttons. Their caps were exaggerated in size, giving them the look of toy soldiers. Some girls had pushed themselves forward to get closer to these bronzed creatures, and William had to feel sympathy for the pimply, pale line of young British officers that held the girls back from the objects of their desire.

A sharp cry had the crowd turning back towards the platform. With military precision, eight men emerged from the side door, marching cleanly to the bark of their leader. The men were dressed in red and their brass helmets pointed to the sky like sundials. The spurs on their high black boots jangled like the rattling of iron chains as they stomped in unison on to the platform and arranged themselves in a line, legs apart, hands behind their backs like prison guards. William thought it most odd to see such a display of German might on English soil. The crowd obviously felt the same, looking around at each other with raised eyebrows.

The ceremonial host, a thin, middle-aged man wearing two sashes emblazoned with the flags of Britain and America, came to the front of the stage. His voice was unexpectedly deep and penetrating as he addressed the crowd. 'Ladies and Gentlemen, please welcome to the city of London our most honoured guests, the Chancellor of the German Empire, Prince Otto Von Rabenmarck and the Vicomtesse Adeline de Bayeau.'

The pair emerged from the Byward Tower. Although the applause was muted, there was much pushing and shoving as everyone attempted to get a good look. William inhaled sharply as the vicomtesse came into view: the flaming hair that rippled daringly across her shoulders was redder than any he had ever seen and her porcelain face and ruby mouth were that of a doll's. Her plain white dress was embellished with some kind of silver thread that caught the sunlight and scattered it in all directions. The hordes were captivated, their applause gaining in enthusiasm as the couple took their seats. It was impossible to reconcile such beauty with her callous words from the night before.

Why did she hunt him? What did she want?

The host of ceremonies silenced the crowd once more. 'Ladies and Gentlemen, the Prime Minister of Great Britain, the Right Honourable William Gladstone.'

William applauded warmly as Gladstone made his way to the platform, one hand raised casually in salute as he lumbered forward. He was a bear of a man, physically imposing despite his late years. This was where he was known to be most comfortable, in front of a crowd, and the few boos that could be heard seemed to amuse rather than dishearten him.

William squinted into the sun to observe Gladstone and Von Rabenmarck greet each other. The handshake looked firm enough, and William was glad to see Gladstone tower over the German chancellor, although he knew one could read nothing into their respective physical statures when it came to assessing the balance of their delicate relationship.

The host addressed the crowd once more. 'Great Britain welcomes to her shores the President of the Tinbergen Corporation and Vice President of the United States, Mr Cornelius Tinbergen.'

William and Savannah were jostled as the crowd erupted into cheers and turned en masse towards the yacht. The sailors stood to attention and, as the man himself emerged from the ship, the band struck up into a deafening and fast-paced rendition of 'Hail, Columbia.' In a suit of cream linen, Tinbergen saluted the crowd with the boater he carried in his hand. White teeth flashed as he fairly bounced along the red carpet in a display of youthful athleticism that seemed to poke a stick at the grey dignity that awaited him on the stage. Many among the crowd were waving American flags and Tinbergen grasped the hands that pushed through the police cordon, laughing easily at the madness of it all.

He greeted Gladstone with a two-handed grip before hugging Otto Von Rabenmarck vigorously. The German chancellor looked happy to see him, a warm smile spreading across his face. As he turned towards the vicomtesse, Tinbergen gave an exaggerated bow before grasping her hand in his and kissing it passionately. There were more embraces for Sir Jasper and flirting with the old dowager with the walking stick, who William thought might shake all the way to the floor as the Vice President of the United States bowed over her hand.

Thankfully the music stopped and the host stepped forward, his arms stretched out, indicating that silence was required. 'And now, please be upstanding for the National Anthem of Great Britain.'

Cornelius Tinbergen stood alongside Gladstone, his face the picture of earnestness as he clasped his arm across his chest and faced the Union Jack.

William joined in the singing of 'God Save the Queen' with vigour, before noticing that Savannah remained conspicuously silent. He bent towards her. 'You do not sing?'

She flashed him a deadpan stare, then leant across and said in his ear, 'I do sing, William. What I do *not* do is give a shit.'

William bristled at the crude word, but forgave her bad temper. In truth, neither of them had anticipated the scale of the police presence at the Tower. They had taken a big risk in coming here.

Once the anthem was over, the prime minister stepped forward, his sonorous voice easily penetrating far into the assembled crowd.

'And so, with pageantry and music, we welcome the Vice President of the United States to our green and pleasant land, and indeed,' Gladstone turned towards the German chancellor, 'to the continent of Europe herself.'

Savannah tugged at William's sleeve. 'Let's start moving towards the back of the stage, find her carriage if we can.'

'You have a plan?' he whispered.

'Yep, your favourite: the "stick a gun in someone's face and see what happens" plan.'

As Gladstone's speech continued, Harry observed the German chancellor. Everything about the man seemed measured: a light pull on his cuff, the occasional smile, every rove of his glance seemed calculated in advance.

' . . . the American constitution is, as far as I can see, the most wonderful work ever struck by the brain and purpose of man. The freedom of all enshrined and respected by all. Vice President

Tinbergen, you find your mother continent struggling with such freedoms. Yet, in that struggle, in the bloodshed of kings and slaves, something much more valuable is so often lost. All the world over I will back the masses against the classes but nothing that is morally wrong can ever be politically right . . .'

Harry scanned the silent crowd, his hackles raised, looking for the tall frame and pale hair of Edward Raycraft. The air was thick, woolly with expectation.

' . . . so the old world does indeed welcome the new, in the knowledge that age is simply a fact and not a virtue. Rebirth is our future always!'

Gladstone stepped back and bowed elegantly towards Tinbergen, who joined in the applause.

The vice president then stepped forward and the crowd hushed immediately. Nonetheless, he raised his hands as if to quieten them still further before he spoke.

'My friends . . .' Tinbergen's voice was soft, his accent warm after Gladstone's clipped tones. 'I am humbled by the sincerity and splendour of your welcome, and thank you for your kind words, Prime Minister Gladstone. It was seventy years ago next month that my father left his homeland in Utrecht and set sail for the Americas, to start a new life and seek out his fortune . . .'

Harry's gaze snatched towards Sir Jasper Raycraft. He was looking out into the crowd, far to Harry's right, unblinking, his face drained and his mouth falling open. It was if he had seen a ghost – and Harry knew exactly what that meant.

Edward Raycraft had shown himself.

' . . . He returned to Europe only once more in his lifetime, a fact that caused a great deal of regret when he finally lay down to meet the great Lord . . .'

His heart racing, Harry looked around for the young Welsh sergeant, finding him five yards behind talking to a pretty girl.

'Sergeant! He is here! Look at Sir Jasper!'

'. . . and if he is watching over me now, I am certain it will mean the world to him to know that his son has finally retraced his footsteps.' Tinbergen turned his face up towards the shining sky and the crowd followed his gaze. But Harry had eyes only for Raycraft's stricken face.

The sergeant followed Sir Jasper's line of sight and made some quick calculations. 'I will pass the message through to the back line on the south-east side; they can approach with greater stealth. If we push through from here it will take too long and he will see us coming.'

Father,' said Tinbergen, gazing to the heavens, 'I came home.'

Harry had to shout over the rapturous applause. 'Very well, I will move toward him from here! Remember, he is dangerous and likely to be carrying a weapon – no man should attempt to tackle him alone.'

'Good luck, sir.' The sergeant strode away, intent on the task.

Trusting to the navigation offered by Sir Jasper Raycraft's frozen gaze, Harry stepped into the throng and began to push his way through. It was slow progress, but he had no wish to alarm the crowd. If they were to take Edward Raycraft by surprise then it was best to be patient. He murmured into a constable's ear and slipped across the red carpet.

The crowd was even denser on the other side of the cordon. He checked back to the platform and saw Sir Jasper's eyes were shifting, following someone through the crowd, moving in the opposite direction to Harry. Damn, he would have to adjust his path once more; he just hoped the line of blue at the far side of the green would do its job. As he pushed on, the crowd began to thin. He checked back to Sir Jasper just as a shout rose up, maybe ten yards further on, followed by the piercing shriek of several police whistles. The crowd in front of Harry stepped backwards, halting his progress. Several women screamed and clutched their children against them as a tall man with flowing fair hair leapt on to the crumbling remains of the original quay.

Harry was momentarily thrown into inaction at this first glimpse of Phoebe's killer. He was undoubtedly a Raycraft: the blond locks, the height of him and the wide mouth all shouted his familial resemblance to Sir Jasper himself. Like a Greek god, Edward was broad-shouldered and powerful, his hair whipping up around him like a lion's mane.

The band began to play a march, ignorant of the unfolding drama, but all eyes were now on Edward Raycraft as he balanced precariously between the green and the river, beyond the reach of the constables in blue that scrabbled beneath him. Harry checked the platform. The prime minister had been whisked away, but Otto Von Rabenmarck stood next to a wide-eyed Sir Jasper, talking angrily into his ear as the uncle continued to lock eyes with his nephew. Colonel Matlock strode across the stage, demanding action from his team of officers.

Harry turned back to the quay. Edward was smiling, a look of triumph shimmering across his face as he lifted his arm and pointed a ridged hunting knife in Sir Jasper's direction. The screams grew and the crowd began to stir in different directions like an awakening beast.

There was only one thing Harry could do. He pulled out his gun. 'Stand back everyone, stand back!'

The crowd backed away rapidly.

Harry pointed the revolver at Edward Raycraft, shouting, 'Drop the knife!'

The man spun his head towards Harry, his eyes obscured by the blond hair that blew across his face. It would not be the first time Harry Treadway had shot a man, but it was disconcerting that he could not see his eyes or read his intentions. All Harry had to go on was a curl of the lips, a smile that seemed to say, *you will not stop me.*

Harry pulled the trigger.

The bullet raced towards Edward Raycraft's shoulder, but at the last moment, the man had jumped to the other side of the wall.

A sea of dark blue uniforms followed him, their whistles blowing in a vain attempt to summon the fleeing man back towards them.

Harry lowered his gun and ran forward, ignoring the horrified stares of the crowd around him. He could not see beyond the crumbling quay, but he knew there was no point in joining the chase. He just had to hope that the posse of blue that had followed Edward Raycraft over the wall and along the south side of the Tower could bring him to task.

Harry turned back. The platform had rapidly emptied, the various grandees husbanded to safety back through the Byward Tower. The crowd was moving in haste towards the bridge, chattering nervously now that the incident was over.

Harry cursed himself. He should have taken the shot a few seconds earlier: he would have had his man, injured but alive. He fought the tide as he tried to reach the platform. He had to update Colonel Matlock – and it was time to speak again with Sir Jasper Raycraft, before the shock retreated and he put on his mask of lies once more.

Harry circled around the platform. As he struggled against the flow, he encountered a startled face staring back at him, a face he recognised – the young man who had escaped Dolly's custody a few days earlier.

William Lamb. That was the rascal's name. Before the man could react, Harry reached out and clamped both hands on his shoulders, ignoring the pushing and shoving around them.

'You're under arrest, son.'

'No! Please!'

'Don't resist me, lad.' Harry kept his grip firm as he looked around, hoping to catch the eye of a constable to assist him, but almost every man in blue was now chasing down Edward Raycraft on the other side of the Tower.

The boy looked terrified, squirming in his hands. Once again Harry scoured the thinning crowd for sight of a uniform but, as he turned, the man broke away and darted north. Cursing, Harry ran after him. The young man had close to forty years on him but Harry wasn't about to let the second murderer of the day slip through his fingers. Away from the crowds, the man ran fast across the green, although Harry could hear him wheezing as he did so. Harry kept up his stride and took his pistol once more from his pocket.

'Stop or I'll shoot!'

William Lamb staggered to a halt only yards from the bastion of Legge's Mount and, with his hands on his knees, placed his head between his legs to catch his breath. He turned back towards Harry, his arm rising in capitulation as he waved the gun away.

'Please,' he gasped, 'you don't understand! Some men have taken my aunt!'

'Save your excuses for Detective Cunningham, I simply intend to deliver you to Scotland Yard and lock the door this time.' Harry kept the gun trained on him. He could hear feet running towards him and assumed the boys in blue were finally catching up.

'Wait!' The young man was really struggling for breath and Harry felt more than a little sorry for him. He really did seem the most unlikely of criminals.

The man continued, his eyes beseeching, 'I didn't kill anybody! The butler was killed by men who work for Obediah Pincott.'

Harry was barely listening, he felt exhausted. He needed someone in uniform to come and take over so that he could get on with the urgent business of interviewing Sir Jasper.

William Lamb continued to babble, the noise simply a backdrop to Harry's own thoughts, but then a name came sharply through the mist.

'Raycraft is connected somehow! I know it seems impossible, but there is this breeding operation, most dreadful. Mr Habborlain has the answers and I know where to meet him, if you would just let me see him I know—'

'Raycraft?' Harry began to lower his gun. 'Sir Jasper Raycraft?'

William Lamb stood up, his eyes blazing with hope. 'Yes! Sir Jasper Raycraft. Although *she* is the real villain of the piece, the vicomtesse, I am sure of it.'

Harry thought quickly, but not quickly enough. Time had run out for him. The last thing he heard as he sank to his knees was William Lamb's desperate cry.

'No!'

The shout seemed to go on for ever, and then there was nothing but blackness for Harry Treadway.

## CHAPTER THIRTY-FOUR

'Well, that's just marvellous, thank you very much.' William looked at the elderly policeman who now lay at his feet, then wiped the back of his hand across his mouth, as if the gesture might undo Savannah's blow.

Savannah bent down to retrieve the detective's fallen gun before putting her own away, ignoring the toy ship that had also tumbled from his pocket. She stared at William, hands on hips. 'Didn't I just rescue you? Isn't that what you pay me for?'

She stood in front of the prone detective and looked back towards the green. William followed her gaze: the crowd were facing in the opposite direction, shoving their way towards the bridge. William took his place beside her, hoping to obscure the man on the ground. It would only take one person to turn about and the alarm would be raised.

Savannah grabbed his arm. 'We need to leave. Right now.'

'I need to talk to him, he—'

'Have you totally lost your mind? He was going to arrest you, William.'

William shook his head vigorously, hope gleaming in his eyes. 'No! He wasn't. He was listening to me, to my story. Just before you struck him he lowered his gun! He was listening to me, Savannah! Do you know how that feels? I think he believed me.'

Savannah snorted her derision. 'What makes you think that?

He was just trying to contain you, make you think you stood a chance.'

William considered the option, his shoulders deflating. Had he read the situation wrongly? Had he been so desperate to be believed that he had seen a friend where there was only foe? He looked down at the man at his feet. The man's polka dot bow tie had turned sideways and William felt a fluttering urge to straighten it for him. 'That was quite some blow. We should at least check his breathing.'

Savannah barely glanced down. 'It's not your problem, William. We should go.'

William folded his arms. 'I won't leave him, not if there's a chance to be heard. I'm paying you, remember?'

'Why else would I be here? But some things are more important than money, William, even for me.'

'Such as?'

'My neck.' She turned towards him, her eyes blazing. 'I won't die for you, William Lamb. I've done things, things policemen don't approve of.'

'What's going on here, then?'

William and Savannah spun around to face two constables approaching them from behind, their frowns fixed on the unconscious detective.

William felt Savannah's arm move to her side and he grabbed her wrist hard. 'I say, what jolly good fortune! I'm afraid my father here has had a little too much to drink, and standing about in the sun has rather done for him. Might you help us carry him into the shade and prop him against the wall just here? Thank you both, you are most kind.'

William reached down to the detective, slinging one heavy arm over his shoulder, hoping his actions would add veracity to his artifice. The two constables stepped forward obligingly and helped William carry the man into the shadows of the bastion's tower and set him gently against the cool stone wall: one of them even retrieved the toy ship from where it had fallen and William shoved it quickly into the detective's pocket.

'Let the old man sleep it off, I'd say.' The constable's smile revealed two missing front teeth. He winked at William. 'My own dad is the same. They forget they're not young any more.'

'You have it precisely,' William offered.

The policemen said their goodbyes and departed. Hidden behind the bastion of Legge's Mount, the detective was no longer visible to the crowd. William turned towards Savannah, who paced up and down with her arms wrapped tightly around herself. Her face was stony when she spoke. 'OK, we'll give him a chance. If you're right, and he believes us, then those women at Pincott's and your aunt stand a better chance of survival if Scotland Yard is in the chase.'

'Exactly!' cried William, thrilled that Savannah was at last seeing sense.

'But if he comes around, listens to your story, and *still* doesn't believe us, then I'll kill him.'

'What?' William couldn't believe what she was saying. 'We can't *kill* him!'

Savannah removed her gun, her mouth set in a determined line as she held William's gaze. 'That's the deal, William. We can leave now and follow the vicomtesse, or we wake him up and talk. If he believes us, and promises me immunity, then all well and good, but if not, then I have no choice.'

'Of course you have a choice!' William shouted.

Savannah stepped closer, her voice hard and low. 'People like me *don't* have a choice, William. The moment he sees my face, there will be no place I can hide. If he doesn't believe us, and the police put a price on my head, how hard do you think it would be to track me in this city? I can't run, William, not far enough or quick enough. We tell him our story, or we don't.

The rest is up to him, but I'm not risking the rope for you or anyone else.'

William slumped under the weight of her logic. 'Why don't you hide around the corner while I speak with him? If he is with us, then you show yourself, but if he is not, and attempts to arrest me again, then I can signal you to come up behind him and biff him on the head once more. That way he won't see you unless he is inclined to believe us! Please, Savannah, I have to try this.'

Savannah shook her head. 'If he doesn't hear directly from me, William, the chances are pretty slim. Look what happened before. We might as well walk away now.'

William was about to speak again in favour of the plan, but another voice intervened. 'I'm afraid she is right, William.'

William stared down at the detective, who was rapidly blinking his eyes and breathing shallowly as his head rolled backwards against the wall for support. The man raised a hand to his head and winced as he continued in a tight voice, 'Besides, I'm really not sure I could take another biff to the head; I'd rather take my chances against Savannah's gun. I do hope I caught your name correctly, Miss . . . ?'

Savannah faced him, feet apart, her gun hand hanging down at her side. A smile that wasn't a smile spread across her face. 'Yep, you got the name right. Savannah, with two n's, in case you live long enough to write it down.'

'Detective Harry Treadway.' The man's head lolled backwards once more. 'Might we find somewhere more comfortable to talk?'

*U*nder the threat of Savannah's gun, they brought the detective to the attic room in Cromwell Road. William had expected Savannah to object, but from the moment that Detective Treadway had opened his eyes, she had behaved as if there was nothing left to lose. Both her name and her face were known to a senior officer: her biggest fear had already materialised. This sudden capitulation scared William, and he knew that she would kill the man if she felt she had no choice.

Now they faced each other in Savannah's quarters: the detective in the battered armchair and William on the neatly made bed. Savannah paced up and down behind them, smoking a cigarette. William could hear the snap of her leather coat as she changed directions, no doubt ready to shoot and run. The air was dusty and hot as the sun drilled down across the rooftops of the city.

'I don't know where to start.'

'I normally find that the beginning is as good a place as any.'

'Very well. I live with my aunt, Esther Lamb, and I work – *worked* – for a man called Nathaniel Bridge.'

William told his story: the unplanned visit to Ambrose Habborlain, the message *the Finder knows*, the mysterious box and the gunshot that changed everything. When he got to the part where he revisited Habborlain's house, he tripped over his words as he described Fischer's mutilated corpse.

'That is when I met Savannah.' He turned around and looked at her.

She stopped pacing. Taking her time, she took a tin from her pocket and removed another tightly rolled cigarette. The sudden strike of a match ripped through the room.

'How do you like it so far, detective? Quite a story, don't you think?' Savannah removed a flake of tobacco from her bottom lip and dropped it to the floor.

Detective Treadway smiled at her. 'Quite a story, indeed.'

'Unbelievable, wouldn't you say? Your colleagues thought so.'

'I am not a man who jumps to conclusions.'

'Very well.' She pulled deeply on her cigarette. 'I worked for a man called Obediah Pincott. He was paying me to watch the Habborlain house.' In pithy but graphic terms, Savannah listed the bare facts of her story, including her encounter with Mildred Whitfield, the captive woman in Pincott's yard. She reached the point where she met William. 'He can tell you the rest.'

The detective asked many questions about the contents of the casket: the antiquarian documents and the list of names. William cursed himself anew for failing to examine them in more detail while he had the chance. A few minutes later, William pulled Habborlain's note from his pocket and handed it over.

Detective Treadway took the note and reached towards his jacket. Before his hand even made contact, Savannah leapt forward, her gun flashing in the bright light. William dived instinctively to the floor.

'Drop your hand!'

The detective's voice didn't waver. 'I need my glasses. You have already taken my gun, and I assure you that I do not have another secreted about my person. If I did, then either I would have used it at the Tower, or I have already demonstrated that I am a man to be trusted.'

William had to admire the man's calm. He might look like an

elderly clerk, but he had nerves of steel. Savannah kept the gun trained at his head, although William thought he could see her wrist shaking. He couldn't allow the tension to escalate. 'There is no point reading it, it's mostly written in ancient Greek.' William supplied the translation: the date, time and place where he hoped Habborlain would be waiting for him.

Savannah dropped the gun to her side once more. Although he did not reach again for his glasses, the detective acknowledged her act of trust with a courteous nod. He turned to William. 'Do carry on.'

William pulled himself back on to the bed and continued the story. He wondered how to portray Savannah's role in disabling his captor at the chambers in Farringdon, but she spoke for herself.

'I shot him. I'd just arrived and I thought he was going to kill William. So I shot him.' Savannah's tone was all defiance.

'Of course you did.' Whether the detective spoke with disbelief or admiration was impossible to tell.

William told of the horror of arriving home and finding his aunt gone. 'I was so sure that Detective Cunningham would believe me and set about looking for my aunt, but when I heard Sergeant Smiley talking about locking me up and ignoring my pleas, I panicked, and ran.'

Detective Treadway frowned for the first time. 'Did they tell you why they were so suspicious of you, William?'

William thought the question odd. 'I suppose it was obvious. Three dead men, and I seemed to be the only witness.'

'And what might they have believed your motive to be, do you think?'

William paused and looked out at the sky. 'I have no idea. I suppose they thought me mad, caught up in a murderous rampage.'

'Indeed, you do look the type.'

Detective Treadway's laugh was gentle and reminded William of how Mr Bridge used to tease him from time to time. He pushed the thought away and moved on to their visit to Pincott's the previous night – the women bound to their beds, the vicomtesse, and the trail they had followed to Whitehall. Detective Treadway seemed particularly interested in Sir Jasper Raycraft, and Savannah offered up the words of one of the pregnant women who had called him *the devil's child*.

Eventually, William sat back in his chair. 'There are many more details, of course: Habborlain's collection, the symbol at the OBA.' William waved them away. 'I could go on, but we have told you everything of import, I believe.'

The detective leaned forward. 'The symbol?'

'Yes. The symbol on the casket and on the building in Whitehall was the same. It is called the Seed of Life, also the name of Tinbergen's ship. I could draw it for you,' William offered.

'There is no need. I believe I know it.'

'You do?'

Detective Treadway turned towards Savannah, who had stopped her pacing and was leaning against the window sill. 'May I please remove my notebook from my pocket?'

Savannah assented. The detective took out his notebook and flicked through the pages. 'Here, is this it?' He held the notebook out towards William.

William nodded in surprise. What relevance did this symbol have for the detective?

Savannah folded her arms, her back now against the door. 'So, Detective Treadway, we've shared our story, guess it's your turn. Raycraft, the symbol – what do they mean to you?'

Detective Treadway shook his head. 'I don't think that is appropriate. I am a police officer. What you have told me has been helpful, and of profound concern, but forgive me if I do not reciprocate. These are grave matters indeed, but now I have a few questions of my own.'

The detective's approach was calm and methodical, but William could tell their answers were frustratingly unhelpful. What was the nature of Bridge's work for Habborlain? *I don't know.* Why was the Habborlain residence being so closely scrutinised? *I don't know.* What connection might you have to the vicomtesse? *I don't know!*

Savannah stirred herself. 'Tell him about your thumb, William.'

William sighed. It seemed so irrelevant now. Branded a murderer, on the run from the police and in search of his missing aunt, his absent thumb seemed to him to be the least remarkable thing about himself.

'I don't have one.' William held up his bandaged left hand. 'I have never had one, this is just a cut.'

Detective Treadway looked thoughtful. 'Tell me a little about your parents, William.'

Trying not to let his frustration show, William told him what little he knew. He handed over the daguerreotype of his mother that still sat on the crate beside the bed and Detective Treadway examined it closely, more closely than William himself had ever done.

'I can see your resemblance to her.'

'She had all of her thumbs, if that is what you are looking for.'

The detective smiled and put the photograph to one side, tucked his notebook away in his pocket and folded his hands in his lap.

William knew the moment had come, all the desperation of the last few days surged up within him and the words came out before he could stop himself. 'Do you believe us, Detective Treadway? Do you believe *me?*'

Detective Treadway sighed. 'I wish I didn't, but I do. I believe every word you have told me.'

William put his head in his hands, relief flooding him with a great and sudden weariness. 'Thank God,' he whispered into his lap. 'At last!'

The detective stood up. 'I see no convincing basis for Cunningham and Smiley's desire to arrest you, or their failure to investigate your aunt's disappearance. I would go so far as to say they have wilfully obstructed the pursuit of justice in this case. I must speak with Colonel Matlock. I will return from Scotland Yard as soon as a plan is in place. So, if you'll excuse me, I should make haste.' He turned to Savannah. 'Unless, of course, you intend to shoot me first.'

William looked at her impassive face. 'Please, Savannah, this is our best chance!'

She closed her eyes briefly, opened them, and nodded to the detective. 'Very well. But we need to speak alone. Outside.'

'I thought we might.' Detective Treadway turned towards William while Savannah unbolted the door. 'If all goes well, these women will be freed and your aunt found before sunset. Be patient, William.'

*Patience.* William thought back to all those days he had spent writing letters and wills and trusts, dipping his pen into the inkwell as the minutes, days and years of his life dripped by. He had once thought of Time as his friend, but now the hours yawned in front of him, unstinting and finite.

## CHAPTER THIRTY-SIX

*H*arry rubbed his still sore head as he emerged on to the landing of Cromwell Road.

Savannah followed, her voice low as she said, 'There are some things that—'

Harry held up his hand. 'I can put two and two together for myself. I assume that somewhere in your past, possibly in another country, there was a degree of *wrongdoing*. If you are to collaborate further, then assurances will need to be given that past misdemeanours will be overlooked. That is what I shall discuss with Colonel Matlock. If he is unwilling to do so, then when I return I will tell you this, and when I negligently turn my back you will have a chance to get away. But do not run yet, Savannah, all could yet go very well for you. Does that cover it?'

Savannah nodded her assent, her head stiff with an unmistakable pride. As he turned to go, she called him back and handed over the gun she had taken from him at the Tower. He saw the indecision in her face, although her words were unambiguous. 'I'm trusting you, Treadway.'

'Call me Harry.'

'I won't, if you don't mind.'

What a strange young woman, although the truth was he liked her in many ways. Despite the blow to the head and her callous, if logical, disregard for his life, there was something honest at the core of her.

Harry had to walk some way towards Chelsea before he was able to flag down a cab. The afternoon sunlight made the city seem magical as it glittered through the plane trees of Gloucester Avenue, but Harry knew that such beauty was only skin deep. There were horrors here in this place, flitting through the shadows like rats in the sewers.

His suspicions that Sir Jasper Raycraft was a villainous man had been confirmed, but where did this lead him? He was investigating Phoebe Stanbury's murder, and once Edward Raycraft was found and convicted, the case and its mysteries would disappear into the streets of the city, pounded to mud beneath the hooves of fresher crimes and tribulations.

Yet the bewildering plot against William presented urgent need for action: to arrest Obediah Pincott, release the captive women, find William's aunt and question Sir Jasper and the vicomtesse. But where was the connection to his own investigations? One of the captive women had called Raycraft *the devil's child*, bringing to mind Anna Raycraft's own assertions. Bad men rarely did only one bad thing. Maybe that was the single link between William's tale and Harry's investigation.

The story of those captive women had horrified him, but he had felt something else too: a resonance. The children were important to the vicomtesse, and presumably to Raycraft himself, the women merely disposable. He thought of Lydia Stanbury, her eyes falling for the first time on the anonymous child her husband had brought home. William was an orphan too, just like Phoebe. Harry had sensed the merest of echoes once more when he had seen the portrait of William's mother – the mother he did not remember. The resemblance to William was there, but something else too, for Harry had a feeling he had seen her before.

When he arrived at Scotland Yard, it was just before four o'clock. The main desk sergeant confirmed that Colonel Matlock had yet to return from the Tower.

'I don't suppose you know if the pursuit of Edward Raycraft was successful?'

'Afraid not, sir. The boys who've returned are full of it. Chased him all over the city, they did, but he lost them. One of the recruits in the Waterloo division got a good look though and is a dab hand with pen and paper. They are printing the likeness later today. By this evening his face will be all over the city.'

'Very good. I don't suppose I could trouble you for assistance on some other matters?'

The desk sergeant readily assented, for it was rare for a CID detective to request help in this way.

'I need to check the missing persons register, and also the list of wanted persons that the United States government have reason to believe may be residing here.'

The sergeant called another colleague to take over his duties and took Harry through to the main administration office where all the records were kept. Row upon row of filing cabinets and bookcases divided the room. The sergeant drew Harry over to one wall where three huge blackboards listed all missing persons: names, age, locations, dates, and the identities of investigating officers. There must have been at least a thousand names, the normal flotsam and jetsam of a city the size of London.

The list was organised in date order, so Harry began by scanning backwards from the last board. He told the sergeant the name he was looking for and the man reviewed the boards from the other direction. When they finally met in the middle, neither of them had found anything.

Harry frowned. 'When were the boards last updated?'

'Saturday evening, I suppose. Any new cases would be in that basket over there.'

Harry rifled through the missing persons reports that had recently arrived and quickly found what he was looking for. Savannah's memory had proved accurate.

Mildred Whitfield, governess. Reported missing by her mother yesterday morning, not seen since Friday when she attended an interview for a new position. No one seems to know where or with whom the interview was to take place.

Harry scanned the report. This was something else to lay before Sir Jasper and the vicomtesse when he interviewed them later today. Harry wondered if they could feel the net closing in around them, or would he take them completely by surprise?

Tracking Savannah proved a harder task. The sergeant sourced two fat ledgers and thumped them down on a reading desk near the window. The ledgers were almost triangular, for so much paper had been stuffed between the pages that they barely closed.

As Harry flicked through, various bills and papers fell out, while others were glued in so firmly several pages had stuck together and he had to tear them open. As he started on the second ledger, a whole sheaf of papers fell to the floor. He bent down to retrieve them, but his hand stopped in mid-air as he spotted Savannah's face staring back at him.

The poster dated from March. The word *Wanted* was written boldly across the top, and beneath was a crude but unmistakable drawing of Savannah, her black hair hanging down and the scar jagging across her striking face in a single thick, black mark. The poster offered little information beyond the bald facts. Savannah Shelton, convicted of three separate counts of murder and sentenced to death by hanging. She had escaped custody in Phoenix, Arizona, and was believed to have gone to New York and caught a ship bound for Europe. The small print advised that she was considered highly dangerous and not to be approached unarmed – permission was granted to shoot to kill on sight.

It was worse than Harry had thought and he couldn't help feeling disappointed in her. He had hoped for something less unforgivable than three charges of murder. Matlock would be unlikely to waive such offences in return for this woman's co-operation. Harry might have to tell her to run after all.

He folded the poster in his pocket and returned to the front desk, just in time to see Colonel Matlock bustle through the revolving door.

'Harry! What happened to you? When the chase finally gave out you were nowhere to be found.'

'I'm afraid I became embroiled in another matter, sir. I would speak with you urgently. People's lives are at stake and we must act quickly.'

Matlock gripped his arm. 'You are having a time of it, Harry.'

When they reached his office, Matlock hung his jacket over the back of his chair, angled the blinds against the sharp afternoon sun and urged Harry to take a seat. 'Tell me everything.'

'I arrested a man called William Lamb at the Tower today, a young lawyer that Dolly has been investigating.'

Matlock leant forward in his seat. 'It's not a name I am familiar with. Is he now in the cells?'

'No. I let him go, sir. I will tell you why.'

Matlock leant back in his seat. His bright smile seemed forced. 'I'm sure you will.'

As Harry retold William's extraordinary story, the smile on Matlock's face began to fade and his ruddy Santa Claus cheeks seemed to visibly pale. He made notes on a yellow legal pad, something Harry had never seen him do before. 'Incredible. I can scarce believe it.'

'Neither can I, sir, but the next steps seem clear. We have to mount a raid on this rogue Pincott, release the women he is holding there. I would also suggest that we take Sir Jasper in for questioning at the same time, and, if you think it is possible without causing a diplomatic incident, we should question this vicomtesse.'

'Yes, of course, on that front I will need to make a telephone call, Harry. Perhaps you could leave me for a moment?'

'Of course.' Harry left the office and shut the door behind him. Dolly Cunningham caught his eye from across the room but Harry turned away. He had not yet had a chance to discuss his concerns about his colleagues with the colonel and a conversation with Dolly was something he wanted to avoid. However, in his peripheral vision he could see Cunningham waddling towards him and it looked as if he would at least have to pass the time of day with the man. Fortunately, at that moment Matlock summoned him back into the office.

'Take a seat, Harry. I have just spoken with the Home Office. I have an appointment to see the Home Secretary tonight. We will take no action until then.'

It made sense, Harry thought. Until they had settled on a plan regarding the vicomtesse, there was no point moving on Pincott or Sir Jasper, both of whom might alert her. In the interim, Matlock suggested that Harry send a telegram to William, reassuring him that all was in hand and he should sit tight and stay out of the way. Matlock called his secretary in and Harry dictated the telegram quickly.

The secretary brought them some tea and, uncertainly, Harry broached the subject of his suspicions regarding Dolly Cunningham's handling of William's case.

'Really, sir, even without the American woman's part in the story being clear at the time, there was little reason for Dolly to point the finger at this young man. I'm afraid it makes me wonder . . . ' Harry knew what he was about to say could sound ridiculous, 'whether it isn't feasible, just possibly, that Raycraft and the vicomtesse have friends within the division itself. It is conceivable, don't you think?'

There, he had said it. Matlock continued to sip his tea, leaving Harry on tenterhooks. Had he sounded irrational? Or like a man seeking vengeance on the colleagues that had treated him so coldly in recent years?

When Matlock finally spoke, it was to answer a question with a question. 'What makes you trust this William Lamb so much?'

Harry considered the question. 'Instinct, partly, and my own suspicions of Raycraft's behaviour. William is an innocent who has stumbled on something inadvertently, I am sure of it.'

'You think you know innocence when you see it, Harry? Sometimes evil lurks behind the most virtuous countenance.'

'Not in this case, I believe.'

'And this Miss Shelton, what makes you trust her also? You say she worked for Pincott, a criminal in her own right.'

'True, but she struck me as ...' Harry paused.

Matlock pressed him. 'As what, Harry?'

Harry lifted the tea cup to his lips, although his insides felt frozen into solid rock. 'I don't know, sir, I was going to say honest, but that's probably not quite the right word.' He smiled, the muscles in his face stretching hard. 'I need to collect something from my desk, sir. I shan't be long.'

He forced himself to walk at a measured pace through the outer office. He heard Dolly's voice call to him from the other side of the room but pretended not to hear. When he reached the stairs he took the first flight slowly before picking up speed. How long had it been since he dictated that telegram and the address at Cromwell Road to Matlock's secretary? Ten minutes? Twenty? By the time he reached the front reception desk, he was running at full pelt.

Harry had not once mentioned Savannah's full name to Matlock, and yet the colonel had called her *Miss Shelton*. His instincts had been right: Raycraft and his cohorts did indeed have friends within the Metropolitan Police, only the rotten apple wasn't Dolly Cunningham.

It was far worse than that.

## CHAPTER THIRTY-SEVEN

Had Savannah done the right thing, trusting Harry Treadway? The minutes had turned to hours since he left. When she had boarded the ship in New York only months before she had made three solemn promises to herself: to stay away from big cities, to find somewhere warm to live where the colour of her skin gave no one cause to stare and, most importantly of all, to never trust another man ever again.

Doing well, Shelton.

William had nodded off in the armchair, relief giving way to weariness. She checked her watch – almost six o'clock. What was taking so long? Her feeling of unease was growing stronger. She got down on her knees, pulled up the loose floorboard at the side of her bed, and retrieved a belt of ammunition, securing it around her waist. Once again she checked the contents of her purse, as if expecting more coin to have miraculously appeared. She shook her head once more at her own stupidity. If only Pincott had paid her dues, she could have got the hell out of this stinking city days ago.

William awoke, stretching his arms above his head. He reached into his pocket. 'Do you have the time, Savannah? I must wind my watch.'

'Six. Your man Treadway left here three hours ago.'

'Good Lord, should we worry?' William's face had already answered his own question.

'I'm not sure we should have trusted him, William.'

William looked crestfallen, and she felt bad for voicing her suspicions, but her feet were getting colder by the minute and itching to run.

A series of rapid knocks sounded like gunfire on the main door below. William's eyes snapped into focus and they stared at each in other in the silence that followed, before a deafening crash announced that the door had been forced open.

She had been right all along. 'Damn that traitorous bastard!'

William was on his feet behind her as she unbolted the door. 'We can take the fire escape!'

The never-used fire escape led off the main landing. The rusty iron would likely pull away from the wall the moment she set foot upon it, but what choice did she have? Treadway and his cronies must already be at the first floor.

Savannah pulled out her Colt and cocked the trigger. 'Follow me.'

William grabbed his bag and followed her obediently on to the landing, his eyes wide like a startled deer's. As they reached the window that led to the fire escape, she could hear voices on the main stairwell below. The police had stopped their ascent and were questioning the neighbours, which made little sense. Even if Treadway weren't among them, surely he would at least have directed the others to the attic floor?

The window opened without sound. Savannah went first, deliberately landing heavily on the staircase with both feet, testing its robustness. If she was going to fall to her death, she'd rather it happened now, before she got her hopes up. The rusted iron grated awkwardly against the bare brick wall, bouncing under her weight, but the staircase held even after William had clambered out behind her.

William slammed the window shut and urged her on, 'Go!'

Savannah held her up her hand to shush him. 'They may have

stationed someone below.' She couldn't see that far down but it made sense to proceed with caution just in case. The steel rasped and squeaked as they descended. The building backed on to another just like it and she could see the face of a child in one of the windows, his mouth formed into a perfect 'o' as he watched them stumble down four flights. Thankfully, she could see no one beneath them. Maybe they could escape without incident after all? She tried to ignore the other voice in her head; what happens then, Shelton? Where will you run when every cop in this city is looking for you? One way or another, you're going to swing.

The ground was only five yards beneath them now and she picked up the pace, but as they turned on to the last flight of steps, the railings gave way with a shudder and the staircase pulled clean off the wall in a cloud of red dust. Savannah's gun clattered through the rungs and fell to the stony ground.

A sharp whistle punctured the air. 'You there! Stop!'

Savannah froze, clinging on to the ruptured staircase as two constables ran around the corner towards them. She could probably jump from here, roll and reclaim her gun before they were upon them. Behind her, William had begun to climb back up the staircase, but the window on the second floor was thrust open and a man in plain clothes leaned out, his gun glinting in the sunlight.

'William Lamb, you are under arrest! Do not move.'

The man had a clear shot at both of them. There was no way she could get to her gun in time. So this was it: Savannah Shelton's particular point of no return. She felt strangely calm, as if time itself had paused in honour of the enormity of the decision she needed to make. Death was no longer optional. She could surrender herself and wait for the noose to tighten inevitably around her neck, or she could die here, shot in the back, still running as she always had throughout her frightened, pointless life.

William read her decision before she was even aware that it had been made. He pleaded, 'No, Savannah! He *will* shoot you. Stay alive, I'm begging you.'

She tried to smile. 'If life was an option, trust me I would take it.'

He grabbed for her, but too late. She jumped backwards and rolled to the ground, two agonising yards from where her gun lay. As she reached forward, a crack of gunfire rent the air but she felt no pain. Maybe this was what it was like? She had always expected that death would hurt but now it made sense to her that it did not. It was life that hurt so much more.

A familiar voice shouted, 'Drop your weapon, Smiley! Next time it won't be a warning shot.'

Savannah looked up, astonished to see Harry Treadway standing a few yards away, revolver in hand.

He kicked her own gun towards her. She scrabbled forward, grabbed her Colt, and stood up, standing side by side with the detective who moments ago she had felt so certain had betrayed them.

The man called Smiley, his face no longer living up to his name, yelled in their direction. 'You're making a big mistake, Treadway, you have no idea what you're up against! No idea at all.'

'Drop your gun, Angus.'

Savannah aimed her weapon. Smiley looked between her and the detective, assessing his situation. Finally he broke into a grin, a forced demonstration of bravado. As he raised his hands above his head in surrender, his gun fell to the ground. Savannah directed William to pick it up. He jumped down from the tangled staircase and, with a look of extreme distaste, picked up the barrel between thumb and forefinger, holding it as far away from himself as he could.

Savannah and Harry marshalled all three police officers back to the attic floor and into Savannah's room, leaving William to loiter on the landing and attempt to explain the goings-on to the neighbours.

Savannah jangled the bunch of keys that would lock the men in once they departed. Her hands shook. Death had been near, close enough to touch, but yet again it had shifted from her path at the last, allowing her to pass once more.

She looked up. It was a pitiful and slightly ridiculous sight, the three policemen forming a glum party of slumped shoulders and furtive looks. Only Smiley looked Harry and Savannah in the eye. 'You can't win, Treadway.'

'I believe I just did.'

'A mere battle, not the war.'

'Tell me more about this war.'

'I don't think I shall, Harry, I don't think I shall.'

Savannah touched the detective lightly on the shoulder. It was time to go before reinforcements arrived. Besides, she had a burning question of her own. Why had Harry Treadway turned on his own men?

❧

## CHAPTER THIRTY-EIGHT

*S*avannah had passed it many times but had never been inside the Natural History Museum before. The thought of dead animals in glass cases seemed absurd to her. You could walk down any street in Whitechapel and find dead dogs, pigeons and, on the odd occasion, dead people left in the street to rot. Were rich folks so dull themselves as to find the dead stimulating?

It was Detective Treadway's suggestion, for the police were unlikely to search for fugitives in a museum. It was also one of his favourite spots and he knew it was open that evening for an event: a man called Darwin was giving a talk on something called evolution. On seeing her blank face, Treadway started on an explanation but she cut him off. 'Wherever I came from, it don't change the fact that I'm here.'

'Quite,' he said with a sad smile.

The main museum was quiet and they found themselves alone in a long gallery, surrounded by stuffed birds of all sizes and descriptions. Savannah found the location creepy in the extreme, but no one else seemed perturbed by their surroundings. Treadway slumped on to an empty bench and explained in gloomy tones exactly what had happened at Scotland Yard that afternoon. When he mentioned finding the handbill and the crude sketch of her face, she looked away, but he made no reference to her crimes.

William grew pale as the tale unfolded. 'I can scarce believe it, a senior officer of the Metropolitan Police involved in some cabal? It beggars belief.'

Savannah shrugged. 'Not where I come from it don't. An honest lawman is as rare as a sober judge.'

William sniffed at her analogy but the detective merely shook his head. 'I have been a fool. I fear that my conversation with Silas Matlock has made matters worse for all of us. I should have known something was amiss when he assigned me to the original case.'

Savannah sat on the bench next to him. 'Why did he? Why didn't he ask the Smiley guy, or that other stooge you mentioned, Cunningham?'

Treadway's shoulders visibly drooped. 'I'm afraid I have a reputation for . . . well, I would call it thoroughness, but others might think me slow, easily distracted. Matlock probably assumed I would get nowhere with it.'

'So they underestimated you.'

'Did they? Really?' His eyes turned to her. 'I'm afraid it is I who has been guilty of underestimating them. I should have smelled a rat earlier.' He rubbed at his nose as if to clear a passage for the odour he had missed.

William patted Treadway's sleeve.

Savannah attempted to jolt him from his reverie. 'Why don't you tell us about your case, detective? No point holding out on us now.'

Detective Treadway obliged with a deft summary of Phoebe Stanbury's murder, her obscure parentage and Edward Raycraft's madness, all of which pointed in one way or another to Sir Jasper Raycraft's villainy.

'Maybe we should look on the bright side?' said William. 'I have won a new ally to my cause, and we have uncovered the identity of yet another hidden foe. We have also managed to keep our best lead intact. You said nothing of the meeting with Habborlain tomorrow?'

'Only that we thought it planned, but Matlock didn't press me for details. Presumably he was waiting to have you in custody and see the note for himself.'

Savannah broke in, impatient with their discussion. 'We can't just skulk around the city. Who can you go to now? Who does Matlock work for?'

'The commissioner, and then the Home Secretary himself.'

'And would they trust you?'

He shook his head. 'They do not know me. I'm afraid I need to amass more evidence before I can go above Matlock's head.'

William stood up, his pretence at optimism abandoned. 'More evidence of *what* exactly? All we know is that this man Pincott is guilty of murder, kidnap and ... ravishment, and that he has done this at the behest of a French aristocrat who hunts me for no good reason at all. And then there is Sir Jasper Raycraft, too? Goodness, we haven't a clue, have we? And now we have all lost our homes, Savannah, even you! Surely they will turn on you now? Where shall we go?'

Savannah could hear the telltale rattle in William's throat, but she could offer no words of comfort. He was right. Having pooled their experiences, they were no further forwards.

A party of Sunday-school children entered the gallery, led by a stern-faced vicar carrying a bible. Detective Treadway rose and led them through to another room where they found a nook behind a row of glass cases. William's outburst of despondency had clearly shocked the detective into action. 'We have another day before we meet with your Mr Habborlain. In the meantime, there is much I can do. I will track down the vicomtesse and see what I can discover. I shall also telegraph a journalist friend and ask him to research a few things. I suggest the two of you take rooms at the Old Bell Tavern in Fleet Street and we will all meet again there tomorrow.'

As the detective spoke, Savannah stared intently at a cast model of a large, ugly bird. The brass plaque identified it as a dodo, announcing the fact of its extinction two hundred years earlier. She wasn't surprised it had lost its place on this earth. With its distended stomach, stupid face and short waddling legs, it was clearly not an animal with the least inclination to fight or ability to run. Well, to hell with that.

She spun back towards William and Harry. 'I will not lay low. I will not wait for them to come and find me like a sitting duck.' She ignored the detective's raised hand and continued, 'I am a person of many talents, Treadway, but with this face, hiding is not one of them. I don't give a damn what *you* do, but I'm going back to Whitechapel to get what I need, then I'm getting the hell out of this city.'

Both men stood mute before her. The look on William's face was hardest to take. 'I'm sorry, William. I can't help you any more.'

He looked down, nodded his head once. 'You should do as you must, but know I am for ever in your debt.'

'You paid me.'

He looked at her then, a smile ghosting his lips. 'Not enough.'

It was her turn to look away. 'I belong in the shadows, William.'

'I can accept it is where you are, not that it is where you belong.'

She wrapped her coat about her, suddenly cold. 'Good luck.'

William proffered his hand. 'I hope you find it.'

'What?'

'Home.'

She ripped her hand away and turned on her heel.

Harry watched her go, then pulled the crumpled paper from his pocket; had she really done those things? Try as he might, he could not see murder written on her heart.

He put the handbill away, and his hand touched the toy ship he had bought for David that afternoon. He thought of his arrangement to meet his daughter-in-law on Tuesday afternoon, the hope that had trembled briefly within. In the next few hours a Matlock stooge was bound to visit his family to enquire after his whereabouts and inform them of his latest perceived treachery. He felt sick, in his stomach and in his soul.

William put his hand on the detective's shoulder. 'The Breeding Association in Whitehall, that is where much of this connects. We should go there.'

Harry drew breath. 'I'm not so sure, William. Either of us could be recognised, we would be entering the lion's den.'

William's face was determined. 'Perhaps we should learn from Savannah. The lion's den is the last place they would expect us to go. Besides, where else does a Lamb belong?'

*I*n a corner of the Devil's Tavern on the damp Wapping foreshore, Savannah nursed a jug of warm ale. Home to smugglers and pirates, the tavern was where the outcasts of Whitechapel came, a deeper layer of fire and brimstone beyond the alleyways of the East End. Probably half the men in the room had found themselves on the wrong side of Obediah Pincott at one time or another. Despite the strong evening sun outside, the room was all shadows. People kept to themselves in this place, nursing wounds and planning vengeance. Today, she was no different.

She ate what she could, replenished her stock of tobacco and even closed her eyes for a while, but the hours were passing slowly and she was growing impatient. She cursed the late evenings of midsummer. She needed the cover of darkness to enter the compound, but the waiting was sapping her resolve and forming a puddle of dread in the pit of her stomach that threatened to drag her down. Maybe if she made her move before sundown, she could use the pharmacist to gain entry, which could make up for the absence of night to shroud her presence.

She drank the last of her ale. Only two things mattered: releasing the women from their chains and stealing enough money to buy a one-way ticket the hell out of there. She'd discovered from the landlord that there was a steamer leaving in the morning for Lisbon and they had space for passengers, no questions asked. The price was steep, but a small handful of gold coins would see her heading south.

She brushed aside the guilt she felt at abandoning William Lamb. She had expected him to plead with her, but he had grown stronger these last few days. Besides, he now had the support of Detective Treadway and was not so very helpless any more. Why should she care if a conspiracy of aristocrats and lawmen were acting together for some iniquitous purpose? Is that not what the rich folks always did? Power meant injustice everywhere, from Arizona to Westminster and Whitechapel. She could not fix the ways of the world.

She stood up and threw a shilling on the table. It was time to go.

When she entered the pharmacy on Dodd's Lane, the dwarf was teetering on a stepladder with his back to the door, rearranging the old glass jars and bottles on the shelves. As the bell clattered, he didn't turn around. 'Yeees?' he drawled, continuing with his task.

'An ointment of hollyhock spleen, if you please.'

He whirled about, almost toppling from his perch. 'You!'

Savannah cocked her pistol, jamming the barrel against his forehead.

His hands flew out to the side to balance himself and he swallowed hard.

'Oh look,' she said. 'Now we're the same height. I hadn't realised how ugly you were before.'

'*You* can talk.'

Savannah smashed the gun across his face and sent him sprawling to the floor. He crawled towards the corner, hands covering his head.

'Shall I tell you what is going to happen now?'

The pharmacist wiped his mouth and Savannah could see blood on his fingers. 'If you don't mind.'

'You're going to be my guide through this rat-infested warren. First, you're going to find me some gold. I don't need the whole stash, just a pouch or two – I'm not greedy. Then you're going to take me to the women and help me get them out of here. All of this you will miraculously achieve without us encountering anyone else. Is everything clear?'

The man nodded, but still asked the question, 'And if I refuse?'

'Well, let's just say that without kneecaps I think you might need more than a ladder to cope with everyday life.'

'He'll know I've helped you. He'll kill me anyway.'

'When we get back here, I'll tie you up. I'm even happy to hit you again if you'd like?'

'That won't be necessary.'

'Then let's go.' She shoved the Colt back into her pocket but kept it cocked and trained on her reluctant accomplice. 'And remember, bullets pass through leather just as easily as kneecaps.'

The pharmacist got to his feet, wiped the blood from his mouth and dusted himself down, his face petulant. 'You know it wasn't really essential to hit me the first time.'

'Oh, trust me, it was. Which way do we go?'

He walked back towards the shelves on the side wall and point- edly moved his stepladder to one side. She rolled her eyes with impatience as he leant into the middle shelf and pushed hard. She heard a click, and a portion of the wall, complete with shelves, swung forward into the room.

'How fancy!' She waved him forward. 'After you.'

They immediately began to climb a steep wooden staircase that led up from the secret door. The wood creaked under their weight. If he were leading her into a trap then whoever might be at the top would easily hear them coming. She prepared herself for the worst-case scenario. She had already decided that, were he to betray her, she would shoot him anyway, even at the cost of her own life. At least she might die with a smile on her face.

However, the corridor they found themselves in was empty. So far he had been true to his word. Savannah calculated that they were somewhere on the south side of the compound, but they would need to find their way to the western side to reach the women. As they crept down the corridor, the dwarf stopped and held up his hand. She could hear voices and laughter from behind a closed door further ahead, growing louder. She tapped him on the shoulder and pointed soundlessly to the door nearest to them, but he vigorously shook his head. Not trusting him, she clapped her hand over his mouth, opened the door and pushed him through into the room beyond.

As they entered, all hell broke loose. A cacophony of thumping and squawking greeted them and she turned to see the most astonishing sight – a dozen or so wooden crates containing the most brightly coloured birds she had ever seen, with ugly black beaks and plumes of feathers sticking up from their heads. Their wings beat angrily against their cages as they railed against their captivity.

'What the hell?'

'Parrots! Worth a fortune!' he yelled. 'I warned you not to come in here!'

She took her gun from her pocket and grabbed his shoulder, spinning him around and back towards the doorway. She hissed in his ear, 'Get out there and explain yourself. Stay where I can see you.'

With a shove she pushed him into the corridor, just as the door beyond was flung open on its hinges and a Scottish voice she recognised boomed, 'What the devil is going on?'

The dwarf did as he was told and stayed in view. 'I was just refilling their food trays. If you had half a brain you would know that even parrots have to eat.'

Savannah winced at his imperious tone but reminded herself that anything else would have been likely to raise suspicion. Dub obviously shared her opinion of the little man, for he simply grunted before retreating back into the room he had come from. She poked her head out of the doorway to check that the corridor was clear before motioning to the dwarf to move on. At the far end of the corridor, he turned in towards the courtyard, pausing before a heavy oak door.

He whispered loudly, 'We will have to go outside briefly to reach the lower gangway. It's maybe five yards to the door below.'

'Is there another way through?'

He turned around. 'What do you think?'

She resisted the urge to hit him again. 'I'm sure the women were higher up than this, not below.'

He raised his eyebrows. 'They are, but the money isn't.'

She paused. Her gut told her that up was a safer direction than down, but she nodded her head and steeled herself to enter the yard.

The pharmacist flung open the door, grabbed the rope beyond and marched down the fragile steps towards the shadows of a covered passageway a few yards below. Cursing under her breath, she stepped into the fading sun. The steps were linked with thick rope but they nonetheless swayed beneath her as she took them two at a time. Out of the corner of her eye she could see people in the yard beneath them but, superstitiously, she refused to look.

She reached the passageway, hidden from view once more. She let out her breath, catching the flash of a smile on the pharmacist's face. He had seen her fear and enjoyed it. She grabbed his hair and smacked his head against the boards, bringing her face close to his. 'Don't enjoy yourself too much, little man, I don't always keep my promises.' She smiled down at him, pleased to see his own smirk fading.

She spun him around and pushed him forward. After a few more twists and turns he brought her to another internal stairwell. She had lost her bearings in the randomness of the building's structure and she wasn't even sure if they hadn't doubled back on themselves by now. As the dwarf began to climb upwards, she grabbed his collar and pulled him back. 'Tell me where we're going!'

The man didn't respond, other than to point his finger at a blank wall opposite them where the staircase twisted round. Another hidden door perhaps? It seemed impossible – the bare wood revealed nothing. She pushed him forward again. On the half landing, he reached down to the skirting board and folded out a well-concealed lever made of the same splintering wood as the board itself. He jerked it forward and she heard a whining noise above her.

She jumped back just as a ladder dropped through the ceiling, stopping only inches from the landing itself. The dwarf cowered on the other side, trapped in the small space between the ladder and the wall.

'Let me guess, I wasn't supposed to get out of the way?'

'I . . .'

'And the money?'

With a trembling finger, he pointed upwards to the top of the ladder. 'Shall I go first?'

She nodded and he squeezed himself out of the corner and began to climb. He yelped when Savannah jammed the barrel of her pistol into his rear end. 'Remember, I could take out your spine and your manhood all with one bullet.'

The room above them was tiny and dimly lit from a skylight above. A black spider scuttled across the dusty pane and a large apothecary cabinet sat against one wall. The little man ran about, opening the drawers one after another. Savannah cocked her gun once more, not trusting him in the slightest. 'What are you looking for?'

'Ah!' The pharmacist spun around, holding up a small leather pouch. 'I trust this will be enough?'

She held out her hand and he threw it towards her. Opening the string with her teeth she saw the glint of gold within. She smiled. 'I can't thank you enough.'

He beamed back at her, rubbing his hands together. 'So, onwards and upwards?'

She pushed him roughly to one side and began to pull open the other drawers in the cabinet. He grabbed at her arm. 'No, please, there is no more. Come, we must waste no more time. Those poor women!'

She threw him off and continued her search. 'A secret stash, eh? What would Mr Pincott say?'

'Please, I beg you!'

Savannah ignored him and kept looking. Opening one of the larger drawers, she found a stack of faded photographs. 'Someone is a very, very naughty boy. Twins, eh?'

She threw them to the ground and he scrabbled around in the dust to retrieve them. Finally she found what she was looking for, three more leather pouches full of gold coin, more than she could possibly have hoped for. The dwarf sat on the floor, his arms cradling his precious photographs. 'That is all I have.'

Savannah could see the agony pulling at the corners of his mouth and judged he was telling the truth. She threw one of the pouches at his feet. 'I'm all heart.'

He picked up the bag of coin and pulled the string taut.

She pushed the other pouches deep within her pockets. 'Do you have a name?'

'Meriwether. Hercules Meriwether.'

Savannah snorted. 'Hercules? Thought he was a big guy? Your mother must have had quite a sense of humour.'

'She was hanged for grand larceny just hours after I was born. The joke of my name belongs to the warden of Newgate, not my mother.'

Savannah was silent for a while. 'Then I shall call you

Meriwether from now on. And if you play the game properly, and help me, then I shall consider handing another one of these back to you. Deal?'

The little man gave a hiccup. 'Deal.'

'So where next?'

He nodded towards the door behind them and she motioned him to go first. Wearily, he got to his feet and with care replaced the photographs in the cabinet before opening the door.

They emerged into a corridor that, with relief, she recognised from her previous visit with William. She followed Meriwether as he led her towards the room where they had come upon the two pregnant women. From here it would be a simple matter of retracing her footsteps from that night across the rooftops and out into the backstreets of Whitechapel. Would the women be able to make such a journey? They would have to try.

Silently, she passed the room where they had found the baby clothes piled carelessly in the centre of the room. She could almost still hear the ancient musical box that William had tripped over, causing it to play its disturbing and broken melody. As they approached the women's room, a piercing cry rent the air. The sound was unmistakable. One of the women was giving birth.

'Oh dear, dear, dear,' Meriwether muttered, pulling back and reversing into Savannah.

She stopped his retreat and whispered hoarsely in his ear, 'Surely you're not afraid of a little pain and blood?'

'And why wouldn't I be?'

'You're a pharmacist!'

He raised an eyebrow and his patronising tone returned. 'Really?'

Another cry interrupted their bickering and Savannah pushed him out of the way. She rattled the handle but this time the door was locked. A voice shouted through the door. 'We need hot water and towels! Immediately!'

'Can you let us in?'

There was a pause, then the voice spoke again, quieter this time. 'Who are you?'

Savannah felt a tugging at her sleeve but she ignored the little man. 'I came before. Is that you, Rebecca?'

'My name is Mildred. I ask again, who are you?'

It was the brave woman in the tartan dress who had called out to her in the courtyard. Mildred Whitfield. Pincott had dragged her away while Savannah did nothing. The memory of her inaction burned hotly. "I've come to help you. Stand back, I'm going to break the door down!'

Savannah stepped back to gather her momentum. At that moment, a crack of laughter tore through the corridor like thunder, a laugh she recognised and which caused her stomach to collapse within.

She whirled around, and came face to face once more with the twin skulls of Obediah Pincott, one arm snaked casually around Meriwether's neck, the dwarf's frightened face glistening white in the fading sunlight. Pincott's other hand held a long slim blade. Instinctively she pulled her pistol from her pocket but before she could raise her arm it was grabbed from behind. She twisted to see Dub leering down at her, his mouth full of cracked teeth like the misshapen gates of hell. He pinned both arms to her side and walked her forward until she stood before Pincott. He smiled then, a rictus grin, although he said nothing. He stroked the dwarf's hair as if he were a pet. She refused to look down, not wanting to see the dread fear she felt inside reflected back to her in the little man's eyes.

The silence was deafening and she could bear it no longer. 'I lost. You won. Get it over with.'

But it was not Pincott who answered. From somewhere behind him, a woman's voice, rich as butter, spoke softly, 'I don't think so.'

Pincott let go of Meriwether and grabbed Savannah by the hair.

He pressed the blade into her windpipe and pulled her forward to an open doorway behind him. She heard Meriwether's feet skitter away from them as, locked in their strange dance, Pincott pulled her inside.

It was the same room she had stumbled into nights before, although then it had been in shadow. The room was extravagantly furnished, with heavy drapes and glinting silverware. Daring to tear her eyes from Pincott's, she saw the vicomtesse arranged on a chaise longue, a vision of green velvet, white skin and fire-red hair. Savannah swallowed, almost causing Pincott's blade to pierce her skin. Dub had followed them into the room and placed her gun tantalisingly out of reach on a sideboard before tying her wrists together with what felt like wire biting into her flesh. Pincott pushed her down into a chair and Dub knelt to tie her ankles to the chair legs. All the while the young vicomtesse watched her, her face as masked as a statue's.

When Savannah was finally secured, Dub left the room and Pincott withdrew the blade. He backed towards the window and folded his arms, his expression saying it all: *this is not my show.*

The vicomtesse rose and took the blade from Pincott's hand before turning in Savannah's direction. As she approached, Savannah could smell something musky and sweet – jasmine, maybe, and power, as old as the world itself. Savannah became aware of her own scent: leather, tobacco and despair. She could feel her heart rising in her chest, so conscious of life now that death approached once more.

She kept her eyes averted, diving deep inside herself in search of a plan, but she found none. What a fool she had been to mistake the dream of escape for a possibility, to believe in another life. It was clearly not her destiny to die in her sleep under a starry southern sky. She would die in pain, in the dirt she had never really left behind.

The vicomtesse slid the blade beneath Savannah's chin and tilted her head. 'Where is he?'

Savannah forced herself to smile. 'Who?'

The young woman smiled back, her even white teeth like an Arabian thoroughbred. 'William Lamb. Your *friend.*'

'I have no friends.'

'Oh, you poor thing.' The vicomtesse tickled the blade down Savannah's neck, lingering at the base of her throat. 'Even a rabid mongrel deserves friends.'

'What do you want with him?'

The woman's eyes clouded. 'I wish to set eyes on him, and then . . .'

'Have you tired of our Mr Pincott already? Maybe rough isn't your type? Although surely William Lamb is a little young for you? There must be almost ten years—'

The slap was sharp and stinging, the woman's hand lightning quick. Savannah's eyes watered as the vicomtesse applied the knife to her skin once more, harder this time.

'Where is he?'

Savannah looked towards the window and thought of William, hopefully tucked up safely at the Old Bell Tavern. 'He's out there, hiding in the dark, just like Edward Raycraft, biding his time until he can hunt you down.'

The vicomtesse appraised her with cold eyes. 'He is weak. He is deformed. The mouse does not hunt the cat.'

'He does if he befriends a rabid mongrel.'

The vicomtesse trailed the knife downwards. Pincott had taken the woman's place on the chaise, his naked chest gleaming and his eyes black as mud as they locked on to the tip of the blade that now slipped through the channel between Savannah's breasts.

'How did you acquire that ghastly scar?'

'The last act of a dying man.'

'Did you kill this man?'

'Yes.'

'Ah, a warrior then.' There was genuine admiration in her voice. 'Perhaps we should breed you like a lioness.' The vicomtesse whipped up Savannah's skirts to reveal her bare legs. 'One might almost believe you have teeth down there.'

This time the knife trailed the length of Savannah's thigh, pushing into the worn linen of her underclothes. Savannah breathed as deep as she could, attempting to diffuse the red mist that filled her eyes, ears and nostrils. She knew this humiliation all too well. It was the easiest way to take power from a woman and, once taken, could not easily be wrenched back. Steeling herself, she looked up into the face of her abuser. The red-painted lips were parted as the woman's eyes tracked the progress of the blade across Savannah's skin.

Savannah shifted slightly from one buttock to the other. The vicomtesse seemed delighted by the ambiguous gesture and leaned her head forward, maintaining the rhythm of the blade. The knife caught Savannah's skin and she gasped, causing the vicomtesse to move closer again and whisper in her ear. 'Where is he?'

Savannah closed her eyes and whispered back, 'I really shouldn't say.'

'Oh, but you can tell me. Nothing bad will happen to you. Call me Adeline.'

'Adeline.' Savannah dipped her head submissively beneath the other woman's chin.

'Tell me where the mutt is hiding and release will be yours.'

The woman's use of that hateful term brought the red mist swirling back into view and, with a savagery that surprised even her, Savannah thrust her head backwards and brought it back down with a sickening crunch on to Adeline's own forehead. The vicomtesse sprawled backwards with a guttural cry, the knife clattering to the floor as her hands covered her face. Pincott leapt forward and helped the woman to her feet. The vicomtesse pushed him away, grabbing instead at a stack of linen napkins and dab-bing them across her bloodied nose. When she finally turned to face Savannah again, her watery eyes were bloodshot and anger had twisted her features into something like ugliness. 'You half-caste bitch!'

Savannah grinned, a smile she meant with all her soul.

The woman pushed her shoulders back and shook out her hair, but when she spoke to Pincott, her voice trembled. 'I must go now, I shall leave *this* in your capable hands.' She dabbed at her nose once more then sniffed, before looking back at Savannah and meeting her smile with one of her own, as cold as winter.

'Make her talk. Once the boy is found, skin her alive.'

William strode along the embankment with a determined step, conscious of Treadway's struggle to keep up. They had already used valuable time in taking a room at the Old Bell Tavern and sending a telegram to Harry's friend Finian at *The Times* before they set off for Whitehall. The faster William walked, the less he thought. Thinking had yielded little reward in recent days, and to dwell on the latest addition of Colonel Silas Matlock to the swelling ranks of his enemies was too much to bear.

The river teemed with traffic now it had reopened. Sailors with meaty, darkened forearms called out to each other, ropes were thrown and the air rang with the cacophony of ships' bells and horns and the slap of water against the debris of the river bank. William heard the music of it, chaotic and full of intent, matching his own discordant mood.

A few streets from their destination, the detective tugged on his arm. 'William, let us forge a plan before our arrival.'

'I am done with planning, Detective Treadway. Plans have a tendency to go awry. At least, mine do.'

'I really must insist,' the detective paused to draw breath, cleaning his spectacles with a handkerchief, 'that you call me Harry.'

William strode on, entering the street where they had followed the black and gold carriage that night. Today the rear gates were flung open and the building appeared to be a hive of activity. There was much commotion as a large dray cart attempted to reverse itself out of the courtyard. Uniformed maids and footmen bustled about carrying baskets and rolling barrels across the cobbles. A Gatti ice van waited in the street to enter the yard, the dappled horse calm behind its blinkers as it relieved itself without effort on to the street. The driver, a young man with a long face, rolled his eyes before grabbing a shovel and clambering down from his perch to clean up the mess. It was Harry who approached him as he went about his distasteful task. 'I say, could you tell me what all this is in aid of?'

The man touched his cap with a free hand. 'Afternoon, guv'nor. It's a ball, I believe. They have one every year, sir, but this one's in honour of the American bloke, Tin-something. I've brought the ice from King's Cross. Need to get it in the basement soon as they let me in.'

'And who are *they*, exactly?'

'Olympian Breeding, some kind of private club. Big, cold cellar is all I know.'

Harry thanked him for his time and turned back to William, who was closely studying a nearby lamp-post as if he might be required to write an essay discussing its attributes.

'William, you look rather ostentatious, old fellow.'

William's confidence had all but disappeared now they were here. The fluttering in his chest had returned alongside his darker thoughts: *I am hunted like an animal; my friends are dead or missing.*

They walked around to the front of the building where more people were coming and going from the front entrance. Despite the hubbub and the scale of the preparations, he was reminded that the building was not particularly grand in size and it seemed surprising that the Vice President of the United States would be attending a ball in such a diminutive space.

Harry pushed up the steps and towards the foyer. Clearly the detective had taken William's momentary aversion to planning to heart and William had no choice but to trail behind, tucking his left hand into his pocket despite the bandage.

The foyer of the building was as humble as its exterior and struggled to cope with the volume of people hurrying through. A Steinway piano was propped sideways on a low trolley as four men attempted to manoeuvre it around the tight corners and through a large pair of doors at the back of the hallway. A stand to their left held a wide array of printed leaflets, with titles such as *Breeding The Perfect Racehorse* and *Stock Management*. As they both perused the selection, William furtively stuffed various copies into his pockets, feeling like a common thief even though the leaflets appeared to be free.

'Please tell me that you are the sculptor!'

William turned towards the voice and was greeted by an old man shuffling towards him, his large frame bent with age although his voice held a strong note of authority.

William forced his face into a smile. 'And you must be?'

The man frowned. 'Mr Lampley. We corresponded, I believe.'

'Ah yes, how do you do, Mr Lampley, I am delighted to make your acquaintance at last.'

'You are *late*, sir.'

'I most humbly apologise.'

Lampley turned towards Harry who was still leaning over the leaflet stand. 'And who is this?'

'My assistant, Mr-Mr Stock.'

Lampley continued, 'Very well, the ice has just arrived, I believe. I will send someone to take you down to the store. I do hope you work quickly, sir.'

'Ah, ice! Of course!' William had read of such things. 'I was thinking a swan or is that considered old hat these days?'

The butler gave William a withering glance. 'I really wouldn't know, sir.'

'Lampley!' A jolly-looking fellow with copious whiskers strode through the front door.

The old butler turned slowly. 'Ah, Colonel Matlock, we were not expecting to see you so early.'

William gasped. Harry still had his back to the room, but William instinctively moved to stand in front of him.

'Just thought I would check up on preparations. We need this evening to be our best yet, Lampley.'

'Of course, sir. All provisions are in and the kitchens are at full gallop. The orchestra has been rehearsing all afternoon and the ice sculptor has just arrived.'

William tried not to cringe as Matlock turned in his direction. He felt Harry flinch behind him and desperately hoped that he wouldn't give in to the urge to run. It took all his nerve to return Matlock's sunny smile with one of his own.

'Jolly good, and what works of wonder might we see this year?'

'Swans.' William hoped the crack in his voice had not been too noticeable.

Matlock frowned. 'Didn't we have a swan last year?'

'Or dogs if you would prefer?'

'Dogs?'

'Yes: poodles, spaniels, beagles . . . and such.'

Matlock raised his eyebrows and turned back towards Lampley. 'Very well, I shall be in my room before our guests arrive. Perhaps you would be so good as to arrange some tea?'

Harry's sigh of relief was audible as Lampley and the colonel skirted the piano and followed the direction of activity through the double doors and beyond. The detective muttered, 'That was too close for comfort, but this proves we have come to the right place. The battle we seek is here, all right.'

William felt a wave of equal exhilaration and fear churn through him.

A maid came rushing through the doors towards them, almost

tripping over the legs of one of the men still attempting to navigate the Steinway to its destination. She approached William. 'I'm sorry, sir, I don't have time to take you down to the storeroom, I have to get these invitations over to the Royal Belvedere before nine. Do you think you could find your way on your own, sir? You have been here before, have you not?'

The girl did indeed look flustered, her face as crimson as the two embossed cards she waved in her hand. They were thick and blood-red in colour and the few words they contained were edged in gold.

*Cornelius Tinbergen greets*
*The Families*
*The Red Ball*
*1st July*

Who were the families? William wondered.

Harry stepped forward. 'No matter, my dear, we shall indeed make our own way.'

'Oh, thank you, sir!' the girl cried as she skittered from the hall.

William whispered to Harry, 'We should leave! This is too dangerous for you with Colonel Matlock here!'

The detective smiled. 'We have come this far, William. Remember, too, that I am armed. Let us be brave.'

Brave, yes, let us be brave. A quality he had never previously required. Was he brave? Could he be? Wherever she was, Aunt Esther's mettle would have been sorely tested. He must attempt to match her courage with his own.

With William in the lead, heart jumping in his chest at the mere thought of discovery, they followed the direction of traffic and through the double doors beyond. They found themselves in a simple antechamber, another set of double doors in the far wall.

The piano had been abandoned here, precariously balanced on the small trolley that was now missing one wheel.

At that moment the far doors banged open and two pairs of soldiers strode through. Despite the panic in his chest and the thrumming in his ears, he recognised the red uniform of the German guard. They were followed by two of Tinbergen's navy personnel, resplendent in their white uniforms, glowing even in the dark. William smiled weakly as they marched past, barely sparing them a glance.

Once they had left, William calmed himself and looked about him. To his right was a familiar bust atop a marble plinth, identical to the one he had seen in Habborlain's drawing room: *Plato, the father of all of us*, the old man had said. Beside the sculpture was a small table covered in a red cloth. As his eyes adjusted to the shadows, what he saw made him gasp aloud.

A simple wooden casket sat upon the table, two as yet unlit candles either side, like a shrine. It was the casket that he had last seen on his very own bedside table and which Mr Bridge had asked him to keep safe. He turned around, eager to inform Harry, but Harry put a hand on his shoulder and gave him a deliberate and reassuring nod. Of course he had guessed already; the Seed of Life symbol was clear to see.

William opened the lid and quickly flipped through the papers within. The list of names was no longer there, but the older documents he hadn't understood seemed to be present.

He closed the lid as the detective whispered in his ear, 'When we come back this way, we shall take it!'

They had no idea what lay beyond the next set of doors. A whole army could be lying in wait for them. *Well, so what?* Savannah's voice nagged at him. *Would you rather wait until they hunted you down?* To hell with that.

He looked at the casket once more. What secrets did those dusty pieces of parchment hold, those ancient symbols scratched in faded ink? He thought back to Mr Bridge's office, the unbearable fear etched across his employer's face, the tears he shed even as he reached for his gun. William's hunger for answers burrowed deep, determined and ravenous.

Going first once more, William gently opened the door at the end of the room, and what he saw beyond took his breath away.

## CHAPTER FORTY-ONE

*In* assuming the modestly proportioned building could not house a ballroom of any scale, William had ignored the possibility that the building might continue *downwards*, below the streets of the city. He stood at the top of a grand oak staircase. On each step was a shining candelabra, complete with red candles, currently being lit by a footman. At the bottom was a cavernous room, twenty feet high and at least a hundred yards long. Even from here he could see the rich detail of the painted walls, like frescoes in a church. At the far end, a full orchestra filled the stage, intently rehearsing a Viennese waltz while a frowning conductor cast spells with his baton. It was late and the ball must surely be commencing soon.

Servants scurried about on the ballroom floor. William caught sight of the elderly butler, who seemed bewilderingly adrift amid the bustle, but saw no sign of Colonel Matlock. He signalled Harry to join him. It was time to explore.

At the bottom of the stairs, William approached the first fresco that adorned the high walls. The painting depicted the birth of a child, the mother's face rapturous as she held the newborn up to the sky, while an elderly man reached lovingly down.

Harry read the inscription aloud. 'The birth of Alexander the Great.' William thought of the painting of Alexander he had seen above Habborlain's fireplace. *It is all connected, don't you see?*

Harry continued, his nose wrinkling beneath his spectacles as he examined the painting. 'Ah yes, many believed his parentage to be divine, sired perhaps by Zeus himself.'

'Zeus?'

'The Greek god of gods.' The detective smiled at him, his tone affectionate. 'Where have you been, young Mr Lamb?'

Hiding, William thought, or rather being hidden, *all my life.*

'Look!' Harry pointed to a corner of the fresco.

The rock upon which Alexander's mother was leaning had been carved with the Seed of Life symbol. Now that Harry had pointed it out, William saw it everywhere. Even the ceiling above their heads showed the symbol in sharp relief, repeated over and over again. He moved on to the next fresco, and then the next: more scenes depicting the childhood of Alexander the Great.

Meanwhile Harry scouted the room, his trained eye clearly analysing the space around him and the frenzied movements of the busy staff. 'Come, William, follow me. If there is a ballroom then there shall be a library. And libraries invariably reveal much about their owners.'

There were no obvious doorways that led elsewhere from the ballroom, other than the panelled section of wall beneath the stairs that swung open as the various staff came and went. It was worth a try – the kitchens would service all areas of the building, not just the ballroom. They pushed through the panelled door and into the busy servant's corridor beyond. Tables were stacked high with crates of champagne and a red-faced man in a cook's uniform was bellowing orders. On seeing the two guests enter, his demeanour shifted to one of polite deference. 'May I help you, sirs?'

Harry jumped in. 'We are looking for the library, the vicomtesse wishes to see us.'

'You've taken the servant's route, sir, but no matter. If you continue to the end here then turn right beyond the door, you will reach the rooms of the seven. You cannot miss the library from there, sir.'

They marched quickly down the corridor. Once they were out of earshot, William whispered, 'The rooms of the seven?'

'Let us see what we can discover.'

They turned right into another servant's passageway, which was empty. It was dimly lit and stuffy, the humidity of the night air reaching down into the earth, and William once more struggled to draw breath. They twisted and turned, following the hallway to its end. William began to wonder if they would ever find their way out of here again. Finally, they came to another door, panelled like the first, and they stopped to gather themselves in preparation for whatever lay beyond.

'If we hit a tight spot, I'll handle it, William.' The detective patted the pocket where he kept his revolver. 'You focus on keeping safe. Run if you have to.'

William nodded. If he had been asked to conjure an image of his ideal knight in shining armour, he would no more have chosen a diminutive old man in a polka dot bow tie than a skinny girl with a scar and a bad temper.

They found themselves in another corridor, this time much grander, and lit with large oil lamps that hung down from the high ceiling. Everything was painted a dark grey, which swallowed much of the light. Harry moved forward and William followed, his attention caught by the doors they passed to their left. Harry had slowed his pace, observing closely the names spelled out in large brass letters on each door. The lettering was in a language William didn't understand, presumably Greek, but helpfully each door also displayed another plaque, smaller and less ornate, in English. William recited the names as they moved along the corridor and past the first six doors – *Warrior, Artist, Scientist, Protector, Bookkeeper* and *Investor*.

'The Bookkeeper! Pincott's men referred to the casket as the Bookkeeper's box!'

'So the Bookkeeper is, or rather *was*, Mr Bridge?'

William didn't respond. The thought of Mr Bridge in this mysterious place was hard to comprehend. His hand reached out to the doorknob and he looked across to Harry. The detective nodded his head, reaching into his pocket as he did so.

The room was empty and quite dark. The light from the corridor illuminated a large walnut desk in the centre of the room. On the desk sat a box of Mr Bridge's favourite peppermints and the sight brought unbidden tears which William let fall. When Harry finally had the oil lamp on the desk lit, William brushed them away and moved to close the door.

The walls were hung with huge oak panels, engraved with tiny gold writing. William's eyes struggled to focus as he approached one of the boards. Thousands of names were etched across the walls, connected with thin gold lines, like an enormous family tree. There were three sections, each headed with one of the words he had seen on the doors: *Warrior*, *Artist* and *Scientist*.

'Look!' whispered Harry. 'The Raycrafts are here!'

Sir Jasper and his son Benjamin were the last names etched on the *Scientist* board. Harry went on, 'How strange, though, that there is no mention of Sir Jasper's sister Sybil. This is not a conventional family tree.'

Harry continued to peruse the names higher up the panel, exclaiming at one point, 'Pascal! Even Bacon!'

William wandered away, daunted by the sheer volume of information. Approaching the *Artist* panel, his attention was caught immediately by the last name etched there: Ambrose Habborlain, a thin line linking him to his forebear, George Gordon Byron.

Could Lord Byron really have been Habborlain's father?

Then he remembered something else. 'The list of names! I remember there were three columns. A hundred or so names in total.'

Harry continued to gaze around him at the web of connections. 'There are thousands of names here. Maybe Bridge just kept a copy of the current generation, those still alive. Bridge's list may be gone, but this is the original record, I would wager. But what does it mean, to be part of these families?'

Footsteps sounded out in the corridor. The marching beat and the telltale clack of spurs sent William diving towards the lamp to extinguish the flame. 'Von Rabenmarck's guard!' he hissed unnecessarily to Harry.

They waited until all they could hear was their own ragged breathing.

'We should move on,' said William.

'Perhaps when the ball is in full swing we may return and examine this room further.' The detective sounded wistful.

William went first into the corridor and they crept forward as they approached the seventh and final door. William's gaze was drawn up ahead, where the corridor opened into a vast cylindrical library, with a spiral staircase enclosed in wood set in the middle. The staircase led both upwards and downwards to another floor below. The circular wall of the library was lined with books and a balcony ran all the way around, dividing the space into something more navigable. The library was quite some feat of engineering, and William wondered when it had been built. He had almost reached the entrance when Harry grabbed at his arm and pulled him back towards the last door in the corridor. The name on the room made him shudder.

*Finder.*

Just then they heard more footsteps approaching from the other end of the hallway. Harry grabbed at the door handle and pushed into the room, but before William could join him, a voice boomed across the hallway, 'Can I help you?'

William turned to see Colonel Silas Matlock approaching along the corridor. His heart lurched in his chest. This is it, he thought, I am undone.

'Should you not be hard at work in the ice store, young man?'

The colonel stopped outside the room marked *Protector* and grasped the handle.

William took a gamble. 'Ah, yes. However the Finder asked me to meet here to discuss the designs.'

Matlock's face split into a wide grin, his rosy cheeks full of bonhomie. 'I bet she did, lad, I bet she did. Enjoy yourself!' Throwing a final lascivious wink in his direction, Matlock opened the door and stepped through it, leaving William to follow Harry into the Finder's room.

As soon as the door was closed he whispered excitedly, 'The Protector! Of course! Matlock is the protector of the group, the one who allows their villainy to go undetected. We have a piece of the puzzle, Harry!'

'Two pieces, I believe. The Finder is a *she*.'

The vicomtesse. *The Finder.* Both Habborlain and Mr Bridge had obviously been terrified of her, and now she hunted him too.

As William turned from Harry he shrieked, clamping a hand over his mouth as he came face to face with a life-size statue in white marble.

Harry bent down to read the inscription. 'It is Olympias, mother to Alexander the Great. This is old, William, very old, possibly from the time of Alexander himself.'

The room was lit with candles, a soft Persian carpet lay beneath their feet, and a huge divan stacked with cushions sat against one wall.

'I say, William, look at this!'

Harry was grinning broadly, standing with his arms folded in front of a series of framed sketches. As William approached, he could see the sketches were simply done in an oriental style, figures of men and women in unusual poses. Very unusual poses, in fact.

'Are they acrobats of some sort?'

Harry laughed. William shushed him but the detective would

not stop chuckling like a little boy. 'It is the *Kama Sutra*. I have had cause to seize copies before now. It is the very definition of obscenity. They are positions, intended to increase enjoyment of *the act*.'

William blushed, but moved in closer nonetheless. Was there no end to this woman's depravity?

'They are beautiful, are they not?'

William spun around.

The vicomtesse was standing in the doorway.

~

## CHAPTER FORTY-TWO

*S*avannah watched the blood drip from her arm and spatter the dusty floor, each red bead landing with a rhythmic patter, tick-tock. She ached to raise her hands above her head and stop the flow but both her arms were held out to her sides, tethered with rope to rough wood panels.

Pincott sat before her now, his long limbs stretching out before him, his mouth pulled wide in a yawn. Throughout the night he had tried many tactics to force her to reveal William's whereabouts. At first, he had simply beaten her, calmly and without relish: a blow to the stomach, followed by a kick to the head, then another to her ribs. One of her molars had been smashed to nothing, and she was certain that one of her ribs was broken. She kept her breathing shallow to avoid the intense pain that came with any sudden movement. At the end of each blow, he had asked the question *where is he?* After a while, she had stopped replying *I don't know*, preferring to retreat far inside herself.

Then Pincott had changed his approach, pouring a large dose of laudanum down her throat, presumably hoping it might weaken her resolve and loosen her tongue. But she had simply grinned at him, enjoying the release from pain that the drug brought her and, at one point, nodding off despite the discomfort of her position.

Now, he had raised the stakes once more. Her coat had been removed and thrown to the floor. She saw the bulge in her pockets where the pharmacist's secret stash of wealth still lay, barely yards away, so near and yet so far. Her bare arms exposed, Dub had helped Pincott to string her up. With a razor, Pincott had then slashed both of her forearms with a surgeon's accuracy, ensuring she would bleed to death slowly enough to give him the answers he wanted: answers she had no intention of giving him. Something told her that he knew she would never give William away. He was simply putting off the moment when he would have to kill her and be done with it.

They held each other's gaze, but Savannah felt her left eyelid closing, swollen by the evening's beating. The silence was broken by a hesitant knock at the door.

'Come.'

Savannah looked up to see JJ enter the room. She had not seen the boy for days, had almost forgotten his existence and the long hours the two of them had spent together in the garden at Red Lion Square. His eyes visibly widened to see her hanging there, beaten and bruised, bleeding to death. 'Shelton?'

She stopped herself from smiling, knowing that her bloodied mouth would scare him even more.

'Well?' Pincott barked at him.

JJ turned towards his master, clearly struggling to find his voice. 'Dub says he's happy to take over if you want.'

Pincott smiled in Savannah's direction. 'I bet he is.'

JJ remained rooted to the spot.

She couldn't bear the look on his face. 'Get out, JJ.'

The boy backed away towards the door, then turned and ran. Pincott chuckled to himself. 'Maybe I let Dub in here. Maybe he make you talk.'

'And maybe I'll bite his manhood clean off,' she spluttered.

Pincott laughed even harder. 'Maybe you will, Miss Shelton.' He wiped his eyes and continued in a more serious tone, 'Tell me this, I am curious, why do you sacrifice yourself for this William Lamb?'

'I don't know where he is.' Her tongue felt huge in her mouth.

'Don't insult me, Shelton. I know you know. But now I ask different question.' He shifted in his chair, allowing his greatcoat to fall open and reveal the tattooed portrait on his chest. 'My client wants him. You, it would seem, will die for him. So tell me, what is so special about William Lamb?'

Now it was Savannah's turn to laugh. She felt light-headed, whether it was the residual effects of the drug or the gradual leaching of her blood she didn't know. 'Well, you see, Mr Pincott, that is the very thing. You have put your finger on it.' She coughed and spat once more. 'There is *absolutely nothing* special about William Lamb, nothing at all. And there is nothing special about me, or you, or that evil whore whose petticoats you trip over. We will all smell the same when we are dead.'

He got to his feet and Savannah steeled herself not to flinch as he approached her. But instead of another blow, he raised his hands and began to clap, the noise like single gunshots rippled through her. 'Well done, Shelton. I am impressed. It is new experience, for which I say thank you. Thank you, Savannah Shelton.'

He stood back and took the razor once more from his coat. 'And now I think it is time to end it, before you change your mind and try to save yourself. That would not do.'

'Your name,' Savannah whispered, 'you promised. The last thing I hear before I die.'

Pincott cocked his head to one side. 'Indeed. You want a bedtime story. I shall tell it.' He held out his coat and turned around slowly. 'This coat? Belonged to the Cossack who plunge a bayonet into my father's belly. I stab the man with the knife we use to scrape potatoes. We were cooks, you see, for the British. But in Crimea, they send us in first. Drag us out last. If at all. That day I came back alone. With this.'

Savannah flicked her eyes downwards, seeing the familiar coat for the first time, the stains still visible.

'Captain Obediah Pincott. A good man. Took pity on the skinny orphan in the greatcoat. Brought me here. Offered kindness. But I had no need for kindness. Just his two gold sovereigns and his name.' Pincott stepped forward, his face inches from hers. 'You see, Shelton, we all have stories.'

Her head felt heavy and her words ran together. 'Mine is better than yours. Wanna hear it?'

Pincott laughed, stopping as suddenly as he started. 'My name is Yaroslav.'

Her death knell. She felt the razor touch her neck.

'Is a shame, to have to do this.'

The razor flashed before her eyes and the next thing she knew, her left arm had been released from its bonds. He had cut the rope, not her neck!

He looked into her eyes. 'If you'd told me what I asked, then you would be dead already.'

Had her resistance won his admiration? And how long would that last? But then it was another voice she heard.

'Stop! Drop the thing in your hand. Drop it now!'

The razor clattered to the floor and Pincott held his hands in the air, a look of delighted surprise on his face as he backed away, his eyes glittering. JJ stood by the door, Savannah's Colt bobbling around in the air as he attempted to hold it steady. Her chest twisted in fear. Pincott would not be intimidated by a small boy waving a gun around. Surely JJ had now signed his own death warrant. 'You don't have to do this, JJ, take the gun and run. Now!'

'I can't let him hurt you, Shelton.'

*Oh but you can. You should.*

He was crying, and almost dropped the gun as he wiped tears from his eyes. With a small boy's ferocity, he shouted to Pincott, 'Untie her! I'll shoot if I have to.'

Pincott grinned; he had still not turned around to face JJ. 'I suggest you do not pull the trigger. You are as likely to hit her as me.' Despite this accurate assessment of the situation, he nonetheless stepped forward and untied Savannah's other wrist.

Savannah was confused. Why was Pincott doing this? He could have ended her life seconds earlier and he could take the boy with one fling of his meaty hand. With her own hands free, she raised them above her head, desperate to stop the drain. Pincott knelt on the floor before her, causing JJ to nervously step closer with the gun. 'What are you doing?'

Pincott touched Savannah's hem and pulled roughly at her petticoat. 'Tourniquet.'

JJ licked his dry lips, clearly as confused as she was by Pincott's submission.

Pincott used his teeth to tear off two strips, tying each one tightly just above her elbows. Then he used the remaining fabric to bind the cuts he had made to her arms.

He was letting her go. She gathered her mind together from the far corners of her brain. Only moments earlier she had prepared for death, now it seemed she must live once more.

Responding to JJ's wild gesturing, Pincott obediently backed into the corner, hands raised, grinning from ear to ear. Savannah winced as she whipped her coat on, before checking the pockets for the pouches of coin and then taking the gun from JJ's hands. She felt unsteady on her feet, but even drugged and beaten, she knew her handling of the weapon would be more adept than JJ's. Pincott looked unperturbed at the Colt's change in ownership.

She ordered JJ to tie Pincott to the rafters in her place, using her free hand to tentatively explore the damage to her ribs.

Pincott smiled politely as JJ fumbled with the ropes. He yanked his left wrist and JJ's knot began to fray. 'You might wish to do this one again, boy.'

Savannah stepped forward. 'Why are you doing this? Why are you helping me?'

'You know why.'

She shook her head. 'I do not.'

The smile slid from his face, his death's head stare returning. 'You amuse me.'

No matter how many of her nine lives she lived, Savannah would never understand the man before her. 'I need information before I go. Where are they holding William's aunt?'

'The Raycraft factory. The basement.'

She wanted to ask more, so much more, but he had already confessed by his own questions to her that he had no idea why the vicomtesse sought William. JJ tugged at her sleeve, but still she was reluctant to leave. 'Did they ever tell you why they are breeding these women?'

JJ's bonds were still loose enough to allow Pincott to shrug at her question. 'Is obvious. Unlike me, unlike you, they fear death and think to conquer it. Every animal in this world believes propagation lends them immortality.'

She had never heard him so articulate. She felt a compulsion to stay and talk, sensed he had answers to questions she had yet to conceive of, but she felt the tug once more from JJ. They needed to leave. She held Pincott's gaze as she backed towards the door. How long would this stay of execution last? He had let her live on a whim, the ground could easily shift again.

The moment they were out of the room, she cuffed JJ sharply around the head, her injured rib burning as she did so.

'What was that for?'

Savannah said nothing as they approached the room where the women had been. Remembering the lock, she stood back and raised her leg, preparing to smash the door down with as much force as her weakened body could muster. Out of the corner of her eye, she saw JJ wave something towards her. A key.

She grabbed it from him, twisted it in the lock and threw the door back. Two of the women stared at her open-mouthed while another screamed in horror. Savannah recognised the screaming woman as the one who spoke no English. The last time she had seen her, the woman had been heavily pregnant; now she nursed a scrawny infant at her breast. Savannah moved towards her but the woman in the tartan dress had already reached across the bed and slapped her hand across the woman's face.

Savannah smiled. 'Mildred Whitfield. We meet again.'

Mildred returned her smile uncertainly. For a moment Savannah though she might have forgotten their encounter in the yard below several days earlier, but then she realised what had caused Mildred's forced smile. Savannah was suddenly conscious of the thick tangle of black hair that fell about her face, matted with blood. Her skirt was ripped and she could feel the crust of blood forming around her mouth. Even for her, she suspected, her appearance right now had plumbed new depths.

'We have to hurry. I can get you out across the rooftops. I know the way.'

'I'm ready,' said Mildred. 'I have nothing to take with me.'

Savannah looked her up and down. The woman stood ramrod straight, a determined set to her jaw. Whatever she had been through, she was not broken yet. Rebecca, in contrast, slumped next to her, her hand on her round belly and a faraway look in her eyes. The foreign woman had remained in her bed, her bloodless face glistened as she held her newborn child in spindly arms.

Mildred spoke in a low voice. 'The birth has left her weak and I fear for the worst. Nor would she want to come with us. I do not think she wishes to save herself.'

Savannah ignored the judgement in Mildred's voice and turned to Rebecca. 'Can you make her leave?'

Rebecca met her gaze and shook her head. Even with the preoccupation of escape, Savannah realised she had never seen such emptiness in someone's eyes.

## CHAPTER FORTY-THREE

They had not heard the vicomtesse enter.

Harry's hand moved to his pocket, an action that William tried and failed to gain assurance from. He swallowed down the rattle in his chest that threatened to explode the air from his lungs. Stay calm, he willed himself, she has not seen me before.

Dimly he was aware of a ballgown of red satin, her pale shoulders and arms bare except for the gloves that reached above her elbows and her loose red curls that flipped across her bosom as she moved. She carried a bottle of champagne in one hand and seemed to sway slightly even as she leant heavily on the open door. She wore a mask the colour of her dress, her ruby mouth a perfect bow beneath, her expression impossible to read.

So here he was, face to face at last. Part of him wanted to reveal himself, to shake her fragile bones until she gave up the answers he so dearly sought. The bigger part of him was too terrified to even breathe. Surely it was written all over his face, shouting his name, *I am the one you seek.* He could feel his lungs constrict but he would not let his body betray him, not this time. He cleared his throat, his voice quaking. 'We wished to see your collection—'

She waved him to a stop with an impatient hand and moved yet closer. He could almost feel her breath upon him, even as he felt Harry tense at his side, no doubt ready to draw his gun if the occasion demanded. Her alabaster skin glowed, as pale as the statue that stood behind in her shadow.

William stared at her full red lips as they parted. Her voice was soft. 'Why have we not met before?'

'It is my first time at the ball.'

'Well, how wonderful!' The woman's attempt at a twirl was more of a stagger and Harry put out a hand to steady her. She shooed him away. 'Your manservant is most forward. Now tell me,' she raised the champagne bottle to her mouth, 'to which house are you related?'

William thought of Ambrose Habborlain. 'Artist,' he lied.

'Really!' She looked at him closely then and it took much effort not to wither under her gaze. Her voice dropped to a seductive whisper. 'You are too handsome to be of that house.'

Up close, he could see now that the mask only partly hid a deep bruise that spread from her cheek across the bridge of her nose. Her examination of him deepened and he could almost see the frown behind her mask. He barely heard her whisper. 'But I know you, do I not?'

He had to distract her. 'Someone hurt you.'

'Someone did.'

'Perhaps you should lie down. You have a long evening ahead.'

She smiled and moved closer, her champagne breath against his ear. 'Maybe you should join me?'

She sought his eyes once more and William tried to look away, uncertain what to do as this astonishing intimacy unfolded, but his feet felt frozen in his shoes. Her face was lifted towards his, their lips barely inches apart. The vicomtesse stumbled backwards and William caught her, encircling her waist with his arms and carrying her towards the divan. He laid her down, taking the champagne bottle from her hand and placing it on the floor. As he knelt beside her, she touched her hand to his brown curls. 'Tell me you love me.'

He said nothing. Her eyes were beginning to close and William was astonished to see tears seeping beneath her mask as she murmured, 'Stay with me.'

'Of course,' he said, uncertain as to why.

She smiled and seemed contented as she drifted off, her hand dropping from his head to the floor. William released a long breath, his mind a tumult of conflicting emotions and thoughts. If this was the lion's den then he had just encountered the lioness – the woman who had exhorted Pincott to kidnap his aunt and slay the defenceless women of Whitechapel. Yet her beauty was a thing of wonder, and the childlike vulnerability of this loveless creature touched him. How unlike the old world the new world was: the former had been made of the simple and the obvious, but the latter swirled with complexity, shifting from one thing to the other, unknowable.

'We should go,' whispered Harry.

William stood, pulling himself back to the moment. 'That was unexpected.'

The detective looked at him, then back to the woman on the divan. 'Let her sleep it off while we explore the library. Then we may return for our answers. That is why we are here, is it not?'

William felt admonished. He had been too surprised by her arrival and too overawed by her presence to press their case. Why had he not revealed himself, confident that Harry's gun would have yielded answers? He had not thought quickly enough, and the shame of what he was to her, the fear of hearing the word *mutt* once more on that beautiful tongue had in part stopped him.

He nodded at Harry. He would not be so overcome on their return to this room. With a purposeful step William pushed past into the corridor and in the direction of the great library. As they neared the central staircase, William saw to his amazement that the stairs circled downwards for a number of floors. He leant forward over the balcony and saw the staircase dip down into darkness. Just how many floors were there? A wave of cool dry air reached him from below. Harry too seemed entranced by the seemingly bottomless nature of the library, moving to the circular wall and beginning to peruse the books there. 'Good Lord, William, what a collection! Let us go deeper, see what the basement holds. That is where the secrets will be kept!'

Just as they entered the spiral staircase, a shout rang out behind them. 'William Lamb, you are under arrest!'

A voice that had yelled the same thing once before and sent a chill through his veins. Sergeant Smiley and Colonel Matlock were both running through the corridor towards them. Harry snapped into action and pushed William upwards. William ran, keeping his head as low as he could beneath the solid banister that enclosed them. A shot rang out and he thought he could feel it whistle past his hair as he forced himself to the top of the staircase. He reached ground level, his sense of direction now hopelessly confused.

Harry flew past him with a shout of: 'This way!'

An open doorway and into yet another corridor. There was a red glow up ahead. They ran towards it. The glow grew brighter and they re-entered the ballroom at the top of the sweeping staircase that had led them down. They skittered to a halt. As Harry fumbled with the doors that led into the antechamber, another shot rang out and he heard a cry of 'Halt!' from the ballroom below, this time in a chilling German voice. The whole building now seemed alive to their presence.

The doors refused to open. William raised his leg and kicked hard. The doors flew back with a loud crash, yielding cries of pain from the two German guards stationed beyond. William and Harry ran headlong into the antechamber, surprise their only ally. Ahead of them, the abandoned grand piano listed on its side.

Harry swooped and grabbed the casket that still sat on the small table and dashed towards the foyer.

William could hear the chaos behind him, the shouts and clatter of weapons, as he dashed hopelessly towards freedom. He almost lost his footing on the waxed floor as he passed the piano. An idea formed and, without further pause, he turned around.

From the other side of the room, a German guard stopped in his pursuit and raised his rifle, training it in William's direction.

Harry had reached the front door and yelled back, 'William! Come on!'

William leant against the Steinway and pushed with all his might. The soldier fired, clipping one of the piano's legs in a shower of sawdust, and began to reload just as Sergeant Smiley came running into the room. William gritted his teeth and roared, mustering all of his strength. The piano toppled briefly then fell with a crash, breaking into pieces that skidded across the floor towards William's pursuers.

William turned and ran through the foyer, vaguely aware of the elderly butler gripping the wall, his mouth open, as William raced past and out into the city streets.

## CHAPTER FORTY-FOUR

*O*ut on the rooftops, they made slow progress. It was a humid night and all three women felt the exertion of their journey. Rebecca was heavily pregnant, but even so seemed reluctant to strive for freedom. Mildred chided her listlessness and pushed her forward as JJ pulled at her skirts. Savannah was struggling herself, the wooziness in her head refusing to go away and the pain of her broken rib stabbing her side over and over.

'Where are you taking us?' Mildred matched her stride for stride.

'Away.' How much time did they have before Pincott was found? She thought it unlikely that he would give her another chance to escape if she failed to take this one. They had to get away, and fast.

'We must go to the police immediately, and I must contact my family.'

Savannah turned towards Mildred. 'That's not such a good idea.'

'Why?'

'Later. Keep moving.' Savannah drove them on towards safety, ignoring Mildred's questions and her own desire to lie down and sleep on the timber roofs of Whitechapel.

When they finally reached the flat roof below the Hog and

Spike's attic window, the sun was beginning to bruise the horizon with the promise of the day to come.

'I need a few minutes.' Rebecca collapsed behind the chimney stack. Savannah, too, needed to gather her strength before finding a way to get all four of them through the attic window and down into the lanes. As they rested, Mildred fidgeted, impatient to continue. To Savannah, Rebecca's silence only seemed louder now they had paused their journey.

'You worked at Raycraft's factory? They're holding my friend's aunt there. In the basement.'

Rebecca's head snapped towards her, suddenly enlivened, although her voice was a monotone. 'Don't go down there. It's dangerous.'

'In what way?'

'Experiments, new weapons. Some people who go in do not come out again.'

Mildred chipped in, 'Apparently they make that ghastly syrup there, the one they made us drink before . . . ' Her voice splintered and her cheeks grew red. She cleared her throat and brushed imaginary creases from her skirts.

'What does it do?' Savannah pressed.

Rebecca replied, 'It heightens fertility, makes the womb more receptive to the male seed. I helped to develop it at the factory before he took me.' There was no trace of irony in her voice, no trace of anything.

Savannah turned her attention to the task of reaching the attic window, her mind beginning to clear. It should be easy enough to hoist JJ upwards and let him use his excellent breaking and entering skills to force it open. Once they were down on the street, she would tell Mildred and Rebecca to meet Harry and William at the Old Bell Tavern and ask them to ensure JJ was safe.

Then, at last, Savannah Shelton could take her leave. She should have plenty of time to make it to the Pool before the ship left for

Lisbon. She could splash out on the most expensive accommodation. The thought of lying in a comfortable bed as the sea rocked her to sleep made her smile, her lips cracking uncomfortably as she did so. She could even afford the attentions of the ship's doctor. She was so close to escape she could almost taste the sea air, salty with promise.

'Rebecca . . . ' Mildred's voice held a warning note and Savannah turned back towards the group.

Rebecca stood perilously close to the edge of the roof, her head bent down to look into the street far below. Savannah ran, ignoring the scream of pain in her ribs, leaping across the ten yards or so that separated her from the desperate Rebecca, but it was ten yards too far.

No jump, no bracing beforehand, just a step forward into nothing.

Mildred screamed, but the rush of blood in Savannah's ears stopped her from hearing what Mildred must have heard: the irrevocable slap of Rebecca's body hitting the ground beneath. Savannah lurched to a halt at the roof's edge and slid to her knees. Rebecca's body had fractured across the stone slab that marked the centre of the little square, her engorged belly pointing skywards, her limbs hanging lifeless either side like a sacrifice to the gods.

Savannah raged: at Rebecca, for refusing to fight her degradation, and at the men who had done this to her, to all of them, down the ages and for ever more. Something was breaking inside, like a sheet of ice cracking open, swift and violent. Self-preservation seemed futile now. What was she saving herself for? Just like Rebecca, she was damaged goods. The thought made her heart swell within her, as if it might burst. Tears streamed down her face and she choked back the sobs that gripped her hard. Crying for Rebecca, crying, she knew, for herself. Mildred's hands gently pulled her head into the folds of that comforting tartan dress. Minutes passed and still she wept, cleansing herself of all dreams of escape, just as Rebecca had done. She knew now that she would never outrun her past, wherever she went, for it was inside her just as Rebecca's had been, twisting in her veins, filling her own belly. There was only one escape to be had in the end and she wasn't ready for it yet.

Mildred's voice was soft when she spoke. 'We should go now before the day comes. Once someone finds her they will know the way we came.'

Savannah wiped her eyes and stood up. To hell with the pain. She took the bags of gold from her coat and tossed them into the square below. The coins scattered around Rebecca's broken body, winking in the early light of dawn.

JJ looked at her, eyes wide. 'Why did you do that?'

'I'm not going anywhere. Not any more.'

Rebecca's death would be avenged. All the deaths of the weak at the hands of the powerful would be avenged and she, Savannah Shelton, murderer, mongrel, and whore, would not stop until they were.

## CHAPTER FORTY-FIVE

*E*dward Raycraft's plan had changed the moment he had seen his father on the podium, his face flecked with fear and as green as his rotting soul. Sir Jasper Raycraft would still die, that was not in doubt, but the difference between slaughtering the innocent and punishing the guilty seemed to be that one did not wish it to be over quite so quickly.

After his escape from the Tower he had retreated to the gloomy shadows of Waterloo until the police had given up their search. It had then taken the best part of the afternoon to hike all the way to Hampstead, keeping to the backstreets and then the open fields, where he had been able to creep through the woods towards Ridgeside unobserved. Leaving the city behind he had breathed fresh air for the first time in twenty years. Now that night had fallen, he had the full run of the grounds, had even approached one of the windows and gazed upon a maid cleaning the silverware in the servants' parlour. She thought herself quite alone and had kissed herself in the polished surface of a serving plate, practising the pucker of her lips.

He remembered this place so well, how he had explored the meadows and woods with such joy during the long days, his head full of tales of adventure, his limbs scratched yet relentless in their desire to crest the next hill. Night had been a different matter, full of different stories; then he would wrap his childish body tightly in his bedclothes, terrified as the branches of oak and ash twisted and waved beyond his window in the overhang of the looming crag beyond. Back then, the day had always returned to snatch him into the light once more. Now the world clawed and conquered him without respite.

He stole into the stable to observe the grooms. Among Sir Jasper's thoroughbreds was a new resident, a black colt that Tinbergen had shipped with him from America to compete at Newmarket. When he heard the groom call the horse's name, Edward wanted to laugh out loud. *Plato.* Of course. The Tinbergens were the investors now, having married into the families only a generation ago. When Edward was very little, he had heard the phrase *new blood* and not known what it meant. His father had used the phrase disparagingly, for what he really believed in was old blood, recycled again and again until it ran putrid in the Raycraft veins. Edward, and then Phoebe. Only Benjamin was pure.

In the stables he overheard that Sir Jasper was not expected home until the early hours. No matter. The night air was muggy as he lay awake beneath an oak tree, his fingers tangled in the grass, the blades whispering against his skin. To think that it was *he* who had spent years incarcerated in that place, that it was *he* the world thought mad, and not his uncle, the man who had forced himself on his own sister in the belief that the old blood could be concentrated into something far greater. He remembered the day his uncle and father had told him the truth of his origins, as if it were something to be grateful for. He had known then what had caused his mother to jump from the rafters with a noose around her neck, days after giving birth in secret to another child.

He had sat in his playroom for at least an hour after Sir Jasper left, among the toys that surrounded him like a sick joke. In that hour, he became a man, and opened himself to all the madness of the world. He remembered little of what followed. The smash of china, his fingernails ripping through skin, and the cry of a child, Benjamin, the brother he loved. His own childish voice echoed through his head once more, *I shall save you!* But there was more rot to be gouged away before the final act of self-sacrifice would cleanse the world for ever of Sir Jasper's sickness.

In the distance, he heard the dull thump of horse's hooves. Sir Jasper was returning. He stole across the grass, cautious now in the approaching dawn, and made for the stables. He would not show his face again until it was time to rid his father from this earth. Tonight was about delivering a message. *As you tortured my mother, so I will torture you.*

He approached the black colt with quiet patience, meeting the huge eyes of that magnificent beast with his own, stroking its nose until the first blink told him his presence had been accepted. He heard the carriage draw up outside the house and leant forward to rest his forehead against the colt's sleek black coat.

'I am sorry, my friend.' With a single movement, he slashed his knife through the beast's neck.

He jumped back as a great spurt of bright red blood flew upwards. The horse screamed and thrashed, bringing everyone running through the stable doors. Edward had already planned his escape and hoisted himself upwards to the hay loft above where he retreated into the shadows to watch.

Sir Jasper was among the first to enter the stables, his red cloak billowing outwards as he ran towards the horse's stall. A stable boy was already there, looking on helplessly as the horse fought certain death.

'His throat's been cut, sir! Who would do such a thing?'

Sir Jasper's head flicked from one side to the other as he turned full circle. His mouth hung open in fright and his arms wrapped tightly around himself. When he spoke, his voice sounded high and girlish. 'Edward! I know you are here! Please, let us talk, enough of this madness. Anything in this world, it is yours, whatever you want, you shall have it!'

*And so I shall, Father, and so I shall.*

## CHAPTER FORTY-SIX

*W*illiam woke early in his bed at the Old Bell Tavern, surprised to find that he had slept at all. He thought again of his encounter with the vicomtesse, the strange alchemy he had felt, fascinating and horrific in equal measure. From the other bed he could hear Harry's gentle breathing. Unwilling to disturb the detective, he dressed quietly and left the room, leaving the stolen casket on a bedside chest.

Like Harry, Fleet Street still slept in the muggy dawn. Exhausted from his efforts the night before, William walked without purpose, finding himself below the dome of St Paul's Cathedral. The clouds swirled and gathered above him and the air turned sticky as his thoughts turned to Westminster Abbey. Today was the day he would meet Ambrose Habborlain once more. The questions burned within him: where would he even start?

By the time he returned, Fleet Street was springing to life. He watched the comings and goings of traders and delivery boys under the grey sky. It was a new day in the city, just like any other. A young lad, pushing a cart full of handbills and advertisements, gaped up at the heavens, concerned for his freshly printed cargo. As he passed William, the cart ran over his foot.

'Sorry, sir!'

William waved the boy's apology away, things on his mind

more important than a muddied shoe. The boy bent down to retrieve a sheaf of handbills advertising Rothwell's Chocolate that had fallen into the dirt. William glanced down at the cart, only to see his own name and face staring back at him. It couldn't be! The drawing of his face was sharp and angular, creating thickly pencilled shadows around his eyes and mouth. Even to William, it was the face of a murderer that glared back at him. The small poster announced that he was wanted for questioning in relation to a number of suspicious deaths. He grabbed at it instinctively, revealing another underneath. What was he going to do, remove them all from the city? Then he noticed two other handbills, side by side with his own. Harry's poster had not bothered with an image, but the words Detective Harry Treadway were boldly printed. Savannah's image was cartoonish, the poster announcing that she was wanted for murder. It warned that she was armed and dangerous and should not be approached. He grabbed one of each and shoved them down into his pockets.

The boy stood up and William immediately turned his back and faced a shop window, desperately hoping the lad had not recognised him. With relief, he heard the cart trundle away. Dare he even face the street again, let alone walk upon it? He leant his forehead against the cool glass. It wasn't real. None of this was real.

Someone touched his shoulder and he wheeled around, ready to protest his innocence, to run, even to fight.

Harry's voice was soft. 'Everything all right, old chap? I found you gone when I awoke.'

William said nothing, but pulled the crumpled papers from his pocket and handed them over.

Harry examined them one by one, nodding his head as if this all made complete sense, when really it made none at all. 'Should I be disappointed, do you think? That there isn't a portrait of me?'

He smiled sadly at William, the joke only half made. 'It was to be expected, William. Our anonymity couldn't last for ever.'

They returned to the Old Bell and ordered breakfast, the only customers so early in the morning. They ate mostly in silence, William's eyes constantly drawn to the pile of crumpled handbills on the table. He unfurled Savannah's poster once more. Three murders, it said. Found guilty and sentenced to hang. No wonder she had been so keen to make her escape when Sergeant Smiley had closed in. Had she been able to steal the funds she needed and help the women of Whitechapel to freedom? No news could equally mean success or failure.

Harry must have read his thoughts. 'I wonder how our friend Miss Shelton has fared. Hers was a most perilous mission and I confess I am anxious.'

'She's a survivor,' William offered.

'We are all survivors, right up to the point when we are not.'

The silence returned and Harry took a toy ship from his pocket and turned it over in his hands.

William remembered how it had fallen out when Savannah clubbed him with her gun at the Tower. 'A present for someone?'

Harry smiled. 'My grandson, David. So like his father, but he's a good boy. He really is.'

William could see the pain in his eyes, and realised he knew nothing of the detective's life. 'You are married?'

'I was.'

'I'm sorry.'

Harry nodded and rose from the table. 'There is much to discuss.'

He went to their room and returned with the casket, suggesting they take the documents to the British Museum later that morning and find a librarian who could aid the translation. Placing his glasses on his nose, he opened the box. 'I have examined some of the documents already. The parchments beneath are unreadable, almost crumbled to dust. The two on top are less antiquated and the language is ancient Greek. My knowledge is more than a little rusty, I'm afraid, but from what I can decipher, one seems to be a copy of a letter written to Aristotle, although I'm not sure from whom. The second seems to be some kind of manifesto.'

Harry delicately lifted the second document out and laid it flat on the table. William had not looked at it when he first examined the box, his inability to read the first document having left him frustrated. The paper was thick and had been folded many times so that the creases had begun to tear. It was covered in a tiny script written in faint purple ink, but William's eye was drawn immediately to the symbol sketched in each corner. The Seed of Life.

Harry continued, 'You'll recognise the symbol, of course. This document is attributed to Aristotle as opposed to addressed to him. There are many references to the number seven – the seven circles, the group of seven and so on.'

William nodded, happy to be distracted from his thoughts. They discussed the corridor of the seven they had visited last night. From the boards they had identified Sir Jasper and Habborlain as the Scientist and Artist respectively. It seemed that Matlock played the role of Protector within the group, Mr Bridge was the Bookkeeper and they finally knew who the Finder was, whatever all those bizarre titles meant.

Harry removed his glasses and looked up. 'That leaves the Warrior and the Investor to be identified, though I have my suspicions. Otto Von Rabenmarck and Cornelius Tinbergen are two possible candidates to make up this . . . ' Harry gestured in the air, 'association.'

William snorted. 'The German chancellor and the Vice President of the United States. The ranks of my enemies swell further!' He shook his head. 'I still find it impossible to believe that Mr Bridge would be concerned with these people and their repulsive schemes.' But whatever this association represented, Nathaniel Bridge had clearly been right at the heart of it. 'And what of the list of names? It's no longer there.'

Harry nodded. 'Those boards hold all the original information, I suspect. We will discover more today, I hope.'

At that moment, the tavern door swung open and an old man lumbered in. William instinctively turned his head away, fearful of being recognised. To his horror, he heard the man approach their table.

'Morning, Harry.'

'Good morning, Finian, may I introduce you to my friend here?'

Finian Worthing took a seat at the table. 'I have the information you require but this time, old friend, I expect something by way of an explanation before I hand it over.'

Harry smiled at his friend. 'Myself and William, well, we're in trouble, Finian, real trouble.'

'That much would seem clear. Perhaps you might expand?'

'It is a long story and I am not sure that we have the time.'

Finian snapped his fingers towards the bar. 'Then a libation will be essential, I believe.'

With deft summation, Harry told their story, from his investigations of the Raycraft family to William's own perplexing tale of misfortune. After his initial wave of mistrust, William considered that it might be helpful to have a journalist in their camp, and from *The Times*, no less. Finian Worthing was not quite what he expected of a journalist. He had imagined someone more wolfish, less benign, although the strong smell of stale whisky that wafted from him conformed to all of William's preconceptions. When the tale was over, the three of them sat in silence, the only customers still, three men in a silent world.

'There is much to fear in this, Harry, much to fear. A conspiracy on this scale? To what ends, I wonder?'

'This clique encompasses influential individuals from at least three of the most powerful countries on earth and, as you said, reason demands that they are intent on something more than just the tyranny of a harmless young man or a breeding experiment, however offensive to common decency their techniques may be.' Harry was grave. 'The Raycraft factory. There is something amiss there. The workers know it but no one has listened to them. I am missing the connections but I know that they are there.'

'I would not dismiss this repulsive Whitechapel activity as necessarily marginal to their plans, Harry,' Finian pondered. 'You partly share an ideology with our man Raycraft, I suspect, that scientific discovery of our past represents an advancement of the human condition. Mr Darwin is undoubtedly a brilliant and well-intentioned man, but in understanding why and how we are here, does it not allow some men to believe they have unlocked the very tools that could control the future of humanity? Some would say that breeding is God's work, as much as war itself.'

Harry swirled the dregs of his tea around his cup. 'I'm not sure I believe in God any more.'

'I would rather believe that God was in charge of who lived or died than a scientist like Raycraft.'

'Amen to that,' said William.

Finian ordered another round of ale for all of them before he continued, 'I bring two pieces of information, both of which will intrigue you. First, I have spent most of the night investigating the name of Habborlain. It is an unusual name, which helped, but it was not until dawn was almost upon us that I found the one and only reference in our library.' He leant forward, clearly enjoying himself. 'Velanya Habborlain was a Serbian artist, and mistress to a certain Lord Byron. They met in Albania in 1810. It is thought that she bore him a child.'

William jumped in. 'That was most certainly implied by the family tree we saw at the association!'

Harry nodded. 'Was this Velanya Habborlain wealthy?'

Finian shook his head. 'Didn't appear to be. Maybe Byron himself is the source of wealth. Although the man had plenty of bastards, so why he would choose to give such a life to only one of them I have no idea. But I looked out his will and there is no mention of a beneficiary named Habborlain. Maybe your man's money came from somewhere else?'

Harry tapped his fingers against his lips. 'I hope we will find out more this evening. We meet with him at the abbey at vespers. And your second piece of news, Finian?'

Finian Worthing polished off his ale and ordered another. William was beginning to find his grandstanding rather irritating. 'As I was leaving the office, a wire arrived. It seems that Cornelius Tinbergen's Newmarket hopeful was slaughtered last night in Sir Jasper's stable. A single slash to the neck.' Finian mimed the action with a grim smile.

Harry nodded. 'I suspect Edward Raycraft is intent on revenge against his uncle. We are not the only ones in the hunt when it comes to Sir Jasper.'

William felt more hunted than hunter but said nothing. He closed his eyes and saw only the red mask and that ruby mouth. Circles within circles. He heard the tavern door open behind him and his eyes snapped open at Harry's words.

'Bloody hell!'

A clap of thunder fractured the air as William turned around. What he saw made his mouth fall open.

Savannah Shelton stood before them, hair wild, her face bloody and her petticoats torn to shreds. Her left arm was slung around the shoulders of a small boy while in her right she grasped a dishevelled woman in a tartan dress.

William and Harry continued to gape at Savannah's appearance.

"What?' she barked, cantankerous as ever.

## CHAPTER FORTY-SEVEN

*H*arry and William ordered another breakfast and marshalled the bedraggled group of survivors to their room
upstairs. Savannah and the boy, JJ, crammed in crude mouthfuls
of warm bread as, beyond the mullioned windows, shards of
lightning jagged towards the earth.

Mildred Whitfield. William had seen her before: the girl who
stumbled from the train at Baker Street on his last morning
in the old world. She had returned his admiring stare with a
frown, and he had looked away, humiliated and unworthy. Now
he met her gaze without shame, a pretty face no longer enough
to terrify him.

Once William and Harry had apprised Savannah of their
evening, they filled in the background for the new arrival.
Mildred asked many questions, her bright mind piecing it
together. Harry persuaded her not to return to her family,
beyond sending a telegram to tell them she was safe. For someone who had endured such an ordeal as she had in the last few
days, she held herself well. She made scant mention of her own
suffering at the hands of the vicomtesse and out of delicacy no
one pressed further. William hoped she had escaped the group's
worst excesses.

Her contributions to the retelling of last night's daring
escape were brisk and to the point. When Savannah told them

of Rebecca's tragic death, she faltered over her words. Mildred squeezed her arm and said, 'Not everyone is as strong as you. It is not her fault. Nor is it yours.'

It reminded William of something his aunt might say.

Mildred glanced up at him. 'Have we met before?'

William thought of the man he'd been only three days ago.

'No,' he said, 'we haven't.' It felt like the truth.

Savannah nodded in Finian's direction, then spoke to Harry. 'You trust him?'

Finian raised an eyebrow as Harry replied, 'I do. He is an old friend.'

'And does Matlock know of your connection?'

'I don't believe so.'

'You're sure?'

Harry paused only briefly. 'I am.'

Savannah rose wearily and came to sit beside William. 'I need to tell you something. Your aunt is being held in the basement of the Raycraft factory.'

He leapt to his feet but Savannah yanked him back down again and related Rebecca's warnings about the place.

Harry mirrored her words. 'I have been there, William, it will not be an easy place to enter or leave. We know they have kept her in the hope that you will seek her out. We will indeed venture there, but not without first securing help.'

'Surely Mildred's testimony would tip the credibility of our tale and allow us to find a favourable ear beyond Matlock's reach?' William protested. 'Once Raycraft and the vicomtesse are tainted with their dirty Whitechapel secret then we can pull the house of cards down upon them!'

But Detective Treadway was immovable. 'Maybe after this evening, William, when we have understood what is in these documents and joined with Habborlain. Maybe then we will have enough to convince those above Matlock to take action.'

'He's right, William.' Savannah's cracked lips cracked some more. 'I cannot fight again today.'

William watched the rain thrash against the tiny panes. He knew there was no point going alone to the factory.

Sensing his frustration, Harry placed a hand on his arm. 'William, I have been thinking. We may have another ally we can turn to.'

'Who?'

Harry paused before continuing. 'Benjamin Raycraft.'

'Raycraft!'

'His son, William. He is a sensitive soul. You remind me of him in many ways. He is not, I am sure, aware of his father's transgressions. He trusts me, and I think he might help us.'

William nodded reluctantly. What choice did he have?

Savannah grinned at him. 'Tell me, did you really manage to get through an entire evening of conversing with the enemy and running for your life without fainting like a girl?'

William returned her smile, for somehow he'd not had the time to feel afraid. He thought of all the years he had avoided upset of any kind, avoided the world even, afraid of its people, people like Savannah. Afraid of so many things.

Finian Worthing took his leave of them. 'I should return to the paper. You know where to find me, old boy.'

Savannah grunted in his direction as he left. 'Be careful.'

'Of what?'

'Strangers. Shadows. That kind of thing.'

He looked her up and down. 'I suspect, my dear, that I have already seen the strangest thing I shall see today.'

Mildred left with him, offering to venture into the storm to search out a new set of petticoats for Savannah and some ointment for her injuries. William found himself thinking of the vicomtesse's bruised face, for it was Savannah who had caused the damage he had seen. He felt ashamed of his own inaction in the Finder's room. Face to face with the enemy he had, in truth, been bewitched.

JJ was still eating. He had said almost nothing since the food arrived and clearly had a relentless appetite. William could hear Aunt Esther's voice in his head, suggesting that the skinny boy was very likely to be sick later. Meanwhile, it was Harry's turn to look through those antique windows, no doubt hoping to find answers in the tempest beyond.

'Ow!'

Savannah had removed her makeshift bandages and was bathing the raw wounds beneath. William winced when he saw them. Truly she had endured a terrible night. She had earlier made light of her torture, but William could see now how astounding her refusal to give him up had really been.

'I cannot thank you enough, Savannah. You have saved me many times over, yet I have done little to earn your protection.'

She looked down then, refusing to meet his eyes. 'I wasn't coming back. I was going to hightail it to Lisbon on a steamer.'

'I know.'

Her voice fell, her words dropping like stones. 'I *hate* them, William. Raycraft, Matlock, the vicomtesse – everyone like them. For what they do to us.'

'I know.'

Savannah sniffed and changed the subject. 'I need money,' she announced to the room in general, not catching anyone's eye.

William rummaged in his pocket and pulled out a single handful of coins. 'Is this enough?'

'It's more than enough.' She grabbed the coins and scattered them on the bedside table. Rolling a cigarette, she summoned JJ.

The boy left his breakfast and trotted eagerly to her side.

Her voice was stern. 'Listen, JJ, I'm grateful, really I am, but I don't want you mixed up in all this. You need to leave.' She nodded her head towards William's coins. 'Take it. What would you do with so much money, eh?'

He looked at the money, then at her. 'Dunno.'

He's just a child, William thought. Lost, like all of us.

'I tell you what, why don't you keep it safe.' She jingled the coins into the boy's pockets, ignoring his inertia. 'If we survive all this, I'll come and find you at the Devil's Tavern. You know where it is?'

He nodded, his eyes cast down. 'You'll come back for me then?'

Savannah said nothing, blowing two perfect plumes of smoke through her nose.

'You look like a dragon,' said the boy. 'Have you ever seen a dragon, Shelton?'

'Yes.'

'They have dragons in America?'

'Yes, I'll come back for you. Now go.'

CHAPTER FORTY-EIGHT

The storm was still raging as they left the Old Bell Tavern and crossed the fields of Lincoln's Inn towards the British Library. JJ had departed as instructed but Mildred Whitfield remained, for it was the safest place for her, and she dare not compromise her family who by now would surely be under scrutiny.

They travelled separately, cautious now that their faces were sketched across the city. However, the inclement weather had kept many indoors and the streets were drained of people. They regrouped on the steps of the museum beneath the grand portico, the stone floor slippery with dirt and rain.

Savannah's weariness had been replaced by agitation. 'I don't like this. We're being predictable. I don't like predictable.'

Harry led the way to the Reading Room, the cylindrical building in the centre of the quadrangle that housed the enormous collections of the British Library. William marvelled at the majestic scale of the buildings around them and, not for the first time, felt ashamed at his lack of education. Aunt Esther had taught him to read and write and to understand scripture, but his patchy knowledge of human history and lack of curiosity appalled him now. He felt mocked by the very splendour of this place that had been here all of his life, offering to share the secrets of human endeavour through the ages, a constant whisper he had failed to hear as he scratched out deeds and watered the roses, happy in his ignorance.

Savannah surveyed the inside of the library as if it were a bank she intended to rob, her eyes quickly scanning the rows of desks and their occupants. She was making William nervous, and he too glanced about the room but could see no faces that caused alarm. Nonetheless, Savannah's gun hand continued to twitch.

When Harry revealed the contents of the box to the elderly librarian behind the counter, the man was clearly excited by what he saw and immediately dashed away to find someone called Professor Middleton. William expected the man to return with someone equally aged, with a walking stick and a cap and gown perhaps, but he was surprised to see instead a sprightly young man, as thin as a sapling, with a tangle of mousy hair, spectacles, and a beaky nose that he constantly wiped with a large, grey handkerchief.

Professor Middleton did not show the same level of excitement as his assistant. He told them in no uncertain terms that it would take him at least an hour or two to conduct even a cursory examination of the papers within and suggested they might like to wait in one of the available study rooms. As he lifted the box, Savannah stepped aggressively forward as if to take it back again but Harry put out a hand to stop her. The professor frowned in her direction and seemed to consider for the first time the group of assorted faces that had brought him this alleged treasure. 'How did you say you came by the casket?'

'This young *lady*,' Harry indicated the scowling Savannah, 'found it among her grandmother's possessions when she passed away. She is *American*.' Harry placed a heavy emphasis on the word, clearly hoping it would explain much. 'I,' said Harry, 'am a family friend with an amateur enthusiasm for the classics.' He nodded towards William. 'And Mr Bridge here is the executor of the will.'

William glared at Harry but Mildred stepped in. 'And I am Miss Savannah's maid, Mildred.'

'So there you have it,' summarised Harry.

Whether he believed them or not was unclear, but they had no choice but to allow Professor Middleton to stride away with the box itself and let themselves be led into an empty side room to wait on his deliberations. As the first hour ticked by, Mildred, who had spent the night awake as they fled across the rooftops of the city, laid her head on the large desk and dozed off.

Savannah paced the room, her eyes red and swollen. Harry took her arm. 'You should rest.'

'We should go. This is taking too long.'

She strode towards the high window but was not tall enough to see out. 'William!' she hissed. 'Take a look. What can you see?'

William sighed but went to the window. 'Just people.'

'What people? Describe them.'

'Lots of people. Coming and going. As you would expect. To describe them would take all day. And,' he stared her down as she was about to object, 'I do believe it would be rather pointless.'

She pulled a chair to the window, thumped her dirty boots on to the rich leather and stood up, belligerently taking up her watch with arms folded.

At that moment, Professor Middleton swept back into the room. William's heart leapt with excitement at the thought of solving one piece of the puzzle, but the professor's words were unexpected.

'I congratulate you on such an elaborate hoax! Very well done, I must say. We have seen many over the years, but the execution is extraordinary! The details, the aging of the papyrus, and the very words themselves of course. Really very tremendous! Now, which of you produced this work of fiction, hmm? Let me guess, one of you is studying at Oxford and hoped this humorous adventure might furnish you with material for your thesis? I'm a Brasenose man myself.' Professor Middleton's eyes loomed large behind his wire-rimmed spectacles as he noticed Savannah standing on the chair. 'Has the young lady lost something?'

They all ignored his last question. William was dumbfounded by the man's allegation of fakery, however impressed the professor seemed to be by such an undertaking. 'It is not a hoax, sir. Or rather, if it is, it is not one of our making.'

'But they simply cannot be real,' the professor persisted. 'If they were, the ramifications within the classical world would be beyond measure.' He turned again to Savannah. 'Do you have any idea how your grandmother came upon these artefacts?'

Savannah didn't shift her gaze from the window. 'Just tell us what's in them, professor.'

Professor Middleton paused, obviously torn between pushing them further on the origins of the documents and his desire to share with them the audacity he believed they contained. 'Very well.'

He removed a pair of fine kid gloves from his pocket and snapped them over his fingers before taking the uppermost documents from the box. He laid them flat on the table.

'It is next to impossible to examine the other papers here, for they are practically turned to dust. I can, however, confirm two things. Firstly, they are written on papyrus and *appear* quite ancient in nature.' Here he flashed a look at William, clearly believing him to be the most likely culprit for such a forgery. 'And secondly, I am fairly confident, in the absence of a more forensic review, that these two documents here are copies of the older ones, made no doubt when the papyrus began to crumble – or at least, that is what we are intended to believe.'

Harry interrupted. 'When do you think the copies were made?'

The professor sighed. 'That would take some time to determine. My guess, however, looking at the form of some of the lettering, for example the shape of this epsilon here, would be that they were made at some point in the thirteenth or fourteenth centuries, or at least this is what—'

'We are intended to believe.' Harry finished the man's sentence for him. 'Please, Professor Middleton, we understand and accept that you doubt the veracity of these artefacts. Let us acknowledge the fact and move on.'

Professor Middleton reddened. 'Very well. I believe this document comes first in the order of things.' He indicated the letter that Harry had earlier suggested was addressed to Aristotle. He paused and shook his head before continuing, 'Its contents are truly fantastical. In summary, it purports to be a letter, written by Plato, the great philosopher, to his pupil, Aristotle, at the end of his life in 347 BC. In this letter, Plato claims to be the father of a child born in Macedonia and he exhorts Aristotle to nurture and protect this child after he is gone. The letter goes on to say that the child is the product of a deliberate experiment. Plato had remained childless for much of his life but, as he reached old age and contemplated death, he wondered whether this childlessness was perhaps selfish of him. How does he put it exactly . . .' Professor Middleton leant over the table and squinted at the letter. '"Removing the seed of my valiant consciousness from the furthering of humanity." Not the most modest of sentiments and somewhat out of character for such a humble man. Nonetheless, the letter states that he set about finding a suitable partner, his intention being "to marry the questioning intelligence of the human soul with the unswerving steel of bravery in battle". He believed that such a combination might yield greatness as the world had never seen before.'

'Intellectual brilliance married to a warrior's strength,' muttered Harry.

'Indeed,' replied the professor. 'Although, in this case, I'm afraid there was no marriage. In fact,' and here the professor paused and glanced in Savannah and Mildred's direction before continuing, 'the letter suggests Plato chose another man's wife with whom to breed this wonder child, a woman who was descended from a long line of fierce warriors who could trace their lineage back to Achilles himself – the wife of Philip of Macedon, to be exact, Olympias.'

Harry whistled. 'Good Lord, then Plato was father to Alexander the Great! That is quite some revelation.'

Savannah simply stared at William, clearly struggling to see why this fact seemed of such interest, but William was beginning to see it too.

'The fourteenth letter.'

All eyes turned to Mildred. 'Plato wrote thirteen letters – that survived, at least. This would be the fourteenth.'

'If it were real,' emphasised the professor before continuing, 'There is more. Plato asks that Aristotle not only watches over the child, but that he makes arrangements to continue Plato's efforts to perfect the lineage across the generations. In effect, to breed over time what he calls a Ploíarchos Agóna.'

'What the hell does that mean?' asked Savannah.

The professor coughed. 'A master race.'

The room fell silent. Mildred turned away from them all and paced the room. 'The vicomtesse was obsessed with my family, their prowess on the battlefield. It was all she appeared to care about.'

Harry picked up the theme. 'Ninety generations, give or take, since Alexander the Great was alive. I wonder what Mr Darwin might think of such a grand scheme. Could anything of significance be achieved in ninety turns?'

The professor shrugged. 'That is not my field. Besides, you are all ignoring the fact that these documents are most likely fake.'

Mildred broke in. 'But it is possible, surely? Aristotle was indeed Alexander's tutor and mentor throughout his life, and there has always been speculation as to Alexander's parentage.'

The professor shook his head. 'Even so.'

William thought of the painting of Alexander above Habborlain's fireplace, and the bust of Plato. '"It is all connected, don't you see? All this. All of it. Me." That is what Habborlain said to me.'

Savannah looked across from her perch by the window. 'Can we hurry this along, please?'

Harry ignored her and pointed to the top of the letter. It appeared to have a title, underlined in ink. 'What does this mean?'

'Well born, perhaps? At least *eu* means good and *genes* means birth. It appears throughout the letter, when the writer describes what he believes will be an exciting new field of study. He intends it as a noun – using our normal etymology in scientific matters we might translate it as *Eugenics*.'

William was eager to learn more. 'And what of this second document? We recognised the Seed of Life symbol but that was all, I'm afraid.'

The professor smiled. 'Well, here the originator gave full rein to his sense of invention. You are correct about the symbol, and the document itself is actually called *The Seed of Life*. It purports to be written by Aristotle in . . . ' the professor hunched over the table once more and wrinkled his nose as he attempted to read the tiny script, '323 BC, the year of Alexander's death and a year, therefore, before his own. In short, the document is a manifesto of sorts, which sets in place a structure called the Seed of Life, intended to breed the line of Alexander over successive generations. Although Alexander himself had died of a mysterious fever in Babylon, Roxanne was still carrying his child at this time, the child that would be born Alexander the Fourth. In this document, Aristotle instructs his successors to breed three lines or *streams* from the unborn child, intended to maximise the development of certain—'

'Police!' yelled Savannah, diving from her chair. She whipped out her gun and leapt across the table at the professor, scattering the precious documents. She pushed him to his knees and jammed the gun barrel into his forehead. 'You called them here, didn't you? Are you with them? Tell me!'

Harry held up his hands. 'Savannah, please!'

William ran to the window. Two constables were strolling through the quadrangle below, hands behind their backs, smiling and nodding as they passed people by.

The professor whimpered and Savannah leant closer, her fierce eyes fixed on his. 'Two of them. Out there. Why?'

William gently moved a startled Mildred to one side and approached Savannah, his tone placating. 'They seem harmless enough, and quite without purpose. There is no need for this.'

The professor finally found his voice. 'C-c-constables Balding and Withers. They regularly look in as part of their rounds.'

Savannah looked up at William and he nodded in reassurance. She returned her gaze to the frightened professor, as if seeing him for the first time. The man slumped as she dropped her arm and jammed her gun back into her skirt. She pushed past William, saying, 'I need to sleep.'

Harry lifted the professor into a chair. 'We apologise, sir. It won't happen again.' William collected up the documents and placed them once more in front of the professor. 'You were saying, about the instruction to breed three lines from Alexander's off-spring. Please do go on.'

The professor pulled the documents towards him with shaking hands, cleared his throat several times, and breathed deeply. 'The manifesto refers to them as Warrior, Scientist and Artist. It is these three streams that are then to be perfected through the generations. The heads of these three families would be chosen in each generation to lead the Seed of Life, alongside four others who would take on key roles within the enterprise, making a group of seven in all, just like the seven rings of the Seed of Life itself.'

His eyes flitted constantly towards Savannah, who now leant against the far wall with her eyes closed. He continued, 'The Protector would be charged with keeping the endeavour secret, and helping it to flourish across the globe so that the best specimens of all mankind could be used to mingle with the three families.

'The Investor would be responsible for ensuring the wealth of the Seed of Life grew over time, again to permit access to the greatest resource of mankind around the known world.

'The Bookkeeper was to maintain records of the family trees as they grew and the Finder, the only role allowed to a female, had the most important job of all, it would seem – to seek out the best breeding stock available and to make the necessary matches. So, as you can see,' the professor sighed and slumped into his chair, 'a work of quite some fantasy, I think you will agree?'

As he looked up, he clearly expected agreement, but they stared at him with stony faces. Harry voiced what William himself was thinking. 'So now we know. It matters not whether there is truth in these documents, whether they are real or not. The fact is, our enemies believe it and are still acting in accordance with this instruction.'

The professor's eyes grew wide once more. 'Excuse me? Enemies, you say?'

'I'm afraid, whatever else may or may not be true, this group exists, and they are indeed engaging in breeding practices of the most heinous nature.'

William broke in, for he had remembered something else. '"The father of all of us" is how Habborlain described Plato. *The father of all of us!*'

The professor shook his head. 'But this is absurd! Roxanne *did* give birth to a child, Alexander the Fourth, but he was murdered before his thirteenth birthday, the only child of Alexander the Great. There are some, of course, who believe he was spirited away to safety but there always are those in scholastic circles who like to doubt and reinvent for no purpose . . . ' His voice drifted away.

Harry was still looking at the document. 'There must be more here, this manifesto, as you called it, is very long indeed.'

'Yes, yes.' The professor was impatient now, clearly desperate for them to leave and take the unhinged American with them. 'Rules, mostly, for the operation of the group of seven and the breeding process. For example, as the families expanded, only one hundred of each numbered generation across the three families would be selected on their fifteenth birthday for the purpose of breeding.'

'The list!' cried William. 'Mr Bridge kept a list of the names of the current one hundred. That would make sense.'

Harry nodded. 'Maybe he was planning on exposing all this after all?'

William urged the professor to continue, keen to know more of the Seed of Life's rules.

'The group of seven leaders would also select their own successors in each generation. And there is much here about the process itself. For example, all conception must be through the process of natural service under the auspices of marriage.' The professor blushed. 'Apologies for mentioning such indelicate matters in front of . . . the lady.'

Savannah opened one eye at his omission, but Mildred waved her hand. 'Apology accepted, go on.'

The professor looked at the manifesto once more. 'There was to be no intermarriage within families for three generations, so that the seed remained undefiled. There are then two more rules, which I really do shudder to discuss in mixed company: a ritual punishment, quite horrifically described, for anyone who breaks the most important rule of the Seed of Life.'

Savannah interrupted. 'Let me guess, it involves a part of one's anatomy being removed and placed in another part of one's anatomy.'

Both Professor Middleton and Mildred looked at Savannah, open-mouthed with shock. She looked from one to the other. 'For goodness sake, I *said* it, I didn't *do* it!'

But something else the professor had mentioned had snagged

William's attention. 'You mentioned the most important rule? What is that?'

The professor recovered himself. 'Well, it is yet another rule that our more gentle age would find distasteful, I'm afraid. The ancient Greeks believed many strange things, even the educated. They thought that physical deformity was a manifestation of evil and disease, that if allowed to propagate it would find a way to infect the entire human race. Like any breeding enterprise, or animal husbandry, Aristotle instructed the Seed of Life to concern themselves not just with breeding the perfect strain of human being, but to eradicate the worst of the rest. According to this document, the most fundamental rule of the Seed of Life seemed to be that all physically deformed offspring of the families should be killed at birth, preferably with fire so the disease might be cleansed. This was their most important rule, and it was the failure to terminate the life of a malformed child which ranked as the highest sin, and therefore incurred this most draconian of punishments.'

William looked down at his bandaged hand, a creeping coldness where his thumb should have been.

## CHAPTER FORTY-NINE

*I*n the east of the city, Adeline watched as Obediah Pincott reached across the bed and closed the woman's eyes. The dead woman's hand still clutched a musical box, although the toy seemed broken beyond repair.

A scrawny child snuffled in a cot on the other side of the bed. The endeavour had ended in disappointment, although it was the death of the other, Rebecca, which peeved her more. To think she had murdered her own child while it was still warm in her belly, ending its life along with her own. Such selfishness! Why would a woman do such a thing? And the Whitfield girl had been lost too, saved by the half-caste whore.

'To think that you were overcome by such a slip of a girl – I can hardly believe it. I do not believe it, in fact.'

'Such a clever puppy.'

'Indeed.' Adeline looked across to the child. 'It isn't fit for purpose. Dispose of it with the mother.'

Pincott continued to stare at the dead woman and said nothing.

'Did you hear what I said?'

'Always.'

Adeline sniffed at his impudence, but refused to let it dampen her spirits. Everything was still to play for.

The baby's lungs gave a weak cry. 'We will need to start again.'

Pincott turned towards her, his eyes flat and dark. 'You search for the perfect recipe, like a child making mud pies in the garden.'

She raised her hand to slap him but he grabbed her wrist, lightning quick. 'Why do you not have your own?'

She pulled away. 'I cannot.'

'You are so sure?'

'I am sure.' She faced away from him, her fingers coiling through a ringlet of red hair, her eyes locked on something that wasn't there.

Pincott's gaze returned to the child. 'Must everything be perfect?'

She smiled at his incomprehension. 'Of course. Otherwise what is the point? If we do not strive for greatness in what we do, then we should not strive at all.'

'Then why not kill all of them? The imperfect ones, whoever sired them.'

'Maybe. Maybe we will.'

He leant forward. 'You have a plan, Vicomtesse? Tell me, when the time came, would I live or die?'

'Well, that depends.' She twirled away from him. 'Where do your loyalties lie?'

He didn't answer. Instead, he leant forward and removed the musical box from the woman's hand. When his voice came, he sounded far away. 'I could tell you a story, about a boy called Yaroslav and a girl named Lata. I could tell you how they loved each other. But the story did not happen that way. Another story took its place. I have no loyalties, Vicomtesse, only stories that never lived.' He plucked at the broken spring and the box tinkled briefly, an echo of its former tune.

It was an answer of sorts. Already she was beginning to regret speaking of such things. There were so many secrets inside her, swirling into soup.

Pincott threw a sheet over the woman's body. 'And what of the young lawyer? Tell me why you hunt him, such an ordinary man. What is he to you?'

Her temper flared once more. 'You say that as if ordinary were *good*! It is not good, it is an evil that does nothing to better who we are.'

'Has he shown himself?'

Her memories of last night were misty for she had drunk too much. She could barely remember William Lamb's presence, let alone his face. But Silas Matlock was on the case and he had a lead to follow. She was not the only one who might yet be betrayed.

## CHAPTER FIFTY

O n the journey back to Fleet Street, William walked ahead of the others. They would think it was his keenness to escape the charging rain; after all, he had a weak chest to go with his missing thumb and countless other flaws in their eyes, no doubt.

Returning to the Old Bell first, he trudged up the steps to their room without caring for his sodden clothes and muddy boots. He took the photograph of his mother from the wooden frame and looked at the familiar features, the ones he so often saw in himself, this time hoping to see through to the secrets beneath. He went to the window and gazed at the turbulent sky. Minutes later, Savannah appeared at his shoulder and silently joined his vigil.

William watched the rain smash down, relentless in its punishment. 'I was born to them. The Seed of Life.'

Savannah said nothing.

William watched the deluge churn the street to mud, splashing filth everywhere. 'My parents failed to do their duty. They perished in a fire. Was the fire intended for me? And now the seven wish to finish the job.'

'You are speculating. You do not know.'

But he did know. The moment Professor Middleton had revealed their most sacred rule, William had known in his very bones what it meant. He was one of their progeny, a deformed child who should have been put to death the moment he emerged from the womb. It followed that one or both of his parents had been part of the families, a supposed descendant of Alexander the Great. Which line did they hail from?

William folded the photograph into his pocket and surrendered his place by the window. Vespers began at the abbey at half past six. Harry kept himself busy writing down extensive notes of his investigations so far, the names of all they knew to be involved and outlining the corroborating evidence that could be found at the OBA. He despatched the notes with the casket of precious documents to Finian at *The Times*, together with a fervent plea to publish if anything should befall them as they pursued the truth this coming night.

William dug through his bag for the leaflets on breeding techniques he had taken from the building in Whitehall. He would know the worst. The booklets provided advice to animal breeders. It was only when William read them in the context of his own species that he shuddered at the appalling inhumanity of it all.

William felt the bitter knot in his stomach harden like stale bread. He looked around the room. He was surrounded by perfect human beings. Damaged maybe, like Savannah's scar, or old, like Harry, but the recipes within them were intact, whereas William's had always been missing an ingredient that could never be stirred through at a later stage, the chance of perfection stumbling at the first hurdle.

William felt a hand touch his shoulder.

Harry spoke gently. 'Come, William, it is time.'

As they stood before the Gothic towers of Westminster Abbey, the sun emerged, intensely bright after the obliteration of the storm. A rainbow sliced through the sky to the east, almost juvenile in its display of primary colours above the murky, subtle stone of the city that mushroomed beneath.

They were early. The plan was for William to sit as close as possible to the Cosmati pavement itself, near the high altar. Harry and Mildred would sit nearby, ready to move closer if and when Habborlain appeared. Savannah, her agitation growing by the minute, decided to stay in the shadows of the north transept, making sure the path was clear if they needed to leave that way.

Harry clapped his hands together. 'This is it, then. Are you ready, old chap?'

William gazed ahead. 'I have never been ready for any of this.'

Before any of them could give him another pep talk, William strode through the ancient portal and into the huge nave of the abbey. The church was sparsely populated, although in such a colossal space it would have been difficult for it to ever feel crowded. William looked around for the shock of white hair and towering form of Ambrose Habborlain, but saw no one of that description. He moved forward through the rows of narrow pews until he reached the centre of the abbey's cross. In front of him lay the Cosmati pavement, a square of mosaic laid in polished stone, the colours now muted. He recognised the Seed of Life symbol everywhere, although here it was but a component part, forming patterns on an even grander scale.

There was no obvious place to sit so he moved towards the north transept, seeing Savannah slip through the north door and lean against one of the columns, looking as out of place as one might expect in a house of Christian worship, although he noticed that she had lowered her new petticoats to cover her ankles. William took a seat in a pew near the front and contemplated the altar before him, ignoring Mildred and Harry as they took their places a few pews away. Although the service would not begin for another few minutes, the choir was already singing a canticle and he closed his eyes. Their harmonies were beautiful, recalling William to another world when he and Aunt Esther would attend evensong at St Peter's church near their home. Then he had believed in goodness as an absolute, before he had seen with his own eyes the evil that men do.

'I am glad you are not alone, William. Shall we call your friends forward?'

William's eyes shot open. It was a voice he recognised, the thin sound that could penetrate the air like an arrow. It came from behind him, but he dare not turn around, so afraid he was that there would be no one there, that the name Habborlain was simply a ghost he would whisper for ever.

He heard more shuffling behind him, then Harry's calm quiet voice. 'You are Ambrose Habborlain? I am Detective Harry Treadway and this is Miss Mildred Whitfield. We are William's friends.'

'I am glad of it.'

At this William finally turned around and looked once more at the ashen face of Ambrose Habborlain, the man responsible for so much.

William heard the steel in his own voice. 'Mr Bridge is dead. Your message, which I dutifully delivered, scared him from his wits. He took his own life, Mr Habborlain, in front of me, *his own life!*'

'I know, William. I thought it a possibility when I sent you back to him.'

William shot to his feet, the pew in front almost toppling over. The congregation nearby turned to stare, but it was Mildred who rose from her seat and touched his arm, pulling him gently back down.

Habborlain continued, 'I understand your anger, William, of course I do. I have stayed in the city myself only to meet with you today. I did not know what Bridge might tell you before he left.'

'He told me nothing! He simply gave me the casket and told me to run.' William did not know which of the two men most deserved the heat of his anger.

'And I have simply come here to tell you the same, William. You must run and leave all of this behind. I have arranged passage for us tonight. I have been making plans from the moment I heard of Nathaniel's death. Many have sacrificed themselves for you and now you must do the same and save yourself. You have the documents?'

'They are safe.'

'Bring them with you.'

'We need answers.'

'If you have the documents, then you will understand much already. Time is against us. We should go now and make preparations.'

William's anger boiled over and he could barely contain his voice as he stared across at Habborlain. 'No, old man, you told me that once before! *Time* is not against us, our *enemies* are against us, and you will *not* leave this place until you have told us everything we wish to know!'

The old man hung his head and Harry gently pushed William back into his seat. Biting his lip, William turned forward, not trusting himself to speak again. He slowed his breathing, not from panic this time, but to control the newborn rage within him.

Harry filled the silence. 'We have been to the Association, and we have translated the documents, so you are right, we know much already. We know of the seven.'

As Habborlain began to list them all, confirming first that Von Rabenmarck was head of the Warrior family, Harry cut him short, for they knew the other identities. What was new to them was the source of Tinbergen's wealth, a subject that seemed to have transfixed the world for years. Tinbergen was indeed descended from the Scientist line, through his mother, a distant Raycraft relation. His father had been plucked from obscurity by the previous Finder, selected for his entrepreneurial, if low-born, skills. Now, as the Investor, the son had been made guardian of the great fortune that the sect had generated over thousands of years, passing it off as his own.

William turned once more. 'And you *believe* in all this? That you are the descendant of Alexander the Great, part of a superior breed?'

Habborlain's downturned eyes met his. 'I believe the former, yes, but not the latter. I believed in it for many years – my father raised me to inherit the line.'

'Lord Byron.'

Habborlain smiled. 'Indeed, William, you have deduced much—'

William interrupted again, 'You were telling us what you believed in.'

'I told you before, when we first met, all the ideas I once believed in died with my children, one by one. Twelve deaths, not one of them living beyond the age of twenty-five. Twelve children by seven different mothers. The disease was in *me*, William, not them. So much for the strength of Alexander's seed! And as for artistic greatness, well, we had some success I suppose throughout the generations, my father in particular. But what of Chaucer, Shakespeare, or Michelangelo? The randomness of God's creation has done far better than us.' He shook his head. 'I no longer believe our sacred mission to be of any value. Poor Bridge never did. He inherited his role from his father, a cousin of mine, but could find no way to leave it behind. He tried, with me, to limit the worst excesses, but we were failing.' He hung his head. 'We *did* fail.'

Mildred's previously restrained anger finally found voice. 'I was kidnapped, taken to a rogue's hideout in Whitechapel. *Forced*.'

Habborlain closed his eyes. 'I refused to have anything to do with it. Our sacred fathers believed only in breeding through consensual marriage; that natural cover was critical for the development of excellence. But the others are impatient, drunk on scientific discoveries. They think to dispense with our rules.' He looked up at William again. 'It is not the only rule they have broken.'

Harry pushed on. 'Their activities at the Raycraft factory. People are dying there.'

William didn't think it was possible for Habborlain's face to grow paler. Harry waited for him to answer the question but there was no reply. The abbey echoed with the canon's sonorous voice, reading the sermon, but all the three of them could really hear was Habborlain's silence.

'Mr Habborlain? It is important you tell me what you know.'

Habborlain's voice was a whisper. 'I share your worries, Detective Treadway. Von Rabenmarck fears political change, the rise of the common man. I thought Cornelius's visit might herald something, though what I did not know. I had suspicions only. It is why Bridge took the documents from the OBA and made a list of the current families. We thought to expose them, if only we could find the right ear. The Raycraft factory you say? I had not thought so ill of him until now.' Habborlain grasped Harry's hand. 'You must go. You must stop them. Otto is a truly great man, with even greater ambitions. I sometimes wondered if he thought himself Alexander, reborn. A conqueror for this new world.'

William grabbed his arm. 'I need my answers too. Was I born to one of the families?'

'Yes.'

'And when I was born, deformed, my parents were supposed to kill me?'

'Yes! Only it was I who was charged by your mother with terminating your life. She was ill after the birth and could not do so herself. But I could not do it either, William. By then I had seen so many of my own children die, I could not take another child's life, whatever the sacred rule said. So Bridge helped me spirit you away. Over the years we have saved many more, Bridge and I, but you were the first, William. I had no idea he had kept you close to him, the fool. We always knew the fate that awaited us if we were caught. That is why Bridge killed himself, thinking he would suffer so horrendously when Adeline's men found him. Now you must go with me. Run, do not let them find you now!'

William ignored his protestations. 'My aunt knew all of this?'

'She is not your aunt, William! She must have been one of Bridge's clients and he arranged for her to adopt you, to bring you up as her nephew. He provided for you both, I suspect.'

William drank up the truth with an eager thirst. 'And the watch my father left me? My trust fund?'

William pulled the watch from his pocket and thrust it towards Habborlain. The old man sighed as he examined it. 'It belonged to Nathaniel's father. I recognise it. He obviously cared for you, William, but it was sentimental of him to keep you close all those years. The others we saved, we sent them away and I was sure no path could be found back to us. Over the years I knew I was being watched, that Fischer was Adeline's man. There were others, too.' William looked across at the pacing Savannah as Habborlain continued, 'I couldn't hide my loss of faith in what we were doing and so they stopped trusting me, rightly so.' He grabbed at William's lapel, his eyes shining wet with tears. 'It was our grand mission, William, to save as many as we could, the only thing that kept me from being buried by grief. He clearly never thought you would come looking for me. He was not a strong man, dear Nathaniel, and not always clever, but he was a good one. Do not blame him, despite his grave mistake. Your deformity was so distinctive there was always a chance it would identify you to those we had deceived.'

William tore the photograph from his pocket and thrust it at Habborlain, not caring for the stares around him. 'What was her real name? Which family did she belong to? Is she still alive?'

Habborlain glanced down. 'He gave you this?' He examined the image, nodding his head as if he understood something. 'She is dead, William.'

'My father then. Who was he?'

Habborlain fumbled for his watch, which hung about his neck on one of the thick gold chains he wore. 'My goodness, there really is no time! You must get the documents and meet me at the port. I have prepared everything. The rest of you should go!' Habborlain stood, unfolding his great height once more. 'Come with me. I will give you the answers you seek once we are away from here.'

'I will not leave without my aunt!'

The old man grasped William by the shoulders. 'Then you will die here and so will she. You cannot beat them, only run!'

William's voice choked on his words. 'Who was my father?'

'Answers won't save you, William!'

Harry grabbed at the old man. 'Stay and help us. Together, we can bring them down.'

A sharp police whistle split the air and the canon paused mid-prayer. Savannah dashed towards them. 'We need to leave right now! The north door, follow me!' she yelled as she ran back through the transept.

William turned to see the west doors swing open, and the elite red guard of the German army march through. They had been found!

Mildred and Harry leapt to their feet, but Habborlain began to laugh. 'Too late. We were always too late!'

The old man removed a sheaf of papers from inside his robe before thrusting them into William's hands. 'Tickets. Money. Everything you need. Go!'

Harry urged him. 'You must come with us!'

But Habborlain threw him off and began to back away towards the advancing men. He smiled at William. 'Maybe I can save you after all?'

William ran to him, grabbing at his clothes. 'What are you doing?'

Habborlain pushed him away. 'I have had enough of life, William! If they have my blood, they might not want yours.'

'No!'

'Perhaps I deserve to be punished? Not for saving children like you, but for inflicting the rot inside me on my own. Now run!'

He pulled away, and marched towards the red guard, as the congregation began to murmur and stir at their approach.

William went to run after him, but Harry grabbed him back. 'Leave him, William, we must go.'

William struggled in Harry's grip, roaring at Habborlain's back, 'Tell me who my father is!'

But Habborlain did not turn. Instead he walked on, into the path of his enemies, raising his arms above his head as if to God.

Savannah cried out. William swung around towards the north door, horrified to see her pinned to the floor by a swarm of constables who struggled to contain her thrashing limbs.

He leapt forward, blind instinct driving him towards her against the tide of the fleeing congregation, even though more men in blue poured through the transept like flies.

'Run!' Savannah yelled. She was hopelessly trapped and he knew it.

Harry tried to pull William back, but his feet wouldn't move, his eyes locked on the futile struggle. He couldn't see her face any more, just one arm stretched out, a savage fist beating on unfeeling stone.

'Don't let her fight be in vain, William!'

How many more would sacrifice themselves for him? He wrenched his eyes away, the hardest thing he had ever done in his pathetic life, knowing he did it for her, and her alone.

He grabbed Mildred by the hand and, with Harry, ran to the south transept and into the cloisters of the abbey. He had no idea how they might escape this place, he just ran and ran, through doors, across grass, skipping over the deep gashes of mud that tore up the streets, leaving a piece of his soul on the abbey floor behind him. He felt as if he were flying, that he could run for ever if only he could find his way home again.

## CHAPTER FIFTY-ONE

*H*arry had almost caught up with William when the young man fell to his knees in the middle of a busy road. Carriages swerved about him, their drivers shouting obscenities. Harry turned back towards Mildred but she waved him forwards. He pressed on, reaching William, and attempted to raise him from the dirt.

It was heartbreaking to see him in such a condition. The William he had encountered only days ago had been fastidious and pedantic, but now he rested on his knees, his arms supporting himself elbow deep in mud, his face spattered with grime as he sucked the stinking air deep inside his exhausted lungs. Harry thought of Edward Raycraft, naked and smeared in filth, driven to madness. He pushed the thought aside and pulled William to his feet and out of harm's way.

Mildred caught up with them. 'We must not stay on the streets, Detective Treadway.'

Harry led a bewildered William into a nearby alley, away from the crowds. Surely the boy's thoughts were tumbling madly, replaying Habborlain's words and agonising over Savannah's fate. Harry also feared for the worst, for he suspected Miss Shelton had finally exhausted her luck.

William caught Harry's eye and seemed to focus for the first time. 'Maybe I should do as he said. Just leave this place behind.

Run.' He still held the filthy, sodden sheaf of papers and money in his fist.

Harry tried to smile. 'It must be tempting, but I know you will not leave the people you love.'

William gave a weak laugh. 'And who are they, exactly? These people I love? An aunt who is not my aunt, who has lied to me for twenty-three years, who along with the man I thought of as my friend brought me up to live in the shadows, to fear everything, to be a *coward*—'

Mildred interrupted him, her tone sharp. 'You heard Mr Habborlain, your aunt probably knew nothing, only that she must keep you safe. You cannot doubt that she loved you.'

William dropped the ball of mush to the floor and kicked it away. He leant his head back against the grimy wall and gazed at the glowering sky. 'I fear Savannah is lost.'

Harry nodded. 'I fear it too, although if anyone in this world can best the odds it is Savannah Shelton.'

Mildred helped William to clean his face and hands. Harry offered his handkerchief, seeing that their own were already brown with dirt. Mildred was a gentle soul, but with a steel backbone. Harry could see William watching her as she went about her ministrations, his eyes naked and raw.

Habborlain had decided not to answer William's burning question, leaving Harry to speculate about the men they had encountered so far who had a connection to the Seed of Life. Could any of them be William's father? Cornelius Tinbergen was surely too young, nor had he visited the country before now, but Otto Von Rabenmarck and Sir Jasper Raycraft were both of the right age, and it was already clear that another Raycraft child, Phoebe Stanbury, had been born in secret. Was William a Raycraft too? Connected somehow to the murderous Edward and the wretched Phoebe?

William broke into his thoughts. 'Why would Habborlain sacrifice himself? Knowing what awaits him?'

'You are young, William. As one gets older, things change; holding on to life seems less important than protecting your family, or something you believe in.'

'He said he didn't believe in anything any more.'

'I think that was a lie. He believes in you.'

William pushed Mildred away and thumped his fist into the wall, his eyes flashing. 'I have been treated like a toy my whole life! Tossed away, retrieved, given away, then found once more, captured and saved and so it goes on. I am weary of it. He had no right to keep me from who I am!'

Harry leant forward, matching William's passion with his own. 'You are who you wish to be! You are a man who loves the woman who raised him, who would do anything to protect her. You are a man with friends. That is who you are, William. Knowing the names of those who conceived of you and then tossed you away will add nothing, *nothing* to the man I know you to be!'

'Well said, Detective Treadway, well said!' Mildred chimed in.

Harry pulled back, weary of his own lies, however well-intentioned. Of course William's parentage mattered. It was in our very soul, the need to know where we came from, a seed that would not be denied.

William's breathing was shallow as he stared down at the bleeding knuckles of his right hand. Harry could see dark shadows had formed beneath his eyes. When he spoke, his voice was hard. 'You are right, Harry. I will do anything to protect my aunt. That is all I am now.' The words were wrong somehow, the look on his face even more so.

Harry reached out and grabbed William's arm. 'We must think through our next steps. Reach out to Benjamin Raycraft. The time has come for that, I think.'

William's gentle laugh was chilling. 'Always, Harry, always we wait. We think. We look for help that never comes. I am done waiting.' William pushed him away as he marched back towards the busy main street.

'No, William!' Harry stumbled to catch up. 'You cannot go to the factory alone!'

William whirred around. 'Then come with me!'

'We need help! We can achieve nothing on our own.'

He grabbed at Harry's lapels as Mildred looked helplessly on. 'I will see my aunt once more! And I will have answers!'

William let go as Harry realised in horror what he had taken – his gun. 'Even if I have to die for it.'

'Please, William!' But the young man turned and ran. Harry gave chase as William sprinted across the street without looking, but he lacked William's careless disregard to his own safety. By the time he had reached the other side, William had hailed a cab and already it was out of reach.

Harry panted for breath, his hands on his knees. So off the pace, always. Why had he not read William's mood? Always the last to sense the wind's direction, or to know the true hearts of men. A poor detective indeed.

Mildred caught up. 'We must follow him!'

'We will telegraph Ridgeside first. Ask Benjamin to meet us at the gates as soon as he can. It is time the son stood up to the father.'

*❧*

*I*t took three constables to hold Savannah down as the police cart rumbled and jolted through the city streets. Where were they taking her?

She still couldn't believe the sheer number of men in blue that had poured through the north door of the abbey, disarming her before she had a chance to reach for her Colt. This had been no accidental discovery of their whereabouts, for the ambush had been planned with military precision. Who, then, had given them away? It couldn't be JJ, that boy would die first. Was he perhaps already dead? The thought sank to her stomach.

They finally came to a stop and she was manhandled out of the cart. She recognised their location at once: the back entrance to the Olympian Breeding Association. Why not Scotland Yard?

She stopped struggling as the constables led her towards the cellar steps. The door yawned open. A smiling, grey-haired man with rosy cheeks and an abundance of whiskers was waiting for her. Colonel Matlock, it must be. She returned his grin.

He ignored her and spoke to her captors. 'Thank you, boys. I appreciate this is an unorthodox location, but this woman will be extradited tonight to the US. Bring her in.'

Savannah recommenced her struggle, landing a clean punch on the side of someone's head, but she knew even as she did so that resistance was useless. They flung her inside a cellar room and left. Matlock gave her a final grin before slamming the door and turning a key in the lock.

So, she was to be extradited back to the US, like a souvenir of the vice president's trip to England, along with some Fortnum's tea and Highland whisky, no doubt. She looked around, her eyes adjusting to the gloom. A weak band of late evening sun crept through a small iron grille set high in the wall. The room held little – a few broken bits of furniture, a rusted press and a crate of stained linen napkins. She was in the junk room, waiting her turn to be cast out with the rest of the rubbish.

She grabbed a chair with three legs. Using the crate to act as a fourth, she dragged both towards the light. Once up on the chair, she could just reach the grille. She poked one hand through and felt around. Sawdust and dirt. Remembering the dogs that chased them that night, she quickly withdrew her hand. She grabbed at the iron bars and pulled hard, but there was no movement. Maybe if she built her platform higher, she could get more purchase.

'I admire you for trying, but personally I think it unlikely to succeed.'

She swung around and in so doing, toppled to the floor.

Matlock stood just inside the door, a smile on his face and a gun in his hand. 'I have been reading of your crimes, those you committed on American soil. Of course, you have since added to the list, but the British government are generously prepared to waive prosecution in order to allow you to return to your home country and do penance there.'

'How kind of them. When do I leave?' she asked. That would be her chance. A journey, out in the open, the docks, a ship. Plenty of opportunities to strike out and run.

'Ah, well there's the rub. The Home Office approved for you to travel back with the vice president, but unfortunately he has had to depart our shores in some haste. President Garfield has been shot and they do not, alas, think he will survive. A terrible business. Tinbergen is to be sworn in as soon as possible.'

'Another ship, then. I am in no particular rush.'

Matlock's smile broadened. 'I don't think so, my dear. We have made alternative plans. Apparently there might be some use for you at the Raycraft laboratory. It would seem you are a fascinating specimen.'

The basement in the factory where William's aunt was being held. She thought of Rebecca's words: *some people who go in do not come out again.*

She only had one card left to play. 'If anything happens to us, the front page of *The Times* might make interesting reading. They know all your shabby little secrets, and they have the box.'

'Ah, Finian Worthing, the journalist, fine fellow.' Savannah's blood ran cold as Matlock continued. 'He was impressively resistant at first, but yes, he betrayed you, and the casket is back where it belongs. I have just this moment read Harry's notes for myself. He was always such an excellent taker of notes.'

She forced herself to smile. 'Never trust a journalist, eh?'

'Goodbye, Miss Shelton. They will come for you shortly.'

He closed the door. She heard the key tumble in its lock, but not the grating sound of it being removed. She waited until his footsteps had faded away and knelt before the door, her eye pressed against the keyhole. Blackness. The key was still there. She felt under the door. There was a gap.

She dived into the pile of broken things, selecting bits of wood that might do the job. She examined the old press. Thin strips of rusted metal ran across the top and she used an old table leg to break one away.

At the door she knelt down again. Using the tip of the metal bar she pushed gently at the key. With a clang, it landed on the other side. She forced the rod beneath the door. It was a snug fit. Slowly she traced an arc with the bar, stopping when she felt it touch something. She pulled the bar towards her, manoeuvring the key towards the bottom of the door.

But progress stopped. The key was too large to slide underneath. She pushed and prodded, trying the key along every inch of the opening to see if it could pass under, but it was no good. Another plan that had come to nothing.

She pulled herself into the corner by the door, arms around her knees. Think, Shelton, think. Her brain was fog. When had she last slept properly? Days ago? Weeks? Months, maybe. She felt in her pocket. Her tin of tobacco was still there. She rolled a cigarette, struck one of the last of her matches and pulled in a lungful of smoke. A fascinating specimen, Matlock had called her. When would they come for her? Maybe she should try to sleep, be ready and refreshed to fight again. Her eyelids were closing. Another puff of smoke, drawn deep, her muscles relaxing.

She woke to the smell of burning. She looked down to see herself smouldering. She scrambled to her feet and tore off her skirt and petticoats, stamping on them. She had almost succeeded in ending her own life, having fought so hard in recent days to save it.

Heavy rain now obliterated the light outside, muddy rivulets running through the grille. They must surely be here soon. No matter, she finally had a plan.

One match left. She pulled the crate of old napkins into the centre of the room and dumped her petticoats on top. She lit the match. Here goes nothing, she thought.

But the petticoats caught, and so did the crate. She grabbed the table leg and stabbed it into the blaze, trying not to think about the consequences if her plan failed. She pounded on the door. 'Fire!'

She ran towards the grille. 'Fire! Please help me!'

The flames were stronger now. She pounded on the door once again. Footsteps at last. She jammed herself into the corner behind the door as someone retrieved the fallen key and rattled it into the lock.

A man ran inside and doused the fire with a bucket of sand. She grabbed the door and slithered through, then slammed it shut and twisted the key.

'Hey!'

She ignored his shouts and stumbled forward, away from the main exit where they might expect her to go. The corridor of dank brick twisted round and she ran up some steps. Another corridor, another series of doors, shouts and the clatter of boots behind her. She grabbed the nearest handle.

The door opened into darkness and she could see nothing. She had no idea what part of the building she had entered. With her arms outstretched in front of her, she began to feel her way around. The floor beneath her was stone, and the air was cool, some kind of storage area perhaps? She kept moving forward, her fingers tentatively stretched out. They made contact with something cold and round, and before she could pull back there was a deafening crash as something smashed on the hard stone floor. Immediately light flooded the room. She shielded her eyes and saw an open doorway to her right. A maid bustled through, astonishment on her face. 'Who on earth are you?' She frowned then, her gaze taking in Savannah's swollen eye. 'I ain't seen you before, are you from the agency?'

Savannah looked behind the maid, but could see no one else approaching. The woman was alone. She stepped forward, her arms out to her side expressing her helplessness. 'I'm so sorry, but I lost my way, I'm with Colonel Matlock.' She knelt down and began to rummage through the broken china. 'Let me help you clear this up.' Her hands grasped a large green jug that had fallen to the floor undamaged. In one swift movement, she smashed it into the side of the woman's head. The maid fell to the floor immediately without uttering a sound.

Savannah checked her pulse, muttered her apologies, and pulled the woman's unconscious body into a corner of what was obviously a large scullery. Quickly she swapped her own clothes for the maid's uniform, pushing her hair inside the little white cap and securing it roughly with pins. She considered swapping her boots, thinking her own might look out of place, but decided against it, once again reminding herself that one never knew when one might need to run like hell.

She entered the room beyond, another scullery where the maid had been in the process of refilling a tray of glasses. She finished the job, grabbed the tray, and opened the door to the next room. A wave of steam rolled over her as she entered the kitchens. A chef was shouting orders as men and women scuttled around in the heat. Savannah dipped her head and skirted around the outside of the room, hoping not to be noticed. As she passed the dresser she grabbed a carving knife from its block and shoved it in the pocket of her apron before hurrying on.

She pushed through another door and almost crashed into a footman coming the other way. Savannah mumbled an apology but he ignored her. She found herself in an empty corridor, not knowing which way to turn. In front of her, what looked like just a section of panelled wall pushed inwards and another maid hurried through with a tray of empty glasses. 'Blimey, they're a thirsty lot tonight! Get them glasses out there then leave 'em to it. Mr Lampley says we've got to clear the ballroom by half past eight.' She leant in close and whispered, 'Some kind of secret ceremony! I used to work at the Mason's hall in Finchley. The things they got up to, really!' She frowned then. 'I ain't seen you before, are you from the agency?'

'Yep. I mean yes.'

'Which one?' The woman looked suspicious.

'Arizona. Now if you'll excuse me, I need to get these glasses to Mr Lampley.' Savannah pushed past her and made for the concealed door.

Like William and Harry she found the scale of the

underground ballroom hard to credit compared to the modest structure of the building above it. There were maybe fifty or so people milling towards the front of the room near the large stage. The gas footlights had been lit as if in preparation for some kind of performance. An elderly man in a butler's uniform beckoned her towards a long table decked in spotless white linen. She hurried forward.

'I don't recognise you.'

'I'm from the agency.' Savannah tried a cockney accent for the first time in her life. It sounded to her own ears as if she had something wrong with her jaw, but Lampley didn't seem the most observant of men.

'Where's Agnes?'

'She's got an 'eadache, sir.'

'Unload the glasses, take the empty ones, and be on your way. We need to clear the room.'

'Some kind of entertainment is it, sir?'

'Never you mind.'

Savannah took her time with the glasses, snatching the odd glance that allowed her to survey the crowd. They were a mixture of ages, including children. The youngest could have been no more than two years old, tugging constantly at his mother's skirts. Others ran around unsupervised, clearly thrilled to be allowed up so late. The atmosphere was convivial and everyone seemed to know each other. One, big, happy family.

Her task completed, Savannah scanned around for somewhere to hide – she had no intention of leaving the party. She could see steps leading to the stage nearby, great black curtains sweeping the floor. She backed away from the table, then dropped to the floor, out of sight. She slid back on her haunches towards the curtain and swung it around her as she pulled herself up on to the stage, fully shrouded now and hidden from view, the only problem being that she couldn't see a thing. She sought out a gap to peer through, but the curtain was made of one solid piece of fabric.

A hush stole over the crowd. She felt the light change, fading from the ballroom itself and condensing brightly on to the stage. Someone passed her, barely inches away, striding out in front of the crowd. The room grew heavy with an expectant silence. Even the children had fallen quiet and Savannah found herself holding her breath as a Germanic male voice addressed them all.

'Friends, family, welcome to this unexpected reunion, so soon after our last. It is humbling to see so many of you in attendance here tonight despite the short notice that is inevitable in these circumstances.' It was the German chancellor, it had to be. 'Sadly, Raycraft has been called away on urgent business and, of course, our dear Investor has had to return to the United States. You will all know that President Garfield's life hangs by a thread. This shameless assassination shows without doubt that the battle I have warned you of is here! In this place, and this time. Across the globe, the natural order of things is being overturned. Unless we act, our days, the days of the elite, will be over for ever, trodden down in the relentless march of the common man.' He warmed to his topic, his voice rising. 'You see, they have been breeding too, the masses. Not for perfection, but for growth. Growth we must curtail! For what is the point of breeding brilliance, only for it to be lost in the crowd?' Shouts of *hurrah* and fervent applause greeted his words.

Von Rabenmarck began again, his voice full of theatrical display. 'Many of you knew Ambrose Habborlain well, some of you belong to his house, *all* of you will, I know, share the burden of responsibility that has fallen on the shoulders of the seven here tonight. But, alas, we are no longer seven. Through acts of the deepest treachery, and most heinous contravention of our sacred covenant, two of our number have abandoned our cause. Nathaniel Bridge, may his soul be damned, took his own life rather than face the sacred penalty. His offence? That most evil of crimes – allowing the weak to survive.' There were murmurs of agreement from the crowd and Savannah heard a young child boo loudly, a sound that chilled her.

The chancellor continued, 'But the main perpetrator, Ambrose Habborlain, head of the Artist family, will stand before us tonight. By his own admission it is a crime he has committed again and again, with flagrant disregard to our noble cause. He has surrendered himself to his fate, acknowledging his own guilt and regret. Our Protector, Colonel Silas Matlock has, with a heavy heart, volunteered to perform the deed. Bring him out!'

The crowd erupted then, a furious sound of catcalling and boos, and Savannah inched back the curtain to view what was happening on the stage. Ambrose Habborlain had been pushed towards the front and stood bathed in light. He wore a long white robe with a sash around his waist, his hands bound behind him. The man was smiling towards the mob that now bayed for his blood, a smile of forgiveness that shocked her. Matlock stood to one side, his rosy cheeks glowing, a knife glinting in his hand. Otto Von Rabenmarck stood nearest to her, smiling as the macabre event unfolded.

What were her options? Surely she had to free Habborlain. She could see no guards or other security waiting in the wings. If she could release the old man, his escape would be the main focus of both Matlock and the crowd, giving her a chance to grab the German and find out what had happened to the others.

Before she could question her own plan, she stepped out from behind the curtain and dashed towards Habborlain, slashing his bonds in one swipe of the knife in her hand. The crowd had barely any time to react before she turned to Von Rabenmarck and yanked him to his knees, the blade of her knife resting against the throbbing vein in his neck. She could see the shadow of the crowd beyond the footlights.

But something was wrong. Habborlain hadn't moved. He should be running, pulling all the attention away from her!

She felt a hand grab her hair through her maid's cap and the cold steel of another knife press against her own neck. Surprise momentarily caused her to lessen her grip on the German, allowing him to scrabble away. Her plan had spectacularly misfired.

Matlock's voice whispered in her ear, his breath sour with red wine, 'Would you be so kind as to drop the knife?'

Habborlain remained still, his eyes looking at her sadly. Why hadn't the man run? Maybe if she could get the knife to him, it would spur him into action. She needed him to do something if she was to stand any chance. The knife in her hand was useless to her now that Matlock held his to her throat.

Decision made, she flung the knife towards the static Habborlain. It arced through the air and landed a few feet away. Immediately, Von Rabenmarck groped towards it on his hands and knees while Habborlain simply stared at her, dumbfounded.

'Pick up the knife!' she roared.

His eyes dropped at last to the floor. As the German lunged, Habborlain bent quickly and grabbed the knife, the steel flashing as it caught the beam of the footlights. Habborlain turned the blade over in his hands then looked towards her, his eyes closing as he slowly shook his head. Matlock chuckled in her ear. 'That was a mistake, Miss Shelton.'

Of course it was. Everything had been a mistake. The old man did not want to be rescued. Just like Rebecca, their choices were made long before Savannah Shelton rode in like a fool. Holding the handle outwards, Ambrose Habborlain plunged the knife through his sternum and into his own heart. The crowd gasped, a few even clapped.

'No!'

Matlock, whose arm still wound about her neck in a deadly

embrace, laughed once more as Habborlain's long body crumpled before them like a tower, built too high and destined to fall.

A shape emerged from the shadows beyond his body, red hair lit up by the footlights. The vicomtesse glided across the stage towards Savannah. No one is coming to save me, she thought, and where is the surprise in that?

As the vicomtesse approached, Savannah knew she brought death with her. She could almost see it, holding the woman's hand like a malevolent child.

Alone in the end. Ah well.

Savannah Shelton did her best to smile.

## CHAPTER FIFTY-THREE

The storm had grown more ferocious as the evening wore on. Edward Raycraft wrapped his coat about him. Realising that he had not eaten for days, his stomach growling with discontent, he abandoned his vigil to steal a half-eaten pigeon pie from the kitchens of a nearby tavern, but took no pleasure in its consumption. He was simply stoking a fire that needed to burn on a short while yet, before it could smoulder into nothingness.

He returned to his observation post across the street from the factory's gates. The minutes turned to hours as he watched the hubbub subside and the workers leave in huddled groups. He remembered the compound only vaguely, the towering chimneys, the riveted iron doors that led down into the earth, intended to keep the world out, and the secrets hidden within.

But he remembered the basement. The beating, secret heart of his father's empire. Memories swarmed, the magic and wonder of an innocent time, when he believed himself whole and human. The things he had seen – shapes etched carelessly on a mind too young to comprehend. In that chamber underground his father had made demons, but the worst of his fabrications he had shaped in the world above.

*I am your grand invention, and I am home at last.*

Glancing at the tower, he saw a light appear in the room at the top. His father must be facing another sleepless night. Just like Macbeth, thought Edward, his father's iniquity had murdered sleep.

*But I will murder more than that.*

## CHAPTER FIFTY-FOUR

The journey was taking too long: the rain, a commotion on the streets. Tonight would be the end of it, one way or another. William closed his hand about Harry's gun, nestled in his pocket, warm from his own incessant touch. It was a prop, no more. The hunk of metal would, he hoped, yield the answers that his own voice had been denied.

When he reached the gates of the factory, he fumbled some coins to the driver and blundered into the rain. It was almost dark now, but he felt a great swell of energy tingle through to his very fingertips.

Aunt Esther was here.

He saw a stack of crates beside a nearby wall, almost forming a staircase, as if someone had known he was coming and deliberately placed them there. Without pause, he clambered up to the lip of the wall and looked down into the factory yard. In the distance he could see a lone shape, battling the storm as it descended a causeway towards a set of iron doors. He was not the only inter-loper tonight.

He looked down. A ten-foot drop. Was he really doing this? He thought of Savannah, her boot in his back as he fell through the window of the Hog and Spike. William felt a loss deep within him, for surely she was gone. Savannah Shelton, his true and brave friend. Vulgar and violent, she had given more than she had ever taken from this world. William wondered if the same would ever be said of him? Living his life as a bystander, while Savannah struggled for so long against the tide, a battle she had now lost.

He landed awkwardly, his boots squelching deep into mud. The rain plastered his hair to his skull and he pushed it from his eyes as he squinted through the deluge at his surroundings. The only light he could see came from atop the nearby tower, a beacon that called him on.

The main door from the yard was bolted as he knew it would be, but William was no longer a respecter of locked doors or the secrets they hid. Using the heel of the gun, he smashed a windowpane, the storm masking the sound as he pushed jags of glass to the floor, making room for him to crawl through. He wasted several minutes exploring dead ends in the dark, before he finally found a lit corridor with a staircase that led upwards. Harry had mentioned a new contraption called a lift, but he had no intention of announcing his arrival to whoever occupied the top floor. As he climbed upwards, his feet felt light and his breathing came easily, so unlike the climb he had made every day to Mr Bridge's office, weighed down by his own limitations. But then, he wasn't William Lamb any more. He was no one.

An outer office, and a room beyond, a light gently glowing within. He strode forward. Gun in hand, he bumped into a chair and the noise produced a gasp from behind the door. He savoured the moment, the sound of someone else's fear, before slamming the door back on its hinges and stepping inside.

Sir Jasper Raycraft sat on the floor, huddled against a bookcase lined with human skulls, both hands gripping a bottle, his eyes wide and staring.

At last, William had cornered one of the seven. He pointed the gun, unable to keep it still and uncertain where to aim.

'Where is my aunt?'

*

Harry and Mildred waited outside the gates, the cab's skinny horse stamping and snorting as the rain lashed down. The driver too was growing restless.

'How much longer, Harry?' Mildred nodded in the direction of the stacked crates against the factory wall. 'William is in there. He needs us.'

Harry rubbed his eyes. It had taken for ever to get to King's Cross. Along with the storm, the hordes gathering in Grosvenor Square following the attempt on the American president's life had caused chaos. Had Benjamin Raycraft even received his telegram, or had he chosen simply not to respond?

'Look!'

Harry glanced up to see a grand carriage with four horses emerge from the flooded shadows on the road ahead. He jumped down from the cab, his thin jacket wet through in seconds as he dashed to greet the approaching vehicle. His heart lifted as he saw Benjamin Raycraft's thin face lean out of the window.

'You owe me an ex-explanation, Detective Treadway.'

Sir Jasper stared, his mouth agape and his face pale.

'I said, where is my aunt, sir!'

A noise, like an animal's whimper, that eventually William recognised. Laughter.

'You're not him!' Sir Jasper rasped.

'Who?'

'Edward! My son. You are not him!' Sir Jasper cackled once more.

Frustrated, William stepped closer, both hands on the gun in an attempt to keep it steady. The man was clearly drunk and more than a little confused. 'Edward Raycraft is your nephew, not your son. And you're right; I am not him. You have taken my aunt and I would have her returned to me!'

Sir Jasper nodded vigorously. 'Yes! You're right! He is both nephew and son.' Sir Jasper giggled once more. 'I am his father, you see? My sister, his mother. Phoebe, too. She was ours. So beautiful. So, so beautiful.'

Could such an abomination be true? Had Sir Jasper been lost to righteousness so long ago? William thought of Harry's investigations, the questions that had been left unanswered. But he would not stray from his own cause. 'Where is she?'

Sir Jasper took a long drink from the bottle in his hands. He wiped his mouth. 'Who is *she*?'

'Esther Lamb – and I am William Lamb.'

William expected his name to cause some reaction but Sir Jasper simply closed his eyes and leant his head against the bookcase. 'I have no idea who you are.'

William thrust the gun into his pocket, leapt forward and grabbed Sir Jasper, shaking him to consciousness. 'I will have no more obfuscation!' He dragged Sir Jasper upwards, his face close enough to smell his sour breath. William's voice tripped over his words. 'I was born to the families. My parents ordered my death, but Habborlain and Bridge saved me. Now the vicomtesse and Matlock hunt me down.' William tore the photograph from his pocket. Grabbing Sir Jasper by the hair he forced him to look. 'Who was she?'

Sir Jasper's eyes struggled to focus. When they did, he raised a finger and tenderly traced the faded image before him. 'Claudine,' he whispered.

'Claudine? That was my mother's name? Do you know who my father is?'

Sir Jasper looked at him, as if seeing him for the first time.

William grabbed him by the lapels and hauled him to his knees, yelling, 'Who is my father? Is it Von Rabenmarck?' His voice broke. 'Is it you?'

Realising the man was about to vomit, William let go, turning away as the retching came, over and over again. William rubbed his eyes, tried to order his thoughts. Why would no one answer his questions? Was he destined to never see his aunt again? To never know where he came from?

'My wife. She is dying. It is my fault.'

William turned.

Tears wetted Sir Jasper's cheeks as he stared into nothing. 'So young. So many mistakes. Anna, Sybil, all of them. And then came the children, such high hopes. But, you see, I have created a monster!'

William's anger flamed once more. He grabbed the gun and jammed it against Sir Jasper's temple. 'And the baby farm in Whitechapel? Was that a mistake too?'

Sir Jasper looked at him, bleary-eyed, inebriated, and uncomprehending. A gun was supposed to unlock answers, see them slithering from their dens like rats from a sewer, but Sir Jasper seemed oblivious to the threat, almost as if he didn't know.

William felt his stomach drop. With abrupt clarity, the truth they had been too blind to see sprang forth.

The names on the board at the association.

How Rebecca had called Raycraft the devil's child.

Sir Jasper had indeed created a monster.

As the realisation landed, a familiar voice shouted from behind. 'Drop the gun, William. Let him go!'

Harry knew William would not fire his weapon, yet he kept the pistol lodged against Sir Jasper's head. Harry wasn't sure who, in that moment, looked more undone, Sir Jasper or William, his hair wild against the sharp angles of his face, looking for all the world like the poster image that named him murderer.

Mildred stepped forward into the room, ignoring Harry's protestations. 'Please, William, this is no way to settle this. Help has arrived!'

William's eyes dropped to the weapon in Harry's hand. 'Where did you get that?'

'Benjamin is with us, William! He gave it to me.'

'Benjamin Raycraft gave you a gun?'

'Yes! Now he has gone to search for your aunt in the factory below. They will be with us at any moment!'

William pushed Sir Jasper to the ground and strode forward, leaving his former captive to crawl towards the bookcase. 'Harry, you have to listen to me!'

Harry remained focused. There would be no more bloodshed here. 'Give me the gun, William.'

William looked down, as if surprised to see what he was still holding. He held the gun outwards. 'I'm sorry. I had to act.'

Harry snatched his old gun back and placed it on the desk. 'I understand, but you are no longer alone in this fight. As soon as he has your aunt, Benjamin is to telephone the Home Office, and send for Mildred's father too.'

Mildred placed a hand on William's shoulder and smiled. 'It is over, William.'

It was the news Harry had longed to give, but William's reaction was not the one he had hoped for.

'Harry, we have to follow him, now. He will not rescue my aunt – *he* is the one who is holding her!'

Harry stared at William. Had the boy unravelled completely?

'What has Sir Jasper said? He is not a man to be trusted!' Harry looked over William's shoulder. Sir Jasper had taken one of the skulls from his display, and was turning it over in his hands as if he hoped to find something left inside.

'It is what he didn't say, Harry! He knows nothing of this, of me, of my aunt, of Whitechapel. He is not the Scientist! At least, not any more. Benjamin is!'

'That makes no sense, William!'

William swung round towards Mildred. 'Did Rebecca ever clarify which Raycraft had so abused her?'

'Yes!' cried Mildred, her face anguished. 'Or maybe not. I don't know!'

William turned back to Harry. 'Rebecca called Raycraft the devil's child, Harry.'

Harry shook his head. William had not met Benjamin, the idea was preposterous. Harry had seen Benjamin for what he was, an insipid young man trodden down by a brilliant father, the underdog, just like the strikers outside the gates, just like William. *Just like me.*

William grabbed Harry's shoulder. 'We rushed Habborlain at the abbey when he talked of the seven. We thought we already knew. And the board at the OBA. Benjamin was named, Harry! Only the elite—'

Harry interrupted, voicing his own inner monologue, 'That proves only that he is one of the selected, but surely that is all that it proves?'

A bell sounded from the outer office and they all turned towards the open door. Harry's thoughts tumbled and he gripped the handle of his revolver. William and Mildred stepped back, their hands clasping together, as two shadowy figures approached.

Benjamin Raycraft stepped into the light. By his side, a middle-aged woman, her hair dishevelled, a fragile smile upon her face.

'Aunt!'

William and his aunt ran towards each other, their long embrace a joy to watch. They held on tightly, William's arms crushing his aunt to his chest, clearly determined to never let go again. Harry snatched a glance at Benjamin Raycraft, whose eyes were cast down, like Mildred's, the intimate scene not something for strangers to gaze upon.

Tears flowing, William gripped his aunt's face in his hands. 'Have they mistreated you?'

She shook her head and straightened her shoulders, her mouth tight and proud. 'I have been told I am safe now. It is all that matters.'

William looked over her shoulder at Benjamin, who nodded

his head briskly to acknowledge the woman's words. The young man had done as he promised. Harry hoped William would see that now.

'And you have not seen this man before?'

William's aunt turned towards Benjamin Raycraft, smiled at him, and then shook her head. 'I would have remembered such a kind soul.'

William hugged her once more, even more fiercely, laughing now through his tears as Mildred brought a handkerchief to her nose.

Benjamin moved away towards his father, still curled on the floor with a dead man's skull for company, his eyes far away. Harry thought of the last time he had been in this office, only a few days before. How much he had disliked Sir Jasper, despite his evident fear of his own nephew, Edward. As Benjamin approached, Sir Jasper cowered away, but the boy simply leant down and stroked his father's hair.

Harry caught the young man's eye and he gave a bashful smile, a smile that became something else as Harry's gaze lingered.

He had missed it, the detail that told the truth, as he had missed everything. Harry could barely hear his own voice as he spoke. 'He didn't go to your engagement party.'

Benjamin Raycraft nodded. 'I am so sorry, Detective Treadway.'

And then Mildred screamed . . .

William swung about to see Colonel Matlock and Sergeant Smiley standing in the doorway. He grabbed Mildred and his aunt and backed away.

Smiley had William in his sights. Matlock's gun was trained on Harry, who mirrored his stance with his own. William glanced at the desk and Harry's gun, but Benjamin Raycraft was already there. William had been right. But the thought brought no comfort.

Matlock smiled at Harry, even as they faced off, weapons in hand. 'I am sorry it came to this, Harry. I liked you.'

Harry was backing away towards the huge windows, trying to keep all of them in his sights. Three weapons against one, for Benjamin Raycraft had already picked up the gun from the desk and was holding it limply in one hand.

Harry's arm did not waver from Matlock as he glanced towards Benjamin. 'This is not who you are, Benjamin! I know it!'

The scrawny young man looked up, no hint of the stammer Harry had previously reported. 'Ah, Detective Treadway. Who am I exactly?'

It was Harry's turn to stutter over his words. 'A-an impressionable young man, brought low by his own father.'

'It would appear we underestimated each other, detective.'

'I do not believe you are capable of this!'

'Don't you?' Benjamin walked around the desk, breaking Matlock's line of sight, and raised his arm, true and steady. 'Maybe it was one of the questions you should have asked.'

The gun exploded and Harry flew backwards. As the window shattered, the detective plunged down into the yard beneath.

'No!' cried William. An animal rage hurled him towards Smiley, sending the man's gun flying and knocking him to the floor. He bolted for the stairs and flung himself downwards, flying towards the earth, and the man who had sacrificed everything for him.

Harry's fall had been broken by an old cart and William threw himself at Harry's side. His body lay awkwardly, defeated and broken. The blood that ran from his shoulder, diluted by the downpour, dribbled towards the barren ground beneath.

'Harry, dear God!'

'It's all right, son.' Harry's eyes stared as if he were afraid to blink.

*No, it is not all right. None of this is all right.* William grabbed

Harry's hand. He wished he was someone else, someone better. Savannah should have been here. Not him.

'Be somebody, William Lamb.' A whisper lost in the rain.

The detective's hand was cold, the movement in his fingers weak. William nodded. 'I can be anyone.' Something he realised he had always known.

Harry's hand agitated the air near his pocket. 'Tinbergen's ship . . .'

William leant across and removed the little wooden model, the red paint already beginning to peel.

'The hull, you remember the colour?'

William swallowed down the lump in his throat. 'It was black, sir.'

Harry's eyes focused then, the light within them as bright as it had ever been. 'Exactly! Exactly so! Tell David . . . tell him we would have laughed.'

And then the light was gone.

William shuddered, a tremor of grief rippling through him like a rope pulled tight. He touched Harry's eyelids with his own fingertips, drawing down the shutters on his world.

Colonel Matlock's voice came from behind him, barely audible above the storm. 'I am sorry for it, lad.'

'Why?' he mumbled. 'Why did you ever involve him?'

'I thought he would fail. He so often did.'

Was that the way of it? Good men fail – fail to see what is in front of them because they wish it were not so.

'I need you to get up.'

William reluctantly turned his face from Harry's body and pulled himself to his feet. Matlock was alone. 'Where are the others?'

Matlock laughed and indicated the gun in his hand. 'This is all the help I need. Come inside, William. Some people are on their way to see you.'

William leapt forward, the hate inside him a weapon beyond measure. He connected hard with Matlock and they sprawled on to the muddy ground, the gun spilling from Matlock's hand. William rolled backwards, ready to fight, but the colonel was upon him in an instant. A fist slammed into his face and he felt his jaw crack against stone. He lashed out blindly but connected with nothing but air. As he pulled himself up on to all fours, a crashing blow to his kidneys sent him slumping to the ground once more. With tears blurring his vision, he looked up to see Matlock crawling forwards towards the gun.

William fought to regain his breath, Matlock's punch still burning in his side. With arms outstretched, he dived forwards and grabbed Matlock by the ankle. The older man was stronger than he looked and kicked backwards, his boot thudding into William's head. William could feel the blood trickling down his forehead, or was it the rain? But he held on, seizing Matlock's other leg too, pulling himself upwards and slowing Matlock's progress.

William wiped the blood from his eyes on his sleeve, his vision clearing enough to see Matlock grab the gun in his right hand. He lurched forward and seized Matlock's arm with both hands. As they fought for control, the gun circled madly between them, Matlock's finger on the trigger.

With all the strength he could muster, William yanked Matlock's arm backwards and pulled him over. Matlock now lay on top, the gun trapped between them. William was astonished to see that the man was still smiling, his face burning red, his cheeks shining with the effort of the struggle.

The gun exploded and William felt a sharp punch in his stomach.

He looked up into Matlock's face. The smile was still there, but the light was fading from his eyes, the pupils grown big. A string of pink spittle dripped from the side of his mouth. William blinked the blood away, while Matlock grinned down, his eyes wide open and staring. William waited for Matlock's smile to sag and fade, but they seemed to lie there for ever before he realised; Colonel Silas Matlock was already dead, his smile no more than a rictus grin.

He rolled Matlock's body away, revealing the bullet wound in the centre of the man's chest. William lay still, the rain washing his face, his breathing ragged. Voices, people coming, he had to move. A boot smashed into his head and his neck snapped to one side. Sergeant Smiley was standing over him, others behind, brass helmets glinting in the moonlight.

Benjamin Raycraft stepped forward, his eyes moving from Harry's dead body, to Matlock's, and finally meeting William's blinking gaze.

'Take him away.'

Two red-coated soldiers yanked William to his feet.

'My aunt ... Mildred ... this has nothing to do with them!' His pleas were pointless but he made them nonetheless.

Someone was prowling behind him, a cold presence chilling the air at his back. William's wet skin tingled. The vicomtesse was here, he knew it. He thought of all those years lived without knowledge of her, of Habborlain, of the Seed of Life. But they had been there always. Now that his ignorance had been ripped away he could sense her behind him as if she were the storm itself.

William forced himself to turn then, to confront the woman who had stolen lives away, including his own.

But no one was there.

## CHAPTER FIFTY-FIVE

*A*t gunpoint, Smiley bundled William through the building and down an iron staircase. A thin light stuttered from globes attached to the walls, connected to each other by thick black wires. They twisted around three flights of stairs before entering a long brick corridor with a high-arched ceiling, as silent and damp as a sewer. They were surely now well below the level of the river.

They passed several heavy iron doors and William jumped when one of the doors opened, releasing terrifying sounds of agony and suffering from within. Instinctively, William moved towards the door but Smiley pulled him back, his laughter joining with the cacophony. 'Save your sentiments, they are but monkeys. Chimpanzees, I'm told. Apparently they make effective substitutes for humans. Like you, they are quite beyond saving.'

William recalled seeing such creatures on a visit to the zoo with his aunt. He had been touched by their antics as they played and groomed one another, and his blood grew colder to imagine what torments might have spawned such haunting cries. The door was slammed shut and the noise abruptly abated. He would have endured it for longer if he could. The ensuing silence was a lie bound in iron and he was sick to his stomach of lies.

Further on, they stopped at another door. Smiley took a ring of keys from his belt and opened it. Before William could react, he was pushed forward and found himself stumbling into the room beyond. The iron door was shut with a clang and he immediately banged on it with his fist.

'Let Mildred and my aunt go, it is me you want, not them!'

He knew his words were futile even as he spoke them. Just like the creatures, his cries would go unheard.

He spun round, his eyes refusing to adjust. William had never known darkness like it, a thick, black obscurity, where his mind imagined shapes and spots of light flashing in and out of the shadows. The air was cool and wet. Beads of moisture prickled his skin and he could hear the drip, drip of water landing with a metallic echo high above.

He sat on the floor and waited. They would come back for him, he knew. What would the endgame be? He thought of Harry, and the fate of all those he cared about, a list that had grown so dramatically in the last few days of his life. Was that something to be grateful for at least? He had wished to make friends and to meet girls. He thought of Savannah and Mildred: one the very epitome of the kind of woman he had thought to marry one day, the other forming a shadow image, the colours reversed so completely. The loss of Harry and Savannah rolled in once more, a vacant place where true friendship had lived.

He heard the scrape of a key being slotted into the lock, and the click of the bolt sliding back. How long had passed? Minutes? Hours? He retreated further into the room, wishing he had earlier explored its depths. He turned his head away as a brilliant light flooded the room from overhead, as if the sun had burned a hole through the ceiling, intent on saving him. The door clanged shut and he shielded his eyes with his arm, blinking rapidly, desperate to see where he was and who had now joined him. There was something new in the air, something sweet mingling with the rotting damp.

Jasmine.

'It is a marvel, is it not? Although I am not convinced it flatters as pleasingly as real flame. I should warn you that Sergeant Smiley and his revolver are standing beyond the door, just in case you are considering another of your miraculous escapes.'

William peered through slits, seeing only a slash of red where the vicomtesse stood before him. 'Let Mildred and my aunt go, they have surely done nothing.'

'How gallant of you!'

Although William couldn't see, he sensed the vicomtesse smiling as she spoke. 'You like her. Mildred. That shows good taste at least. You may have her, if you wish.'

The lasciviousness in her voice drove his anger deeper.

'That would be her choice, not yours.'

'You are a prude.'

'And you are a monster.'

'Maybe I am, William, maybe I am. But I am also your mother.'

William dropped his arm from his face, his eyes snapping open. He saw the moist brick walls around him, the grey-green mould eating away at the mortar. He saw a spider scuttling upwards away from the circle of light. He saw the woman in red before him, her glossy curls beginning to fray in the moist air.

He saw everything.

He took the photograph from his pocket, now crumpled and damp, the image soon to be lost. The vicomtesse snatched it from him.

'They gave you this? How clever. But this is *my* mother, not yours.' She crushed the fragile paper in one hand and tossed it to the floor.

'But there cannot be more than ten years between us!'

'Eleven, almost twelve to be exact. Not that it is polite to discuss a lady's age.'

'You . . . you were forced?'

Her green eyes held his own, but the connection between them shifted. With all the weight of the world, she shook her head in answer to his question. She was a monster indeed.

'Why?'

'I wanted a child as soon as I was able. I was impatient. I believed – *I knew* – that the blood of Olympias was strong in me. I am a woman in a man's world. We have only one power.'

It was impossible to believe, yet he knew it was true.

He had always thought that he had wasted little energy in his life on imagining his mother, had simply been content with the blurred vision of the past sealed in a wooden frame. Now he realised how far from the truth that was. He had conjured her often, painting her in white lace and summer dresses, with a soothing hand and undoubting love in her heart. The vicomtesse could not have been further from that vision. It was one more thing she had taken and ground into the dirt. Something gave within him, like a door to a secret cellar yawning wide.

He looked down at his left hand, still bandaged. When he spoke, he didn't recognise his own voice. 'So, it would seem I was something of a disappointment.'

He looked her in the eye once more but again she held his gaze without shame, her sadness holding only to herself. 'You were not the first in our line to be born with this deformity. But our rules are clear. Weakness and deformity poisons the lineage.'

'There are many forms of weakness.'

'Only a few that matter, I think.'

William stepped forward, watched her flinch. 'I am stronger than you know.'

'Maybe so.'

'Did it take strength to ask Habborlain to murder your own child?' He began to unwrap the bandage from his hand.

Her voice hardened. 'Murder is a strong word, William. If we must use it then think on this. When you *ripped* yourself from my womb, squalling for air, you took half of me with you. I bled for days – and then never again. I gave birth to a cripple and it left me childless. You murdered all the others, left them unconceived, stillborn inside me.'

Her tears were like melting ice, turning his heart colder. He held up his left hand. 'Are you not grateful for it now, Vicomtesse? I have no weapon, and I doubt I can strangle you with only one thumb.'

He held his hand out toward her, twisting his wrist to display the object of her fascination from all angles. She followed the movement of his hand through the air, seemingly transfixed.

'Aren't you revolted? You do not fear infection?'

She grabbed his hand with both of hers and stroked her fingers across the nub of bone where his thumb was not. Had she touched him like that once before, perhaps? A child's tears falling on his infant face before she sentenced him to his death. A week ago he would have felt the shame of his deformity spiral up within him at such intimacy, but no longer.

'Who was my father? I will know it all.'

'Who would you like him to be?'

'A good man.'

She laughed. 'If I told you your father was Nathaniel Bridge, no doubt that would make you happy.'

His right hand snapped around her throat. 'I will have the truth.'

Her face betrayed no fear and her eyes said it all: *you are not the first man to hurt me.*

He dropped his hand to his side.

'You have some gumption, William, to hunt me even as I hunted you. Maybe you have survived for a reason?' Her eyes shone up at him. 'If you are willing to prove yourself, maybe you can live after all?'

Her face was close to his and he saw it then for the first time: the same nose maybe, the set of her chin, the same symmetry, even the trace of red in his own brown hair. She had always been there, behind him in the mirror, a ghost he had not seen.

'And what must I do to prove myself?'

She twirled away from him and clapped her hands, like a child who had just invented a new game. 'It's obvious, when you think about it. What marks us out, the families, the seven even more so? What is it that we take on ourselves while the rest of humanity cowers, passing all responsibility to a God that doesn't exist and a world that doesn't care?'

His brain, like his heart, could not follow her and he shrugged his ignorance.

'We choose, William. We choose who lives and who dies. Now that choice can be yours.'

## CHAPTER FIFTY-SIX

The vicomtesse left him in the dark as suddenly as she had arrived, but there was barely any time to recover before the door slammed open once more and Smiley snatched him into the light. William stumbled forward, pushed on through the warren of corridors beneath the factory by the barrel of Smiley's revolver. He had lost all sense of direction and time since he entered the bowels of the factory. As for the vicomtesse and her monstrous secret, he felt only numbness where feeling should have been.

The floor beneath his feet began to slope downwards. The corridor wound tightly in circles that spiralled further into the ground. The glowing orbs were gone, the walls lit by guttering candles in rusted sconces, the wax falling on to hardened puddles. The fetid smell of the river grew thicker and finally they reached a wide iron door. Smiley brought them to a halt and thumped his fist against the metal. What fresh hell lay beyond?

The door cranked open, and they were greeted by Benjamin Raycraft.

'Come in.' As if they had dropped by for afternoon tea.

Smiley gave him an unnecessary shove as he passed through the doorway. His gaze was immediately drawn upwards to the domed brick ceiling high above. The room was circular. Halfway down the walls a gallery with wooden benches ran the full diameter, encircled by a cast-iron balustrade. It was as if he were in some kind of theatre. A door led away from the gallery, presumably to a higher level within the factory. His eyes travelled downwards to the centre of the room and what he saw made him cry out.

Aunt Esther stood before him, a tremulous smile on her lips and her hands pressed up against a filmy pane of glass. It took a moment for him to realise that she was encased in some kind of conservatory. The steel framework was all curves, and the panes of glass bulged outwards. The overall effect was of a huge cloche shaped like a flower, mirroring the Seed of Life itself. A swirling moat surrounded the structure, the stink of the river unmistakable as it sloshed around the island of glass and gushed back on itself through a tall iron grate. He could see no doorway into the chamber, on this side at least. He saw Mildred too, further away and blurred by the misshapen glass.

William rushed forward towards them, striding across a green tiled walkway that linked the glass island to the main chamber. He placed his palms against his aunt's. 'Can you hear me, Aunt?'

'Yes, my dear boy, yes I can!'

Although her voice was flattened by the glass, it was music to his ears to hear it once again, so convinced had he been that he never would.

He turned towards Mildred. 'Mildred, I am so sorry, I—'

'Don't, William, it is not necessary for you to apologise. I came here of my own free will.'

'Are you hurt?'

'No, I am not, but . . . ' She turned to look back inside the glass dome. William followed her gaze. Lying on the floor beyond them was an indistinct shape, like a black dog curled around itself.

'Pardon me if I don't get up.' The third occupant of the chamber broke off into a fit of coughing, as harsh as a crack of thunder.

'Savannah! You are alive!'

The coughing continued, as if she might turn herself inside out.

When it subsided, she spoke again. 'Alive? I'm not sure.' Savannah appeared to laugh at her own joke but the racking coughs came once more. His joy at seeing her again was tempered by that miserable sound. What had they done to her? She had yet to rise from the floor.

'This is all very moving but I'm afraid you have work to do, William,' said the vicomtesse from somewhere behind him. 'Bring him here.'

Smiley yanked William's arm and spun him round. Another path of green tiles led to a raised platform where Benjamin Raycraft and the vicomtesse stood behind a large, curving desk. They were both smiling at him, like indulgent parents watching their child take his first steps. Smaller versions of the glowing orbs he had seen in the corridors lit either end of the platform, fading in and out with a fizzing noise.

On reaching the platform, he looked back towards the glass chamber. Only Aunt Esther's hand was still in focus, pressed against the glass like a disembodied relic of another time. The roof of the chamber was linked to a thick copper tube that snaked up into the dome above them. The desk was fitted with a metal panel, adorned with dials and levers, just like the control panel of a train he had once seen as a boy.

Smiley had flung himself into a swivel chair behind the desk, his gun still firmly trained on William as he faced Raycraft and the vicomtesse.

Raycraft took a phial from a wooden tray and held it up to the light. A thick amber liquid swirled within. 'Do you know what this is?'

'Judging by the rest of your work, Raycraft, it is nothing good.'

Raycraft laughed and ran his hand through his thin blond hair. 'Ah, I suspect you have rather conventional notions as to what *good* really is. You think kindness is good, no doubt, and charity. And if you saw a bedraggled kitten in the street, you would save it?'

'You think I should not?'

'I think you should not interfere with what God intended.'

'And you are familiar with his intentions?' William could feel the anger rise within him at the man's condescension and cruelty.

'Anyone who studies the world is familiar with his intentions. The survival of the fittest, William – it is how we evolve. Without it, we would still be climbing trees.'

The vicomtesse laughed. William looked at Benjamin Raycraft, his round shoulders and indistinct features. Even without his fake stammer, he understood how easy it had been for Harry to believe Sir Jasper the villain, not this pale mouse of a man, as far from the epitome of a master race as it was possible to imagine. The irony had cost Harry his life.

William fought for time, to what end he wasn't sure. 'You *knew* your fiancée was your sister?'

Raycraft closed his eyes. 'Such a beauty. You should have seen her. She should have been mine but my brother took her away.'

'Your father did not approve?'

'He got "cold feet", I believe is the expression. As he got cold feet about many things.' Benjamin straightened, his voice a whisper. 'I am the strongest yet!'

The man's lavish self-deceit was plain, but then William thought of himself, of how only hours before he had so believed he could yet triumph. We are all the heroes of our own story, he thought. Something Harry might have said.

William looked back at the amber liquid in Raycraft's hand. 'So what does your liquid do?' He could still hear Savannah's coughing, more distant but no less wretched.

'It is not a liquid. In its most active form it is, in fact, a gas. What it does, William, is the will of creation. It improves the stock.'

'It makes one stronger?'

'Not in the way you mean. It kills the weak. Even diluted in the air it eats away at tissue like acid, burning through skin and destroying the ability to breathe within minutes.' The delight of a child at its own invention.

William despaired that someone would willingly create such a devastating weapon of war.

Raycraft took another phial from the tray and held it up. The liquid was clear. 'And this is the antidote. One phial of this solution and the effects of the gas will never be felt. Even as it is unleashed on the population of towns and cities, those who have taken the antidote are protected while all others perish.'

Time seemed to stand still for William as the blood slowed in his veins. So this was it. The endgame revealed. How naive to think this a weapon of war, confined to the battlefield. It was a weapon of indiscriminate mass execution. He thought of the leaflets he had taken from the OBA, and of the rules he had first heard at the museum. Breed the strong. Kill the weak. The clues had been there, pointing towards this place beneath the earth. The massacre of populations, countless lives destroyed. That it was possible seemed impossible. That anyone might desire it, even more so.

'Why?'

Raycraft cocked his head to one side and smiled. 'Improving the stock is as much a matter of culling as it is of propagation. You have seen us do the one, surely you expected us to consider the other?'

William's voice deserted him. *No we didn't. God help us but we didn't.*

The vicomtesse continued the lecture. 'We have always been in control, William, the only thing that has changed is the science that helps us along. The blood of the greatest human being that ever lived, Alexander the Great, flows through our veins, yours too. As our knowledge of science has grown, so have our dreams of what is possible.'

The dreams of monsters, brought up to believe in their own superiority. Dreams whispered down through generations – polluted, vicious, and pitiable.

William found his voice once more. 'It is not your knowledge of science that has led you here. It is fear of your own imperfection. You're worried that God has done better than you. You are a coward, Raycraft, nothing more. Your ancestors would not be proud of you. They would be ashamed.'

Raycraft's face had turned red and ugly and he looked as if he might smash the phials to the floor. The vicomtesse stepped forward and placed her hand gently on his arm. 'Come, Benjamin, we have a game to play, do we not?'

Benjamin turned his face towards her and she smoothed his brow and cupped his cheek. William watched as the madness slipped away once more.

The vicomtesse turned to William and, grabbing both his hands in hers, pulled him toward the panel of controls, forcing him to again face the glass chamber. Standing behind, she nuzzled against him, her cheek finding his as he shuddered at the smell of her perfume, the touch of her wintry skin. It was a connection he wished to break for ever.

'Remember what I told you, you have impressed us against all the odds: you can live if you choose.' She nodded towards the chamber. 'But there is another choice you must make first, to prove yourself capable, then I shall call you son.'

She continued to talk in his ear but her words faded as he looked towards the chamber. Aunt Esther's hand had dropped away, and all he could see now were three shapes, two standing and one lying prone, like fish below the surface of an icy lake.

William knew what would be asked of him even before Raycraft spoke again. 'So who will receive the antidote? Which one will you save, William? There can be only one.' Raycraft inserted the phial of amber liquid into a device on the control panel. He tipped it up and turned it twice, locking the poison in place.

'And if I refuse?'

The vicomtesse replied, her voice soft as silk, 'Then they all die.'

Raycraft appeared at his other side. 'And so do you.'

A shadow passed across the gallery above but William's gaze stayed rooted to the chamber before him and the women he could no longer see.

'Shall I advise you?' The vicomtesse moved closer. 'Let us use the principles of the Seed of Life. Your aunt, if I may call her that, is old and of little use to you now. The mongrel gutter-snipe has a certain strength of character, I will admit, but I fear there is something irrational, unbalanced, within. I also suspect that my brother's guards may have caused irreparable damage before they brought her here. So, that leaves us with Mildred, who is another kettle of fish entirely. Full of potential I would say. I intended her for my brother, but why not you? Save her, William, breed with her. What a family we might make!' Her voice dropped to a whisper. 'How alike we are, you and I. I think you have chosen her from the crowd already, just as I did. Like mother, like son.'

And so he had, days ago on the train. What ancient lust had seen him desire her so strongly? He was the Finder's son indeed. William turned to see his mother's eyes glinting up at him, the mouth he had almost kissed that night in her room. Now he knew himself to be well and truly cursed. Was it possible to be haunted by the living so much more than the dead?

A voice called out from the chamber. 'William, do what you must! Save one of your friends – and darling, please save yourself. I shall always love you. What fun we had, always.' Aunt Esther's voice broke and William choked back his own tears, for they would not help him now.

Mildred too cried out, 'Whatever you do, William, I will

understand. This *choosing* is not your fault. I will know who has killed me, the same woman who stole my honour!'

The vicomtesse giggled like a child. 'Oh, the *gumption*! You have to save her, William, really you do.' She clasped his arm in excitement.

William looked down at the panel before him, the controls swimming before him. One lever was marked with the symbol of a key. Might it somehow open the chamber? Even if it meant a bullet in his own brain from Smiley's gun it was a far better alternative to anything else.

The sound of Savannah's watery cough exploded once more and he looked across. She was trying to sit up. Her words were mumbled though and he could not hear them through the glass or over the sound of the churning river.

Mildred shouted, 'She says the enemy of your enemy is your friend! She says to look to heaven for the answer! Oh yes, William, I agree, look to God, William, look to God!'

Since when had Savannah Shelton ever turned to God? The enemy of your enemy is your friend? What did she mean?

Raycraft sighed loudly. 'Time is up, William, make your decision.'

The vicomtesse moved away and William felt Smiley's gun press against the back of his head as Raycraft dangled the phial of clear liquid in front of William's eyes, his voice spiteful and girlish. 'Who lives?'

A movement caught William's eye – and at the same instant he understood Savannah's message. Above them on the gallery stood Edward Raycraft, within jumping distance of the platform on which they stood. With an exaggerated cry, William pointed upwards.

All heads turned towards Edward as he sprang down, part of the balustrade crashing to the floor with him. Benjamin shrieked in horror. As Smiley's gun swung away, William seized his chance. He pushed the astonished vicomtesse aside, took hold of the lever marked with a key and thrust it forwards, desperately hoping he had made the right choice.

A gunshot rang out, but Edward Raycraft clubbed the misfiring Smiley with a single swipe of his powerful fist and moved towards Benjamin, who huddled against the desk as he fumbled for his own weapon. He mishandled the revolver and it skittered away. With a yelp, he wrapped his arms around his knees, as if they could protect him from the glint of steel that flashed in Edward's hand.

William looked around to see the vicomtesse running across the platform towards the main door. He threw himself forward, grasped her foot and brought her crashing down against a row of shelves that he only hoped contained none of the lethal toxin.

Smiley was scrabbling for his gun as Edward Raycraft grabbed Benjamin by the hair and pulled his head back. William could see the veins on his neck pulsing rapidly, but, like Benjamin himself, couldn't tear his eyes away from the hypnotic arc of Edward's knife as he raised it high, tears running down his cheeks as he bellowed, 'I thought you were pure!'

The knife swooped down, but Smiley's gun went off once more. Edward fell to his knees. William released the vicomtesse and lunged towards Benjamin's gun before Smiley could take aim once more, but it was just beyond reach. There was a sharp cry and the air was smacked from William's lungs as Smiley crashed on top of him.

A sharp hacking cough announced a new presence on the platform.

'Well, ain't this dandy?'

## CHAPTER FIFTY-SEVEN

William's spirits soared. Savannah had been released from the chamber!

He rolled out from underneath Smiley's dead weight. The man's head was caved in on one side. A metal spindle from the broken balustrade lay beside him, Savannah's lethal makeshift weapon.

Edward Raycraft slumped backwards against the shelves that surrounded the platform, a crimson pool spreading around him. His eyes seeped hatred as they followed Benjamin's movements. Benjamin held Edward's knife limply in one hand, his mouth hanging slightly open in disbelief as he looked down upon his brother.

Savannah waved Smiley's gun in a circle to grab Benjamin's attention. 'Put the knife on the desk if you wouldn't mind, Mr R.' Her voice sounded as if it had blown across thousands of miles of desert.

William would not have imagined that a human being could look so terrible and still be alive. Savannah wore the remains of a maid's uniform, torn and stained with blood. He recognised her boots, but not her face, which was puckered and bruised, the left eye closed and swollen. Her black hair streamed outwards as if it had taken fright all by itself. She looked as if she had been buried underground for days, but when she smiled at him, her crooked grin flashed white, and he smiled as if it was the first time he ever had. My enemy's enemy. My friend.

Savannah rasped, 'You may join us now, ladies!'

William grabbed Benjamin's fallen gun and ran forward to greet Mildred and his aunt as they emerged from behind the glass chamber. As he threw his arms around his aunt, he could still smell her lavender toilet water clinging to her bedraggled clothes. He turned to Mildred, intent on embracing her too, but remembered himself at the last moment. 'The two of you must leave immediately. Matlock is dead. You must go to the police.'

His aunt grabbed his arm. 'Mildred has explained much. I knew none of it, William, none of it! My poor boy.' Her fingers touched his cheek. 'Come with us.' She glanced back towards the platform. 'This is no place for you.'

He followed her gaze. 'This is exactly where I belong. Now go!'

Mildred ushered his aunt through the main door and clanged it shut behind them. He could only pray that safety was within their reach.

William turned back to the platform. Edward Raycraft lay dying, Benjamin was still crouched by the desk while the vicomtesse huddled against the shelves of chemicals, cradling a phial of amber liquid in her hands. Dragging one leg across the tiles, Savannah limped towards her, but the woman in red did not look up at her approach.

'She was my sister!' Edward Raycraft's eyes glittered in the artificial light as he stared across at Benjamin, his lifeblood leaking into his words as he spoke. 'I saved you from us, monstrosities both. I saved you from our blood, from our rancid, ruined, evil blood!' He started to rise, loathing fuelling his veins as the blood drained away. 'I had no choice to be what I am. But you!'

Savannah swung her gun in Edward's direction as he lunged towards the desk. In one swift movement he grabbed the knife and fell atop Benjamin, rolling them across the platform in a fatal embrace. The vicomtesse cried out, Benjamin's own shrieks of pain muffled against his brother's chest as Edward plunged the knife into his side again and again. The screams stopped long before Edward Raycraft's arm grew weary, finally coming to rest with a final thrust of the blade. One foot twitched with a steady rhythm, beating out the fanfare to death as he clutched his dead brother to his own silent heart.

William looked down at the gun in his hand. He could have stopped him. Savannah could have stopped him.

'Benjamin . . .' the vicomtesse whispered.

Savannah turned towards her, grabbed her arm and yanked her to her feet. She pushed the barrel of the revolver into the flesh beneath the other woman's chin, forcing her gaze to meet hers. William saw his mother's eyes flash through a gamut of emotions – fear and hatred and life, fighting to carry on. There was something else too, a weariness in the soul of this woman who had never grown up. William felt certain that Savannah would pull the trigger, could see her finger itching to do it.

'Please, Savannah . . .' William spoke without hope.

'Do it!' The vicomtesse spoke through clenched teeth.

'You think I don't have the . . . what was your word? The *gumption?*'

'You're a savage. I think you will do it.'

'I am a savage. And you're right. I will.'

Savannah cocked the trigger. 'For Rebecca.'

'*Lass Ihre Waffen Fallen! Sie sind übertroffen!*'

A voice from above. William turned to see shadows everywhere on the gallery, massing upon each other. Savannah raised the barrel of her gun upwards but a bullet tore through her arm and sent her spinning towards William. His own weapon fell from his hands as he caught her and dragged her behind the desk, the only protection between the platform and the gallery above and behind them. He watched, helpless, as an arsenal of bullets rained down around them. The vicomtesse scrambled to the far side of the platform, back flattened against the shelves of chemicals as the Germans avoided firing in her direction.

William helped Savannah sit upright. Dark red blood dripped from her arm as her face screwed up in pain. William grabbed at what remained of her maid's petticoat and with a firm grip tore a strip of material away. Careful to keep his head low, he bound the makeshift tourniquet around her upper arm and pulled it tight.

'We've made a soldier of you after all.' Savannah spoke through gritted teeth.

With an effort, she cracked open Smiley's revolver. Four bullets remained.

Savannah pointed across the platform. Benjamin's gun was lying a few yards away where he had dropped it. It was too far to reach without moving into the line of fire.

'Cover me.' Savannah dumped her gun in William's lap and shifted round, ready to pounce.

'You seem to have forgotten that I have never fired one! At least, not on purpose or with any skill!'

'We need more bullets. We'll die anyway, but I'd like to take a few of those bastards with me before I go.'

'Mildred has gone for help.'

'Harry? Where is he?'

William shook his head, the words too awful to form.

Savannah's ravaged face smiled at him. 'Then I'm afraid the cavalry is already here.'

No one was coming. His protectors had fallen one by one, like the layers of a chrysalis peeling away, only Savannah left at his side.

It was time, at last, for William Lamb to save himself.

He grasped the weapon in his palm, feeling its heft, the warmth of the barrel against his skin. 'What do you need me to do?'

'When I say go, you stand up, turn and fire once at the gallery. Then you sit down again. Hopefully we will both still be alive.'

'Just the once, you say?'

'Yes. Or twice maybe. Try not to think about it too much, William.'

'Very well.'

'One, two, three. *Go!*'

William stood and turned. With his eyes closed, he pointed the gun upwards and pulled the trigger. The weapon bounced backwards in his hand and he almost dropped it. He randomly aimed and fired once more. There was a cry of pain from above and a loud crash as something fell to the ground. He felt a sharp tug on his trouser leg and dropped to the floor.

'You got one, William! Damn me to hell, you got one!' Savannah held Benjamin's gun in her hand.

William was breathing hard. He felt as if his lungs had expanded threefold, that he could breathe this deeply for ever and still not fill them. He had brought death to another, yet he had never felt so alive.

Hopelessly outnumbered and with fewer resources, they took it in turns to stand up and fire a random shot while the other took surer aim from below, resting their weapons on the edge of the battered desk. The bullets had done their worst, splintering the wood and blowing clouds of sawdust in the air.

Across the platform the vicomtesse was edging her way towards the moat, trusting the soldiers to avert their fire. She groped her way along the shelves, which were beginning to shake with her efforts, the glass bottles tottering perilously.

Savannah saw her too. 'Maybe I should—'

'Save our bullets! We need them.' Was that really why he stayed her hand?

'I have another idea.' Savannah shifted round and began to remove her boot, her face grimacing at the pain in her shoulder.

'What on earth?'

Savannah launched her boot into the air. It flew towards the vicomtesse, who ducked to avoid the missile. But she hadn't loosened her grip on the shelves behind her and they toppled forward, spilling their contents and trapping her beneath. The glass bottles shattered, their contents pooling on the floor, a rainbow of colours and vapours swimming upwards. Shimmering lines of heat fractured William's vision as the gunfire stopped.

Then they heard the scream, a sound full of horror and nothing else.

The shelves moved and the vicomtesse emerged, a blaze of red as she scrambled forwards towards the churning waters. Her clothes were smoking and a terrible stench found his nostrils as the vicomtesse plunged into the green depths of the moat.

'Adeline!' A German voice, etched in pain.

The red skirts billowed in the roiling surf as her body was dragged down by the current. William stared, surely damned if he cared and damned if he did not. Indecision trapped him, unable to move even as his heart leapt towards the river, hungry for the thing he had never known. But it was too late and there was no point. The water couldn't return what the past had stolen so long ago.

The guns remained silent. There was nothing but the gurgle of the river as it frothed and spun.

'Good riddance,' whispered Savannah, her voice hard.

'She was—'

'What?'

*My mother. My enemy.* He said nothing.

The powerful German voice rang out once more. 'William, I am Otto Von Rabenmarck. We share the same blood. Let us stop this, for I wish you no harm.'

William shouted back, feeling the power in his own voice. 'That is hard to believe, sir, after everything that has befallen us!'

'We have our traditions, William. Foolish ones in your eyes, I suspect, and Adeline cared for them more than I. She told you the truth, did she not? Surely you can understand her feelings towards you, she lost everything—'

'Understand?' William flung his gun to the floor and stood up, ignoring Savannah's attempt to pull him down once more. He faced Von Rabenmarck, a pacing shadow on the gallery above, surrounded by his army of blond giants. Three of their number had perished, one of them at William's hand, and every remaining gun was now pointing at William's head as he spoke. 'Let me see you.'

Von Rabenmarck pushed aside the concerned hand of the nearest guard and stepped forward. Only one globe light had survived the battle between them and now it cast the light upwards on to the chancellor's face. 'Come with me, William, let us start the line again. I see you are a warrior, a rightful heir of our family, an Alexander reborn. Let us make the world what we would have it be.'

'You would have it tamed, chained to the past. I would not!' As the words tumbled out, he felt the truth of them. Only days ago, he too would have had a world without Savannah, without Harry, without evil or the bravery needed to bring it down. Now the world around him felt rich beyond measure. Finally precious. 'I am no warrior, I am not Alexander reborn. I am *ordinary*, sir, and I am your equal in this world.'

Von Rabenmarck's face turned cold once again. 'Very well, William. Then you will die here.'

William dropped to the floor as the barrage of gunfire resumed, the desk disintegrating with each shot. Savannah had already retrieved his gun and snapped open the barrel. 'One bullet left.' She handed it back to him. 'I have two.' She smiled. 'Ah well. Fancy speech, by the way.'

William smiled back as the desk behind them began to buckle

under the onslaught. The control panel for the glass chamber was partly shielded from the line of fire. Even so, a single stray bullet could unleash the poison into the open chamber at any moment. He closed his eyes tightly, hoping that Aunt Esther and Mildred had made it to safety.

'So how is that weak chest of yours holding up at the thought of your impending demise?'

William smiled, strangely calm as the bullets landed closer and the air filled with splintered wood. 'I have lived a lifetime these last few days.'

'You sure have. Just one more thing to experience, I believe.' She leant across and kissed him full on the lips, her mouth soft and warm. 'Sometimes kissing the wrong girl makes up for not kissing the right one.'

He wanted to laugh, to sing out, to dance and shout with life. How dear it all was. Even as he faced the end, he felt no sadness now that it was over, only joy that it had existed at all.

'So,' she said. 'Shall we die standing up?'

William took a deep breath and closed his eyes. I am special, he thought.

I lived.

He made to stand for the final time.

'Wait!' Savannah grabbed his arm. 'Look!'

On the platform, the swirl of chemicals from the fallen shelves had caught light even upon the slick green tiles, a fluorescent purple flame spreading closer. Savannah reached for a length of splintered wood.

'Here goes nothing.'

She leant forward and dipped the wood into the flaming pool. A blast of light leapt upwards as she stood and flung the exploding torch towards the gallery. The rush of heat was immense as the chemical fire finally met with combustible timber. William could hear the howls of pain, audible above the booming rumble of fire that rolled around the cavernous chamber. William stood up to see men tumbling forward, splashing into the water below. Savannah grabbed him and they ran across the platform to escape the flames that now licked at the battered desk. William could scarcely believe what he was seeing.

The purple fire ripped through the gallery, incinerating the wooden structure and sending great chunks of wood and iron crashing down. One of the German guards had jumped to the ground and was calling to the German chancellor, marooned midway down the dislodged staircase that led to the other side of the glass dome.

But the damage was done. Fire raged across the platform towards them. The single remaining guard was still pleading with Von Rabenmarck to jump. Savannah stepped forward, moving perilously close to the flames as she raised her gun. The guard was an easy target, his back turned towards her as he grasped the bottom of the broken staircase and raised his hand high. Von Rabenmarck grasped the hand in his, just as Savannah shot the guard in his back. He fell to the floor, the German chancellor tumbling forward beside him.

William looked around. 'We must get back to the door before we are trapped!'

Von Rabenmarck was on his knees beside the fallen guard, tears streaming as he cradled the man's head and kissed his brow, seemingly disinterested in the fire that raged about him.

Savannah shouted above the blaze, her face glowing in the now unbearable heat, 'We can't get out that way!'

The German chancellor looked across at them, leapt to his feet and disappeared behind the glass dome.

Savannah pointed towards the tunnel where the tide of the river sloshed the water to and fro. 'We must go through it!'

The tunnel was barred with an iron grate. 'We can't get through!' cried William.

Savannah mimed a swimming stroke, and William realised that this really was the end for him. 'But I can't swim!'

They dropped to the floor as a unit of shelves behind them crumbled to the floor, its contents exploding across the platform and adding to the rampant inferno. Savannah ignored the chaos and ran towards the remains of the desk, her attention riveted to the glass dome beyond as the flames licked around her. William ran to her side.

He could see the blurred shape of Von Rabenmarck moving behind the glass. The German chancellor, his uncle, his flesh and blood. The control panel was still intact and Savannah pulled the lever marked with a key, sealing the chancellor inside.

Before she had a chance to find the control that would unleash the poison, William covered her hand with his own. 'No, Savannah, there is no need to kill in cold blood. Leave him here, we must find a way out and save ourselves!' Even as he said the words, he doubted that it was possible. Savannah was right. The only chance now was to give themselves to the water, and hope the river's tide would carry them below the grate and out into the city beyond.

Desperately, William grabbed Savannah's hand and dragged her forward. There was still a way through the flames that would take them to the moat. As they twisted their way through the heat, William could see Von Rabenmarck, his palms pressed flat against the curved pane, his face just visible, his eyes pleading as he mouthed something over and over. William slowed down, his vision obscured by the heat haze around him as he tried to make out the chancellor's words.

But, just as they reached the moat, Savannah broke free and ran back towards the platform, sprinting through the fire. William knew what she would do, Savannah Shelton, avenging angel, and felt the awfulness and the rightfulness of it all at once.

With both hands she seemed to pull every lever and twist every dial.

William turned back towards the chamber, to Von Rabenmarck's pleading face, pressed even closer now to the blurry glass. His hands were around his own neck as the air inside dimmed to a grimy yellow. His face distorted further. Was it the glass or something else?

William looked back towards Savannah, but he could not see her behind the wall of flame. He cried out, but there was no way back for her now.

In the chamber Von Rabenmarck sank to his knees. William mirrored him, a child copying a parent's gesture, his uncle's mouth still moving as his features grew more and more indistinct. What was he saying? William knew it didn't matter but could not tear his eyes away, enraptured by this final intimacy when there had been no other.

Habborlain's words returned. *It is all connected, don't you see?* And, finally, he did. Pull one thread and we all unravel, roots running deeper than the heart can ever know.

The heat of the fire finally blurred his vision and he could see no more. William turned and stumbled towards the moat and the water that had taken his mother to its churning depths. Would her phantom come for him, he wondered? Her greedy hands tugging him down, clammy tendrils of hair choking him like weeds, a Jonah that would never let him go.

A sudden movement caught his eye, a shadow beyond the flames, growing more distinct. Savannah burst through, her clothes and hair catching fire. She barrelled towards him and drove them both over the edge, the rushing water dragging them down and spinning them forward. They crashed into the grate and finally broke the surface.

Savannah yelled, 'There is a gap below, a few feet at most, push under and let the current do the work!'

William turned his head back towards the glass chamber but Savannah pulled him round, her eyes firm as she shouted, 'There's nothing there for you. Just the past. And to hell with that.'

Taking a deep breath, he filled his lungs and surrendered his destiny to the flowing river, trusting the current to carry him home.

## CHAPTER FIFTY-EIGHT

*A*utumn was stealing across the city, the cool air blowing the truth away like fallen leaves.

The bell clanged as they entered the Pestle and Mortar. Hercules Meriwether had his back to them, rearranging a row of glass jars. 'One moment, if you please.'

'Whatever,' she said.

The dwarf swung around, a look of sheer horror on his face. 'Shelton!'

'Meriwether.'

Savannah prodded JJ and he doffed his cap respectfully.

'I had very much hoped that our paths would not cross again.'

'I'd hoped the same. Still, you begin where you begin and you end up where you end up.' She moved further into the shop, dumping a large canvas bag on the floor. 'Wasn't sure you'd still be here. Mr P around?'

Meriwether nodded. She instructed JJ to remain in the shop and made her way through to the yard. The weather had turned colder now. She needed to buy new clothes, not to mention another gun.

It was business as usual for Obediah Pincott. She found him in the same room, wearing the same coat. His twin skulls greeted her, but neither of them smiled.

'Howdy.'

He looked her up and down. 'Why?' Economical as ever.

She shrugged. 'You still owe me two weeks' wages, and I never forget a debt. Figured you might also like to give me a tip. For not telling tales.'

The moment the churning river had spat them out of the factory, she had argued with William that Pincott's role should be relegated to the margins of their story, along with her own.

'You think he is a good man?' William had looked incredulous.

'He did a good thing,' she had replied, ducking the question, thinking of the night Pincott had let her go, knowing she would also try to save the women chained to their beds.

An unmistakable snuffle interrupted the memory. There was a cot in the corner of the room. She smiled, 'Aww,' and looked back at Pincott. 'Seems the worm did turn after all.'

He leant forward. 'They are all dead?'

'Yep.' A proud smile lit up her face. 'The clever puppy, the rabid mongrel – whichever, she did all right in the end.'

'And what now?'

'A holiday. In the sun, I think. With a young friend. Lisbon, maybe.'

He stood up and stretched his arms. The memory of those dangerous limbs still tugged at her, but she held her ground, not so afraid this time.

He looked down. 'You know there is price on your head, courtesy of your government, no less?'

She nodded, though she hadn't known. 'So, what am I worth?'

He went to a cupboard at the rear of the room, returning with a leather pouch.

He threw it on the table. 'That is what you are worth.'

She picked it up, felt its weight. 'Thank you.'

He waved her thanks away.

She got to her feet and moved towards the door. 'What's the kid's name?'

'Yaroslav.'

She smiled. How the vicomtesse would have hated that.

Hunched over a table in the Old Bell Tavern, William shook his head. 'It's a cover-up!'

'Of course it is,' said Finian, as sanguine as ever. He walked with a cane now, but had made light of the injuries he had suffered when Matlock's men had beaten the location of the Habborlain meeting out of him and stolen back the box.

'Harry sacrificed his life to bring this conspiracy to light, yet you steeple your fingers as if simply contemplating a clue in your own crossword. Please don't respond to that.' William sighed. He knew he sounded childish, whimpering about justice as if it were the simplest and most attainable of concepts, when in fact he knew the opposite to be true.

Finian spoke quietly. 'They are dead, William. Printing the truth will not bring our friend back.'

'And what of Tinbergen? With Garfield gone, he is now the President of the United States! Don't you think the American people deserve to know where all that money really came from?'

Finian laughed. 'William, my dear chap, do not lose all sense of perspective here. There is no proof. Besides, Cornelius Tinbergen may well have been helped to power by this insane faction, but he is now on his own. Nor will he be the first leader to have scrambled to power on the backs of others, dead or alive.'

William said nothing, his anger deflating as Finian continued, 'The world is a better place. Von Rabenmarck and his sister are gone, Matlock too, and Benjamin Raycraft's lunacy is at an end. There is much to be proud of.'

'And we have no duty to warn people of the lengths some will go to in order to hold on to power?'

Finian Worthing gave a sad smile. 'I think they already know.'

\*

William left the Old Bell Tavern and returned home. The conversation had left him exhausted. The authorities had failed to elicit any useful information from Sir Jasper Raycraft, who had committed himself to Bedlam the very day after the fire destroyed the factory. Detective Superintendent Dolly Cunningham, as he now was, had shown little inclination to follow Harry's investigations through. The Olympian Breeding Association lay abandoned and Cunningham had returned the casket of documents he found there to William, as if it was no more than a curious family heirloom that had somehow gone astray. But the cabal was broken. Maybe Finian was right and it was enough.

At breakfast the following morning William opened the paper and spread it wide on the tablecloth, avoiding the greasy stain where Sarah had earlier dropped the butter dish. 'Gladstone to introduce a new reform act in the next parliament. Hoorah, I say.'

'I don't suppose it shall include votes for women?'

'Aunt Esther! I had no idea you were such a radical.'

'Is that such a radical idea? Mildred, what do you think?'

Mildred swallowed a large bite of toast, her eyes twinkling as she brushed the crumbs away. 'I care little for politics, and even less for politicians.'

William smiled at them both. His family.

He had married Mildred at the end of July. Her family had questioned their haste, but they had both insisted. Although the reason had remained unspoken between them, when Mildred had told him a few weeks earlier that she was expecting a child, she had broken down and wept. 'I am so sorry, my love, so sorry.'

He had grasped her hands in his. 'The child is of my blood, Mildred, I know it.'

She had wept in gratitude at his willingness to believe it was so, and he allowed her to make her assumptions. He vowed to himself that they would have no secret but this one. William had not discovered the identity of his father, and likely never would.

He thought of Nathaniel Bridge and Harry Treadway. From now on, when he had need to think of his father, he would conjure them both.

At the memorial service he had organised for Mr Bridge, the handful of mourners had barely filled the front pews. A contrast to Harry Treadway's funeral, where so many people had attended they had spilled out of the little church. William had given the toy ship to Harry's grandson and told him of the wrongly painted hull. The boy looked bewildered but his mother smiled through her tears. Someone, at least, had got the joke.

Aunt Esther interrupted his thoughts. 'After breakfast, we must make a start on clearing the nursery. We have preparations to make!'

Mildred laughed and patted her still flat belly. 'We have plenty of time, Aunt, there is no reason to rush.'

Aunt Esther looked pointedly at William. 'Still, there is no time like the present. I believe it is the perfect day for a bonfire, clear some of the rubbish we have up there.'

William knew what she was referring to. The Seed of Life box languished in the spare room. He went upstairs and opened the casket for the first time in months. Touching the fragile documents within, he thought of the families, the one hundred considered the brightest and best of their generation. Where were they now? In his darker moments he wondered if any among them still presented a threat.

He built a fire in the corner of the garden. As he consigned his inheritance to the flames, William felt sure his ancient ancestors would understand. Their belief in the potential of humanity had become a quest for superiority, a desire to create a master race, a plan that must never again flourish. As the smoke billowed upwards, he looked at the clouds that blew across the sky. The past was turning to dust and the twentieth century was coming.

William Lamb wanted to live there someday.

## CHAPTER FIFTY-NINE

The woman waited until it was dark to go out. As the nights drew in, she spent more time outside, wandering the streets, her hood pulled low. It was not the life she wanted, but it was a life nonetheless.

She had waited weeks for tonight to come. The costumier had promised her his best work, that the long wait through the endless summer would be justified, so she had forced herself to remain patient as the man strove for perfection.

She knocked twice at the back door to his salon, pulling her hood across one side of her face. The costumier's assistant answered and, without words, she brushed past him and into the workshop. She waited for the assistant to leave before taking her place in front of the mirror and removing her hood. She breathed deeply before allowing herself to look. Tonight would be the last time she would gaze upon the burned flesh of her forehead and cheek, the misshapen brow, the ridges of scar tissue that knotted her hairline.

Once she was whole again she could leave the city, go to Cornelius, maybe. They would rally the families, begin again. Without her brother she had thought the world might end, but it had not. Possibilities fluttered inside her. She was in charge now, a woman, for the first time. The phial of amber liquid she had snatched from the factory was safely locked away, and somewhere to the west of the city, a very special child would be born soon.

The costumier arrived and fussed about her. He held a blue velvet cushion in his hand, and upon it lay her future: a porcelain mask, contoured perfectly to match the unblemished side of her face. He secured it in place, snug against the horror beneath.

She combed forward a few glossy red curls and smiled at her reflection.

It was a symmetry of sorts.

# HISTORICAL NOTE

❧

*I*f you had to pick the decade that gave birth to the modern world we now live in, the 1880s would, in my humble opinion, be a major contender. Electricity, cinema, the motor car – just a handful of modern phenomena that can trace their origins back to this signature time in human endeavour. But it wasn't just science that led the way. Ideas themselves had never been more catalytic, able to ignite the touchpaper of a growing but still disenfranchised working class, and kick-start revolutions with bewildering speed.

1881 was a tumultuous year in world politics. The assassinations of Alexander II in Russia and President James Garfield in the US, which form the backdrop of this novel, rocked the power brokers of old Europe. Universal suffrage, *real* democracy, was The Big Idea that wouldn't go away. Some leaders coped better than others. For Gladstone's speech at the Tinbergen rally in chapter thirty-three I used many of his own words, taken from a number of speeches he gave across his career in support of the working classes of all nations.

But Britain was becoming increasingly isolated. The European race to colonise the world, and the start of the Scramble for Africa, was driving old divisions deeper and sowing the seeds that would so devastatingly taint the battlefields of northern France thirty years later. The League of the Three Emperors, an historic pact between the Russian, German and Austro-Hungarian empires, was indeed revived on 18 June 1881 by Otto Von Bismarck (1815–1898), only weeks before the events in this novel take place.

A word then on Otto Von Bismarck. In creating the character of Otto Von Rabenmarck, I borrowed a little from his namesake, chiefly his role as German chancellor, his ambition and political ingenuity, his dislike of British politicians (documented in many a *Times* editorial), and strangely, his name. John Lothrop Motley (1814–1877), an American author and lifelong friend to Bismarck, used the name Otto Von Rabenmarck when he wrote a thinly disguised portrait of his friend in his first novel, *Morton's Hope* in 1839. The similarities end there, however, and the rest of Von Rabenmarck's words and deeds are purely my invention.

Von Rabenmarck is not the only character that drew on real life for inspiration. Cornelius Tinbergen is entirely fictional, but his family's story borrows heavily from that wave of European migrants, such as the Vanderbilts, who made their fortune in the States during the Gilded Age of the late nineteenth century. I should point out that the real successor to the presidency following James Garfield's assassination was Chester A. Arthur (1829–1886), who bears no resemblance as far as I can see to the tanned and toothsome Tinbergen.

The Vicomtesse Adeline de Bayeau was partly inspired by her namesake, Adeline de Horsey (1824–1915), the second wife of the Seventh Earl of Cardigan, who led the Charge of the Light Brigade at the Battle of Balaclava. She published her memoirs to a scandalous reception in 1909. I omitted many of her more fanciful endeavours, from organising steeplechases around her local graveyard at midnight to sleeping in her coffin, for fear they would seem too outlandish. But her spirit lives on, I hope, in my Adeline, who, I think, would happily have done either of those things if feeling sufficiently bored or petulant.

There are many more real-life individuals that served as

inspiration for characters in the book. Edward Raycraft bears some resemblance to Richard Dadd (1817–1886), the English painter who spent much of his life incarcerated in Bedlam. In describing Edward's paintings, I borrowed heavily from Dadd's most famous work, *The Fairy Feller's Master-Stroke*, now part of the Tate Britain Collection.

Pietro Rotari's painting of Alexander and Roxanne does exist and can be found in the Hermitage. Lord Byron (1788–1824), of course, will be familiar to many, and he did indeed travel to Serbia and also became obsessed with Alexander's tomb. But the connection between either of them and anyone called Habborlain is entirely fictional.

Dolly Cunningham borrowed his name from Frederick Adolphus 'Dolly' Williamson (1830–1889), the first head of the Metropolitan Police CID when it was founded in 1878. Readers of *The Suspicions of Mr Whicher* will be familiar with his character, which stands in marked contrast to his fictional namesake in this book. The CID unit was created following the Turf Fraud Scandal, where three senior officers had stood trial and been sentenced to two years in prison. This incident prompted Harry Treadway's backstory: the man who sacrificed everything to see his colleagues face the justice they deserved.

I so wish I could tell you that Savannah Shelton was a real person. I'd certainly like to think there are real Savannahs out there, fighting their battles with raging hearts and a bravery I could never emulate. But the appearance of a sharp-shooting, straight-talking American woman in Victorian London is not something I made up. *Buffalo Bill's Wild West* toured Europe in the late 1880s, and featured over time both Annie Oakley and Calamity Jane – a command performance was even given to Queen Victoria.

Sir Jasper Raycraft owes much to the well-known scientist and arms manufacturer William George Armstrong (1810–1900).

The house he built in Northumberland, Cragside, has obvious parallels with the fictional Ridgeside, home to the madness of the Raycraft family. It was the first house in the world to be lit using hydroelectric power, and included early prototypes for a lift, a dishwasher and a washing machine. One of Armstrong's goals was to 'emancipate the world from household drudgery'. But it was his work in armaments that saw him most lauded, and his advancements in the technology of warfare were deployed around the world, from the Crimea, to Japan and the trenches of the American Civil War.

In fact, all of the science in this novel is genuinely rooted in the breakthroughs of this amazing decade. The telephone saw a rapid take-up on both sides of the Atlantic and, by 1880, telephone exchanges had opened in most of the major cities across the UK. But of course not all scientific endeavour can be seen as progress. Opinions vary on when the formula for mustard gas was first stumbled upon. Some believe experiments date back as early as 1822. The nascent formula was definitely in existence by 1886, when Viktor Meyer (1848–1897) published the first paper outlining its synthesis, yields and devastating impact. More primitive forms of chemical warfare, such as chlorine gas, were considered for use as early as the Crimean and American Civil Wars. Senior generals by and large dismissed them, although it is hard to say whether it was a distaste for their impact, or a refusal by the old guard to engage with modern weaponry, that saw chemical weapons largely sidelined until the First World War.

In terms of the ancient history referenced in this book, the stories of Plato, Aristotle, Alexander and his son, there is little to add to the text in the novel. The timelines and the connections are all there, and are all factually correct to the best of my knowledge. Thirty-five dialogues and thirteen letters are traditionally ascribed to Plato, although the authorship of several of these is now under question. My fourteenth letter, and the idea that Plato might have fathered Alexander the Great, is pure fantasy. But it is a fantasy built on two very real foundations.

Firstly, in many ways Plato really *was* the father of all of us, at least those of us in the Western world, because he is so often seen as the father of how we think. He founded the Academy in Athens, one of the first institutions of higher learning in the world. He opined on almost every subject, from science to philosophy, religion to politics, and psychology to mathematics. What's more, most of his work has survived for almost two and a half millennia.

Secondly, and less benignly, we come to the subject at the heart of the book: eugenics. The idea of selective breeding to improve the human race has been with us since we first looked upwards and outwards at the world around us and sought ways to control it. Plato, inevitably, was enamoured of the idea – he talked of selective mating to breed a guardian class, for example, encapsulating this idea that you could breed humans for physical and mental traits just as you could animals. In the nineteenth century, Charles Darwin's *Origin of the Species* appeared to legitimise eugenics as a genuine field of scientific study. Indeed, it was his cousin, Francis Galton (1822–1911), who first coined the term in 1883. Darwin struggled in his own lifetime to reconcile the scientific robustness of natural selection with his distaste for where many were so keen to take it. He cautioned that although enabling the weakest to survive would lose the benefits to our race of natural selection, not to do so would endanger our instinct for sympathy, which he described as 'the noblest part of our nature', and maybe the reason why, as a race, rather than as individuals, we had come ultimately to dominate the world.

But eugenical theory continued to thrive. International conferences were held in 1912 in London and 1921 in New York. Eugenics societies existed in most Western countries by the early twentieth century. It is easy to dismiss this as a scientific novelty of a more innocent time; it probably depends on where you sit on the cultural relativism spectrum. Me? I'm not so sure. Nor, when you look at the tensions around immigration today, am I so sure that our enchantment with the possibility of our own perfection was ever fully exterminated in the gas chambers of Nazi Germany.

## ACKNOWLEDGEMENTS

*I*'m enormously grateful to Ed Wood at Sphere for his encouragement, enthusiasm, and storytelling brain. Nor would this book be what it is without the wisdom and insight of my agent, Jonny Geller at Curtis Brown.

The whole team at Sphere have been a pleasure to work with. So thank you to Thalia Proctor and Kati Nicholl, for their forensic eye for detail in all matters historic and grammatical, and to Emma Williams and Ella Bowman for their commitment and creativity.

In the early days, I received much assistance and support from the Writer's Workshop, specifically Nikki Holt and Debi Alper. They went above and beyond in helping me to tame the beast and move forward.

I would also have been lost without Wikipedia. I'm no academic, and can't enter into a debate about accuracy and integrity of information, but the ability to move through history, to see connections and jump down creative rabbit holes at the click of a button, inspired the very heart of this story and made its ambition possible. Any factual errors in this book are entirely my own, and I'm not sure I care that much. It's fiction, after all.

I have to thank my fantastic support group of family and friends that read my very first draft (all 190,000 words of it. Don't ask.). Their feedback was invaluable and their encouragement equally priceless.

Howard Evans, for his unwavering identification of all rogue apostrophe's, except this one.

Victoria Farrow and Peter Powlesland, for choosing to live in the nineteenth century and telling me there are no bicycles there, and for giving me a place to stay and lots of wine to drink.

Lorraine Mollins and Beth Hamer for being such enthusiastic readers, Michael Dynan Oakley for telling me when I was being pretentious, and Sarah Earl for falling in love with all the bad characters you're not supposed to like.

A huge thank you to Gillian Jones and Sonia Beldom for forcing me to be brave, and to Helen Vangrove, for being my very first reader and not letting me give up.

And finally to my mum, Margaret Evans, gone but never forgotten, for making me love stories so much in the first place. I'm sorry I ruined your antique copy of *David Copperfield* by reading it on a beach, and that I never got to read your own novel before you tore it up. My story is yours.